# The Australian's Proposal

MEREDITH WEBBER
ALISON ROBERTS
MEREDITH WEBBER

Published in Great Britain 2014
by Mills & Boon, an imprint of Harlequin (UK) Limited,
Eton House, 18-24 Paradise Road, Richmond, Surrey, TW9 1SR



*The Doctor's Marriage Wish*, *The Playboy Doctor's Proposal* and *The Nurse He's Been Waiting For* were first published in Great Britain by Harlequin (UK) Limited.



ISBN: 978-0-263-91213-5
eBook ISBN: 978-1-472-04508-9

05-1214

Harlequin (UK) Limited's policy is to use papers that are natural, renewable and recyclable products and made from wood grown in sustainable forests. The logging and manufacturing processes conform to the legal environmental regulations of the country of origin.

Printed and bound in Spain
by CPI, Barcelona

# THE DOCTOR'S MARRIAGE WISH

BY

MEREDITH WEBBER

**Meredith Webber** says of herself, 'Some ten years ago, I read an article which suggested that Mills & Boon were looking for new medical authors. I had one of those "I can do that" moments, and gave it a try. What began as a challenge has become an obsession, though I do temper the "butt on seat" career of writing with dirty but healthy outdoor pursuits, fossicking through the Australian Outback in search of gold or opals. Having had some success in all of these endeavours, I now consider I've found the perfect lifestyle.'

Meredith Webber says of herself: 'Some ten years ago I read an article which suggested that Mills & Boon were looking for new medical [illegible] I had one of those [illegible] and [illegible] What [illegible] [illegible] has [illegible] though [illegible] the [illegible] of writing with [illegible] [illegible] the Australian [illegible] [illegible] [illegible] [illegible] [illegible] [illegible] of [illegible]

# CHAPTER ONE

WELCOME TO CROCODILE CREEK!

The writing was gold on green, very patriotic, but what was a woman who'd grown up in a penthouse in inner city Melbourne, and to whom wildlife was a friend's pet galah, doing in a place called Crocodile Creek?

She'd overreacted.

Again!

Though flinging her engagement ring at Lindy hadn't really been overreacting—it had been a necessary release of tension to avoid killing either her erstwhile best friend or her stunned and now ex-fiancé, Daniel.

Overwhelmed by the sign telling her she'd finally reached her destination, Kate pulled the car over onto the grass verge and stared at the name of the town, heart thudding erratically at the magnitude of what she'd done, and with apprehension of what might lie ahead.

Could this unlikely place with the corny name—Crocodile Creek, as if!—possibly provide the answers she so desperately needed to rebuild her life?

She then considered the implications of the town's name again. Nah! Surely nobody would build a town on a creek that actually had crocodiles in it.

But she glanced behind her towards what looked like, well,

more like a river than a creek—and, just in case, put the car into gear again and drove on.

Up here in North Queensland anything might be possible.

'Go through the town, over the bridge, past the hospital to a big house on a bluff.'

The directions the director of nursing had given on the phone last night had been clear enough. The road led through the town and over another rather rickety bridge. Looking out her side window, Kate was tempted to stop again, for there, virtually in the middle of the town, was a sandy beach, lapped by lazy waves that frilled the edge of a blue-green sea. Hot and sticky from this final day of a five-day drive, she looked with longing at the water, but someone called Hamish was expecting her at the house.

The house!

Could that be it?

The one perched on the bluff at the southern end of this magical cove?

As a child she'd dreamed of living in a house by the sea, a longing frustrated rather than satisfied by holidays at the beach.

Excited now, she drove on. Yes, that was definitely a hospital on her right. Low set and relatively modern, it was surrounded by palms and bright-leafed plants, but still had the usual signs to Emergency, Admittance and parking areas.

Past the hospital she went, to the house on the hill—by the sea—parked the car in a small paved area to one side, unloaded her suitcase and climbed the steps to the wide veranda.

The front door was open, but she tapped on it anyway, then called out a tentative hello before venturing slowly down the wide hall that seemed to lead right through the middle of the old building.

'Have you any idea how difficult it is to organise a rodeo?'

The big man appeared at the far end of the hall, waving the

handset of the phone as he spoke. A soft Scottish accent spun the question from bizarre to fantasy and when he added, 'You'll be Kate, then?' in that intriguing voice, Kate smiled for the first time in about six months.

Well, maybe not quite six months.

'I will be, then,' she said, dropping her suitcase and coming towards him with her hand held out. 'Kate Winship. When I phoned last night the DON said Hamish would show me around the house, so you'll be Hamish?'

His large firm hand engulfed hers and the voice said, 'Hamish McGregor,' but something apart from the accent made Kate look up—into eyes so dark a blue they looked almost black, here in the shadowy hall of the big old house she'd been told was called 'the doctors' house'.

She removed her hand from his and backed away. One step. Two. Then she realised she must look stupid and backed far enough to turn her panicky retreat into a suitcase retrieval.

'I'll take that.'

He only needed one long stride, lifting it from her unresisting fingers.

'We've put you in here. This was Mike's room, but he and—Well, you'll get to know everyone soon enough. Suffice it to say there're more people sharing rooms these days than there used to be, which is why we've room for some of the nursing staff while the nurses' quarters are renovated.'

He turned a teasing smile on Kate.

'Fair warning, Nurse Winship. There's been an epidemic of love racing through Crocodile Creek these past few weeks, so watch how you go.'

'Love! That's the last thing I'll catch,' she assured him. 'I'm immunised, inoculated *and* vaccinated. The love bug won't bite *me*.'

He set her suitcase on the bed and turned to look at her, dark eyebrows rising to meet brown-black hair that flopped in a heavy clump over his forehead. The eyebrows were asking questions, friendly questions, but there was no way she was going to answer them. The hurting was too new—too confusing—too all-encompassing. She had to learn to cope with it herself before she could share it with anyone—*if* she could ever share it.

But he was still watching her.

Waiting…

Diversion time.

'Why are you organising a rodeo?'

His smile returned, softening his rather austere features, parting lips to reveal strong white teeth.

All the better to eat you with, Kate reminded herself as a niggle of something she didn't want to feel stirred inside her.

'It's for the swimming pool.'

'Of course—a swimming pool for bulls and bucking horses.'

A deep, rich chuckle accompanied the smile this time. Had she not been immune…

'We're raising funds for a swimming pool at Wygera, an aboriginal community about fifty miles inland. The kids are bored to death—literally to death in some cases—sniffing petrol, chroming, drag racing, killing themselves for excitement.'

The smile had faded and his now sombre tone told her he'd experienced the anger and frustration medical staff inevitably felt at the senseless loss of young lives.

'And when's this rodeo?'

'Weekend after next. That's why the house is deserted. Whoever's off duty is out at Wygera, organising things there—not so much for the rodeo as for the competition for a design for the swimming pool. Entries have to be in by today and the staff available are out there registering them and sorting them into categories. All the locals are involved. I'm on call for the emergency service. Did you know we have both a plane and a helicopter based—?'

The phone interrupted his explanation, and as he walked out of the room to speak to the caller, Kate opened her suitcase and stared at the contents neatly packed inside. But her mind wasn't seeing T-shirts and underwear, it was seeing young indigenous Australians, so bored they killed themselves with paint or petrol fumes.

*You're here to trace your mother's life, not save the world.* But the image remained until Hamish materialised in the doorway.

'Look,' he said, brushing the rebellious hair back from his forehead. 'I hate to ask this when you've just arrived, but would you mind doing an emergency flight with me? There are fifteen kids from a birthday party throwing up over at the hospital so the staff there have their hands full.'

Kate closed her suitcase.

'Take me to your aircraft,' she said.

'When you've put something sensible on your feet. Nice as purple flowery sandals might be, they won't give much protection to your ankles if we have to be lowered to the patient.'

'Are you criticising my footwear?' she said lightly, embarrassed that he'd even noticed what she was wearing on her feet. Embarrassed by the frivolous flowers.

She opened her case again and dug into the bottom of it to find her sensible walking boots. The rest of her outfit was eminently practical. Chocolate brown calf-length pants, and a paler brown T-shirt with just one purple flower decorating the shoulder. But a woman couldn't be sensible right down to her toes—especially not when these delicious sandals had called to her from a shop window in Townsville the day before.

Pulling off the sandals, she sat down on the bed to put on her boots, uncomfortably aware that Hamish hadn't answered her.

Uncomfortably aware of Hamish.

'You don't have to wait—just tell me where to go. Is it to the airport? I passed that on the way in.'

'Regular clinic flights leave from the airport. And retrievals leave from there if the aircraft is being used. But today it's the chopper.'

He didn't move from the doorway and Kate was pleased when she finally had her boots laced tightly and was ready to leave.

She followed him through the house, out the back door and into a beautiful, scented garden. She glanced around, trying to identify the source of the perfume that lingered in the air, but Hamish was striding on, unaffected by the beauty. Too used to it, she guessed.

'We've a helipad behind the hospital to save double transferring of patients,' Hamish explained. 'The service has two helicopter pilots and one of them, Mike Poulos, is also a paramedic, so we can do rescue flights with just him and a doctor, but when he's off duty and Rex is flying, we take two medical staff.'

'Is it a traffic accident?' Kate was glad she'd been running every morning. Keeping up with Hamish's long strides meant she had to trot along beside him.

'Apparently not.'

It was such a strange response she glanced towards the man who'd made it and saw him frowning at his thoughts.

'It was a weird call and, now I think about it, maybe you shouldn't come,' he added.

'I'm coming. Weird what way? Domestic situation?'

'No, just weird. The caller said there was an injured man in Cabbage Palm Gorge and gave a GPS reading. You know about satellite global positioning systems?'

'I've heard of it but, generally speaking, street names are more useful in Melbourne. Corner of Collins and Swanson kind of thing.'

A glimmer of a smile chased the worry from his face, but not for long.

'Because it's a gorge, we might have to be lowered from the chopper.'

'Been there and done that, though not, admittedly, into a gorge. But I have been lowered onto an oil-rig in Bass Strait in a gale, and that's not a lot of fun, believe me.'

They'd reached the helicopter, and the conversation stopped while Hamish introduced Rex, a middle-aged man with a bald head and luxuriant moustache, then they clambered into the overalls he handed them.

'It's three-quarters of an hour to the head of the gorge, but until we're over it and get the right GPS reading, we won't know where the bloke is. I can't land anywhere in the gorge itself, and going down on the winch without a landing spot marked isn't an option in that country—too thickly treed. So I'll land where I can at the top of the gorge and you'll have to abseil down.'

Rex was talking to Hamish, but glancing warily at Kate from time to time.

'That's fine,' she assured him before Hamish could answer. 'I'm qualified for that and did a winch-refresher weekend only a month or so ago.'

Taken because she'd thought she'd be going back to the emergency department at St Stephen's and on roster for rescue missions…

'We'll see,' Hamish objected. 'I think I should go down first to find the patient. If he's mobile, we won't need two people.'

'No go, Doc!' Rex told him, hustling them into the cabin, handing Kate some headphones then checking she'd found her seat belt. 'It'll be dusk by the time we get there and, though it's not as deep as Carnarvon or Cobbold Gorge, Cabbage Palm's no picnic. Even if you find a suitable place to lift him from, I won't be able to do it tonight. And RRS rules say two staff for overnighters.'

RRS—Remote Rescue Service, Kate worked out. She hadn't realised when she'd asked the agency for a job at

Crocodile Creek that it had such wide-ranging services. She glanced at the man with whom she was about to spend the night. He was frowning again.

'Do you suffer some kind of knight errantry towards women, that you're looking so grim?'

Because he wasn't yet wearing his headphones, she had to yell the question above the noise of the engines. He turned towards her and shrugged, but didn't reply. Which was fine by her. Helicopters weren't the best places for casual conversation.

They lifted off the ground and Kate wriggled around so she could see out the window. The hospital was cradled by the curve of a creek—no doubt called Crocodile—to the west, but to the east there must be a view of the blue waters of the cove. She could see the doctors house on the bluff overlooking the cove, then the stretch of sand and water and another bluff on the northern end, on which perched a sprawling, white-painted building set in lush tropical gardens.

Beyond the creek, on the landward side, was a reasonably sized town, a cluster of larger buildings lining the main road. She'd driven past them earlier, noticing a pub, a grocery store and a hairdressing salon.

The helicopter swung away, and now all Kate could see were the slopes of hills, many of them covered with banana plantations, while beyond them rainforest-clad mountains rose up to meet the sky.

'It's cattle country once we're over the mountains.'

She turned to Hamish and nodded acceptance of his statement, soon seeing for herself the open stretches of tree-studded plains. Rex seemed to be following what appeared to be a river, with more closely packed trees marking its meandering course. Then more hills appeared, rugged, rocky sentinels rising sheer from the plains, the setting sun catching their cliffs and turning them ruby red and scarlet.

So this was what people talked about when they used

phrases like 'red centre' to describe Australia. Kate pressed her face to the window to get a better view.

'You'll be seeing it firsthand before long,' Hamish reminded her, and, right on cue, the helicopter began to descend. It took another twenty minutes but eventually Rex found somewhere he could safely set down. He turned off the engine and, with the rotor blades slowing, he climbed back into the cabin and began to unstrap the equipment they would need.

'I'll send you down first, Doc, then the gear, then you, Sister Winship.'

'Kate, please,' Kate protested, but Rex just shook his head.

'Rex is an old-fashioned gentleman. He calls all the women by their proper titles,' Hamish told her. 'Tried to call me Dr McGregor for the first few months I was here, but I kept thinking he must be talking to my father and didn't answer, so he finally gave it up.'

Hamish was checking the equipment bags as he spoke. Once satisfied that each contained what it should, he'd lower it out of the helicopter. Rex set up a belay rope, using one of the helicopter's skids as the anchor point, and Kate was reassured by the professionalism of both men.

'You've got the radio but once I leave the top of the gorge you won't be able to contact me until I'm back overhead in the morning. Use the hand-held GPS to find the patient. When it's light, if you can see a space—maybe near the waterhole—that's clear enough for me to do a stretcher lift, you can radio me the position.' Rex was looking anxiously at Hamish, obviously unhappy that he had to abandon the two of them. 'I'll fly over to Wetherby Downs for the night, refuel and be in the air again at first light. Back here soon after six.'

'We'll be OK,' Hamish assured him, handing an abseiling harness to Kate, then fastening himself into a similar one. He followed this up with a helmet, complete with headlamp. 'Kate, you're sure you're happy about this? You could stay with Rex.

It wouldn't be the first time we've broken RRS rules in an emergency.'

'Not on my first day,' Kate joked, hiding a tremor of trepidation. The gorge wasn't all that deep, and dropping down the cliff-face would be simple, but the sun had already left the bottom of the cleft and the shadowy gloom beneath them seemed…unwelcoming somehow.

She watched Hamish disappear, and when he gave the signal helped Rex haul the reinforced rope back up. They hooked the two backpacks, one with medical gear and the other with the stretcher and stabilising equipment, onto the rope, then added another which, Rex explained, held emergency rations.

'There's a little gas stove so you'll be able to have a hot cuppa later tonight,' he said. 'No fires, though, it's a national park.'

Kate nodded, though she was certain park rangers would forgive a small fire should it be needed for warmth or survival.

She watched as Rex lowered the rope. Hamish would undo the gear, then send the rope back up, and it would be her turn.

Strong arms caught and steadied her as she found her feet, then Hamish unclipped her harness and signalled to Rex he could haul it back up. But the pilot was obviously anxious for he repeated all his warnings and instructions about contact before Hamish finally signed off.

He reached down and swung one of the backpacks onto his shoulders, then lifted the other one.

'That's mine,' Kate told him. 'If you want to be gallant, take the smaller bag.'

He grumbled to himself, but held the medical equipment pack up for her so she could slip her arms into the straps.

'We've a way to walk,' he warned, and Kate grinned at him.

'My legs may not be as long as yours, but they'll get me anywhere we need to go, so lead on.'

He muttered something that sounded like 'damned independent women,' then turned his attention to the GPS, marking their current position as Landmark One, then keying in the position of the injured man.

'It's about eight hundred yards in that direction,' he said, showing Kate the route map that had come up on the small screen.

They set off, picking their way through the wide-leafed palms that gave the gorge its name, clambering over the rocks littering the banks of the narrow creek that had cut through the sandstone over millions of years to form the deep but narrow valley. The creek was dry now, at the end of winter, but, come the wet season in late October, and it would roar to life, marks on the cliffs showing how high it could rise.

Darkness was falling swiftly, but they'd left the creek-bank and were walking on more stable ground, the light from their torches picking out any traps for their feet.

'It shouldn't be far now,' Hamish told her. 'I'll try a "coo-ee."'

The thought of a Scot using the Australian bush call made Kate smile, but Hamish's 'coo-ee' was loud and strong, echoing back to them off the cliffs. Then they heard it, faint but clear, definitely a reply.

'Well, at least he's conscious,' Hamish said, reaching back to take Kate's hand to guide her in the right direction—hurrying now they knew they were close to their patient.

The man was lying propped against the base of the cliffs, an overhang above him forming a shallow, open cave. A very young man, haggard with pain, trying hard to hold back tears he no doubt felt were unmanly.

'Digger said he'd let someone know, but I thought he was just saying it to make himself feel better about leaving me,' the lad whispered, his voice choking and breaking on the words.

'Well, he did the job and here we are,' Hamish told him. 'One doctor and one nurse, all present and correct. I'm Hamish and this is Kate, who'd barely set foot in Crocodile Creek when we whisked her off on this adventure.'

'Crocodile Creek? You're from Crocodile Creek?'

He sounded panicky and Kate knelt beside him and took his hand, feeling heat beneath his dry skin.

'We're the Remote Rescue Service,' she said gently. 'And now you know us, who are you and what have you done to yourself?'

She brushed her free hand against his cheek, confirming her first impression of a fever, then rested it on his chest, unobtrusively counting his respiratory rate. Twenty-five. Far too fast. She'd get him onto oxygen while Hamish completed his assessment.

The Scottish doctor was already kneeling on the other side of their patient, taking his pulse with one hand while the other released the clasps on the backpack. Kate swung hers to the ground and moved so her light swept over the patient's body, picking up a rough, blood-stained bandage around the young man's right thigh.

'There's a bullet in my leg,' he said, and the phrasing of the answer made Hamish frown, although he didn't question how or why, simply repeating part of Kate's question.

'And your name?'

The lad hesitated for another few seconds then finally said, 'Jack. My name's Jack.'

He was radiating tension that Kate guessed was more to do with his circumstances than his condition, although he seemed very weak. But if his tension arose from being abandoned, injured, in the middle of nowhere, surely their arrival should have brought relief.

And the name? Had he opted for Jack as a common enough name or was he really a Jack? Kate didn't know, but she did know it didn't matter. Jack he would be while they tended him, and part of tending him would be getting him to relax.

Hamish was doing his best, chatting as he ran his hands over Jack's head and neck, asking him questions all the time, satisfying himself there were no other wounds and no reason to suspect internal damage. Where was the pain? Could he feel this? This? Had he come off his horse? Off a bike? Hit his head at all?

Jack's responses were guarded, and occasionally confused, but, no, he hadn't fallen, he'd stayed right on his bike. It was a four-wheeler.

And where was the bike?

He looked vaguely around, then shook his head, as if uncertain where a four-wheeler bike might have disappeared to.

The smell hit Kate as she fitted a mask and tube to the small oxygen bottle she'd taken from her backpack. She looked up to see Hamish unwinding the bandage from Jack's leg. Necrotic tissue—no wonder the boy was feverish and looked so haggard.

'How long since it happened?'

Jack shrugged.

'Yesterday, I think. Or maybe the day before. I've been feeling pretty sick—went to sleep. Didn't wake up until Digger moved me here this morning.'

'Where's Digger now?' Kate asked, holding the oxygen mask away from his face so he could answer.

'Dunno.'

Hamish raised his eyebrows at Kate, but didn't comment, saying instead, 'His pulse is racing. He needs fluid fast. I don't want to do a cut-down here, so we'll run it into both arms. If you open the smaller pack you'll find a lamp. Set it up first then in your pack there'll be all we need for fluid resuscitation—16g cannulae and infusers for rapid delivery. You'll see the crystalloid solutions clearly marked.'

Kate found the battery-operated lamp and turned it on, a bright fluorescent light pushing back the shadowy evening.

Now it was easy to see what they had—sterile packs of cannulas and catheters, bags of fluid, battery-operated fluid warmers, boxes of drugs.

'Good luck,' she said to Hamish as she handed him a venipuncture kit. 'We're going to get some fluid flowing into you,' she added to Jack, as she found the fluid Hamish wanted and began to warm the first bag. 'And that means inserting a hollow needle into one of your veins. But because you're pretty dehydrated, your veins will have gone flat so it won't be an easy job. I'm betting Hamish will need at least two goes to get it in.'

'I'll have you know, Sister Winship, I'm known as One-Go McGregor,' Hamish said huffily, taking the tourniquet Kate passed him and winding it around Jack's upper arm, hoping to raise a vein in the back of his hand or his wrist.

The needle slipped in. 'See, told you!' Hamish turned triumphantly to Jack. 'Aren't you glad you didn't bet?'

Kate had tubing and a bag of fluid ready, and she turned her light onto the cliff-face behind their patient in search of small ledges where they could place the bags.

They changed places, Kate starting the fluid flowing into Jack's vein, then setting the bag so it would continue to gravity feed through the tube. And all the time she talked to him—not about how he'd come to have a bullet in his leg, but about what she was doing, and how it would help.

'Once Hamish has you hooked up on that side, we can start pain relief and antibiotics. It's the infection from your wound that's making you feel so lousy.'

'Actually,' Hamish said mildly, 'getting shot in the first place would make me feel pretty lousy.'

Jack gave a snort of laughter, and relief flowed through Kate. Surely if he could laugh he'd be OK. But he was very weak and the wound, now she could see it, was a mess. A deeply scored indentation running from halfway down his thigh towards his hip, then disappearing into a puckered, blue-rimmed hole. Dried blood on the bandages suggested it had bled freely—but not freely enough to keep infection at bay.

Hamish set the second bag of fluid on the ledge behind Jack, then probed through the contents of the backpack.

'I'll get some antibiotics into you with that fluid, then I want to check your distal pulses and test sensation in your foot and lower leg. Kate, would you watch for renewed bleeding from the wound? We know you've been lucky, Jack, in that the bullet didn't go into your femoral artery. And how do we know that?'

Hamish had found what he wanted—a small bag of fluid Kate recognised as IV antibiotic medication diluted with saline. He spiked it with an IV administration set, connected it to a second port in the IV line he had running, then placed the small bag on the ledge so the drug could be administered simultaneously with the fluid.

'Because you'd have bled to death by now—that's how we know the bullet didn't hit your artery,' he said cheerfully. 'But it might have damaged a nerve, which is why I'm going to prick your foot, or the velocity of the bullet might have chipped a bone and sent that as a secondary missile to squeeze against the artery, which is why I'm going to check to see if blood is still flowing in your foot.'

Kate watched Jack's face and saw that Hamish's matter-of-fact approach was just what the young man needed. In fact, he was interested enough to ask, 'Why does Kate have to watch for bleeding?'

'Good question! Go to the top of the class.' Hamish smiled at him. 'Kate has to watch because you'll have damaged some blood vessels, but smaller veins and capillaries have the ability to close themselves off if that happens. Problem is, once we build up your fluid levels, they might get all excited and open up again—bleeding all over the place.'

'Ouch!'

Jack jerked his leg, and the bleeding Kate was watching for began right on cue.

'Well, you've feeling in your toes and a weak but palpable pulse in your ankle, so I'd say you've been a very lucky young man. Unfortunately, that luck's about to change. I need to clean up that wound and, although I'll anaesthetise the area around it with a local, it won't be comfortable. Kate, how about you shift over to Jack's other side and talk to him while I work? Can you talk and pass instruments and dressings?'

Kate stared at the man who was taking this situation so calmly, chatting away to Jack as if they were sharing space on a city bus, not a cave at the bottom of a gorge at nightfall, while someone with a gun lurked somewhere in the darkness.

'Well?'

Hamish smiled at her and she shook her head, then realised he might think she was answering his question.

'Of course I can talk and pass things,' she said, immediately regretting the assurance when his smile broadened and he threw a conspiratorial wink at Jack.

'I thought so,' he gloated. 'Most women can talk and do other things, can't they, mate?'

Jack smiled back while Kate glowered at the pair of them. She'd walked right into that one.

'Local anaesthesia is in the green box,' Hamish continued, 'and sterile swabs in the white one with the red writing. You might pass me the sharps container and a plastic bag out of that pack as well, so I can put the soiled stuff away as I use it.'

Kate handed him what he needed, then checked the contents of the pack again, trying to anticipate what Hamish would want next. A scalpel, no doubt, to cut away some of the infected tissue, and more swabs to mop up blood as he got down to clean flesh.

Sutures? Would he stitch it up or leave it open until they got back to the hospital where further surgery would be necessary?

She set out what she thought he'd need immediately, placed

them on a large flat stone and lifted it across Jack so it was within Hamish's reach.

'You're supposed to be talking to me,' Jack reminded her, but his voice was weaker than it had been earlier. Seeing them had probably prompted a surge in his adrenaline levels which had now waned. Did Hamish want her talking to the young man to distract him, or to keep him awake and stop him slipping into unconsciousness?

Not that the reason mattered.

'I will,' she promised, checking his blood pressure, pulse and respirations. He had the mask across his mouth and nose, but was talking easily through it. His breathing was still far too fast, but his pulse, though still tachycardic, was more regular than it had been when she'd automatically felt it earlier. 'You start. Tell me all about yourself.'

'Not worth talking about,' he muttered weakly. 'In fact, I'd have been better off if you hadn't come.'

'And here I thought you were pleased to see us,' Kate teased, aware a little self-pity was quite normal in someone so ill.

'Well, I was at first,' Jack grudgingly admitted, 'but only because I was feeling so lousy. Really, though, I'd be better off dead.'

'Don't we all feel that at times?' Kate sighed.

'I bet you don't,' Jack retorted, buying into the argument she'd provoked, although he was so weak. 'Look at you—pretty, probably well dressed under those overalls, good job. What would someone like you know about how I feel?'

'I would if you told me.' Kate smiled at him. 'In fact, you tell me the Jack story and I'll tell you the Kate story, and I bet I can beat your misery with my misery—hands down.'

'I bet you can't.'

'I bet I can.'

'Bet you can't!'

'Can!'

'Children, just get on with it.'

Hamish's voice was pained, but Kate heard amusement in it as well. He knew they had to find out Jack's background, and had guessed this was her way of goading Jack into telling it.

'My family didn't want me,' Jack began, anxiety and pain tightening the words so they caused a sympathetic lurch of pain in Kate's chest. 'They all live in Sydney and they sent me right up here to work. Can you imagine a family doing that?'

'Not to a nice boy like you,' Kate told him, taking his hand to offer comfort even while she tried to stir him into further revelations. 'But mine's worse. My father died, then my mother, then my brother told me they weren't my parents at all. They'd just brought me up because they'd felt sorry for me. So I didn't really have a family at all. Beat that.'

Jack frowned at her, but had his comeback ready.

'Mine'll disinherit me when they find out about this,' he said.

'Well, that sounds as if they haven't already done it. You've still got time to redeem yourself. And now you're hurt, you can play the sympathy card. My brother—or the louse I thought was my brother—is contesting my mother's will because he says I wasn't ever properly adopted. How's that for the ultimate disinheritance?'

'That *is* a lousy thing to do,' Jack agreed, but he was thinking hard, obviously not yet ready to concede in the misery stakes. 'My uncle kicked me off his property.'

'I traced my birth mother but found out she'd died the week before I got there.'

'Wow! That's terrible. So you don't know who you are?'

'Nobody—that's who I am,' Kate said cheerfully. She didn't feel cheerful about it, but that wasn't the point. Keeping Jack talking was the point. 'Beat you, didn't I?'

He looked at her for a moment then shook his head.

'I lost my girl.'

His voice broke on the words and Kate squeezed harder on his hand.

'That's why my uncle kicked me out.'

'Ah, that's terrible, but can't you get in touch with her again even if you're not working for your uncle?'

Jack shook his head.

'I tried. I really tried. I worked on another property. It didn't pay much so I got this other job, then I had some time off so I thought I'd go and see her—tell her what was happening. But I couldn't get a lift—I tried, I really tried—and I had to get back, and it turned out— Anyway, if I had got to her place, her dad would probably have killed me. It was her dad broke us up. He rang my uncle and told him we'd been seeing each other. Apparently he went mental about it and that's why my uncle sacked me.'

The story had come tumbling out in confused snatches, but Kate was able to piece it all together.

'Love problems are the pits,' she sympathised, 'but, really, yours are chicken feed, Jack.'

'Chicken feed?' He perked up at the challenge she offered him. 'I'm shot and I lost my girl.'

'OK, but what about this? I stop work to nurse my mother—'

'Who wasn't your mother,' Jack offered.

'That's right, but I loved her.' It was only with difficulty Kate stopped her own voice cracking. This wasn't personal, it was professional, and Jack was sounding much more alert. 'Anyway, I took two months off to nurse her at the end and my ever-loving fiancé and my best friend began an affair right under the noses of all our colleagues. OK, so I didn't lose my job, but can you imagine going back to work with the pair of them billing and cooing all over the place, and everyone laughing about it?'

'More swabs.'

The gruff demand reminded Kate that Jack wasn't the only one hearing the story of her recent life, but Hamish had told her to distract Jack, and her strategy was working. She opened a new packet of swabs and passed them over, giving Hamish a look that warned him not to say one thing about her conversation.

'No, I wouldn't have gone back to work there either,' Jack said. 'But you've got another job now, haven't you? I'll never get another job.'

'Piffle! Of course you will. Young, healthy, good-looking chap like you. You'll get another job and another girl, both better than the ones before.'

Silence greeted this remark, a silence that stretched for so long Kate checked his pulse again. Then he said quietly, 'I don't want another girl, and I don't know how to get…the one I want back now I've messed things up so much.'

'We'll help you,' Kate promised rashly. 'Won't we, Hamish? We'll get you better then we'll help you find your girl.'

Hamish looked up from the business of debriding infected tissue from Jack's leg.

'We can certainly try,' he said, but the frown on his face was denying his words.

Did he think they wouldn't find the girl?

Or…Kate's heart paused a beat…did he think they wouldn't get this young man better?

## CHAPTER TWO

'OKAY, THAT'S ABOUT as clean as I can get it without actually removing the bullet,' Hamish announced. 'I'd like to go in and get it, but without X-rays to show us exactly where it is and where I'd have to cut, I wouldn't risk it. You're also losing a fair bit of blood, Jack. Had any problems with bleeding before?'

Jack ignored the question, closing his eyes as if the effort of talking to Kate had exhausted him.

Which it might have, though Hamish was thinking otherwise.

'At least, doing it back at the hospital, we'll have blood on hand should you need it. The helicopter will be back at first light, and we'll have you in Theatre in Crocodile Creek a couple of hours later.'

Jack's eyes opened at that, and he tried to sit up straighter.

'Shouldn't I go to Cairns? Or what about Townsville? That has a bigger hospital, doesn't it?'

'Bigger but not better,' Hamish told him. 'Besides, it's too far for a chopper flight. Something about Crocodile Creek bothering you? We don't really have crocodiles in the creek—well, not where it flows past the hospital.'

Jack didn't answer, but turned his head away, as if not seeing Hamish might remove him from the cave.

And the prospect of a trip to Crocodile Creek…

Hamish watched Kate bend to speak quietly to the young man, no doubt reassuring him he'd have the very best of treatment at Crocodile Creek, but Hamish was becoming more and more certain that Jack had reasons of his own for avoiding that particular hospital.

But how to confirm what he was thinking?

He walked around to the other side and squatted beside the open pack, delving through it for what he needed. Then, from this side, he looked directly at Jack.

'I'll add some pain relief to the fluid now, so you should be feeling more comfortable before long, and then I guess we should do the paperwork. You up for that, Kate? Did you see the initial assessment forms in the pack?'

Kate's frown told him she disapproved of the change in his attitude from friendly banter to practical matter-of-factness, but she didn't know about a feud between two neighbouring families up here in the north, or the connection of one family to the hospital. Or about a baby called Lucky who was now called Jackson who had a form of haemophilia known as von Willebrand's disease.

Or about the search for the baby's father—a young man called Jack.

'I've got them here,' she said, putting ice into her words in case he hadn't caught the frown.

'Then fill them out. You and Jack can manage all the personal stuff then I'll do the medication and dosages when you get down to that section. And while you're doing it, I'll take a look around to see if there's a patch of clear ground from which we can winch Jack up in the morning.'

He found a stronger torch in the equipment backpack, turned it on and walked away, hoping his absence might help Jack speak more freely. If he'd talk to anyone, it would be to Kate. Nothing like a baring of souls to create a bond between people. But had she really been through so much emotional trauma or had she made it all up to keep Jack talking? He had no idea, which wasn't surprising, but what did surprise him was that he wanted to find out.

Hell's teeth! He'd been in Australia for nearly two years, and while he'd enjoyed some mild flirtations and one reasonably lengthy and decidedly pleasant relationship, he'd remained heart-whole and fancy-free. So now, three weeks before he was due to return home, was hardly the time to be developing an interest in a woman.

Yet his mind kept throwing up the image of his first sight of her, a slight figure, dressed all in brown, except for those ridiculous purple sandals, standing in the gloomy hallway, with a stray sunbeam probing through the fretwork breezeway above the door and turning the tips of her loose brown curls to liquid gold.

'Is he a good doctor?' Jack asked, when Hamish had disappeared into the darkness.

Kate looked in the direction Hamish had taken, but already she could see nothing but inky blackness beyond the glow of the lamp.

'I've just started work so I don't know, but from the way he treated you I'd have to say he is.'

Jack closed his eyes and lay in silence for a while, but just when Kate had decided he'd drifted off to sleep he opened his eyes again and looked at her.

'So you don't know anything about the hospital?' he asked.

'Not a thing, except its reputation is excellent. Apparently the boss, Charles Wetherby, insists on hiring top-class staff and only buying the best equipment, so it has a name for being far in advance of most country hospitals.'

But her words failed to reassure Jack, who had not only closed his eyes but had now folded his lips into a straight line of worry.

Seeking to divert him, she pulled out the pad of assessment forms.

'You must be tired, but before you drop off to sleep, how about we fill this out. There aren't many questions.'

Jack opened his eyes and looked directly at her.

'I should have died,' he said, then he closed his eyes again and turned his head away, making it unmistakably clear that the conversation was over.

'Full name?' Kate asked hopefully. 'Address? Come on, Jack, we have to do this.'

But the young man had removed himself from her—not physically, but mentally—cutting the link she'd thought she'd forged when they'd played their 'whose life sucks the most' game earlier.

She lifted his wrist and checked his pulse then wrote the time and the rate on the form. She filled in all the other parts she could, remembering Jack's initial respiration rate, systolic blood pressure—she'd taken that herself before Hamish had started the second drip—and pulse, writing times and numbers, wondering about all the unanswered questions at the top of the form.

'Asleep?'

Hamish's quiet question preceded him into the light. She stood up, careful not to disturb their patient, and moved a little away.

'He wasn't—just closed his eyes to avoid answering me—but I think he's genuinely asleep now. I've just checked him. His pulse is steadier but his systolic blood pressure hasn't changed as much as I'd have thought it would, considering the fluid we're giving him. Do you think there could be internal bleeding somewhere?'

'It's likely, and though I've sutured part of the wound and put a pressure pad on it, I'd say it's still bleeding.'

'That's more than a guess, isn't it?' Kate looked up at the man who sounded so concerned. They'd moved out of the lamplight, but a full moon had risen and was shedding soft, silvery light into the gorge.

'It's a long story but we've time ahead of us. If you dig into the equipment backpack you'll find a space blanket to wrap around Jack—there should be a couple of inflatable pillows in there as well. Put one under his feet and one behind his head and cover him with the blanket while I get a cuppa going and find something for us to eat.'

'And then you'll tell me?'

Hamish smiled, but it was a grim effort.

'I'll tell you what I'm guessing.'

Kate cupped her hands around the now empty mug and looked out at the broad leaves of the cabbage palms that filled the gorge. Hamish's story of a newborn baby found at a rodeo, the dramatic efforts that had saved his life, the finding of his dangerously ill mother, and the fight to save *her* life, was the stuff of television medicine, while feuding neighbours and heart attacks turned it into soap opera.

Maybe she'd got it wrong.

She turned to Hamish, sitting solidly beside her at the entrance to the cave.

'So you think Jack is Charles Wetherby's nephew, sacked from the family property, run by Charles's brother Philip, for consorting with the Cooper girl, daughter of the Wetherbys' sworn enemies who live next door. And you've put all this together because his wound is bleeding and you think he has von Willebrand's disease.'

'Lucky—the baby—has von Willebrand's disease and it runs through the Wetherby family,' Hamish said patiently. 'Originally, back when Lucky was found, Charles had no idea his nephew had been working at Wetherby Downs, because Charles and Philip rarely spoke to each other. But since Jim Cooper was admitted to hospital with a heart attack, Charles has been anxious about the Coopers' property and that forced him to speak to Philip—'

'Who told him about Jack and Megan—OK, I get that bit.'

Kate assured him. 'And the family feud—I can understand that. But if Jack is Charles's nephew, and Charles and Philip don't get on, why's Jack so against going to hospital at Crocodile Creek? It's a good uncle and bad uncle scenario—like good cop and bad cop. You'd think he'd be happy to be under his good uncle's care. Family does count, you know.'

Before the words were fully out, she knew they were a mistake. She didn't need to look at Hamish to know those darned expressive eyebrows of his would be on the rise.

'Look,' she told him, wishing she was standing up and a little further away from him but resigned to making the best of things. 'The story I told Jack—well, that comes under the heading of nurse-patient confidentiality so, please, pretend you never heard it and don't you dare breathe so much as a word of it to anyone. I went back to work for a week after my mother died, and if one more person had put their arm around me or thrown me a "poor Kate" look, I tell you, I'd have slit their throat with the nearest scalpel. Stuff happens, and you have to move on. I've moved on, and that's it.'

He nodded but didn't speak. In the end she had to prompt him.

'So why's Jack worried about going to Crocodile Creek?'

'He has a bullet in his leg.'

Kate turned to frown at the man beside her.

'This is the bush. Out here, from what I've heard, people tote guns all the time. They shoot things—wild pigs and water buffalo and snakes. From the evidence of road signs on the drive up, they even shoot road signs. So he shot himself, gun going off as he climbed through a fence—isn't that what happens? Or maybe Digger shot him by accident.'

'So where's Digger now? If he shot Jack by accident, why would he call for help then disappear?'

'Because he had to be elsewhere. Had to take his cattle to market or organise a rodeo. I'm a city girl, how would I know where he had to be?'

She saw the glimmer of white teeth as Hamish smiled, but the cheerful expression passed quickly.

'Outback people aren't like that. They don't desert their mates. And Jack's worried about being disinherited for something that's happened since his uncle sacked him. My guess is he met up with some unsavoury characters—no doubt innocently, he's a city kid too, remember—and when he realised something was wrong, he tried to leave.'

'And someone shot him? To stop him leaving? Someone who's out there? With a gun?'

Kate must have sounded more panicky than she'd realised, for Hamish put a comforting arm around her shoulders and drew her close. It was probably a 'poor Kate' kind of hug and she should have been reaching for a scalpel, but the heavy arm was exceedingly comforting so she let it stay there—even snuggled a little closer.

Not a good idea as far as the immunity was concerned. She unsnuggled and thought a little more about Hamish's hypothesis.

'What kind of unsavoury characters might you have out here?'

'Cattle duffers.'

'Stupid cattle?'

Hamish laughed.

'Cattle thieves. They steal cattle from properties in the area. These properties are the size of small countries so their boundaries can't be watched all the time. The duffers keep the cattle somewhere safe—this gorge would be ideal—until they can alter the brands, then truck them to the markets.'

'So Jack meets these guys who say come and steal some cattle with us and he does?' She turned to study their sleeping patient for a moment. 'He doesn't look that dumb.'

Hamish turned to look as well, bringing his body closer.

'No, but say he meets a couple of guys at a pub, and their story is that they're droving a mob of cattle to a railhead. Something like that. Jack joins, thinking they're OK, then slowly works out there's something wrong. I'd say he recognised his uncle's brand on some of the cattle. He tries to leave and the boss, who's about to reap a good reward for his thievery, tries to stop him.'

'With a bullet?'

Bother the immunity. Kate scooted back to snuggle position by Hamish's side.

'They play for keeps.' He tucked his arm back around her as if it was the most natural thing in the world. 'It's my guess he didn't shoot to kill the kid. In his mind, that gave Jack a chance of survival and himself time to get the cattle away from here. Jack was lucky the second guy, Digger, had a conscience.'

'That does explain Jack's concern, but surely if he went into the job innocently, he can't be charged with cattle... What was the word you used?'

'Duffing.'

Kate nodded. 'I like it. Cattle duffing. It has a ring to it, doesn't it? Not quite as nasty as stealing.'

'Apparently it's gone on ever since Australia was first settled, but that doesn't make it right, or legal. No, our Jack will be in trouble. For a start, we have to report bullet wounds to the police.'

'But if he's the father of the baby, and we know he loves the girl because he told us so, then it's not very lucky for Lucky if his father's in jail. We'll have to get him off the charge. Don't people get a second chance? Or if he's responsible for the police catching the duffers, won't he be rewarded, not punished? Perhaps we could help catch the duffers?'

'Well, that gives me hope,' Hamish said.

Kate shifted reluctantly away from him so she could turn and look into his face.

'Hope for what? What kind of hope?'

He grinned at her.

'Well, I thought earlier you'd only come closer to me

because you were worried about a gunman lurking out there somewhere, but if you're brave enough to take on a couple of armed desperados, then I guess you were cuddling up to me because you like me.'

He touched her lightly on the head, lifting one of her curls and twirling it around his finger.

Dangerous territory, finger twirls in hair that felt very… comforting?

Kate took a deep breath, sorted her thoughts into order, shifted out of hair-twirling distance and tried to explain.

'I do like you, what little I know of you, but I meant what I said about immunity, Hamish. Coming to Crocodile Creek is the first stage in getting on with my life. My birth mother came from here and I want to find out more about her—and who my father was. At the moment, I'm lost. Everything I believed in—the very foundations of my life, even love—proved to be a lie and right now I need to find some truths. Something to rebuild on. Can you understand that?'

He nodded, then stared out into the gorge for a few minutes before saying, 'I could help you, Kate. Everyone at the hospital would help you. Some of the staff have lived in Crocodile Creek all their lives.'

'No!'

The word came out far more strongly—and more loudly—than she'd intended, and she turned automatically to see if she'd disturbed Jack. He was still sleeping peacefully, so she repeated the word more quietly this time.

'No, Hamish. I know you mean well, but this is something I have to do myself.'

She'd edged further away from him and Hamish knew she was withdrawing behind whatever feeble defences she'd been able to build up since her callous brother and unfaithful rat of a fiancé had delivered their separate but equally devastating blows. He could understand her reluctance to accept help because accepting help meant getting close to the helper, and right now, with everything she'd ever trusted in stripped away from her, getting close to someone wasn't an option.

'OK,' he conceded. 'But just remember, if ever you need anything at all, a little help, a hug—especially a hug—I'll be there for you.'

'Thanks,' she said, but Hamish knew there was no way she'd be coming to him for a hug. She'd felt the same chemistry he had between them and hugs plus chemistry equalled trouble for a woman who claimed to be immune to love and who was fresh out of trust.

'I'll check our patient, then we should try to get some sleep,' he said, standing up and moving back into the cave. 'There are a couple more of those space blankets in the pack. It could get cold towards morning.'

Grateful to have something to do, Kate also stood. She'd noticed a couple more packs of the flimsy silver sheets they called space blankets when she'd pulled one out to cover Jack. She was aware they prevented heat loss from the body but was dubious about how warm they'd be if the night grew cold. Still, it was something to do and having something to do was important because it stopped her thinking about the mess her life was in. She'd talked bravely to Hamish of having to do this on her own, but it was the aloneness of her situation—the total stripping away of all she'd believed to be true—that frightened her the most. Far more than a man with a gun somewhere out there in the darkness of the gorge.

Hamish was attaching a new bag of fluid to one of Jack's IV lines. He nodded towards the blood-stained bandage.

'I'm just hoping it's not running out faster than it runs in.'

'Should we give him a clotting agent of some kind—or don't the packs carry such things?'

'They contain Thrombostat, which is topical thrombin. I put some on when I was dressing the wound. Because of Lucky, everyone at the hospital knows a lot more about von Willebrand's disease than most non-specialist physicians would but I don't know as much as I'd like to know. I know some coagulants work for some haemophilic patients and not others, depending on the missing blood factor in their particular disease. I wouldn't like to try anything on him without checking a pharmacology text for contraindications or complications…'

He paused and sighed, but Kate understood his dilemma.

'You don't want to take the risk,' she finished for him. 'Well, hopefully the thrombin will work well enough to stop some of the bleeding.'

'Externally!' Hamish reminded her, hanging the second fresh bag of fluid. 'Internally we haven't a clue what's happening. Damn that Digger for not leaving Jack's gear with him. He'd have some kind of coagulation drug in it for sure, probably an inhalant.'

'Unless he didn't know he had von Willebrand's. Some people don't, do they?'

Hamish nodded. He was counting respirations. Their patient would make it through the night, he was sure of that. And providing they could stem the infection, he would recover from this wound. What he wasn't sure about was what would happen after that. Lucky was the hospital's miracle baby, but his mother, Megan, and her family had been going through a rough time for years, and now, right when it looked as if things might be coming good for them, Lucky's father could end up in jail.

Hamish looked out into the darkness. Kate's idea of finding the cattle duffers and bringing them to justice was suddenly very appealing.

*And* very stupid, he admitted to himself, but he turned to study the spunky woman who'd suggested it. She was unfolding a space blanket, her head bent as she concentrated on spreading it out, neat white teeth biting the corner of her lower lip. He saw her again as he'd first seen her, and heard her voice saying 'piffle' in a no-nonsense way to Jack.

You don't fall in love because of a sunbeam turning brown curls golden, or because a husky voice says 'piffle.' But if he wasn't in love then he must be sickening for something. Elevated heart rate, shallow respiration, a slightly nauseous feeling in the pit of his stomach, as if something disagreeable was lurking there—and all this without taking into consideration the stirring in his groin whenever he looked at the woman.

She's not interested, he reminded himself. And who could blame her, after what she's been through? Even if she was interested, she's here on a mission and you're going home in three weeks. Home to a position you've waited two years to secure, home to specialise in paediatrics—your life-long dream-come-true scenario. You cannot fall in love with Kate Winship.

'Here's your blanket. Do you want another of those dreadful biscuits from the provision pack?'

'Those dreadful biscuits are proven to be life-sustaining. They probably contain more nutrition than your regular three meals a day.'

It would be nice to eat three meals a day with Kate…

'But they taste terrible,' Kate reminded him with a smile.

And have her smiling at him all the time…

'Should we take turns to watch him?' She nodded towards their patient.

'I'll doze beside him. I'll need to change the fluid bags during the night, and probably see to fluid output as well. I think he'd prefer I tended him.'

Kate nodded, knowing this was an indication she should move a little further away to give Jack and Hamish privacy, but there was someone out there who might not want Jack rescued.

'Bring the backpack to cushion the rock, and sleep on the other side of me,' Hamish suggested, apparently reading her thoughts with ease. 'I'm big enough to block Jack's view of you, and to shade you from the lamplight. Come on. We'll be warmer if we're all close together.'

Not too close, Kate warned herself, but she lifted the pack and carried it around to Hamish's side of the patient, opening it in the light first so he could get out what he'd need during the night, then pushing it into place against the rock wall.

'I'm not sure that a backpack full of medical supplies makes the perfect pillow,' she said, as she tried to shift box-shaped lumps around inside it.

'Try sleeping against a folded aluminium stretcher,' Hamish countered, but he leaned over and removed some of the boxes from her pack, stacking them neatly on the ledge. 'Better?'

His face was shadowed but she knew he was smiling, because she could hear the amusement in his voice. He was a nice man, she decided—the kind of man a girl would be lucky to meet should she be on the lookout for *nice* in a man.

Or anything in a man.

Or a man…

Was it a sound that had woken her? Hamish must have turned off the lamp, for the cave was dark. Kate lay still, knowing any movement would rustle the silver blanket tucked around her body. Someone—or something—was moving out there.

'Shh!'

She didn't need the barely breathed warning but it was comforting to know Hamish was awake—comforting to feel his hand find her shoulder and give it a reassuring squeeze.

He'd be a nice man to hug.

Good thing he couldn't see the eye-roll that was her reaction to the stupid thought. She had to get a grip. What she needed was a big rock to hide behind, not a hug. What use were hugs if whatever was out there was a man with a gun?

'Look!'

The soft word made her turn, and there, exposed in the moonlight, was a family of wallabies.

'Rock wallabies,' Hamish whispered, as the biggest of the three lifted his delicately shaped head and looked around, scenting some alien presence in his domain. The middle one was also curious, but anxious about the youngster, who was braver in his exploration of the world. Kate sighed at the wonder of it.

'I didn't know they were nocturnal,' she murmured, fascinated by the threesome who had paused, as if posed for photographs, right in front of her.

'It's nearly dawn. They'll feed now until the sun gets too hot then rest in the shade for the remainder of the day.'

A shot rang out, then echoed frighteningly back at them again and again. Two of the wallabies had disappeared, but the third lay still in front of them, the long back legs twitching one or twice.

'That's Todd! He's out there. It's a warning.'

Jack's voice quivered with fear, and Hamish's 'Get back here' was far louder, but Kate was already bending over the injured wallaby, trying to turn the body to see the wound. Then she was lifted from the ground and carried back into the cave.

'You stupid woman! He had a clear shot at the 'roo from wherever he was and you go out there and make a bigger target for him. Are you insane?'

'It might not be dead.'

Kate couldn't believe the dampness on her cheeks could possibly be tears. She hadn't cried when Bill had told her she'd been fostered. She hadn't cried when she'd found out about Daniel and Lindy. She hadn't even cried when she'd discovered she'd missed meeting her birth mother by one lousy week—so why was she crying over a dead animal?

'We'll check later.' Hamish was still holding her, but more gently now, brushing his hand over her head and repeating the words as if he knew she needed the reassurance. 'We'll check when we hear the chopper overhead. If it's only injured we can take it out with us, but experienced 'roo shooters shoot to kill, Kate.'

'He'll shoot us all.' Jack's panic reminded Kate she had a patient to tend. She pushed away from Hamish, swiped her hands across her face and knelt beside the young man, who was frantically trying to free himself from tubes and bags of fluid.

'He's just trying to scare us,' Hamish said, but his Scottish accent didn't make the words any less ridiculous.

'Well, he's succeeded in that part of his plan. What's next?' Kate muttered, holding tightly to Jack's hand—finding as much comfort as she was giving.

'I doubt he wants three bodies on his hands. It's not as if he has the luxury of time to get rid of any trace of us. Having heard the chopper yesterday, he'll know it will be coming back for us at first light. I'd say the gunshot was a warning to Jack not to talk about what's been going on.'

'As if I would!' Jack muttered, and though Kate wanted to argue with him he was still feverish and they had a difficult time ahead of them, getting him safely out of the gorge.

Which reminded her.

'Did you find an open space we can use to winch Jack up?' she asked Hamish, though the thought of how vulnerable they'd be when they left the cave, she and Hamish carrying the stretcher, Jack strapped to it between them, made her shiver.

'I did, and not too far away. It's getting lighter by the minute, so Rex will be on his way. Once he's overhead we'll have radio contact with him and I'll let him know there's some unfriendly person out there. He'll buzz around and hover over us when we move, but I'm sure this Todd person fired his shot to frighten Jack, then took off.'

'I should have died. You should have let me die!' Jack said, and Kate rounded on him.

'If you moan like that once more I swear I'll finish you off myself. Think of it as a big adventure in your path to adulthood. As a great story you can tell your kids in the future. How many young men your age have been shot at and had to huddle in a cave in a gorge in the middle of nowhere, and been rescued by…' She turned to Hamish. 'Could we be Batman and Robin, do you think? Swooping out of the sky in our Bat Helicopter?'

She looked up at Hamish. 'Bags I be Batman!'

Hamish was kneeling on the floor of the cave, fitting the long sides of the stretcher together. He turned towards her and smiled.

'And that would make me Robin?'

'Or Jack could be Robin and you could be the butler guy who answered the phone at the mansion.'

'That's not very fair,' Hamish protested, moving the now-assembled stretcher over to their patient. 'I flew in too so I have to be Robin.'

'I don't need that. I can walk—or hop—if the two of you support me,' Jack protested. He sat up to prove his point, and as the colour faded from his cheeks Kate caught him and rested him gently back against the pillow.

'Not just yet,' she said, helping Hamish position the stretcher where they needed it. 'It's far easier to carry you if you're lying down, and much safer winching you up in a stretcher harness. I imagine Hamish will go first so he can get you safely inside, then you, then I'll follow.'

She glanced up to see Hamish frowning at her.

'It's the only practical way to do it,' she pointed out, though she knew he'd know it. It was the knight errantry thing again—he didn't want her down here on her own. 'I'll be fine—I'm Batman, remember.'

Her reward was a brief smile, flashing across his tired, unshaven face, but the smile was almost immediately replaced by a new frown.

'Just remember Batman wasn't indestructible,' he warned,

then he turned his attention to Jack, explaining how they would move him onto the stretcher.

'When it's time to move, we'll take you off the oxygen and stop the IV fluid until you're on board. The fewer tubes you have around you, the less likely it is we'll foul the winch ropes.'

'Boy, that's a comforting thing to be telling a patient,' Kate remarked, fitting a strap across Jack's chest. 'Less likely to foul the winch ropes! And just how often does this service have trouble with winch ropes?'

'Never in my time,' Hamish reassured Jack, then he smiled again at Kate. 'But I believe when it does happen, it's usually on the third lift.'

'Great! Might have known!' she said, poking Jack's arm with her finger. 'Told you my life was worse than yours.'

Hamish studied her for a moment, and saw the small even teeth once again nibbling at the corner of her lower lip as she fastened the straps on the stretcher. She must be scared stiff, but she was dealing with it her way—with teasing humour. He wasn't exactly unconcerned himself. Dangling on the end of a winch rope, all three of them in turn would make perfect targets for a man with a rifle.

Hamish could tell himself any shooting at this stage would bring the full might of the Queensland police into the gorge, so the man called Todd would be stupid to take aim at any of them.

But believing it was harder.

How badly did Todd want to protect his secret?

How far would he go?

# CHAPTER THREE

IN THE END, the airlift was completed safely, though delayed for several hours, Rex insisting the three on the ground remain in their cave until the rescue helicopter from Townsville arrived with armed police. Two of this contingent, carrying serious 'don't mess with us' rifles, were lowered to the ground to escort Jack, Hamish and Kate to the retrieval area. The second helicopter then flew surveillance while Hamish, the patient and finally Kate were winched aboard the Crocodile Creek chopper.

'Now everyone in the whole world knows I'm in trouble,' Jack muttered to Kate an hour later, as he was lifted from the helicopter at Crocodile Creek, TV news cameras capturing the scene.

'I doubt the *whole* world will know,' Kate retorted. 'North Queensland maybe, if it's a slow news day, but this kind of footage never makes the national news. They're taking it for a local station.'

'Big deal,' Jack grumbled. 'Both my mother's brothers are locals.'

He closed his eyes as he had done back in the cave, and Kate, tired as she was, felt a wave of sympathy for him. She took his hand. 'It will be OK,' she promised. 'We'll work it out. You're not on your own, you know. Even if your family is upset with you, Hamish and I will stick by you.'

Having made this promise on Hamish's behalf, she glanced

around. The man in question had spoken briefly to the two orderlies who'd met the chopper, then walked away. Ah, there he was—over on the edge of the gathered crowd, squatting down so he could speak in confidence to a man in a wheelchair.

Still holding Jack's hand, she was moving further and further away from the pair, and as they approached the hospital she felt a sense of… Surely it wasn't loss? No way. She hardly knew the man, so why should he stick around? Escort her into the hospital? Introduce her around?

Because he seemed so nice, that's why.

You don't need nice, she reminded herself, dredging up a smile for a good-looking man with burnt red curls who was coming towards them now.

'You must be Kate!' the man said, holding out his hand towards her, though she knew most of his attention was on Jack. 'I'm Cal Jamieson, the surgeon who'll be digging the bullet out of your patient's leg.'

He introduced himself to Jack and gave directions for the orderlies to take him into the emergency department first. The men wheeled their charge onto a wide veranda, turning right and entering through a door into a long, bright room, with curtains hanging from ceiling racks to divide off cubicles.

Kate undid the straps and the orderlies lifted Jack onto an examination table.

'We'll take a good look at it here,' Cal explained to Jack, then he looked across at Kate. 'You can stay if you want—meet some of the staff—but I imagine a shower and a sleep might be more of a priority.'

'Is that a tactful way of telling me I'm on the nose?' Kate lifted her arm and sniffed at her T-shirt. Not too bad, considering.

Cal laughed.

'Definitely not. I just know how those overnighters can be.'

'Stay with me, Kate.' Jack decided for her. 'You promised.'

'I didn't promise to stay with you for ever and ever,' she told him firmly. 'But just for now, I will. Until Dr Jamieson puts you under for the op. Then I'll go home and shower and be back when you wake up. That's if I'm not rostered on duty.'

'I think they'll let you have the rest of today to yourself,' Cal said. 'And here's someone who can confirm that. Jill Shaw, Director of Nursing, meet Kate Winship, new nurse and local heroine.'

'I'm not a heroine!'

Kate's protest cut across Jill's quiet, 'How do you do, and a belated welcome to Crocodile Creek.'

Jill held out her hand, and as Kate shook it she sensed a quiet strength in the older woman. Here was someone, she knew immediately, who would stand firm in crises, and who would be there for her staff should they ever need her.

'We were giving you today to settle in,' she said, confirming Cal's words. 'And tomorrow we thought you might like to go on the clinic run to Wygera, so you can see a bit of the countryside and meet some of the people out there.'

Kate opened her mouth to ask about this place, but Jill was already bent over Jack, talking quietly to him. Did she know him?

'Uncle Charles'll kill me!' Jack protested, and Kate realised Hamish's surmises had been correct.

'Don't overdo the drama,' Jill said, but she was smiling fondly at the young man. 'Besides, his job is to save people from death, not cause it. You're in trouble, yes, but Charles and Philip will both stand by you. You should know that.'

'Charles might, but Philip certainly won't,' Jack muttered.

'I think we should get this bullet out of your leg and worry about who kills who later,' Cal said. He nodded towards a young woman who'd wheeled an X-ray machine into the room. 'Right thigh, top and side views. Everyone out.'

Kate gave Jack's hand an extra squeeze and left the cubicle.

'He's really worried about the repercussions of whatever been up to,' she said to Jill.

'He should be,' Jill replied, frowning in the direction of the wounded young man. 'Hamish radioed Charles from the helicopter. Cattle duffing—if that's what he's been involved in—is a serious business up here—anywhere in outback Australia really. The sentences and fines have recently been increased. Oh, here's Charles now.'

Kate looked around to find the man in the wheelchair had silently joined them.

'I believe I owe you a debt of gratitude,' he said. He, too, held out his hand. 'Charles Wetherby.'

'Kate Winship,' Kate replied. 'And no gratitude required. I was only doing my job.'

'And doing it very well, from what I hear,' Charles told her, a warm smile lighting up his craggy face. 'Thanks, Kate. I haven't seen much of young Jack lately, but as a kid he often holidayed up here and I'm very fond of him. I didn't know he was at Wetherby Downs let alone that he'd fallen out with Philip and left. Silly young ass—he should have known he could come here. I'd have found him another job somewhere in the area.'

'He might have thought you'd side with your brother.' Hamish's voice made Kate look up to find he'd come in through another door and was standing behind Jill. Kate smiled at him, then realised she shouldn't have. Not that smiles meant anything. Not hers, nor the warm, friendly one Hamish bestowed on her in return. 'Now, Kate, shouldn't you have returned to your unpacking and settling in?'

'I promised Jack I'd stay until he goes to Theatre,' Kate told him, and Charles laughed.

'I notice Jill's standing guard over him as well. The young rascal wormed his way into her heart when he was a kid, always heading for her place if he was in trouble with me or his grandmother.'

Kate wished Jack could hear the affection in Charles's voice as he spoke of his nephew. Jack's fears he'd be disinherited were obviously baseless. She was relieved for him, of course, but somehow it made her own aloneness more acute.

And her desire to find her father even stronger—her father and perhaps some other family. Both her parents—the ones she'd known—had been only children, in their forties when they had taken Kate in, so though she'd known and loved her mother's father, there were no other relatives.

'The wound's infected but the X-rays don't show any nasty surprises, apart from a groove along part of his femur and some serious blood pooling further up around his hip.' Cal appeared from the curtained cubicle to deliver his good news. 'I want to get the clotting time down in his blood. I've got cryoprecipitate running into him now in a rapid infusion, and I'll give Alix more blood to test when that's done. I spoke to a haematologist after Hamish radioed in and described the patient, and Charles confirmed it was his nephew. The haematologist says minor surgery is OK once we get the blood-clotting factors up to thirty per cent of normal. The cryoprecipitate should do that.'

'Do you want us to thaw some FFP just in case?' Charles asked, and Kate realised just how sophisticated this country hospital was, to have fresh frozen plasma on hand.

Cal thought for a moment.

'It's such a waste to thaw it if we don't need it within twenty-four hours. What's thawing time?'

'Twenty minutes.'

An attractive young woman with a long plait of dark hair swinging down her back answered the question as she came briskly into the room. She nodded at Kate then turned to Cal.

'His clotting time is up to fifty per cent of normal. You can go ahead.'

'Thanks, Alix.'

Cal disappeared back behind the curtain.

'Alix, this is Kate. Kate Winship, meet our pathologist, Alix Armstrong.'

'Hi,' Alix said. 'You've had an exciting introduction to Crocodile Creek. I'd love to hear about the gorge some time, but right now I need to talk to Cal about what he'll need in Theatre.'

'Alix is bush-crazy,' Charles explained to Kate. 'All her time off is spent bush-walking. She's serious about wanting to hear about the gorge.'

Kate shivered, memories of the echoing gunshot sending icy tentacles along her spine.

Had Hamish noticed, that he put his hand lightly on her shoulder?

'I'd better go in and see Jack before he goes to Theatre,' she said, moving away from Hamish as swiftly as she could, but Charles was before her, shifting the curtain aside and wheeling silently towards the bed. He reached out and touched Jack's cheek with the back of his hand.

'Silly young fool,' he said gruffly, and Kate swallowed hard. It wasn't that she begrudged Jack this familial affection, just that once again it emphasised her own lack.

She took Jack's hand, promised to see him later and left the cubicle, assuring herself it was lack of sleep and a letdown after the tension of the night that was making her so stupidly sentimental.

A small boy who looked just like Cal was sitting on the top step when she arrived back at the house. Beside him, spreadeagled like a fireside rug, was the weirdest dog Kate had ever seen. Part cocker spaniel and part something spotty, she guessed, greeting both boy and dog with a smile.

'Hello, I'm Kate. Who are you two?'

'I'm CJ and this is Rudolph, and his nose isn't red because he's not called after a reindeer but after a dancing man. I'm hiding.'

'I thought you might be,' Kate said easily. 'From anyone in particular?'

'I'm supposed to be at that stupid child-care place, but Rudolph followed me and sat outside so I decided to take him home, and he won't stay home on his own so I'm here, too.'

'Of course,' Kate said, not understanding much of the conversation. 'Do you think the people who mind you at the child-care place will be worried?'

'They won't notice 'cos they don't know me 'cos I'm new. Or they might think I'm sick.'

'Well, that's OK, then,' Kate said, climbing the steps and sitting beside the pair.

Rudolph raised his dopey head and soft brown eyes looked deep into hers, then he dropped his head onto her leg and went back to sleep. Going to child care and back must have been a tiring business.

'I'm waiting for Hamish, he'll know what to do.'

'I'm sure he will,' Kate agreed. This was obviously a job for Robin rather than Batman.

Fortunately, the top of Hamish's dark head appeared above the foliage in the garden, and the dog, perhaps sensing his presence, woke up, then loped off down the steps, the huge grin on his canine face making him look even dopier.

The boy followed the dog, disappearing round a bend in the path then reappearing on Hamish's shoulders, the dog lolloping around his legs.

'You've met CJ, then?' Hamish greeted her, and Kate nodded. 'He's absconded from child care again,' Hamish continued, apparently unperturbed by the child's delinquency.

He set CJ back down on the top step, then sat himself down in the space between the child and Kate. Rudolph found this unacceptable and proceeded to spread himself over all three of them.

'Off! Sit!' Hamish ordered, and the dog looked at him in surprise, then, to Kate's astonishment, obeyed.

'I've been teaching him to sit, like you told me,' CJ said, giving the dog a big hug and kiss. 'He's a very clever dog, isn't he?'

'Yes, he is,' Hamish told him. 'It's just a pity he's going to have to go and live somewhere else.'

'But he can't go somewhere else to live,' CJ protested. 'He's *my* dog!'

He gathered an armful of dog to his chest as he spoke, and glared at Hamish over the spotty head.

Hamish nodded.

'He is, but if he keeps causing trouble, like making you run away from child care, your mom will just have to give him away.'

Silence, and Kate, who thought Hamish's chiding had been unnecessarily harsh, reached around behind his back to pat CJ on the arm.

'They laugh at me.'

The whispered words were barely audible, but understandable enough to make Kate's stomach clench.

Hamish, however, seemed unmoved.

'Who?'

'Some of the kids. They say I talk funny.'

'Bloody kids,' Kate muttered under her breath. OK, so CJ appeared to have a slight American accent, but did that make him so different? At child-care level? What age would the kids be? Four? Five at the most?

'Of course you do—that's because you're half-American—and it's not funny, it's just an accent, like mine is. But kids love to pick on anyone who seems different. The trick is to ignore them and eventually they'll get tired of it and pick on someone else.'

'Then that someone will be sad,' CJ pointed out, and Kate glanced at Hamish, wondering how he'd handle that one.

'Why don't you make your difference count?' he suggested, ignoring the bit Kate had wondered about. 'Think of all the great things that have come from the United States of America—spaceships and astronauts and all the movies those kids at school go to see, not to mention most of the television they watch, and X-Boxes and video games.'

'Could I tell them my father was an astronaut?' he asked, and Kate looked at the burnt red curls and raised her eyebrows at Hamish.

'It's complicated,' Hamish said in an aside to her, before tackling CJ's question.

'I wouldn't tell a lie,' he said mildly. 'Lies are hard because you have to remember what you said the first time you told it, and then they grow bigger and bigger and it all gets very complicated. But you could tell them that you're going to be an astronaut when you grow up, and you could take spaceship stuff along to child care to show them.'

'I don't have any spaceship stuff.'

Kate smiled. The kid had Hamish now.

'Cal will help you make some,' he said. 'Cal knows all kinds of things about space and the solar system and other solar systems. You ask him to help you.'

CJ considered this for a moment, then he nodded.

'He does know a lot of stuff. I like Cal. But he's working and so's Mom, so would you take me back and tell the teacher I was late because the man with the gun made the helicopter late?'

Hamish sighed.

'I'll take you back to child care and tell the teacher you had trouble getting Rudolph to stay home,' he said. 'Remember what I told you about lies?'

CJ nodded, and lifted one of Rudolph's silky ears.

'I'd like child care a whole lot better if he could come with me.'

The wistful statement made Kate smile, but Hamish was getting to his feet, giving orders for Rudolph to stay and sending CJ to wash his hands and face before they departed.

'Mom, Dad, Cal?' Kate asked him, when the boy had disappeared.

'I'll explain later,' Hamish promised. 'In the meantime, would you mind seeing that Rudolph doesn't follow us? The dopey dog once chased my car right up the main street of the town, just because I had CJ with me. I'll get his lead—Rudolph's, not CJ's, although maybe he needs one too—and if you can just hold him while we get going, then tell him to stay, he should be OK. The child-care centre is just the other side of the hospital, so I won't be long.'

Hamish disappeared inside the house, reappearing with CJ a few minutes later. He waited patiently while CJ kissed the dog goodbye, clipped on the lead and handed it to Kate, then he herded CJ through the house and out the front door.

Kate shifted from the step to an old settee set back in the shade of the back veranda. Rudolph needed no invitation to climb up and flop beside her.

'Dog-minding duties? I assume you're Kate and no doubt Hamish roped you in to hold that hound.'

A woman with a cascade of deep brown curls and a soft American accent was taking the steps two at a time.

'Is CJ with Hamish? Did Hamish take him back to child care?'

Kate nodded, and the woman pushed the dog to one side and flopped down on the couch.

'I'm Gina,' she said, 'CJ's mother, in case you hadn't guessed. I don't think it's the child-care place that's bothering CJ so much as not being here. From the day we arrived, he's been petted and spoilt by everyone in the hospital, so now he thinks he might be missing out on something if he's not here. What was his excuse this morning?'

Kate stared at the woman who was frowning at the spectacular view beyond the garden.

'He had to bring the dog home,' Kate offered, and Gina gave a scoffing laugh.

'This dog could find his way to Mars if he had to,' she said, patting the head of the dog in question with absent-minded affection. 'I keep wondering if it's because of Cal. CJ's more or less had me to himself since my husband died, and now he has to share me with Cal, but he seems to love Cal and the two did boy things together all weekend, so...'

She sighed, then added, 'I don't know! Perhaps I should stop work and be a full-time mother, though I know I'd hate not working and the hospital needs a cardiologist.'

She stopped again, and flashed a smile at Kate.

'Heavens, but you're good! You arrive here and get whisked away on a rescue mission, then get shot at, then left to mind a dog, and now some total stranger is unloading on you—and you're just sitting there and taking it. Tell me to go get a life!'

Kate smiled at her vehemence.

'I'm really too tired to tell anyone to do anything,' she admitted. 'I'd be inside sleeping only once I go to sleep I might not wake for twenty-four hours and I promised Jack—the young man we brought in—I'd be there when he comes out of Theatre, so I may as well be dog-minding and listening to anyone who wants to unload.'

Gina reached across the dog and gave her a hug.

'Thanks,' she said. 'But now I know CJ's gone back—one of the carers rings me as soon as they realise he'd done a bunk. Problem is, they can't work out how he gets out, with the child-proof locks on the gates. Anyway, that's my problem, or theirs, really, because they have to stop it happening. For now, this mongrel...' she brushed his ears with loving hands '...can be shut on the side veranda, so why don't you have a shower and lie down? I promise I'll come over and wake you when Jack comes out of Theatre. Have you got a room? Did you get that far when you arrived?'

'I have and I did, but I haven't unpacked. Maybe I will have a shower and unpack, then see about a sleep.'

Kate looked anxiously at Gina.

'You *will* wake me?'

'Promise!' Gina said, then she took the lead from Kate. 'Cal and I have a kind of flat on the hospital side of the house,' she explained. 'There are two of them—ours is two-bedroom and the other is a one-bedroom. Mike and Emily are using the other one, though not for long. Mike's parents are building a place for them beside their house and restaurant on the other side of the cove.'

'You and Cal, Mike and Emily—is this pairing off to do with the love epidemic Hamish said was happening in Crocodile Creek?'

Gina laughed.

'I guess you could call it that. You're lucky Christina and Joe are over in New Zealand, or you'd have three pairs of love-birds under your feet.'

Kate looked at the still smiling woman, seeing the translucence of love in her eyes and the sheer delight of it in her smile. Gina might be worried about her son settling into the child-care centre, but there was no doubt the rest of her life was richly rewarding right now.

'See you later,' Gina added, leading Rudolph away along the veranda.

Kate stayed where she was for a little longer, then decided she really, really needed a shower, and if she didn't get up and have one right now, she'd fall asleep on the settee and be there until nightfall.

She found the room she'd been allotted, and was surprised to see her case had been unpacked, her clothes hung in the wardrobe and her toiletries set out on a small dressing-table. A plastic folder on the bed held a plan of the house, the rooms or suites marked with the occupants' names, while the kitchen had a note beside it, giving the times breakfast and dinner were served at the staff dining room at the hospital should the tenants not want to cook.

A second sheet of paper showed a plan of the downstairs

area of the old house. This was obviously the rec room—with a bar, pool table and a big-screen TV marked. Below that was a note explaining when and where laundry could be left, and a phone number for her to contact someone called Dora Grubb, should she need any more information.

A place like this, she realised, with resident doctors and nurses working irregular hours, would need someone to keep it running, and from the look of the spotless room Kate had been given, Mrs Grubb did a wonderful job.

Kate set the folder aside, noting as she did so that the closest bathroom was two doors down the central passageway. Gathering up what she needed, she headed straight there. Suddenly a shower seemed infinitely appealing, but she'd get dressed again after it and sleep in her clothes, knowing Gina could return to wake her any time.

Hamish knocked, then opened the door very quietly. Kate was sleeping soundly, fully clothed but with a throw across her legs. He'd called in at the hospital after dropping CJ back at the child-care centre, and Gina, after thanking him for his help, had asked him to wake Kate and tell her Jack was about to be shifted to Recovery.

She couldn't have been asleep very long, he knew that, but he also knew she'd want to keep her promise to Jack.

'Kate!'

Not wanting to enter her room, he called her name from the doorway, but when she didn't stir he ventured inside, telling himself that looking at a sleeping woman wasn't really voyeurism. Yet looking at her disturbed him and he finally nailed the reason. It was something to do with the total vulnerability of a sleeping woman—anyone asleep, he supposed, though he doubted he'd get knots in his stomach watching Cal sleep.

'Kate! Wake up.'

He put his hand on her shoulder and shook her gently,

watching her eyes snap open, her expression confused at first then clearing as the dark brown irises focussed on him. Her full lips curved into a smile.

'Jack's awake?'

She sat up, dropped her legs off the side of the bed and thrust her feet into the flowery purple sandals. 'Thanks for waking me.'

That was it? *Thanks for waking me?* Well, what had he expected? Sleeping Beauty after the Prince's kiss?

Weird thoughts were still muddling around in his head while Kate pulled a brush through her loose curls, dropped it back on the dressing-table then left the room, poking her head back inside a moment later.

'I think you've done enough good deeds for the day, Dr McGregor. Go have a sleep.'

Hamish looked down at Kate's bed, still with the indentation of her body on it, and thought of his own bed awaiting him next door. An urge to lie on her bed—feel the warmth of where she'd been—was so strong he very nearly gave in to it. After all, he'd heard her sandals tap-tap-tap their way along the hall and through the kitchen to the back steps. She'd be well on her way to the hospital by now.

Then, shaking his head at the folly of his thoughts, he left the room. A shower and a sleep would surely sort him out. Tiredness, that was all it was, not love at all.

# CHAPTER FOUR

A TALL POLICEMAN with cool grey eyes and floppy black hair was leaning against the wall in the ED when Kate entered it, looking for someone to give her directions to Recovery. He smiled at her and she found herself returning the smile, though this probably wasn't an occasion to ask a policeman for directions.

A nurse with a badge that said her name was Grace appeared from inside a cubicle, and flashed another smile in Kate's direction.

'Recovery is through that door, down the corridor, turn left and it's the first door on your right,' she said.

'Am I the only stranger in town, that everyone seems to know who I am?' Kate asked.

'The only small, dark curly-haired stranger at the hospital,' Grace told her, then she introduced herself. 'Actually, Harry here is waiting to see Jack as well. You could take him with you if you like.'

Kate looked up at the policeman. He was no longer smiling but neither was she.

'You want to see him right now? He'll be in terrible shape, just out of an op. Is that fair, talking to him when he'll be woozy as all get out?'

'Probably not,' the policeman called Harry said. 'But there's someone out there with a gun and, as far as we can tell, he's not too fussy about where, when or at whom he points and fires it. The sooner we have information about him, the safer it will be for anyone in his vicinity.'

Kate couldn't argue with the theory, but in practice, if this man tried to badger Jack…

She followed Grace's directions, very aware of the man walking beside her. A local policeman—if he was a local—could be very useful in her search for information about her birth parents, so perhaps she shouldn't antagonise him.

Like hell she shouldn't. Jack was her patient—kind of—and she wasn't about to allow this policeman to bother him.

'Are you a local?' she asked, as they turned the corner and she saw the recovery room in front of them.

'Born and bred,' he said, pushing open the door and holding it for her. 'My family have owned the sugar mill here for generations.'

So he *would* be useful.

But Jack wasn't only physically unwell, he was emotionally upset. He was also awake, and looking around. A pretty woman with honey blonde hair and grey-blue eyes was on the other side of the bed, studying the monitors to which Jack was still attached.

'Hi, I'm Emily,' she said, barely turning her attention from the screen in front of her.

Kate nodded in response then hurried forward, taking Jack's hand and holding it in both of hers.

'I thought you weren't coming,' he said, and Kate saw the tears in his eyes.

'You came out of that anaesthetic far faster than I thought you would,' she told him. 'You are one tough guy.'

The tears were blinked away and he smiled, then must have noticed Harry standing right behind her, for he paled and closed his eyes.

But before Harry could ask questions, the cavalry arrived. Charles wheeled himself into the room, Jill and Cal not far behind.

'Sorry, Harry, but we need you out of here.' There was no mistaking the authority in Charles's voice. 'The surgery's shown up an unexpected complication. We need scans and more blood tests and some expert advice on what to do next. I'm expecting he'll need to go back into Theatre today, or tomorrow at the latest. Kate, Cal will fill you in on what's happening—Cal, take Kate through to the dining room for a coffee. Jill and I will stay with Jack until you get back.'

Harry left without an argument, but what surprised Kate even more was Jack's acceptance of the orders. Here she was, being hustled down the corridor by Cal, and Jack hadn't even protested.

'Did Charles do that to prevent the policeman questioning Jack just yet, or is there a problem?' she asked Cal.

'Big problem,' Cal said gloomily. 'Big, big problem. Here.'

He directed her in through a door into a reasonably sized dining room, where the smell of coffee and the enticing aroma of a hot meal reminded Kate it had been a long time since she'd eaten the dreadful dry biscuits.

'Do you want food? There's always something hot in the bains-marie along that side, and cold sandwiches and salads in the fridge.'

It was closer to dinnertime than lunch, but Kate chose a pack of salad sandwiches while Cal fixed their coffee. They were heading for a table at one side of the room when Hamish appeared.

'Problems?' he said, raising his eyebrows at Cal this time.

'And then some. Did you find out about it through osmosis?'

Hamish grinned and slipped into a chair between Cal and Kate.

'Much the same thing. Mrs Grubb. She came over to make sure there was food in the house for me and Kate and told me Harry Blake had been turned away from questioning Jack in Recovery because of some complication.'

Cal sighed.

'The bullet is lodged in bone. The X-ray wasn't clear because there was a lot of blood pooled around the actual site, and when I went in I could see the bullet had scored down along the periosteum.' Cal turned to Kate. 'That's the fibrous vascular membrane that covers bones. Then it entered the greater trochanter.'

'The ball-shaped head of the femur that fits into the hip bone?' Kate checked.

'A job for an orthopod?' Hamish asked.

Cal nodded.

'Which means flying Jack out to Townsville,' Hamish said.

Cal shook his head. 'Charles doesn't want to do that. He says we have all we need here, and the flight could further weaken the lad. He *is* very sick—the infection is still causing fever—but I think that's just an excuse. Damn, but it's complicated!'

Cal stirred sugar into his coffee then tapped the teaspoon fretfully on the side of the cup.

'I suppose Charles is worried that if Jack goes to Townsville and the police there become involved, Jack could be placed under arrest,' Hamish suggested, taking the teaspoon out of Cal's hand and setting it on the table.

'Placed under arrest? Why?' Kate demanded. 'He hasn't confessed to anything. All we know is that he's been shot. The rest is just guesswork.'

'No, Hamish is right. That's a definite possibility. Apparently there's been a special federal police squad working on organised cattle thefts in this area,' Cal explained. 'One of their officers went under cover some months ago, and only last week his body was found—in a state of advanced decomposition and with a bullet in his chest. If that bullet matches the one in Jack's leg, it's enough of a connection for the police to hold him pending further enquiries.'

'But he was the one who was shot, not the shooter,' Kate protested, looking at Hamish as she recalled the saga he'd told her. 'And what about Megan and Lucky and Mr Cooper? What will it do to Mr Cooper's fragile health if his grandson's father is arrested?'

Hamish shrugged his shoulders.

'I'm sure Charles is considering all of that,' Cal told them. 'He probably feels he might have more control over the situation if we keep Jack here and Harry does the investigation. But there's more to it than the police side of things. First, the kid's Charles's nephew and Charles will want to keep an eye on him. It was a dumb accident with a gun when he was a kid that put Charles in a wheelchair and I'm betting there are a whole bunch of memories being stirred up right now that Charles is trying to keep a lid on. Charles's accident caused the family feud which is maybe how Jack got to be in this mess. So Charles is going to want to hold him close.'

'But doesn't Jack have parents? Do they have a say in this?' Kate asked.

'That's the next hassle,' Cal explained. 'Charles has to let them know he's injured, and if they hear we're moving him to another hospital, Charles believes they'll want him flown to Sydney—to top specialists down there.'

'But if he's in Sydney and Megan's up here, what chance will they have to sort out their feelings for each other?'

Cal answered Kate's new protest with a nod.

'Exactly!' he said. 'That's the other reason we really need to keep him here if we possibly can.'

'So, what's the answer?' Hamish asked Cal. 'Will you do the op? Do you feel confident of handling it?'

Cal hesitated.

'With expert help, yes. Charles is trying to set it up now. He has a friend, an orthopaedic surgeon, in Brisbane. If we set up a video camera and link it via computer to Charles's mate, he can virtually guide my hands. In a less complicated form, this system's being trialled in a number of country areas where there's a nurse but no doctor. It's mainly been used for diagnostic purposes but some operations have been performed this way.'

'You OK with it?' Hamish asked, and Kate sensed a bond between the two men.

Cal nodded.

'The worst part will be the timing. The surgeon we need is in Theatre right now, and he has a full list for today. It could be midnight before we get going.'

'Late night for all the staff. Because of the von Willebrand's you'll need Alix on hand and Emily for the anaesthetic—do you want me to assist?' Hamish asked.

Cal grinned at him.

'You'll probably be more useful as a babysitter. Knowing Gina, she'll insist on assisting. I know it's not heart surgery, but as soon as she heard you'd found Lucky's father, she's been itching to get involved.'

Kate was only half listening to the conversation, aware more of the interaction of the two men and the sense of belonging that being part of a hospital staff engendered. Dangerous stuff—belonging. She finished her sandwiches, drained her coffee-cup and stood up.

'Speaking of babysitting, I'd better get back to Jack,' she said, and if Hamish looked surprised by her abrupt departure, that was too bad. She'd opted to go through an agency to get this job, rather than applying direct to the hospital. She knew from experience with agency nurses in the hospital in Melbourne that they worked set contracts. They came, they did their jobs, remaining uninvolved with the people around them because they were moving on. Her contract was for two months. Long enough, she'd decided, to find out what she wanted—needed—to know. Then she'd move on.

Yes, she wanted to find her father, and to learn the circumstances of her birth—she needed to know these things to give her new life some foundation. But her new life would not be dependent on other people. From now on, she was depending solely on herself.

'He's sleeping, and so should you be,' Charles told her, when she arrived in Recovery where Jack was being held awaiting his second operation.

'I feel I should stay,' she said, but Jill, on the other side of Jack's bed, shook her head.

'I'll order you to bed if I need to,' she said, smiling to soften the words. 'But common sense should tell you, you need to sleep.'

Kate nodded her agreement but as she walked away she wondered why she felt a little lost now Jack had so many other people to be there for him. This wasn't how someone who depended solely on herself should be feeling.

She made her way back to the house, pleased Hamish was still over at the hospital with Cal, then, as she heard voices in the kitchen, contrarily wished he was here so she wouldn't have to face a roomful of strangers alone.

'Here she is—the elected judge,' someone said, and Kate looked helplessly around the smiling faces, catching sight, eventually, of Gina's.

And CJ's.

CJ and Rudolph and another little boy were cutting and pasting something in a corner where the kitchen opened onto the back veranda.

'Elected judge?' Kate echoed weakly. What on earth were they talking about?

Gina took pity on her, coming forward and introducing her to Mike—the paramedic chopper pilot Hamish had spoken of—and Marcia, a fellow nurse. There was also Susie, a pretty woman with short blonde curly hair and blue eyes who was apparently the hospital physiotherapist, and Georgie Turner, O and G specialist, a stunning young woman with very short shiny black hair and long legs encased in skin-tight jeans. The only other man there was someone called Brian—someone

Kate realised she should have met earlier, as apparently he was the hospital administrator.

'Poor Kate, I bet she doesn't even know about Wygera and the swimming pool,' Georgie said. 'And here we are appointing her judge of the designs.'

'Judge of the designs? I'm a nurse, not an architect.'

The others all chuckled.

'We don't need an architect—well, not yet. We need an unbiased person, someone who doesn't know any of the people of Wygera, to choose the best model or design then we'll pass it on to an architect to draw up the plans for us.'

Kate was about to protest that surely the architect should be the judge when Susie spoke.

'We've been arguing about it for ages, then decided you'd be the best, not only because you don't know anyone and can't be accused of bias but because you're going out there tomorrow. Doing the clinic run. Jill always puts new nurses on the clinic run to give them an idea of the area we cover.'

As everyone was smiling encouragingly at Kate, she couldn't argue, so she accepted the dubious honour of being the judge of the Wygera Swimming Pool Competition.

'Is there a prize? Do I have to give someone something?' she asked, sitting down in the chair Mike had brought over for her.

'The prize is free entry to the rodeo for the entrant and his or her family—within reason, the family part,' Mike explained. 'The company who brings a truck to all the rodeos, selling clothes and rodeo equipment, is also donating a western shirt and hat, so whoever wins gets that as well.'

'We want to win the hat,' a small voice said, and Kate turned to see CJ looking up from his task. 'I've got a hat, but Max hasn't.'

'Max is mine,' Georgie explained, but then everyone was talking again—this time about the barbeque they were planning for dinner—so Kate couldn't ask on what criteria she should judge the contest.

'Are there rules for this contest? I don't want to choose some stupendous design whoever's paying for this pool can't afford.'

'We're paying for the pool,' Georgie said, and Kate looked around the group, arguing amiably about who would do what for the barbeque. None of them looked as if they had fortunes tucked away.

'We're running fundraising events like the rodeo,' Brian explained, 'and soliciting donations from local businesses. The local council has guaranteed to match us on a dollar-for-dollar basis so I think we can afford to build something fairly special.'

Kate smiled to herself. The 'fairly' in front of special showed Brian up as a number-cruncher. Hospital administrators had to be cautious in their spending—after all, it was their job to see the place ran within its means.

The group had by now delegated tasks, and were scattering in various directions, although Gina, Susie and Marcia remained in the kitchen, pulling things out of an old refrigerator and starting work on salads.

'Can I help?' Kate asked, but once again Brian had spoken over her, offering to show her around the hospital, saying they may as well get her paperwork in order.

Kate's apologetic smile at Gina was greeted with a grimace, but directed more at Brian, Kate thought. Was he one of those administrators who insisted on all the paperwork being perfect and always up to date? She'd worked with ward secretaries who'd thought paperwork more important than patients, and it had driven her to distraction.

But she followed Brian out of the house—through the front door this time—and across to the hospital, while he talked about bed numbers, and clinic flights, and retrievals, and how expensive these ancillary services were.

'But people living in isolation five hundred miles away can't rely on an ambulance getting to them, surely,' Kate reminded him, and although he nodded agreement, he didn't seem very happy about it.

'Ah, Kate. I was coming to get you. Jill tells me you're off to Wygera tomorrow so I thought I'd show you around.'

Hamish loomed up as Brian was explaining how much it cost to run the emergency department, giving Kate figures per patient per hour that made her mind close completely. Maths had never been her strong point.

So Hamish was a welcome relief—he, at least, would make the grand tour patient-oriented.

Providing she concentrated on what he was saying, not what she was feeling. The feeling stuff was to do with having spent a fraught night together, nothing more. She knew that, but at the same time knew she should be on her guard.

Feelings could be insidious. Creeping in where they were least wanted.

'No, no, we've paperwork to do. You go on back to the house and help the others with the barbeque. I'll bring Kate when we finish here.'

Brian's assertions cut across her thoughts, so it seemed that even if she'd wanted Hamish as her tour guide, she wasn't going to get him.

By the time they'd seen the hospital, met dozens of staff, completed the forms Brian required for insurance purposes and walked back to the house, the party on the back veranda was in full swing. The smell of searing meat hung in the air, while sizzling onions tantalised Kate's taste-buds.

'After a dry biscuit for breakfast and some sandwiches for a meal at afternoon teatime, that certainly smells good,' she said to Brian, who had put his arm around her waist to guide her into the crowd.

Cal was there, so she headed towards him, anxious to know when Jack's operation would take place, only realising who he was with as she drew closer.

'So, seen all you need to of the hospital?' Hamish asked, frowning at a point over her shoulder.

'More than I could take in,' Kate told him, feeling a new touch on her back and realising Brian had followed her. 'It's far bigger than I thought and I'll be getting lost for at least the first week.'

'I'm sure you won't,' Cal said kindly. 'Did you look in on Jack?'

'He was still sleeping and Charles was with him so I didn't go in. When's the op? Have you heard?'

Cal shrugged.

'Between ten and twelve's the best timing we've got so far,' he said. 'Though we should know more by nine when the surgeon in Brisbane is due to start the last patient on his list.'

Brian had moved to her side and was asking if she wanted a drink, and politeness decreed she answer him.

'Something non-alcoholic—I haven't had much sleep,' Kate told him, pleased he would have to move away so she could ask Cal about the operation. But to her astonishment Brian simply turned to Hamish and said, 'Hamish, would you get a squash for Kate?'

Hamish—Cal, too, for that matter—seemed equally surprised, but Hamish moved obediently away, while Brian, perhaps sensing everyone's reaction, explained, 'I don't live here so don't want to be poking around in their kitchen.'

It was an acceptable excuse, yet Kate felt uncomfortable that Brian was sticking to her like Velcro. She knew it was probably kindness on his part—after all, she was the new face in this gathering of friends and colleagues—but the discomfort remained.

Although being uncomfortable about Brian was certainly distracting her from thoughts of Hamish.

Setting both aside, she returned to her mission—finding out from Cal what lay ahead for Jack.

'I'm virtually doing a hip replacement. We have prosthetic devices here because we have a visiting orthopaedic surgeon who comes once a quarter, operating in Croc Creek to save the patients travelling to him. It will depend on the damage to the neck of the trochanter. If the bullet is deeply lodged, the orthopod in Brisbane suggests we take if off completely and insert a new-age ceramic replacement and ceramic acetabular socket for it.'

Cal smiled at her.

'Want to watch?'

Kate shuddered.

'I had to do a certain amount of theatre work during my training, but the noise of the saws in orthopaedic work put me off that kind of surgery for life.'

'Besides, she needs to sleep,' Gina put in, arriving with Hamish and the lemon squash. 'She'll need all her wits about her to judge the pool entries tomorrow.'

Hamish handed her the drink, and somehow he and Gina managed to detach Brian from her side. Kate wasn't sure but she felt it had been deliberate, a sense confirmed when, a little later, Gina whispered, 'Brian makes a play for all the new female staff and Hamish felt you might be too polite to escape his tenacious clutches.'

Hamish felt that, did he?

Kate scowled at the man in question who'd moved, with his arm around Brian's shoulders, over to the barbeque. She was about to launch into a 'What right had he to make that decision?' tirade to Gina when she realised that she'd given Hamish that right—had told him she wasn't interested in a relationship with anyone.

Gina suggested they find a chair before they were all taken.

'Nothing worse than trying to eat barbequed steak standing up,' she said. 'Besides, if we're sitting down, someone might serve us—saves getting in the queue at the salad table.'

Someone did—Hamish bringing two plates piled high with meat and assorted salads across to where they sat.

'CJ's eating with Max and Georgie, and Cal's nabbed us a table at the end of the veranda,' he said, adding, rather obscurely, 'With only four chairs.'

Gina stood up and moved away immediately, though Kate followed more reluctantly. Hamish was only being kind, she knew that, but his kindness—she was sure it was just that—made her feel warm inside. Actually, quite hot in places.

Funny that kindness could have that effect…

'Oh!'

The table Cal had snagged was beyond the old settee and had the most wonderful view out over the cove. The moon had just risen, so it hung like a slightly squashed golden lantern just above the horizon, spreading a path of light across the sea.

'Nice view?' Cal teased, and Kate shook her head.

'I can't believe it,' she whispered, not wanting to break the spell beauty had cast around her.

'It's what makes Crocodile Creek so special,' Hamish said. 'And what I'll miss when I go home. Although I do have a view of the Firth from my flat, and moons do rise in Scotland, though not in quite the same majestic splendour as these tropical moons.'

'You're going home?'

Kate's question came out far louder than she'd intended it to, and she certainly hadn't meant to sound shocked.

'In less than three weeks.' Cal answered for him. 'And, boy, are we going to miss him. I know Charles has a replacement lined up—several replacements, in fact, because we're down about three doctors and we don't know if Joe and Christina will be back—but we've kind of got used to having a big, useless Scot around the place.'

'Useless? I'll give you useless!' Hamish growled, and the others laughed.

'We thought he'd be useless when he first arrived,' Cal explained. 'He was so polite to everyone, and so correct, and he'd never been in a light plane or a helicopter and didn't trust either of them.'

He smiled at his friend. 'But we brought him up to speed, and now, just when he's become a reasonably useful member of the community, he's going back to cold, dreary Scotland.'

'To specialise in paeds,' Gina added, giving Cal a nudge in the side, 'which is what he's always wanted to do, remember. You should be happy for him, not giving him grief.'

Once again Kate was struck by the warmth and camaraderie between these colleagues and housemates—and once again it emphasised her aloneness.

Or was it the news that Hamish was leaving so soon causing the empty feeling inside her?

Not possible.

She was still debating this when Brian appeared, a plate of food in one hand, cutlery poking out of his pocket and dragging a chair behind him.

'Thought I'd lost you,' he said to Kate, pulling his chair into position between her and Gina. 'Great moon, huh? Maybe we can take a walk up onto the headland when we've finished eating. I often take a walk after dinner. Helps me sleep.'

'I doubt Kate needs a walk to help her sleep,' Hamish said, before Kate could think of a reply. 'We had precious little last night and today she's spent most of her time with Jack.'

Kate looked at Hamish, who appeared to be glaring at Brian, although with Hamish's rather severe features it was hard to tell. But, glaring or not, he was going back to Scotland in a couple of weeks so he couldn't possibly be warning Brian away for his own sake.

Did he not like Brian?

Or was he just genuinely interested in her need for sleep?

Whatever! She felt uncomfortable allowing him to take over her decision-making.

'I'd like a walk after dinner,' she said, more to the table in general than to Brian.

'Oh, good, we'll all go,' Gina said.

Which was how Kate's first evening in Crocodile Creek ended in a moonlit walk over the headland above the house with Brian and Hamish, Cal and Gina, Susie, Marcia, Mike, and Georgie, CJ and Max, while a lolloping, lovable, dopey dog called Rudolph gambolled along beside them.

## CHAPTER FIVE

'WHAT DO YOU mean he's gone into shock? What kind of shock? Septic from the infection? Hypovolaemic from the blood loss? He's in hospital—how could they let him go into shock?'

Kate was vaguely aware she was shooting the messenger, but Hamish was right there in front of her, so why not vent her anxiety and distress on him? He was big enough to take it.

She had clambered out of bed while he was explaining why he'd woken her for a second time, and was now pulling a pair of sweats over her skimpy pyjama pants. Thrusting her feet into her sandals, she hurried towards the door.

Hamish didn't move.

'Come on, let's go,' she urged.

'You're going like that?'

She glanced down at the amiable hippo on the T-shirt top of her pyjamas.

'I'm decent, Jack's very ill, why not?'

'No reason,' Hamish said, but he shook his head in a bemused manner and followed her through the quiet house.

Were all the occupants over at the hospital, or were some people actually getting some sleep?

As they walked through the garden, an imminent dawn ghosting the foliage into strange shapes and patterns, Hamish explained. The operation to remove the bullet, with the guidance of the surgeon in Brisbane, had apparently gone well, and no replacement devices had been required. Jack had made the transition to the recovery room safely. Even there, Emily had been pleased with his responses as he'd come out of the anaesthetic, then they'd transferred him to the ICU for monitoring, and everything had gone haywire, his blood pressure dropping, pulse rate rising and his mental state confused and lethargic.

He wanted to die, he kept repeating weakly, then closing his eyes in response to any comment or question.

Desperate with concern—had he made the wrong decision doing the op here?—Charles had paged Hamish, asking him to wake Kate in the hope she might be able to rouse the young man.

'The ICU is through here,' Hamish said, guiding Kate with a hand on her elbow to an area she hadn't explored with Brian.

Talk about state of the art. Many city hospitals Kate had seen would have been pleased to have such a set-up. Five rooms, all monitored from a central desk, but only one of them occupied. Behind the desk, a nurse and Emily frowned at the monitor.

Jack's was the room crowded with people in spite of ICU protocols that discouraged such practices.

'Kate!' Charles greeted her with relief. 'I'm sorry, but we thought if you could speak to him—rouse him. Alix is running new blood tests but as yet we can't find any physical reason for his sudden collapse.'

'He's been through a lot,' Kate reminded him, slipping past the man in the wheelchair to reach the side of Jack's bed and take one limp hand in both of hers.

'Hey, Jack, it's me, Kate. Sorry I was a bit late getting here, but you were ages in Theatre and a girl has to sleep some time.'

She was keeping it light, as she had earlier, but although Jack acknowledged her arrival by opening his eyes, that was all the response she got.

Cal, who'd been standing at the foot of the bed with his arm around Gina, nodded tiredly at Kate, then led Gina away. Jill, who looked as if she hadn't slept for days, also departed, her shoulders slumped as if Jack's failure to respond was somehow her fault.

Kate continued to talk, while Charles sat beside her, watching the screen for any kind of response from his nephew.

Nothing—well, not nothing, but the changes were all negative. They were looking on while a healthy young man died for no apparent reason.

Hamish stood outside the room, watching through the window, seeing the urgency in Kate's pose as she bent over the bed, trying to force a reaction of any kind from Jack.

Apparently deciding there was nothing he could do, Charles left the room, wheeling to a stop beside Hamish so he, too, could watch through the window.

'I tried to phone his mother, but got an answering-machine. Philip thinks she might be skiing in New Zealand. Even if we ask the police over there to track the family down, it could be days before she gets here.'

The anguish in Charles's voice told Hamish far more than the words. The man was blaming himself for insisting the lad stayed here in Crocodile Creek.

'You did all you could,' Hamish assured him. 'His whole blood clotting time was within acceptable limits, we had the desmopressin on hand for Lucky, so you were able to infuse that into him before the op. They couldn't have done any more in a major city hospital, and shifting him again might have provoked this problem earlier.'

But Charles refused to be comforted.

'I shouldn't have assumed my way was the best way,' he said bitterly. 'Damn it all, Hamish. There's far too much bad blood in this family already, without me having more of it on my hands.'

'You've already done what you can to get Jim and Honey

Cooper back on their feet and to end the feud between the Coopers and the Wetherbys,' he reminded Charles.

'Sure!' Charles growled. 'I patch things up just fine then let the father of their grandchild die. It'll start all over again!'

'Not if Kate has any say in it,' Hamish said, nodding to where Kate was ordering the young man to live.

Standing helplessly beside the bed, her gaze snapping from Jack to the monitor and back again, Kate thought about the story Hamish had told her. A family feud that had torn this modern-day Romeo from his Juliet.

His Juliet! His girlfriend! The baby! She swung around to see Hamish talking to Charles outside the window.

Leaving Jack's side, she headed out the door.

'Megan? Where's Megan? Is she still in the hospital? Or in town? Can we get her here? She's the one person to whom he might respond.'

Hamish, who'd heard Jack's insistence that Megan was the only girl for him, caught on fastest.

'She's living at Christina's house. I'll go there now.'

But Charles held him back.

'You think he cares about her? According to Jim, he hasn't seen her for six months.'

'He cares,' Hamish said, and Charles nodded.

'Then go and get her. I'll handle Jim.'

Satisfied she'd done what she could, Kate returned to Jack's side, and continued urging a response from him, but through the window she saw Charles wheel away—to tell Jim Cooper his daughter's boyfriend was now in the hospital?

Would Megan come? Kate was frustrated that she didn't know more about the dynamics of the relationship between Megan and Jack. There was a baby—but did Megan care about its father?

The question was answered very soon afterwards when a

plump young woman came racing into the ICU, Hamish hurrying rather ineffectually behind her.

'Where is he? Where's Jack?' she demanded.

Emily came out from behind the monitor to intercept her.

'Hush, Megan,' she said quietly. 'Calm down, love. You're not long out of here yourself.'

But Megan was beyond stopping. With one swift glance around the sterile space, she found which room held the man she sought and, stepping around Emily, headed straight for it.

But was it love or anger driving her? Kate had no idea, but she wasn't going to take any chances. She intercepted Megan as the excited young woman burst through the door.

'He's very sick. Don't shock him,' she warned, then put her arms around the newcomer as Megan's face crumpled and she let out an anguished cry.

'I wouldn't hurt him,' she whispered. 'I love him!'

The plaintive declaration speared pain deep into Kate's heart, but she held her ground, talking quietly to Megan to calm her before she approached Jack's bed.

'Hamish said there was no reason for him to be so sick,' Megan whimpered, allowing Kate to hold her while she stared at the pale, depleted figure on the bed.

'No, it just seems as if he's given up.'

'He can't do that. He's got a baby,' Megan protested. 'He can't die without knowing about Jackson.'

'He won't die,' Kate promised—both fiercely and foolishly—then she led Megan close to the bed, took Jack's hand and spoke to him again.

'Hey, Jack, I've got a surprise for you. This will make you open your eyes.'

She put his hand into Megan's and stepped back, while Megan collapsed into the chair beside the bed and brushed her lips across his hand. Tears spilled onto his skin and dampened the sheets, and Kate backed up against the wall and waited, knowing Megan needed to get her own emotions under control before she could speak to Jack.

'Jack, I'm here, and I love you so much. Please, don't leave me again. I tried so hard to believe I didn't love you. I even told myself I could live without you, but seeing you again I know I can't, so don't leave me, Jack, don't leave me again.'

Megan used his hand to wipe away fresh tears, and Kate found herself swallowing hard and hoping her eyes weren't brimming too obviously.

'I need you, Jack,' Megan continued, her voice steady although she was trembling all over. 'You have no idea how much I need you—especially now.'

She glanced up at Kate, despairing questions in her eyes. Was she talking too much? Was it doing any good?

And the big one—should she tell him about the baby?

Or maybe Kate imagined that one. She hoped so because she had no idea how a young man might respond to the unexpected news he was a father.

'Keep talking, that's all you can do,' she said.

Megan obeyed, telling Jack she'd been here in hospital herself and though she'd been sick she'd kept thinking of him and that had kept her going.

'We need each other, Jack,' she said, imploring a response from him. 'We're meant to be together.'

But Kate, who was watching the monitor all the time, willing a change in the slowly declining peaks, knew the words were being lost somewhere in the caverns of emptiness inside the young man.

Megan gave her one last despairing look, then threw the last dice.

'We have a baby, Jack. A little boy. I called him Jackson—you know, Jack's son. He's been sick too, Jack, he has a bad heart, but he's a fighter, our baby, a real little champ.'

There! The spike Kate had been praying for happened, and

she turned her attention from the monitor to the patient. Jack had opened his eyes, startling Megan so much she began to cry again.

'A baby?' Kate lip-read the question, as his voice was strangled by the tubes in his nose and mouth.

Megan held both his hands now, and nodded, tears falling all over him.

'A baby called Jackson. I'll bring him in to show you just as soon as you're well enough.'

'Now!'

Neither Megan nor Kate could decipher the word, until Jack repeated it.

Megan turned to Kate.

'The baby's still here in the nursery because he ran a temperature last week and he's still not feeding well. Can I bring him now?'

Kate had no idea of the protocol of tiny babies in this ICU, but Charles had obviously heard the conversation, for he was at the door.

'I'll get Lucky for you,' he said to Megan, then he smiled apologetically and added, 'Jackson! I must remember Jackson!'

He wheeled away, Megan returning to Jack's side to tell him the baby was on the way, and that he looked just like his father, and now Jack was back they could be a family.

And although Jack's eyes had closed, Kate could tell he hadn't slipped away from them again. He'd left that no-man's land between life and death and, hopefully, wouldn't return there for a long, long time.

Leaving the little family in the ICU in Charles's hands, Kate returned to the house, but now, in daylight, she knew she wouldn't sleep. Not that there was time for sleep. It was after six and she'd been told the hospital car left for Wygera at eight. She changed into her running gear, slipped on her trainers and once again went quietly out of the house.

This time, however, she heard noises in the old building, voices from the side veranda—CJ and Cal, she guessed, while Mike was sitting at the kitchen table, talking into a mobile phone.

He lifted a hand in salute to Kate, then jotted something in a small notebook on the table in front of him.

Kate waved back and continued on her way. A good run over the headland would shake away the cobwebs her interrupted night's sleep had left behind, and prepare her for whatever lay ahead.

She began slowly, pacing herself as she crossed the dewy grass, relishing the salt tang of the air as she drew it deeply into her lungs. Then her rhythm picked up and she extended her pace so she reached the sun-drenched summit winded enough to need to bend over to regain her breath.

So it wasn't until she straightened that the full beauty of the place struck her—the blue-green of the sea, the curved hump of an island on the horizon, the golden sands curling around the cove.

Finally, a house by the sea. Maybe she'd extend her contract.

Maybe if her father wanted her…

Best not to think about it, she reminded herself, but the warning came too late. Thinking about the father she didn't know had disrupted the blissful serenity her run had given her, and now, as she stared out at the peaceful sea, disquiet was growing again within her.

Or was the disquiet because she sensed she was no longer alone on the bluff?

She turned, wondering if it was one of the housemates she hadn't yet met who was joining her in her silent communion with the sea.

It *was* a housemate, but one she knew—one she'd been trying not to think about as she'd run across the tough, springy grass of the headland.

'Kate.'

Hamish was close enough to shield her from the breeze that had been fidgeting at her clothing, and her name was both an acknowledgement and a greeting.

She nodded in reply then decided to walk along the clifftop, assuming, if he wanted her company, he'd fall in beside her.

But instead he grasped her elbow, effectively halting her progress and, at the same time, turning her towards him.

He stared at her for a moment, as if uncertain who she was.

'This is the most ridiculous situation,' he grumbled at her.

'Walking on a clifftop?'

'No!'

The grumble had become a growl.

'Then what?'

Batman would never have asked that question.

Batman would have known the answer without having to ask.

In actual fact, Kate knew the answer, too, because she could feel the attraction between them simmering in the clean morning air.

Pollution, that was what it was…

And, as Hamish had said, it was a ridiculous situation. They'd barely met. He was going away.

'Do you know how badly I want to kiss you?' His voice was tight enough to make the words sound clipped and harsh.

'I can guess,' Kate admitted, as her own body hummed with a quite absurd desire to do the same to him. 'But I'm sure it's just proximity that's doing this to us. We shared a night of tension, out there in the gorge with Jack, and it drew us closer together than a month of normal company might do.'

Did she sound down to earth and together, or had her internal flutters botched the job?

'Do you honestly believe a work-related bond would make me want to kiss you? I've worked with Cal for two years and never wanted to kiss him. Or Emily. Or Christina.'

Hamish didn't seem to be moving but his body was narrowing the gap between the two of them so now she could feel its warmth.

'I should hope not,' Kate retorted, edging backwards because the warmth was dangerous. 'You can't go around kissing all your colleagues. And that includes me. Apart from anything else, with me, anyway, it's impractical. Think about it, Hamish! Starting something would be idiotic. You're going home in less than three weeks and I'm here on a mission. It's a perfect example of the wrong time and the wrong place.'

She was trying hard not to look directly at him—looking at Hamish being something more safely done from a distance—but she knew for sure he'd greeted this prime example of common sense with a frown.

Knew for sure he'd closed the gap between them once again!

'Wrong time? Wrong place? Is there such a thing with kisses?' he demanded, then, without waiting for her answer, his lips closed on hers, warm and firm and all-encompassing, claiming her mouth like a trophy, tempting her lips open with an inciting tongue, luring from her a response she knew she shouldn't give.

The kiss lasted until her knees gave out and she slumped against his body.

'Hamish!'

The word she'd intended as a protest came out more like an endearment, encouraging him to lock his arms around her body and draw her close against him, supporting her, so he could continue to plunder her mouth at will.

The sweet invasion warmed the lonely places in her heart, seducing her with its promise, and although her head knew kissing Hamish was not at all a good idea, her heart longed for more—her body demanded more.

No! Kate broke away, frightened by the intensity of whatever it was between them.

'I'm going back,' she said abruptly, and ran away, heading

down towards the house—hoping she might find her lost sanity along the way.

CJ was on the top step again, but as Kate drew close Cal appeared, hoisting the child onto his shoulders and carrying him down the steps.

'I'm taking a spaceship to child care,' CJ told her, waving a cardboard contraption in the air above Cal's head. 'And Mr Grubb's taken Rudolph to get his shots so he won't follow me today.'

Kate congratulated them both on the excellent spaceship, wished CJ a happy day then took the steps two at a time, crossing the veranda and finding Emily in the kitchen with Mike.

'Hi, Kate. Have you met Mike? Our second chopper pilot and paramedic.'

Emily had a possessive hand resting on Mike's shoulder, and the same sheen in her eyes that Kate had noticed in Gina's the previous day.

The love epidemic?

'We met last night,' Kate explained. 'Jack OK?'

Emily beamed at her.

'More OK than he was earlier. We'd thought of bringing Megan in, but we had no idea if he'd want to see her or not. He hadn't been in touch with her for six months, so we thought maybe he'd be more upset than he already was.'

She paused for breath, then added, 'Hamish said Jack told you both how he felt about his girlfriend, and how he'd tried to go and visit her.'

'It's often a case of whatever works in medicine, isn't it?' Mike said, patting Emily's hand, which still rested on his shoulder. 'How was your run?'

The change of subject was somewhat abrupt and Mike's question was innocent enough, yet Kate felt colour surge into her cheeks. Could people see the headland from the kitchen? Or had Mike been outside and seen her kissing Hamish?

'It was fine,' she said, 'but I'm very sweaty. I've got to change for work.'

And with that she escaped to her room.

It didn't matter who saw what, she told herself, but she knew it did. After the public humiliation she'd endured with Daniel and Lindy, Kate was determined her private life would be just that—private.

Not that she intended having a private life with Hamish.

She'd have a shower, grab a bowl of cereal—she would have to find out about cooking and shopping rosters—then go over to the hospital well in time for the trip to Wygera.

If she was early enough, she could get her roster from Jill. Maybe she could get the doctors' rosters as well. Then all she had to do was make sure she was always busy if she and Hamish happened to have corresponding time off.

Avoidance—that was the answer.

The white station wagon with the 24-hour-rescue emblem she was beginning to recognise as belonging to the hospital, pulled up in front of her, the driver—from his sheer size—unmistakable.

'Charles or Cal usually do Wygera clinics,' Hamish said cheerfully, reaching across to open the door for her, 'but Cal's got a theatre list today and Charles wants to stay close to Jack, so you're stuck with me again.'

Kate eyed him with suspicion. It wasn't so much that he might have engineered this togetherness—after all, he didn't know about her avoidance decision—but the way he was acting so…well, colleaguey!

Weird!

Uncomfortable, even.

But two could play at pretending they hadn't exchanged heated kisses on a headland a bare hour earlier.

'Will you be helping me judge the swimming pool designs?'

'Oh, no, not me! That's your job, Sister Winship. Yours

alone, although remind me when we get there, I've got young Shane's model in the back of the car. He came in a few days ago with a burst appendix and as he had to finish his model in hospital we gave him an extra couple of days to get his entry in.'

Kate remembered the talk about the competition she'd heard the previous evening. And CJ's words as well.

'And CJ and Max's entry? They were working on it last night. Have you got that on board?'

Hamish turned and smiled at her, and she forgot swimming pools, and models, and a small boy who needed a cowboy hat.

This could *not* be happening!

'Cal has already ordered a cowboy hat for Max and he and CJ will get it as a consolation prize,' Hamish said. 'That was arranged after Rudolph ate the dressing sheds which they'd made out of dog biscuits.'

Kate had to laugh, but Hamish's tone made her feel uncomfortable.

He was either far, far better at this colleague stuff than she was, or his words about needing to kiss her had been just that—words.

Or maybe he tested women with a kiss.

Maybe he'd tested her and she'd failed.

The thought made her so depressed she remembered she was going to Wygera so she could see something of the countryside, and she looked out the window at the canefields through which they were passing, seeing nothing but a green blur, while her mind wondered just what the man beside her might have expected from a kiss.

Kissing ineptitude—was that why Daniel had chosen Lindy?

'Aboriginal community.'

Kate tuned back in to Hamish's conversation but it was too late. Not a word of it could she recall.

'I'm sorry, I missed that,' she said, facing him again, although that was dangerous when he might smile at any time.

'Canefields *are* fascinating,' he said, eyes twinkling to let her know he knew she hadn't seen them.

He knew too damn much!

'I was saying that as well as a swimming pool, Wygera needs some kind of industry. Perhaps industry is the wrong word, but a number of aboriginal communities like it are self-supporting. They run cattle stations, or tourist resorts. In the Northern Territory there are artists' colonies. The problem is Wygera's close enough to Croc Creek for some of the men to be employed there, but there's not enough employment in town for all of them. Nor does everyone want to drive fifty miles back and forth to work.'

'So kids grow up and leave home,' Kate said, understanding the problem of the lack of employment in small towns.

'Or don't leave home and get into trouble,' Hamish said, sounding more gloomy than she'd ever heard him.

'You sound as if you really care,' she said, thinking how different he was from some city doctors she had known who felt their responsibilities ended when a patient walked out the door.

'Of course I care!' he snapped. 'I've worked with these people for two years and become friends with a number of them. Just because I'm going home, it doesn't mean I'll stop thinking about them. But until something happens to change things at Wygera, these clinic runs—well, doctors and nurses will go on treating symptoms rather than the problem.'

They'd turned off the main highway onto a narrower road which ran as straight as a ruler towards a high water tower.

'Wygera!' Hamish said, nodding towards the tower, and gradually, beneath it, a cluster of houses became evident. Dilapidated houses for the most part, with dogs dozing in the dirt in the shade cast by gutted car bodies. Kate recognised the look—there were suburbs in Melbourne where car bodies were the equivalent of garden gnomes in front-yard decor.

Beyond the houses, the ground sloped down to where thickly grouped trees suggested a creek or a river.

But if the town had a creek or river, why would it need a swimming pool?

# CHAPTER SIX

HAMISH PULLED UP in front of a small building with a table and three chairs set up outside and a group of people lounging around on logs, chairs, or small patches of grass.

'Medicine, Wygera-style,' he said to Kate. 'If the weather's good we work outside, although there are perfectly adequate examination, waiting and treatment rooms inside the building.'

He nodded towards a stand of eucalypts some distance away, where more people lay around in the shade.

'They're your lot. We come out a couple of times a week, and today's well-baby day, but if you see anything that worries you, shoot the person over to me. Eye problems are the main worries with the kids, diabetes with the mums. They'll all have their cards with them—the health worker sees them before we arrive.'

Kate accepted all this information and advice, then, as a young man opened her door with a flourish, she stepped out and looked around her.

The place was nestled in the foothills of the mountains that divided the coastal plain from the cattle country further inland. The ground was bare and rocky, with grass struggling to grow here and there, mainly in the patches of shade.

'Your bag, ma'am,' Hamish said, handing her a square suitcase from the back of the station wagon. 'Scales, swabs, dressings and so on all inside, but Jake here will act as your runner if you need anything else.'

Kate took the bag, but the young man—presumably Jake—who had opened the car door lifted it out of her hand and led her towards the trees, where the shapes became women and children as Kate drew closer. Another table was set out there, with two chairs beside it, but Kate wondered if she might be better sitting on the grass with the women.

'Sit on the chair, then the women can put babies on your knee,' Jake told her, while another woman who Jake introduced as Millie got up from the grass and took the second chair.

'I'm the health worker here,' she said, unpacking the case and setting up the baby scales. 'I do the weighing.'

'Thanks,' Kate said, but she glanced towards the clinic building. Strange it didn't have its own scales.

'People take them to weigh fish and potatoes and bananas, not so good afterwards for babies,' Millie said, while Kate wondered if people in North Queensland had a special ability to read minds or if she'd always been so easy to read.

Though Hamish was a Scot, not a North Queenslander.

She almost glanced towards him, but remembered Millie and caught herself just in time.

'I'm Kate,' she said to the assembled throng, then she took her chair. 'Now, who's first?'

Some of the women giggled, and there was general shuffling, but Millie called a name and a pretty girl in blue jeans and a short tight top came forward, a tiny baby in her arms.

Kate looked at the girl's flat stomach, complete with navel ring, and decided she couldn't possibly have had a child, but Angela was indeed baby Joseph's mother.

'He just needs weighing and I'm worried about this rash,' she said, putting the baby on the table and whipping off his disposable nappy. 'See!'

The angry red rash in his groin and across his buttocks would have been hard to miss.

Kate delved into the bag, assuming she'd find a specimen tube and swab. Yes, it was as well equipped for a well-baby clinic as the equipment pack had been for Jack's retrieval. She wiped a swab across the rash, dropped it into the tube, and screwed the lid shut and completed the label, taking Joseph's full name from the card.

'Nappy rash, I told her,' Millie said. 'Said to leave off his nappies or use cloth ones on him.'

'I did leave his nappy off,' Angela protested, 'and it didn't get better, and I tried cloth nappies.'

'Actually, the latest tests seem to find that disposable nappies are less irritating to the skin than cloth ones,' Kate said gently, not wanting to put Millie off side, but wanting to get the message across to Angela. 'Also, if we look at the shiny surface of the rash and the way there are separate spots of it here and there, I think it might be candida—a yeast infection.'

'Like women get?' Angela asked, and Kate nodded.

'A similar thing. It's caused by yeast from the bowel and by bacteria and is more uncomfortable for poor Joseph than simple nappy rash, but there's a cream you can use that should clear it up.'

What next? From what she'd seen of the town, it didn't have a chemist's shop, so getting Hamish to write a prescription seemed pointless.

'Cream in the bag,' Millie said to Kate. Millie obviously knew far more about clinic visits than Kate did! 'This stuff stains his nappies so don't you be worrying about it,' Millie continued, addressing Angela this time, while Kate found the cream, one per cent hydrocortisone and three per cent iodochlorhydroxyquin—and, yes, the tube said it could leave a yellow stain.

Millie certainly knew more than Kate did!

'Spread it thinly over the sore part twice a day,' Kate told Angela. 'Like this.'

She used a treated cloth to wipe the little fellow's nether regions clean and another cloth to dry him off, then smeared a little of the cream over the bright scarlet rash. 'You really need just a thin smear—putting it on more thickly doesn't make the slightest difference. If it hasn't shown signs of improvement, come back…'

There wouldn't be a well-baby clinic more than once a fortnight but Kate remembered Hamish saying they did clinics, plural, each week.

'Come back and see whoever comes later in the week,' she finished, while Angela handed the baby and his card over to Millie for weighing and recording.

'You give Joseph to his gran and get back to school,' Millie told Angela when Joseph had his nappy on again and was ready to go.

'She's still at school?' Kate asked Millie, while they waited for the next patient.

'Last year, university next year. Wants to be a doctor. She'll do it, too. Her mother'll go to Townsville with her to mind Joseph while she studies. Girl's got guts and brains—just stupid in the heart.'

Stupid in the heart! It was such an apt phrase it stayed with Kate as she examined another eight babies and listened to the problems their mothers had. She brought some up to date on their triple antigens, administered Neosporin drops into weeping eyes, gave advice to mothers on weaning, solids, diarrhoea and contraception, Millie letting her know in unsubtle ways whether she agreed or disagreed with the advice dispensed.

'Lunch and judging time.'

Kate looked around to see Hamish approaching.

Stupid in the heart, Kate reminded herself just in case the reaction inside her had been something other than hunger manifesting itself.

'Why doesn't Millie take the well-baby clinic?' she asked Hamish as they drove further into the town. 'She knows the people and certainly knows as much if not more than I do.'

'She says the people take more notice of someone from the hospital. They go to Millie in between our visits then come to see us to confirm what she's told them.'

'And that doesn't drive her wild? That they don't believe her in the first place?'

Hamish smiled.

'I think it would take a lot to drive Millie wild. She just accepts that's the way things are and gets on with her job.'

And that's a salutary lesson for you, Kate told herself, then she gazed in astonishment at the building in front of her.

'What *is* this place?'

'Local hall. Funded by the federal government and designed in Canberra, which is why the roof is steeply pitched—so snow can slide off it.'

Kate was laughing as she got out of the car into the searing heat of what in North Queensland was considered cool spring weather, but once inside her laughter stopped, though a smile lingered on her lips.

The models, dozens of them, were set out on tables in the middle of the hall.

'So many? Boy, the people here are really enthusiastic about having a swimming pool.'

'You'd better believe it! But we'll eat first. Wygera does the best lunches of all our clinic runs,' Hamish said, leading her past the tables of exhibits to the back of the hall, where three women waited in a large kitchen.

'Cold roast beef and salad. That all right?' asked an older woman Hamish introduced as Mary.

'Sounds great,' Kate said, though she felt uncomfortable sitting at the table with Hamish while the women served and fussed over them, offering bread and butter to go with the salad, tea or coffee, then finally producing a luscious-looking trifle, decorated with chocolate curls.

'I bet the female staff refuse to do more than one Wygera trip a week,' Kate said, smiling at the women. 'I'd be the size of a house if I came here more often.'

'We like visitors, so why not show them how we feel with good food?' Mary said, then she cleared the table while one of the other women walked back into the hall with Kate.

'All the plans and models have numbers and the doctors who were here on Sunday, they have a list of the number and the names, so all you have to do is choose one and tell them the number. Dr Cal, he has the list.'

Kate turned around, thinking she might co-opt Hamish into helping her, but he was still in the kitchen, talking to Mary.

So she pulled her little notebook and pen out of her pocket and did an initial survey of the entries.

Round and round she went, slowly eliminating designs, until finally one was left. It had bits of dying bushes where trees would be planted, and tiny plastic animals sliding down plastic rulers to show waterslides. Scraps of drinking straws indicated where water would stream out from spa jets and what looked suspiciously like a hospital kidney dish represented the main pool.

'This is it,' she said to Hamish, who, with the other women, had now joined her in the hall and were eagerly awaiting the decision.

'But that's Shane's,' Hamish said, apparently recognising the model he'd brought into the hall earlier.

'Does that disqualify it in some way?' Kate asked.

'No, no, of course not,' Hamish said quickly, then he smiled. 'In fact, I think it's great. Poor kid's been sick as a dog since his appendix op, and this will cheer him right up.'

He turned to the three women.

'Will you keep it quiet or should we announce it straight away?'

'People will know straight away whether you tell or not,' Mary said. 'People always know things.'

This was no more relevant to her situation than the 'stupid hearts' comment had been, Kate told herself, yet 'people know things' joined the 'stupid in the heart' phrase in her head, as if both were philosophical concepts of prime importance in her life.

You do not *know* you're attracted to Hamish—you just think you could be, she reminded herself. But the phrase refused to budge.

'This afternoon we work together, usually doing a bit of minor surgery in the clinic itself. Some days there's a long list and other times we get an early mark.'

Hamish explained this as he carried Shane's model out to the station wagon. They would take it back to Crocodile Creek and pass it on to the architect, hoping he would at least follow the concept of this winning design.

Still in colleague mode, Kate registered, which was good—at least one of them would be totally focussed on work!

But Kate's mind found focus soon enough. Their first patient was a middle-aged man, Pete, with a fish hook caught in his wrist. As he peeled off a grubby bandage, Kate could see the angry red line that indicated infection running up his arm from the wound.

'You did the right thing, cutting off the barbed end and trying to pull it back through,' Hamish said, as he injected a local anaesthetic around the injured part. 'But slashing at yourself with razor blades to try to cut it out wasn't the brightest follow-up treatment.'

'M'mate did that,' Pete told them. 'We were up the river in the boat, and we'd had a few tinnies, and he thought he'd get it out.'

Now the wound was cleaned, Kate could see the slashes across the man's wrist, making it look like a particularly inept suicide attempt.

Or was it, and the fish hook just an excuse?

She glanced at Hamish, who was now probing the wounds carefully and competently, talking quietly to Pete about fish and fishing.

He was obviously a doctor who saw his patient as a person first while his easy camaraderie with the women at lunchtime had suggested they saw him as a friend.

'Ah, I can see it now. Forceps, Kate.'

Recalled to duty, Kate passed the implement but, try as he might, Hamish couldn't pull the hook free.

'I'll have to cut down to it,' he said, and Kate produced a packaged scalpel for him, carefully peeling off the protective covering and passing it to him.

'Soluble sutures for inside and some tough thread for the skin—these guys don't treat their wounds with any consideration,' Hamish told her, as he cut into the man's wrist. 'And check Pete's card for his tetanus status.'

Kate found the sutures Hamish would need, prepared a tetanus injection and another of penicillin, certain Pete would need an antibiotic boost even if Hamish gave him tablets. Another check of his card showed he'd had penicillin before so they had no need to worry about allergies.

But it was the need for his last dose of penicillin that drew Kate's attention. A fish hook in his foot?

'Was Pete plain unlucky or are fish hooks particularly aggressive up here in North Queensland?' she asked Hamish as, three hours later, they drove away from Wygera. 'He had one in his foot only six months ago.'

Hamish turned to smile at her.

'Pete's mad keen on fishing. He took me out once, but once was enough. I know the boat we were in was bigger than the crocodiles I kept seeing lazing on the bank, but not by much. In fact, it got flimsier and flimsier the longer we stayed out, especially when some of the crocs got off the bank and started swimming towards us.'

'Real crocodiles?'

Kate knew it had been a stupid question as soon as she'd asked it, but she'd just blurted the words out.

'Too, too real,' Hamish said, 'although before that day I thought Crocodile Creek was just a name. You know, like Snake Gully. Maybe someone once saw a snake there, but it doesn't mean there are dozens of the things in the gully.'

'But there are dozens of crocodiles in the creek?'

Kate looked nervously out the car window. How far from creeks did crocodiles travel? And hadn't she heard they could run faster than a horse?

Could a horse run faster than a car?

'Hey, we're safe,' Hamish said gently, slowing the car and resting his hand on her shoulder.

'I know that!' Kate snapped. Now she compared the two experiences, thinking of crocodiles in a creek not far from where she'd sat and looked at babies was freaking her out far more than the man with the gun had.

Then she'd been able to snuggle close to Hamish for protection. Now she'd look stupid if she straddled the gear lever to get close to him, which, from other points of view, would not be a good idea anyway.

'I can see why they need a swimming pool. I wouldn't want to swim in a creek with crocodiles.'

Somehow talk of swimming pools and crocodiles kept them going for most of the journey, though tension built inside Kate until she wondered if she'd burst with it.

But when Hamish pulled off the road into a parking area that gave a view over the town and the cove and the sea beyond it, she guessed she wasn't the only one feeling the crackling in the air between them. He was just better at hiding it.

He turned towards her, his eyes looking black in the shadowy car.

'Is it the wrong time and the wrong place, Kate?'

He kissed her gently, but even a gentle kiss fired her heartbeats.

'Can you deny there's something special between us? Can you deny you feel what I feel when we're together—deny there's magic in our kisses?'

Kate tried, she really did, but she couldn't, and in the end she had to shake her head.

'But it's not about magic, Hamish, it's about trust.'

He kissed her again.

'I know that, which is why we don't need to hurry things—don't need to put the pressure of a three-week time limit on getting to know each other. I know you want to find your father, but there's every chance, particularly if we involve people from the hospital, you can do that in a few days. Then why don't you come to Scotland with me? No pressure or promises. Just come, to see how things might work out.'

The strength of his hands, and the warmth they generated, seeped deep into Kate's body, but it was all too soon, and taking warmth from someone else was far too dangerous.

'I don't think so, Hamish,' she said quietly, and sat back in her seat.

At least now crocodiles weren't the main worry in her mind.

Hamish paused for a few seconds, then reversed out of their parking space and pulled out onto the highway, starting up a conversation about the necessity to watch out for kangaroos on the roads around dawn and dusk.

It was, she was learning, typical of this kind, caring, empathetic man—not play-acting at being a colleague but genuinely trying to set her at ease.

She was beginning to admire Colleague Hamish.

Back at the hospital, they unpacked the car then, as Hamish went to report to Charles, she walked through to the ICU to visit Jack.

* * *

Jack was lying with his eyes closed, and though he opened them when Kate said hello, his eyelids soon drooped, but the smile on his face, even as he slept, told Kate all she needed to know.

She dropped into the chair beside Megan, who was anchored to the bed by Jack's hand clasping both of hers.

'Are you OK?'

Megan nodded, a tremulous smile on her lips.

'Dad came to see him,' she whispered to Kate, 'before they transferred him to Townsville for his bypass. He told Jack he'd better hurry and get better, because he was needed out at Cooper's Crossing.'

Megan's smile improved as she added proudly, 'That's our place. Dad wants him there, but not right away. Dad and Charles have been talking. They think Jack and I should get agriculture training—they say we should spend a few years at university so we're sure we know what we're doing. Charles says there's enough money to fund it and that there's child care at university.'

She paused and her smile, if possible, grew even more radiant.

'University, Kate! Can you imagine? Then we'll come home and with water we'll make Cooper's Crossing viable again. It'll be as good as Wetherby, good enough to support two families—the Ransomes and the Coopers. Together.'

As Megan's expression suggested this was the most wonderful of ideas, Kate gave her a hug and told her how happy she was, hiding her own reservations about this happy-ever-after-ending until she'd left the ICU.

Charles and Hamish were talking outside the ED and though she didn't want to interrupt—and certainly didn't want to get entangled with Hamish again, as colleague or kisser—she did want to know if Harry was proceeding with his enquiries.

She hesitated, and Charles saw her and settled her indecision.

'We were just talking about you,' he called to her.

'Surely I haven't been here long enough to be in trouble,' she said lightly, smiling at Charles.

'Far from it,' Charles assured her. 'No, we were talking about Jack. Harry really needs to see him and, for Jack's sake, the sooner the mess with his mates Todd and Digger is sorted out, the better. Emily says, providing there's no setback, we can move him out of ICU tomorrow, and once he's on a ward it will be hard to keep Harry away from him.'

'You'll stay with him when Harry interviews him?' Kate asked anxiously.

Charles looked at a point somewhere over her head.

'That's actually why we were talking about you. I know you were employed to work the ED here, but I wondered if you'd mind working the men's ward for the next few days. I don't want to seem as if I'm standing guard over the lad, it will make him look bad, but I'd like to think he has someone he knows and trusts hovering around. I'll tell Harry he's still sufficiently ill that I want a nurse with him while he's interviewed. Would you do it?'

'Of course,' Kate said. 'Do I see Jill? She'll need to change someone else's shift as well as mine.'

'I'll fix it up with Jill. What were you working tomorrow?'

'Early shift,' Kate told him. 'Six to three.'

Charles smiled at her.

'Well, isn't this your lucky day? We'll transfer Jack in the morning, and he'll need to rest after the move, so I won't let Harry near him until the afternoon. If you could do the afternoon shift, midday to nine, that should cover the time Harry's likely to be there, and if you're already on the ward, it won't look as if we've brought in someone especially to be with Jack.'

Kate smiled at Charles's obvious satisfaction with this plan. In fact, it pleased her as well. She'd have the morning free to explore the town and, once she'd found out how shopping and cooking rosters worked in the house, maybe shop as well.

She nodded to the two men and walked away, her thoughts veering between Hamish, who'd been silent throughout her talk to Charles, and Jack—was he well enough for Harry to question him?

'Are you happy taking on the role of protector?' Hamish fell in beside her. 'Do you feel you'd be able to stop Harry's questioning if you felt it necessary?'

Kate stopped and turned towards him.

'Medical question?' she asked, feeling warmth within, although he wasn't touching her.

'Medical question,' he confirmed, though the look in his eyes suggested he was feeling things not entirely medical.

'You bet your life I'd stop the questioning if I felt it was affecting his recovery in any way.'

'Mama bear protecting her cub?' Hamish teased, and Kate had to agree.

'I'm probably the very worst person to have there, because I do feel over-protective about Jack, but the slightest sign he might be tiring and Harry will be out of there.'

Hamish smiled at her.

'Word gets around the hospital quickly. When I hear Harry's arrived I might drop by, in case you need moral support.'

'And you're not over-protective?'

Hamish shrugged in a way that suggested agreement, leaving Kate to wonder if it was Jack or her that Hamish was protecting.

They walked out into the scented garden that drew Kate like a magnet, together only as colleagues, she was sure.

Its potent spell filled her head with pleasure, so worries over Kissing Hamish and Colleague Hamish were banished to the far reaches of her brain, and even her concern for Jack lost its hard, knobbly edges of doubt and dread.

# CHAPTER SEVEN

HARRY FAILED TO arrive the next day, and Jill explained she'd like Kate to stay on the ward until he did come. Not a bad idea, as far as Kate was concerned, as she hadn't seen Hamish all day, whereas in the ED, if a child came in, she'd have had to call him as he was the doctor with the most paediatric experience in the hospital.

And being on duty until nine meant she could eat dinner at the hospital, and by the time she'd signed off and walked back to the house, it was late enough to go straight to bed, pleading tiredness should any of her housemates be hanging around.

The arrangement was perfect as far as Hamish-avoidance went.

Until she had to walk through the kitchen on her way to her room! He was over by the bench, waiting for the electric kettle to boil.

'Cup of tea?'

She checked her watch and studied him suspiciously.

'Were you waiting for me to come off duty?'

'Me?'

All innocence!

But then he smiled. 'Of course I was. I haven't seen you all day. Do you think I'd miss this opportunity? Now, did you say yes to tea?'

'No, I didn't,' Kate said crossly, although her mouth had

suddenly gone dry and she could kill for a cup of tea. 'And not seeing each other is a good idea, Hamish. I don't want to get into another relationship—not now, not here, not anywhere.'

He had turned his back, busying himself with cups and the kettle, and finally turned back and set a cup of tea on the table in front of her.

'You'd deny the magic?'

He spoke so softly she barely heard him. She wanted to yell, to tell him she'd had magic before and it had let her down, but she knew that what she and Daniel had shared had been an illusion—a magic trick, not the real thing at all. Only it had taken her longer than it had Daniel to work that out.

She picked up the cup of tea and sipped at it, eyeing Hamish cautiously over the rim.

'I'm not answering that, and I'm taking my tea through to my room.'

Would he argue? Pursue her?

Not Hamish. She answered her own question even before she heard his quiet 'Goodnight, Kate.'

So with a cup of tea in her hand, and loneliness beyond measuring in her heart, she walked through to her bedroom.

Hamish watched her walk away then took himself out onto the back veranda, settling into the old settee.

He needed to get rid of the baggage of his feelings and think this through with cool, unemotional logic.

Was he stupid, pursuing this attraction Kate obviously didn't want?

Yes.

So he should stop.

Right.

Would he?

Didn't even need to ask that question. This was different. This was special. This was something he'd never felt before…

* * *

Jack's condition improved steadily, and the following afternoon he watched Megan feed the baby, then held his son for a short time, before nodding off to sleep.

Megan was in the nursery, bathing Jackson before returning him to his crib, and Kate was putting a new dressing on Jack's wound when Harry wandered in.

'OK if we talk a bit?' he said to Jack, while Kate tried to act as if she was part of the furniture.

Jack did his eye-closing thing, but Kate knew he was refreshed and this was probably a good time for Harry to question him.

'You have to talk to Harry some time,' she said quietly. 'Why not at least start now. I'll be here, and if I see you getting tired I'll send Harry away, but at least start, Jack.'

He opened his eyes, looked at her for a moment, then nodded and turned to Harry.

'I honestly had no idea that they were anything more than cattle drovers,' he said. 'Not at first.'

'And who were "they"?'

Jack looked startled.

'Todd and Digger of course.'

'That's all the names you knew?'

Jack nodded.

'Met them in a pub out past Gunyamurra. They had a camp in an old station house way out on the edges of some property. Could even have been Wetherby Downs, but it was a place I'd never been. Todd said they had to hold these cattle there because they were expecting more.'

Kate had finished the dressing and now she took Jack's arm, unobtrusively holding his wrist so she could feel if his pulse began to race or falter.

Jack sipped from a glass of water, then continued.

'About the time of the Gunyamurra rodeo they gave me some time off—I tried to visit Megan but couldn't get the right lifts. I thought they were going to the rodeo because they kept talking about it, but when I got back they'd brought more cattle in. That's when I saw the brands.'

'What brands?' Harry asked, as Megan walked back into the ward and, seeing Harry with Jack, came flying across to the bed.

'It's OK, Megan,' Kate said quietly, but Megan was not to be stopped.

'He's still too sick!' she yelled at Harry. 'Can't you see that?' Then she turned her fury on Kate. 'You should have stopped him.'

Behind her, Kate sensed another presence and turned to see that Hamish had come in quietly.

'He has to answer questions some time, Megan,' Hamish told her, but Megan refused to be appeased, and as Jack had closed his eyes again, this time with a finality Kate recognised, she indicated to Harry to walk away. She followed him out of the room, leaving Hamish to reassure Megan that her loved one was all right.

'Jack *was* getting tired,' Kate said to Harry. 'Why don't you come back in the morning? Patients are always fresher then. And in the morning Megan is due to spend some time with Susie, learning massage techniques for Jackson.'

Harry smiled.

'She was as fierce as a mother bear protecting her cub, wasn't she?' he said, and Kate nodded, though she was thinking not of Megan's behaviour but of Hamish, who had said the same thing to her the previous evening.

Hamish who was now holding Megan in his arms and no doubt whispering all the soothing, special, comforting things she needed to hear.

He *was* special…

Get your mind off him and onto your patient! Think Jack!

Kate set her mind to it, recalling the questions and answers. Jack had been talking easily about the cattle until he'd come to the bit about the brands.

'Worries?'

So much for getting Hamish out of her mind by thinking about Jack! But, then, maybe Hamish could help.

Kate glanced back into the room to see Megan sitting quietly at Jack's side, while he apparently slept, and turned her attention to the man she'd been determined to avoid.

'Jack was upset by the questions before Megan came in,' she explained. 'Remember when you were telling me what might have happened and you said Jack might have recognised the Wetherby Downs brand and realised the cattle were stolen?'

'In the cave?'

Kate nodded.

'Well, what if they weren't Wetherby cattle but Cooper cattle he recognised? Would he want to admit that? When Jim had just welcomed him to the family and Megan was nearby to hear?'

Hamish put his hand on her shoulder.

'Do you always take on the worries of the world?'

'It's not the world, it's Jack,' she retorted. 'And if Harry comes back in the morning to cover this tricky stuff, I'd like to be there, but I'm not a lawyer and maybe that's what he needs.'

She used her own hand to lift his away and determinedly ignored the effects of both touches, but he wasn't going to be put off.

'It's your tea-break—I checked,' he said. 'Let's go talk to Charles about it.'

He led the way, guiding her along corridors and tapping quietly at the door before entering. Jill was there, which pleased Kate who was beginning to feel she was making a fuss about nothing but obscurely felt Jill might understand.

Jill could also change her shifts!

Charles greeted them as if he was used to small staff delegations wandering through his door, and asked how he could help.

'Kate will explain,' Hamish offered, so she brought Charles up to date and explained her worries.

'So,' she added, directly to Jill this time, 'I know it's a nuisance to keep switching shifts around, but if I could work maybe nine to six tomorrow, I'd be there in the morning when Harry comes, and still there in the afternoon if he happens to be held up.'

Jill assured her it would be OK but she was obviously as worried about Jack as Kate was.

'Is it time to bring in a lawyer for him?' Hamish asked Charles.

He thought about it for a minute, then shook his head.

'At the moment it's all pretty low key. Harry's getting the information he needs—there is an old homestead out on one of the back blocks of Wetherby, by the way, but no one's kept cattle on that block for years so Jack wouldn't have known of it. Anyway, Harry's happy and Jack's not too distressed, and the way I look at it, if he can prove he had time off when the cattle were stolen—'

'He hitched lifts to try to get to Megan,' Kate broke in. 'We only have to find the people who gave him lifts and we can prove he wasn't there.'

Charles smiled at her.

'We'll find them,' he promised, but, though he sounded confident, when Kate turned to close his office door behind her and Hamish as they left, she caught him frowning.

Had he only said it to make her feel better?

'Now tea?'

How could someone make such ordinary words seductive?

'No!'

The single word snapped out and hung in the air for so long she finally had to add a feeble 'Thank you' before she marched off back to the ward.

Didn't he know she was avoiding him?

Of course he didn't! She'd practically leapt at his suggestion that they talk to Charles together.

Harry arrived at ten the next morning, while Kate was hanging a new bag of fluid on Jack's drip stand.

'You getting preferential treatment here, Jack?' he asked. 'A pretty nurse all to yourself?'

'I've only just got to him,' Kate protested, knowing Jack would be embarrassed by the question. 'I didn't like to disturb him earlier when Megan was here, and Mr Roberts needed a bit of TLC.'

She checked the calibrations on the drip and picked up Jack's chart, knowing she had to look busy if she wanted to hang around.

'So, we were up to where your mates—'

'They weren't my mates!' Jack snapped, then, as Kate brushed his arm with her hand, he relented. 'Digger was OK.'

'Well,' Harry continued, 'we were up to where Todd and Digger took you back to the old homestead and there were more cattle there.'

Jack nodded.

'I saw the brands and asked if they'd bought the cattle from Jim Cooper—that's Megan's dad. I'd sometimes helped her, you see, mending the fences. It's how we met. Some of their cattle got in with ours and Philip went berserk, saying they were rubbish and he didn't want them polluting his stock, but although they were in poor condition, they were good cattle.'

Kate smiled to herself. Jack might have been a city kid like she had been, but he'd soon learnt.

'Anyway, I asked Todd if he'd bought them and he said yes, the place was going down the drain and Jim wanted rid of them—and I knew things were bad with the Coopers so it seemed OK. But then Todd and Digger started fooling around with the brands and that didn't seem right. So I left.'

'Did you tell them you were leaving?'

Jack shook his head.

'But I had to take the bike—Todd had two two-wheeler bikes and a four-wheeler he let me use. And taking the bike was stealing—so I left a note to say I'd leave it up near the highway, and as soon as I had some money I'd send him some for the inconvenience.'

'So he knew exactly which way you'd head?'

'I guess!'

Jack sounded more defeated than tired, but Kate felt he'd had enough, so she signalled to Harry that it was time to leave.

To her surprise, he didn't argue, and Kate wondered if he'd been as affected by Jack's patent honesty as she had been. Here was a kid from the city, helping his girlfriend mend fences on her property, worrying about her father's cattle, escaping from criminals, yet leaving a note to say which way he was going!

She smiled at the young man on the bed. Some might say it was stupidity rather than honesty, but she couldn't believe any jury in the world would find him guilty of whatever charges Harry might choose to lay against him.

In fact, if she could find out who had given him lifts and prove he hadn't been with the men when they'd stolen the cattle, Harry couldn't lay charges at all.

Another job for Batman and Robin?

Shaking her head at the intrusion of the stupid joke she'd come up with in the cave, she got on with her work. The whole idea of avoidance was that it got the other person out of the forefront of your mind.

Kate loved the walk from the hospital to the back of the house. There was a path, of course, from the front of the hospital to the front of the house, but that didn't go through the garden.

The Agnes Wetherby Memorial Garden, she'd discovered it was called. Planted in honour of Charles's grandmother—Jack's great-grandmother.

Jack was doing well—medically—and Harry hadn't reappeared to ask more questions in the afternoon, so Kate, Jack and Megan had all decided to take that as a good sign.

But apart from finding out who had given Jack a lift—and she had no idea how to go about that—she couldn't do much to help, so she wouldn't think of Jack's problems now. Although not thinking of Jack left a space in her mind, which was dangerous because spaces in her mind inevitably filled up with thoughts of Hamish.

The Hamish who had kissed her on the hill, not Colleague Hamish who had first appeared when he'd driven her to Wygera. Hamish kissing away her fear of crocodiles. Or had he been kissing away her fear of commitment? Hamish looking hurt when she'd refused to have tea with him yesterday.

It had been tea, for heavens' sake, and there'd have been a dozen people in the dining room, yet she'd seen the flare of disappointment in his eyes and had felt the touch of that flare in her heart.

'You're stupid in the heart,' she muttered to herself, and turned her attention to the garden.

Yesterday she'd discovered the source of a new perfume in the garden and she wanted to pick a stem of the pale pink pendulous flowers and ask someone to identify them for her. Actually, she'd pick the top of the stem—the whole stem, like the leaves that sheltered them, being taller than she was.

She had just succeeded in her task and was sniffing the rich, sweet scent when she heard the strumming of a guitar, but it wasn't until she reached the bottom of the steps she recognised the tune.

'K-K-K-Katie swallowed a ha'penny, a penn'orth of fish, a ha'porth of chips the day before—'

'The day before that,' Kate joined in, 'she swallowed the doormat, now she's trying to swallow the key of the kitchen door!'

She beamed up at Hamish, who was slumped in the old settee on the back veranda, his guitar across his lap.

'My grandad used to sing that to me. I always thought he'd made it up, but if you know it, too…'

Hamish saw the radiant smile fade from her face and read the cause of its disappearance with ease. Unexpected pain stabbed deep into his gut. Getting to know how this woman thought wasn't all beer and skittles.

And the fact that she was trying to keep him at arm's length wasn't doing one thing to curb his body's reaction every time he saw her. Rather the opposite, in fact.

'Come here!' he ordered, setting aside his guitar and standing up to enforce his order should it be necessary.

But Kate obeyed, coming wearily up the steps towards him, halting in front of him, summoning a shadow of her earlier smile and snapping a cheeky salute with a spray of flowers she'd been holding in her hand.

'Oh, Kateling!' he whispered softly, then he put his arm around her shoulders and led her to the settee.

It had been sat on so often by courting couples that it sagged conveniently in the middle, so any attempt to not sit close was met by defeat. This helped him tuck her small body close to his far larger one, the closest to a hug or cuddle Kate would allow.

'Just because he wasn't a blood relation, it doesn't mean he didn't love you with all of his heart.'

She turned and stared at him.

'How do you do it?' she demanded. 'How do you know what I'm thinking?'

He had to smile.

'Never play poker, kid!' If he kept it light he could tighten his arm and give her half a hug. Half a hug was friendship, not involvement. 'You've got the most expressive face I've ever seen.'

Kate sighed then, joy of joys, rested her head on his shoulder and gazed out over the placid waters of the cove.

'I know that in my head—about Grandad and my parents loving me,' she admitted sadly. 'It's in my heart I'm having trouble.'

*Tell me about it!* But Hamish kept his comment to himself. Having Kate this close was bliss, but one false move and she'd skitter away again, hiding behind the barricades of remembered pain.

'In my heart I've got this alone thing happening. I know it's stupid, but I can't seem to get around it. Anyway, smell this.'

She thrust her frond of flowers under his nose.

'Isn't it beautiful? Do you know what it is? Do you know why Charles doesn't like me?'

'Charles doesn't like you? You're asking me to identify a flower for you—it's ginger, by the way. I liked the scent so much myself I asked Jill about it. Then you switch to some cockamamie question about Charles not liking you. Has he said so? Did he roll right up to you and say, "Kate, I don't like you"? What is going on in that head of yours?'

He tightened his hold—in friendship of course.

'He frowns at me. Well, not at me when I'm looking at him, but you know how silently he gets around—someone should have found a way to make his wheels squeak by now. Anyway, sometimes I kind of sense his presence and I turn around and there he is, frowning at me.'

'You're imagining it,' Hamish said stoutly, though in his head and heart he was remembering that he spent a lot of his own time frowning at this woman when she wasn't aware of his presence. His frown was because he was pretty sure he loved her, and couldn't work out how to get past her determination to avoid love at all cost.

Could Charles also be in love with her?

Hamish could well understand if he was, and the clenching in his gut suggested he didn't like this idea one bit. Charles was far too old for her.

Not that old…

And Charles could certainly be charming…

'I'll talk to Charles,' he said firmly, and Kate laughed.

'And ask him to stop frowning at me? Oh, please!' She turned and kissed him on the cheek. 'You're a really good friend, Hamish, and I appreciate the offer, but I'll live with Charles's frowns. I only mentioned it because it happened again when we left the room after we'd been talking to him about Jack.'

She was silent for a moment, moving away a little before the settee tipped her back towards him.

'You don't suppose he thinks— He couldn't think I've got something going with Jack, could he? I mean, apart from me being far too old for Jack, he's really only interested in Megan…'

She sounded confused enough to need comfort so Hamish drew her close again, and they sat like that for a while, watching the moon come up over the horizon, spreading a silver path across the water of the cove.

'Moonlight and water—made for romance, isn't it?'

The murmured words slid seditiously into Kate's ear and her heartbeats upped their intensity, bringing heat to the innermost parts of her body.

Kissing Hamish was back!

'We can't have a romance, Hamish,' she said, betraying the words by wriggling closer to him, because being close to Hamish was extremely comforting. 'Leaving aside my hang-ups about relationships—which are huge—you're going home in a couple of weeks. It would be stupid to start something we can't finish.'

He kissed the top of her head then his lips moved down and pressed against the corner of her right eye. His tongue slid out to lick a tiny patch of skin—surely eye-skin shouldn't be erogenous.

'My leaving isn't an issue. We could finish it in Scotland. Or not finish it at all.'

Even hushed, his deep voice sent shivers down her spine. It *had* to be the accent. Daniel's voice had never made contact with her spine at all—with any of her bones, come to think of it.

'Come home with me. Be *my* family. Make a family that is ours.'

His lips had reached the corner of her mouth. He couldn't have any idea how tempting that suggestion had been—how much she longed to regain some concept of 'home' and 'family'.

Damn, she should have been concentrating on the progress of his lips, not thinking about nebulous concepts of home and family. He'd taken advantage of her distraction and was kissing her!

Perhaps she hadn't got an F for the cliff kiss…

'Are you with me on this?'

He raised his head far enough to free his lips and ask the question, but the aftershocks of the kiss were such that she couldn't answer. Bones—it was all to do with bones. His voice had affected her spine; now the kiss had made the rest of her bones turn to jelly.

Not possible.

'Apparently!' Hamish said, presumably to himself as she certainly wasn't carrying on a conversation with him. She was trying to get her bones to solidify again, and worrying about the warm feeling in the pit of her stomach that Hamish's kisses was generating.

He resumed kissing her.

She should be protesting, or at least not kissing him back, but there was something so deliciously delirious about being kissed by Hamish that shoulds and shouldn'ts didn't count.

'Oh, dear,' she managed when they drew apart to breathe some time later. 'This really shouldn't be happening, Hamish.'

'No?'

He tipped her chin up and smiled into her eyes.

'But how else can I convince you this is special? Yes, it's sudden, *and* surprising, *and* barely believable, but that doesn't mean it's not real, Kate. So I'll keep kissing you because I know words won't build the trust you need to overcome your doubts—and admit it, woman, you're kissing me right back!'

His gruff words shook her jellied bones.

'Yes, I know, and it's very nice—lovely kisses—very special, but, Hamish…'

Kate couldn't find the words she needed to tell him about the hurt inside her—about the scars so new they had no protective scabs—about the hurt against which she had so few defences.

To open herself up to pain like that again, it was unthinkable…

'No buts,' he said gently, and he kissed her again, so thoroughly she wondered if they'd leave scorch marks on the settee.

'No, I won't go to the fire on the beach with you tonight,' Kate said firmly, pushing past a lounging Hamish to get into the ED office. With Harry apparently satisfied he'd got all he could out of Jack, Kate had been shifted back to the ED for the weekend.

She'd been happy about the arrangement as there was usually less time for chat and gossip in ED—until Hamish had wandered in.

Searing embarrassment still swamped her when she remembered her behaviour on the settee the previous night. They'd eventually been startled apart by a round of applause from the kitchen, Cal announcing with unabashed delight that they'd broken the settee kissing record, set only recently by himself and Gina.

Kate had skulked off to her room, not knowing the others well enough to laugh it off, though Hamish had stayed, apparently unaffected by the fact any number of their housemates had seen them kissing.

Now here he was again, wanting her to accompany him to the fire party at the beach, making public a relationship that didn't exist.

'You'll enjoy it,' Hamish persisted.

'Yes, I will, because I'm going anyway,' Kate told him. 'With Susie. She was talking about it yesterday while she was massaging Jack's leg. And as it's in celebration of getting Megan and Jack back together, Megan's coming with us. Girls' night out.'

'Oh!' For a moment Hamish looked so downcast Kate wanted to change her mind, but when he smiled just seconds later she was glad she'd stood firm. Hamish's smiles were nearly as addictive as Hamish's kisses and neither were the kind of addiction a woman who was determined to make her own way in life could afford.

'Susie and Megan, huh? Well, that's OK.'

He wandered off, leaving Kate to get on with her work, which, today, because the ED secretary hadn't appeared, was recording patients as they came in and prioritising them to see the doctor on duty, who happened to be Charles—making it the first time Kate had worked directly with him.

She glanced cautiously around, but he was still out the back where ambulance patients were admitted or in treatment room five where a small boy who'd been vomiting all night had been shifted up ahead of a young woman with stomachache and a drunk who'd fallen out of his mate's car and taken a lot of skin off one leg.

'OK, I'll take over here while you make yourself useful out there.' Jane, a cheerful secretary who usually worked on the front desk, came bustling into the small office. 'Charles phoned to say Wendy hadn't arrived, and asked if I could come. Don't worry, I started work in this cubbyhole, so I know what to do.'

Then she nodded to the drunk who was singing a song neither Kate nor, by the looks on their faces, anyone else in the room could recognise.

'Who's your friend?'

Kate smiled.

'I'll do him first,' she said, and went out, taking the man with the gravel rash through to a treatment room. With any luck, all his leg needed was to be cleaned up and dressed, then he could go on his way.

Easier said than done. She managed to get him into the treatment room, but he'd no sooner lain down on the examination table than he gave a helpless yelp then threw up all over her.

A hastily summoned aide came in to clean up while Kate grabbed some clean scrubs and headed for the bathroom. But no matter how much water she splashed over herself, she knew she'd smell all day.

Damn the man!

Back in the treatment room, he was sitting up and at least had the decency to look embarrassed.

'Room went round and round when I lay down,' he explained, which was when she realised she'd misread his embarrassment as he began to sing again, this time about a room going round and round.

Kate shifted him so his leg was propped on an absorbent pad on the table and she could get at the bits of gravel in the wound. She flushed it first, but the grit remained embedded and she knew it was going to be a piece-by-piece job.

Using small tweezers and wearing a magnifying loupe, she painstakingly removed every grain, while her patient alternately serenaded her and asked her to marry him. She had nearly finished when Charles appeared in the doorway.

'Need me?' he said, and this time she was sure the frown accompanying the words was because of the way the two of them smelt. 'Phew! Talk about ripe!' he added, confirming her thoughts but making her smile nonetheless.

'You might like to take a look, but he's up to date with his tetanus shots, there are no deep wounds that need stitching and there's no infection, so I thought I'd swab it all over with Betadine and let him go. Leave it without a dressing to dry it out?'

'Yes,' Charles said, then he frowned again, though he should have got used to the smell by now.

He wheeled away and, because the line-up for treatment hadn't become noticeably longer, Kate finished tending her drunk then ducked over to the house to have a proper shower and change into clean clothes. She didn't want people coming into the ED and going home feeling worse than when they'd arrived.

Susie knocked on her door at eight that evening.

'You ready?' she asked, when Kate called to her to come in.

'As I'll ever be,' Kate told her. The quiet morning had turned into a hectic afternoon and she'd only come off duty fifteen minutes ago. But she'd had a quick shower and dressed in jeans and a light cotton knit sweater, thinking the breeze on the beach might be cool in spite of the fire.

'Then let's go,' Susie said, leading the way out of the house.

'Where's Megan? Weren't you going to pick her up?'

'I was, but Hamish said he had to go downtown so he said he'd get her.'

Girls' and Hamish's night out?

Had he offered deliberately? Would that explain his smile?

Kate shook her head. She was here to find her father, not to get caught up in thinking about Hamish. Not about his kisses, or his Colleague Hamish days—just to find her father.

Harry might be there tonight.

She'd ask Harry about her mother. Say she was a friend of a friend in Melbourne—from a long time ago.

'Hi you two.'

Mike and Emily greeted them, and Kate was relieved to see Emily was at last taking some time off. She worked in Theatre when Cal was operating and did shifts in other parts of the hospital, but mostly Kate had met her in the ICU where Emily had spent her free time fretting over Jack.

So her presence at the fire party was not only good for her, it meant she had at last accepted he was stable and his recovery would continue.

Susie unfolded the blanket she'd been carrying and spread it by the fire. She and Kate settled on it, though they had to move only minutes later when Megan and Hamish and Hamish's guitar arrived, all three joining Susie and Kate on the blanket that had become, in Kate's eyes, almost minuscule.

Not that Hamish was bothering her—not deliberately. Oh, no, he was being Colleague Hamish again, cheerful, chatty, making Megan laugh at silly jokes, asking her about Jackson's progress, although every member of the hospital staff personally checked Jackson's progress every day.

'He's coming home tomorrow,' Megan said happily. 'Well, home to Christina's house with me. I'm not sure how I'll manage, what with Mum over in Townsville with Dad.'

'You know we'll all do anything we can to help you with Jackson,' Susie said, putting her arm around Megan and giving her a hug. 'Anything you want, just yell, and half the staff will come running.'

Megan nodded.

'You've all been so kind—and with Jack, too, although he's still too sick for me to tell him all that happened.'

She turned to Hamish.

'Should I tell him?'

'About having Lucky at the rodeo?'

So Hamish's ability to read minds wasn't restricted to reading hers, Kate thought as Megan nodded.

But how would he reply? Kate held her breath, glad Megan hadn't asked her.

'I think you will eventually,' Hamish said. 'Not necessarily right away. But one day there'll come a time and you'll know it's the right time. Then you'll tell him and he'll understand.'

He took one of Megan's hands and held it in both of his.

'You've been very sick, too, and have been through tremendous emotional pressure, so think about yourself as well as Jack and Jackson. Do what's right for Megan sometimes, not just what's right for them—or for your parents. That's been a burden you carried on your own for far too long.'

Megan rested her head on his shoulder, and Kate heard her whispered thanks.

Kate was glad of the shadows as she blinked moisture from her eyes. Colleague Hamish was definitely something special as doctors went.

Drinks were passed around and Hamish shifted from the blanket, settling on a rock nearby and strumming lightly on his guitar. People started singing, soft ballads they'd obviously sung before, around other fires blazing on the beach. But the togetherness of it made Kate feel lost and alone again, and she remembered why she'd come on contract—and why she'd come at all.

She looked towards Hamish—strumming quietly on his rock. Could she forget her quest? Go back to Scotland with him?

Did it matter who her father was?

She no longer knew the answer to that one, and not knowing made her feel more lost than ever.

Helpless.

She waited until Susie had gone to get more wine and Megan stood up to talk to Emily and Mike, then she slipped away, heading for where the casuarina trees threw shadows across the top of the beach—shadows deep enough to hide her departure.

'Leaving so early? I'll walk you home.'

Brian's voice came from the very deepest of the shadows and, certain she hadn't seen him approaching as she'd walked up the beach, she wondered if he'd been standing there.

Watching…

A shiver she didn't understand feathered down her spine, and when Hamish spoke from close behind her, she was so relieved she nearly flew into his arms.

'Sorry, had to say goodbye to Mike,' he said, catching up with her and slipping his arm around her waist. 'Oh, hi, Brian! You going down to join the party?'

'Well, I was but then I saw Kate leaving and thought I'd walk her home.'

'Kind of you, but I'd already offered. You go and join the fun.' Hamish's arm tightened, drawing Kate closer to his body.

'Oh, well, I guess I might as well,' Brian said, and he walked slowly out of the shadows towards the beach.

Reluctantly, because standing hip to hip with Hamish was very comforting, Kate drew away from her rescuer.

'I might have wanted to walk home with Brian,' she told him, angry because she couldn't handle the way Hamish changed from colleague to, well, some kind of lover with such consummate ease.

'You could have said so,' Hamish pointed out. 'You could have said, "Thanks but, no, thanks, Hamish, I'm going home with Brian."'

'I wouldn't have gone *home* with Brian,' Kate retorted. 'Not the way you make it sound.'

'Even to avoid me? Because that's what you're doing, isn't it, Kate?'

She heard his pain but had to argue.

'It's best that way.'

Hamish put his arm around her and drew her close again.

'Is it? I don't think so. And is it just me you're avoiding or are you afraid to let anyone, even colleagues, get close to you in case you're hurt again? Is that why you walked away from the fire? Is that why you've suddenly got doubts about finding your father?'

'That's ridiculous! You don't know that!' Kate snapped, irritated beyond reason by too many sensations ricocheting through her body.

And by the fact he always seemed to get things right!

He was holding her just lightly enough that she knew she could break away.

If she wanted to…

'Don't I?' He drew her just slightly closer. 'Oh, Kate!' he sighed. 'You've every right to feel vulnerable, but is hiding away from emotion the answer? You're braver than that, Kate. You're a fighter. I saw you in action with Jack.'

She didn't feel like a fighter. She felt like a wimp—weak and feeble, and nervy from the touch of this man's hands. All she wanted was to lean against him and feel his lips on hers, and let the sensations of a kiss drive all the demons from her mind.

She was obviously quite, quite mad!

She moved away from him, remembering avoidance, but he tugged her closer, then somehow they were in the darkest shadows, and he was kissing her again, kissing her with such ferocious intensity she couldn't breathe, let alone think.

'I know you've got a good heart that reaches out to touch all those around you,' he said, what seemed like hours but was probably only minutes later. 'And I know you've been immeasurably hurt by people you loved and by circumstances beyond your control. I understand your fear, my Kateling, but your kisses tell me something else. So if you want me to stop kissing you, then…'

Kate heard his words coming to her through a fog of well-being, and she leaned against the man who still held her in his arms.

'You'll have to tell me!' he said crossly, tucking her closer and pressing his lips against her hair. 'You'll have to stop kissing me back.'

'Not tonight,' she whispered. 'Let's, just for tonight, forget about everything else and kiss again. Maybe we'll get sick of it—like chocolate if you have too much.'

She felt his chest move as he chuckled, then his hands clasped her head, tilting it up again so his lips could claim hers.

Stupid in the heart, she told herself when, drunk with kisses, they turned and, arm in arm, walked back towards the house.

'I'll leave you at your door,' Hamish announced, as they climbed the front steps. 'I don't know about you, but the chocolate analogy didn't work for me. However, I've always had one guiding principle that fits most situations, and that's never to make a decision at night. An idea that after a few pints is absolutely foolproof and bound to bring in millions is often revealed as flawed in the sober light of day and, though I don't want to equate women with bright ideas, the same rule works with relationships.'

'Or non-relationships, as the case may be,' Kate whispered, thankful she didn't have to make a decision because the desire humming through her body made thinking nigh impossible.

But, true to his word, he left her at her door, Colleague Hamish back again, placing a chaste kiss on her forehead before opening her door for her and wishing her goodnight, his deep voice with the soft Scots burr making magic of the simple words.

Kate shut her door and leaned against it. She heard his footsteps going along the passageway, bypassing his door, growing fainter as he walked through the kitchen. Was she imagining she could hear the springs on the old settee squeaking?

Was he sitting out there now?

Regretting his gallantry at leaving her at her door?

Half expecting her to join him?

Her body remembered the electric charge their kisses had

generated, and yearned for the release and forgetfulness that spending a night with Hamish would surely bring.

But it would only be for a night and after that—awkwardness, embarrassment, regret. All of those and more—the big one—guilt, because casual sex wasn't her way.

Worse, guilt because he was far too nice a man to use that way.

Kate shook her head, changed into pyjamas and climbed into her lonely bed.

Hamish slumped down onto the settee—again.

He was obviously mad!

Leaving Kate at the door like that—going all gentlemanly when what he should have done was ease the two of them through that bedroom door and let nature resolve the fragile barriers Kate kept erecting between them.

He held his head in his hands and applied pressure to his skull with his fingers, though it wasn't his brain that was hurting.

It was all the rest of him, hurting in a way he'd never felt before—like an all-over cramp, which proved all the rot you read about love being joyous and uplifting was totally wrong. Love hurt like hell, that was what love did.

If it *was* love, not some as yet unidentified tropical disease.

Don't joke about it, this is serious, he told the flippant self that had, up till then, ruled the emotional part of his life.

But if he couldn't joke, how else to handle it?

Grown men didn't cry.

Though he didn't feel like crying. He felt like hitting something, like raging and ranting and yelling at whatever callous Fate had decreed he fall in love right here and right now.

Not only fall in love, but fall in love with probably the only woman on the entire planet who had excellent, viable, irrefutable reasons for not loving him back!

Well, there were probably quite a few women who wouldn't want him. But only one he wanted…

* * *

Sunday in the ED was far quieter than Kate had expected it to be. Hamish, who was on duty elsewhere in the hospital, drifted in, in search of Mrs Grubb's chocolate-chip cookies, which he swore he could smell somewhere on the premises. He explained that people in country towns really didn't like bothering doctors on a Sunday.

'Or perhaps they don't like giving up their Sundays for minor medical problems when they can just as easily take Monday off work and bother doctors then,' Kate suggested, and Hamish tutted.

'So young to be so cynical! It seems you've got out of the city just in time. But you're right in one thing—Monday is always frantically busy.'

'My day off,' Kate said smugly, pleased to be handling what could have been an awkward post-kissing conversation with Hamish so well. Or maybe it was Hamish who was directing it so well…

But she kept up her end. 'Monday and Tuesday this week, then back in ED again from Wednesday through to Saturday,' she explained with a lot of false cheer.

'But you'll miss the rodeo,' Hamish protested. 'You're working this weekend—shouldn't you be off next weekend?'

Kate shrugged off his concern.

'I'm a contract worker, and I said when I was employed I'd be happy to work weekend shifts,' she explained, not adding that she'd thought having weekdays off would be more advantageous in her search.

What search?

Hamish leaned against a convenient wall and studied her.

'My decision in the sober light of day was that I was wrong in my decision last night,' he said quietly, and Kate had to smile.

'So the chocolate-chip cookie search was a scam.'

'Not entirely. They're here somewhere—but I did want to see you.'

'And having seen me?'

'I thought I'd put a proposition to you. Let's talk to Charles—no one else—about your family.'

'But Charles grew up at Wetherby Downs—that's hundreds of miles away from here.'

'OK, scrap Charles—talk to Harry. He'll be discreet. He can find out what you need to know then you can decide whether or not you still want to make contact with your father.'

Kate stared at him.

'What are you talking about? Why wouldn't I want to make contact with my father?'

He smiled—the gentle smile that curled around his lips and lurked so sympathetically in his eyes. Yet he couldn't *know* that the rash, grief-laden impetus that had propelled her thousands of miles north had turned to doubt and dread.

'I imagine because it finally entered your admittedly beautiful head that maybe a middle-aged man might not want an unknown daughter turning up on his doorstep.'

He came closer and took her hand.

'I know you care about people, Kate. Care deeply for those you love. That's been obvious since I first met you. So it's not so hard to take the next step and imagine how disturbed you must be feeling about disrupting the life of a man you don't know but might want to care about. Of course you're wondering and worrying about the damage your appearance in his life might do, not only to him but to his entire family. And, being Kate, you're prepared to sacrifice your own happiness in order to not disturb his—whoever he might be.'

Kate stared at Hamish, unable to believe this man could so easily read the thoughts that had been festering in her head all week. To the extent that when she'd gone to the library one morning and found old electoral rolls, she hadn't been unduly disappointed when she hadn't found her mother's name—or any voters with the same surname.

'Go find the cookies!' she snapped at him, snatching her hands from his grasp and moving crossly away. 'I hope they make you fat!'

He was right, of course, which was what had made her angry—him being right plus the fact that her mind was now so muddled she was barely aware which way was up.

And most of the muddle was Hamish-oriented.

The more doubts she had about finding her father, the more appealing the idea of a trip to Scotland sounded.

She could always come back. What was one more broken heart?

*Are you mad? Of course you don't want to take that risk!*

A loud, demanding car horn cut through her helplessly circling thoughts and she went through to the ambulance bay to meet it, arriving in time to see Georgie Turner pull up on her motorbike behind the car.

'Bed, Kate. One of my patients about to pop.'

An orderly had already wheeled a bed out to the car, and Grace, who'd been dozing in a treatment room, also appeared.

'This patient's mine,' she said to Kate, helping Georgie settle the woman on the bed. 'Love deliveries, love babies, and, besides, I'm on duty in the nursery this week so I deserve to be the first to meet this little person.'

'You're so clucky it's a wonder you don't lay eggs,' Georgie said to Grace, and, with the help of the husband, the two of them took their patient through to the birthing suites.

'I'll shift your car and bring you the keys,' Kate told the husband, who looked too stunned to really take in what she'd said, but as the keys were dangling from the ignition, it didn't matter.

Kate parked the car safely in the car park and took the keys in, arriving in time to see the new life emerge into the world. A little girl to take Jackson's place in the nursery. She looked at the love and wonder on the faces of all those present—even that of Georgie, who must deliver a dozen babies a month.

Everyone loved a newborn—but a new daughter who was twenty-seven?

She made her way back to the ED. So far, coming to Crocodile Creek had thrown up more questions than it had answers.

# CHAPTER EIGHT

'BATMAN AND ROBIN ride again.'

Hamish's voice startled Kate out of a reverie about the man who had spoken—a man she'd been avoiding, and about whom she definitely should not be thinking!

But though he'd made the joking comment, the coolness in his voice told her he was well aware of her avoidance tactics. And perhaps that he'd been hurt by them.

She glanced at him, but his face gave nothing away. Still, somehow, deep inside she hoped she hadn't hurt him.

Hamish didn't deserve that.

'Why are you doing this flight?' she asked, her work self ignoring all the palaver going on in her head. 'Mike's flying and you're not on call.'

'Mike's got that twenty-four-hour bug that's been going around. Rex is flying, and the patient's a child, so why not me?'

Hamish spoke with such exaggerated patience that Kate wanted to grind her teeth.

Batman probably wasn't a tooth grinder, but Batman probably didn't get collywobbles in his stomach when he got into the Batmobile with Robin.

With a decidedly unfriendly, though meticulously polite, Robin!

'The patient's a child?'

'Out on Wallaby Island.' Hamish nodded his confirmation. 'Apparently the silly kid disobeyed his parents and went wandering out on the reef without protection on his feet.'

'And?' Kate prompted, hoping to get more of the story before they took off.

'Walked on a stonefish.'

'A stonefish? What on earth's a stonefish? A fish that eats stones?'

Hamish turned and his cold demeanour cracked to the extent she was sure a small smile slipped out, then quickly disappeared.

Kate felt the chain reaction of quivery delight along the nerves throughout her body, even though what she thought had been a smile might just have been a grimace.

But the quivery delight reminded her why she'd been avoiding him.

'You're the Aussie and you don't know what a stonefish is?'

His question jerked her back to business, and she was about to remind him she was a city person when Rex handed them headsets then began take-off procedures. It was easier to wait until they were in the air to pursue the conversation.

'A stonefish?' she prompted Hamish.

Bad move as he smiled at her again, a real smile this time, but quivery delight was soon replaced by concern as he explained.

'It's a nasty beastie that looks very like a largish rock. It hides among other largish rocks, so unsuspecting prey rests on it then gets poisoned by venom from one of the glands along the dorsal fin spines.'

'That's unbelievable!' Kate muttered. 'I mean, I know we have a good range of poisonous snakes and spiders, but I thought, apart from sharks and stinging jellyfish, the seas were fairly safe. Is it bad venom? Do people die?'

'Never in Australia, although there are recorded cases of deaths overseas.'

It was Rex who provided this answer, then Hamish took up the explanations.

'The venom can have nerve, muscle, vascular and myocardial effects. We have antivenin, and normally there's some in the medical kit out at the island, but apparently when they looked at it, it was out of date.'

'Oh, for heaven's sake, doesn't anyone check these things?' Kate muttered. 'Cal insisted we check the medical kits in isolated places when I did a clinic flight with him. Isn't there a rule that the person with the key to the kit has to check it?'

Hamish nodded.

'Unfortunately, they've had so much trouble with the kit at Wallaby Island, Charles has been thinking of removing it. The island is only a twenty-minute flight away— Look, you can see it now.'

Kate peered out the window at the rounded shape of the island, jutting out of the azure sea, the waters around it paler shades of translucent green.

'That's the reef,' Hamish explained. 'One of the reasons Wallaby is so popular as a tourist destination is the magnificent fringing reef.'

But although she was stunned by the beauty of the place they were approaching, she was more worried about the child who'd been stung by the stonefish.

Hamish must have been just as worried. The moment they touched down, he was out of his seat, unstrapping a small backpack, another backpack that contained resuscitation gear and the lightweight stretcher.

'I'll yell if we need the stretcher,' he said to Rex, who had come through to open the door. 'Come on,' he added to Kate, dropping out of the chopper then racing, doubled over, to where a small group of people was clustered beside the helipad.

The child, eight or nine, Kate judged, was sitting, white-faced, on his mother's knee, an oxygen mask on his face and one foot in a bucket of water.

Beside the pair, a young man wearing a bright Hawaiian-print shirt stood uncertainly. A second man detached himself from the group and headed towards the helicopter.

Hamish nodded at the young man, acknowledging his presence but at the same time conveying the utmost disapproval.

'That's Kurt,' he muttered to Kate. 'Wallaby Island's current keeper of the medical kit. At least he's done something right, with the hot water.'

'Hot water?' Kate echoed.

'The pressure immobilisation we use for most venoms is useless with stonefish. In fact, it can worsen the pain,' Hamish explained as he knelt beside the child. 'Immersing the injured part in hot water—forty to forty-five degrees—is the best thing to do until we can get some antivenin and regional anaesthetic into the patient.'

He'd let his pack slide to the ground and Kate put hers down beside it, grateful resus equipment wasn't needed. She opened the one Hamish had carried, while Hamish introduced himself to the boy—Jason—and his mother, Julie.

'It hurts so much,' the boy whimpered.

Kate found the ampoules of stonefish antivenin easily enough. She broke one open and filled a syringe, while Hamish checked the child, asking questions about allergies and examining the wound.

'We'll need another ampoule of the antivenin, Kate,' he said quietly. 'We use one for every two puncture wounds and young Jason here has managed to tread on four of the beastie's thirteen spikes.'

'This is going to hurt when I prick you, Jason, but it won't be nearly as bad as the pain from that rotten stonefish, so just hang onto Mum for me while I get it in.'

He injected the antivenin into the muscle on Jason's thigh,

and though the boy did no more than wince at the injection, his mother's face lost colour and Kate put out a hand to hold her steady.

'Not much good around needles,' Julie said weakly, smiling her thanks at Kate.

'I don't know anyone who is,' Kate told her.

'OK, now we'll see what we can do to stop some of that pain, young Jason,' Hamish said. 'Kate, you'll see a pack with a sterile syringe of bupivacaine in there somewhere,' he said. 'Twenty mils at 25 per cent. That'll provide a regional block, which works better in these cases than narcotic analgesics.'

Kate found the pack he needed and handed it to him. She watched the child, and Hamish handling him—so gently competent and comforting Kate could see why paediatrics should be his specialty.

'I'll get this into him and we'll check him out while it's working. A couple of minutes at this stage won't make a difference.'

Check out the mother, too, Kate thought, noticing for the first time that Julie was pregnant.

Hamish was asking her if Jason was on any medication, and Julie was answering calmly enough, but a flutter of fear trembled beneath the words and revealed itself in the tremor of the hands that rested lightly on her son's shoulders.

'We'll take you both back to the mainland,' Hamish said, when Kate had finished jotting down Jason's details on the initial assessment form. 'Stonefish toxin can affect many parts of the body, so we need to keep an eye on Jason, at least overnight. We also need to treat the wounds themselves. I want an X-ray to make sure no fragments of the spines broke off in his foot, and it's possible he'll need antibiotics if the wounds become infected.'

'What about my husband?' Julie asked. 'He went off on a fishing trip early this morning—he doesn't know about this. What will he do?'

'Do you want us to let him know? We can radio the fishing boat,' Kurt offered.

Julie thought about it for a moment, then turned to Hamish. 'Should I let him know?'

Kate knew the question behind the question was, *Is my son's life in danger?* And she silently applauded Julie's courage in asking it.

'We'll watch Jason carefully for any signs the venom is affecting him. The resort has a small helicopter and I'm sure if you needed your husband urgently, they would fly him over, but the decision about whether you tell him now or later is up to you.'

Kurt nodded his agreement, adding they could always airlift him off the fishing boat.

'Then let him enjoy his day out,' Julie said. 'He'll be angry I didn't contact him but he's been working far too hard and been under a lot of stress. He needs whatever relaxation he can get.'

'The fishing trip gets back in time for him to take this afternoon's flight back to the mainland,' Kurt offered. 'I'll get the housemaid to pack up your things, then I'll meet the fishing boat and tell Mr Anstead what's happened. Our agent in Crocodile Creek can meet the chopper and take him to the hospital.'

Hamish nodded his approval of this arrangement, though he was still furious with Kurt for neglecting to keep the contents of the medical kit up to date.

'OK, let's get you into the helicopter, young Jason,' he said, reaching down, removing the oxygen mask and lifting the child into his arms. Kate had already slung one backpack across her shoulders and she carried the second as she herded an anxious Julie across the helipad.

And though 98 per cent of Hamish's concentration was on his patient—feeling the steady rise and fall of the child's chest against his, watching the throb of a pulse beneath Jason's chin—

the other two per cent had been enticed into consideration of Kate—and the way she'd been avoiding him for the last few days.

Perhaps it was for the best. He could understand her reluctance to get involved again, yet he couldn't clear his head of the daft idea that she was the only woman in the world for him.

He, who had never believed in such nonsense! As if there would only be one perfect match for every person in the world!

But the deep ache inside him gave lie to his argument. It told him there was only one person in the world for him.

Kate…

'Want to sit up front?' he asked Jason, knowing young children who didn't need mechanical support or monitoring were usually happier if they could ride up front.

'Yes please.'

Jason's response was so wholehearted Hamish was reassured that his initial assessment of the child—that he hadn't taken in a huge dose of venom—had been correct. Whether the stonefish was immature or Jason's bodyweight was so light the spines didn't penetrate deeply, Hamish didn't know, but apart from the excruciating pain Jason hadn't shown any of the toxic effects of stonefish venom.

So far!

Rex helped him settle the boy into the copilot's seat, and pointed out what all the controls did.

'You can help me fly it if you like,' Rex offered. 'Just hold on here and do what I do.'

He fitted a pair of headphones to the small head.

Kate, who was helping Julie fasten her seat belt, looked towards the cockpit with alarm, and Hamish smiled. As far as he knew, she hadn't ridden up front on a flight yet, so wouldn't realise the second set of controls wasn't effective unless a special switch was thrown.

Hamish handed Julie a second pair of earphones.

'Here. You can talk to Jason through the mouthpiece.' He

pointed to the small attachment, then passed Kate one of the white helmets she'd worn on her first flight—helmets that held both earphones and a microphone.

A microphone so those in the helicopter could converse without shouting, yet it couldn't help him talk to Kate—even if they'd been alone. You couldn't talk to someone who didn't want to hear.

Charles met them at the helipad.

'The boy all right?' he asked Hamish, as Kate helped Julie out of the chopper and Rex lifted Jason out, settling him on the stretcher two orderlies had waiting nearby.

'You get a ride to the hospital, kid!' Rex said, and Hamish saw the look of hero-worship in Jason's eyes.

'I liked the helicopter best,' he assured Rex, and Hamish nodded to Charles.

'Yes, I think the boy's all right,' he said, 'but we're going to have to do something about the medical kit at Wallaby. They don't deserve to have it there if the person in charge can't be bothered to check it regularly.'

'I'll go over myself later this week and sort it out,' Charles promised, then he frowned, not at Hamish's concern but at Kate, who was walking beside Jason on his wheeled stretcher.

It was the first time Hamish had ever noticed this reaction—the frown Kate had mentioned to him before she'd started avoiding him.

'She's a good nurse—very empathetic,' he told Charles, although he knew Kate wouldn't thank him for sticking up for her.

Charles turned his frown on Hamish.

'Do you think I don't know that?' he demanded.

Frowns all round! Hamish was sure one was gathering on his forehead.

'You were frowning at her,' he pointed out, then saw a look of sadness cross Charles's face.

'Frowning at my own bitter thoughts, Hamish, not at your Kate.'

'She's not *my* Kate!' Hamish snapped, and he walked away, moving swiftly to catch up with the cavalcade of stretcher, patient, mother and nurse, which was now inside the hospital grounds.

He tagged along as they entered the ED, in time to ask the orderlies to take Jason straight to a treatment room. He could use a portable X-ray machine to check for spines in his foot, then debride the wounds and dress them. If he had to operate to remove pieces of spine, it was a minor procedure and could be done in the treatment room.

She'd never be his Kate, unless he could come up with a miracle.

Grace met them as they came in, introducing herself to Jason and explaining she'd be helping Dr Hamish look after him.

Hamish caught the look that passed between Kate and Grace. Was Kate really so worried about propinquity between them that she'd enlisted Grace's help in avoiding him?

The thought saddened the two per cent of his brain he was allowing to linger with Kate, but as he followed Grace into the small treatment room he pushed even that small portion aside. Jason deserved one hundred per cent.

'We'll be banished from the room while they take the X-ray,' Kate said to Julie. 'Would you like a cup of tea or coffee?'

'Please!' Julie said. 'Weak tea with plenty of milk. I'm trying to totally avoid caffeine but I think I deserve a cuppa today.'

Kate sent an aide to get tea and biscuits, then settled Julie on a chair outside the treatment room.

'When's the baby due?'

Julie turned to her with a puzzled expression, then pressed a hand to her stomach.

'Do you know, I'd almost forgotten about the baby!' She patted her bulge as if apologising to it. 'I'm thirty-two weeks. My husband had a week off and we took the opportunity to take a holiday before the baby arrived. Heaven knows when we'll get away again once we're a family of four.'

Kate waited with Julie until Hamish was satisfied he'd cleaned out Jason's wounds and the boy could be transferred to the children's room, so called because it looked more like a magical playroom than a hospital ward.

'I want to watch him overnight,' Hamish explained to Julie, 'and start him on a course of oral steroids. The antivenin is made from horse serum and in some cases can cause serum sickness. The steroids guard against that happening.'

'Aren't steroids bad for kids?' Julie asked.

'Only if they're taking them to improve their sports performance,' Hamish teased. 'We're not talking massive doses—fifty milligrams of prednisolone daily for five days. It's a drug used often for children—particularly those with chronic asthma. We'll divide the dose into three so he takes three tablets a day.'

Julie accompanied Jason and Hamish to the children's room, but Kate caught up with her later that day when she finished work and went to see how her small patient was faring.

Bad move as Hamish was there, but Kate was happy to see Jason's father had arrived and was to spend the night with his son, while Julie went to the hotel to rest.

'I think we connect more to patients we bring in on emergency flights,' Hamish said, walking with her out of the hospital.

Kate nodded, but didn't answer. It didn't seem to matter how much she avoided Hamish, because the instant he was back in her presence again all the attraction came roaring back to life, made stronger rather than diminished by her stringent avoidance tactics.

Did he know she always walked back through the garden that he guided her that way?

It was early evening, the moon not yet risen, and though bright stars threw mellow light the path was darkly shadowed.

'I'm sorry I left you at your door on Saturday night,' he said.

It was the last thing Kate had expected to hear, although he had said something similar before. She stopped—quite close to the ginger plant, for she could smell the flowers—and looked at her companion.

'Why?'

Hamish drew a deep breath. If he told her he loved her, would it destroy the very fragile thread that linked them?

Or was he imagining even that?

But for days he'd gone along with her avoidance tactics, thinking space might clear his brain, but all it had done had been to confuse him even further.

And if she'd asked Grace to help her avoid him? Well, that hurt!

He took another breath.

'Because if I hadn't we'd have made love, and maybe, during love-making, if I'd told you I loved you, it might have meant more than baldly coming out with it in a garden with no moonlight and that damned ginger plant overwhelming me with its perfume.'

'It is rather strong,' Kate remarked, and Hamish wondered if she'd even heard his declaration.

He was no good at this. He was good at detached. Very good at flippant. Heartfelt declarations of love were too new. Even thinking about them, practising what he had to say, had made him feel raw and exposed.

Now he'd messed things up with the ginger plant.

Had he actually said the love bit? Had he told her?

If he had, she showed no inclination to reply, merely walking a little further along the path.

He followed, feeling like Rudolph when he'd had a scolding.

'Well?' he demanded. Rudolph would have barked.

*Much* better at flippant!

But the cramp was back, and his knees were shaking, and he knew flippant wasn't any use to him at all.

He steadied himself, took hold of her elbows and looked down into her shadowed eyes.

'I love you, Kate,' he repeated, just in case he hadn't said it earlier.

Or she hadn't heard it.

'I know, Hamish,' she whispered. 'But I don't know how to answer you. I'm just so confused.'

It wasn't much but Hamish felt considerably heartened.

'Let's go to dinner at the Athina and talk about it. Talk it through. There has to be an answer to this somewhere. Besides, you haven't been there—it's the most ro—' he caught himself just in time '—beautiful place. Mike's parents own and run it.'

He took her hands, lifted them to his lips and kissed her knuckles one by one. Would physical contact strengthen his invitation? He took more heart from the fact she didn't draw away, but even in the shadows he saw her shake her head.

Anger came so swiftly he had no time to stem it!

'You didn't say no to a trip to the pub with Harry last night.'

The accusation hung in the air between them, then Kate said softly, 'There's no danger in a drink with Harry at the pub. And we were celebrating the fact that Jack's off the hook. Todd and Digger have been arrested, and because Jack's agreed to testify against them and Digger's story backs up Jack's, it means he's free and clear. It was a celebration.'

'Dinner with me could be a celebration!' he snapped, angry beyond reason, although her explanation had made sense.

'We've nothing to celebrate,' she reminded him.

'Because you won't give in.' He was speaking far too loudly, but the hot rush of emotion welling inside him refused to be capped. 'You must feel something for me, or you wouldn't be avoiding me. You'd be treating me the way you treat Cal, or Mike, or—dare I say it?—bloody Harry! But you're not. You've even got Grace helping you—'

'Grace? Helping me what?'

'Helping you avoid me.'

He knew as he said the words they were wrong. Kate was such a private person there was no way she would have talked about her feelings to Grace, or anyone else.

He wanted to unsay it, but it was too late.

The thread—real or imaginary—had surely broken.

Or had it?

Kate had taken back her hands but she hadn't moved away.

He tamped down the still smouldering anger and took her in his arms, holding her close, reminding himself that this emotional vulnerability was probably far harder for her than it was for him.

Although he couldn't imagine it!

He took a steadying breath and tried another tack.

'Did you ask Harry about your mother?'

The movement of her head against his chest told him she hadn't.

'For some reason?'

A nod this time.

'Still having second thoughts, Kate?'

She edged away and looked up at him, a pathetic attempt at a smile trembling on her lips.

'And third and fourth and fifth thoughts, Hamish,' she said quietly. 'Does it matter? Do I really care? I don't know any more.'

She kissed him gently on the lips then drew away again.

'I was running on emotion as I headed north. The idea of finding my father helped me set aside things I couldn't cope with—grief and loss and anger. And I believed having something to do—a quest—would give me time to arm myself in some way—build defences to protect myself against hurt like that again.'

Another kiss brushed against his lips.

'Then I met you, before the defences were in place—and that's terrifying, Hamish.'

He held her closer, wrapping her tightly in his arms, desperate to protect her from the hurt she feared, his own hurt and anger forgotten in the rush of love engulfing him.

She nestled against him.

'I know I've hurt you these last few days, avoiding you the way I have, but it was only to avoid a greater hurt later on.'

Hamish kissed the top of her head.

'To borrow your own word—piffle!' he said, sounding more like a frog than a prince as emotion choked the words on their way out. 'Greater happiness, that's all there'll be later on. We'll work it out.'

'Will we?' she asked, moving away. 'I don't think so.'

'Well I do!' he said, releasing the reins on both anger and flippancy.

There were times when only they would do.

'But I'd like you to know this is not exactly a walk in the park for me,' he grumbled. 'How do you think I'm feeling—thirty years of age and finding myself in the clutches of the phenomenon I've scoffed at all my adult life? Romantic love, I've pontificated—usually after several single malts—is an illusion, perpetuated through the ages by merchants with a winning way with words. Think back to the seers and witches who sold love potions—it's always been a commercial con.'

He paused, looking down into her face and brushing her hair back from her forehead.

Could she feel the change in him? Guess how just looking at her made him feel?

How to explain?

'And until one afternoon a couple of weeks ago, I believed this foolishness,' he said quietly. 'Until one afternoon, when a sunbeam shone on a brown curl and turned it gold…'

He knew he sounded strained, and though he'd tried to make light of his emotions, Kate must have heard his pain. She reached up and kissed him on the lips, her kiss denying all the things she'd said. Passion, deep and hot and hard, stirred his blood until he could feel it thrumming through his veins.

## CHAPTER NINE

'I CAN'T BELIEVE you did all that organising for the rodeo then opted to work the day it was on,' Kate said, looking at the man who'd come lounging into the Emergency Department in search of distraction.

Hamish shrugged broad shoulders in a gesture so familiar she couldn't believe she wouldn't be seeing it for ever.

'The others will all have an ongoing relationship with Wygera and the people out there. I leave next week and probably won't ever see them again.'

He sounded regretful, but it wasn't regret that tightened Kate's stomach when he talked about leaving. It was like the shoulder shrug. The familiarity. And a lot of things she didn't want to think about.

Except that she did.

Most of the time…

So, she could go to Scotland with him. The offer was there…

But it would take a leap faith and she didn't have much faith these days.

Except when she was kissing him…

Or he was kissing her…

'Besides,' he continued, for once not attuned to her thoughts, 'you weren't going to be there and if you ask me which I'd prefer—a rodeo without Kate or a hospital with her—then there's no choice.'

Uh-oh, maybe he was attuned to her thoughts…

He spread his arms wide and smiled at her.

'Stop it!' she snapped, glad the place was as quiet as a tomb so no one heard her. The entire population of Crocodile Creek must be out at the rodeo.

'Stop what?'

Dark blue eyes projected injured innocence, making Kate madder than ever.

'Stop smiling at me. And talking like that. You know I don't want a relationship.'

His smile became gentler.

'Don't you, Kate?' he said, then he put his hands on her shoulders and drew her closer.

'Don't you?' he repeated as his lips closed on hers.

'Don't you?' he breathed, a long time later, when they drew apart to catch their breath.

'Don't do this, Hamish,' she murmured brokenly, shaking her head to emphasise her words. 'I really, really, really don't want this.'

'Only because you've been hurt—because everything you knew and believed in turned out to be a lie. But this isn't a lie, Kate. Deep down in your heart you must know it's more than a passing fancy—more than physical attraction or lust or whatever other excuse you make to yourself to fend me off.'

She looked at him and shook her head, but before she could reply Mike burst through the door.

'You two on call for the Rescue Service?'

Kate nodded.

'Do you need us both?' Hamish asked.

'I think so. Multi-vehicle traffic accident up on the pass. The ambulance is on the way. It was at the rodeo and left from there. The rodeo's over and the hospital staff who were out there are all on their way back here, so this place won't be short-staffed for long.'

'I'll just let someone know we're going,' Kate told him. 'It's been so slow today I've been restocking the dressing cupboard and sent the others off for a second afternoon tea. Mrs Grubb's been baking chocolate-chip cookies, so they didn't need to be persuaded.'

Kate whisked away, and Hamish watched her go.

'Not winning her over?' Mike said, and Hamish turned back to his friend.

'*What* did you say?'

Mike laughed.

'Come on, mate. You must know the whole hospital is talking about you and Kate. The staff have been laying bets on how long you'd take to—well, to get her into bed.'

'They'd better not have been!' Hamish growled. 'How dare they talk about her that way?'

Mike touched his arm.

'Relax,' he said. 'You know how it happens. It doesn't belittle you or Kate. If anything, it shows the affection in which people hold you. And sometimes it also shows how stupid we are when it comes to love. Apparently Walter Grubb was running a book down at the Black Cockatoo on when Emily and I would get together—and that was years before we finally did.'

Mike's lack of concern over the groundsman's behaviour cooled Hamish's anger—slightly. Walter Grubb had better not be running a book on him at the local pub.

Though maybe he should take whatever odds Walter was offering on him losing her.

Because, in spite of the passion of Kate's kisses, and the heat that roared between them, he *was* losing her. Or maybe not winning her was a better way to put it, as she'd never really been his to begin with.

He followed Mike out to the chopper, wondering what she'd been about to say when Mike had walked in—knowing in his heart it had been another rejection.

So why didn't he give up?

He couldn't, that was why. Somewhere deep inside him was a certainty that Kate was his future, and all the avoidance, and denial, and, yes, joking in the world couldn't kill that notion.

He glared at the woman in question as she arrived at the helipad. She took her overalls from Mike, chatting away as if she hadn't a care in the world.

Which she had—lots of cares—so it just proved how much better she was at hiding her emotions than he was!

Growling quietly to himself because, distracted, he'd stepped into the wrong leg of his overalls, he turned his mind from Kate to what lay ahead.

'Where's the accident?' he asked Mike. 'Right at the top of the pass, or further down?'

'Further down. There's a lay-by about a kilometre from the top where I can land. Apparently a fully loaded cattle road train lost its brakes coming down, and as it crossed the road to go up the safety ramp it struck a vehicle coming from the other direction.'

'A fully loaded cattle train? You're talking three trailers? A hundred head of cattle, many dead or injured, the others loose on the highway? Anything could happen.'

'And probably will,' Mike said.

The flight was short, but as they came into land in the fading daylight they could see the chaos beneath them. Dead and dying cattle lay across the road, policemen with rifles shooting those beyond saving.

'Pity we're not vets,' Kate muttered, wincing as Mike opened the door and another shot rang out.

'We'll have enough injured people to worry about,' Hamish said, but Kate, seeing the mangled cabins of two semi-trailers, was doubtful. The fire brigade's crash unit was already on the scene and men with giant tin snips were cutting at the tangled metal.

'Have you got anyone out?' Hamish asked, as Harry joined them by the side of the road.

'Not yet,' Harry said, his voice not hopeful. 'The smaller semi is the Alcotts'—the people who supplied the rodeo bulls. They had four bulls at the rodeo so presumably there are four in the trailer. We haven't looked at them yet—too busy trying to clear the cattle from the other wreck off the road.'

He shook his head then left, answering a call from one of his men.

'Let's see what we can in the cabins,' Mike suggested, and the three of them headed for the centre of the action, Kate and Hamish carrying bags, while Mike had the lightweight stretcher.

The prime mover of the cattle train had ridden right over the smaller vehicle so it was hard to see where one ended and the other began.

'One more cut and you'll be able to get at the bloke up the top,' one of the fire crew told them, and they stood back to let the experts work. 'Once he's out, we can cut through to the other vehicle, though it doesn't look too good for anyone in it.'

The cattle train driver was barely conscious but responded both to Hamish's voice and to sensory stimulation. Aware they had to get him out before attempts could be made to rescue anyone else, Hamish worked swiftly, starting oxygen, protecting the man's neck with a cervical collar, sliding a short spine board behind him and securing it so they could lift him out in a sitting position without moving his spine more than necessary.

Within minutes they had him on the ground, well away from the firemen who were continuing their efforts to untangle the two vehicles with the jaws of life and a small crane attached to their unit.

Hamish worked with his usual thoroughness and Kate

thought what a loss he'd be to emergency services when he began his paediatric specialty.

In Scotland…

'Breathing OK, carotid pulse strong, BP 149 over 80, high but not disastrous, no sign of tension pneumothorax or flail chest, minor contusions without too much blood loss, no facial injuries indicative of hitting the windscreen, no obvious damage to his skull—but he'll need scans—damage to left patella, broken right tib and fib.' Hamish was listing the injuries while Kate did the documentation and Mike started an IV infusion. 'That's all I can see, and he's stable enough to move. Let's get him to the chopper. Mike can take him back to town while we wait to see if they get someone out of the other vehicle. The ambulance should be here soon. We'll ride back in that.'

Kate looked over at the flattened cabin and wondered if it could be possible for someone to have survived. She carried the bag of fluid while the men carried the stretcher back to the helicopter, then waited while Mike and Hamish secured their patient inside.

'Get Harry to radio if you need me back here,' Mike said, then he shut the door and Hamish steered Kate away before the rotors started moving. A tow truck had arrived, its winch lifting dead cattle off the road, but back at the scene of the accident a very much alive animal bellowed for release from the trailer that held the rodeo bulls.

'We've checked,' Harry said. 'Although the Alcotts had four bulls at the rodeo, the only passenger in the trailer is this huge fellow—I think he's the one they call Oscar. He's stamping and pawing and bellowing like crazy, but I daren't let him out without someone here who knows how to handle him.' He frowned in the direction of the cranky bull. 'I guess the other option is to shoot him.'

'You can't shoot a healthy animal,' Hamish protested, and Harry shrugged.

'You want to try calming him down?' he said, nodding towards the trailer that had jackknifed and tipped onto its side in the middle of the road.

Kate walked towards it, seeing the tear in the top that had allowed Harry to check for dead or injured animals. A huge head, grey-black, with curved horns and, below them, floppy grey ears looked back at her. Somehow, the animal had managed to turn himself so he was upright, stamping and bellowing with either pain or frustration.

Knowing there was no way he could get out, she moved closer, talking softly to him, but he refused to be placated and kept up his complaints, his roars an accompaniment to the awful screeches of tearing metal.

'We're in, Doc,' one of the men called, and Kate left the irate bull to follow Hamish to the cabin.

Both its occupants, a man and a woman, were dead.

'It doesn't matter how often I see it, I hate the waste of life road accidents cause,' Hamish said, as he straightened after examining both bodies. 'Is the ambulance here?'

Kate nodded and waved the vehicle closer.

'It can take them into town. We'll do all the formalities at the hospital. I guess Harry will know who they are and who we need to contact.'

'It's Jenny and Brad Alcott,' one of the ambos said gruffly. 'They met on the rodeo circuit when they were young kids. Brad was a runaway who somehow hooked up with a rodeo stock contractor, and Jenny's mother ran a food van at rodeos for years. She died about six months ago from pancreatic cancer. These two nursed her to the end.'

After a fortnight in a country town, Kate was no longer surprised about how much people knew of each other's business, but she was saddened by the regret in the ambo's voice as he talked of the young couple.

'They were making a good job of providing quality rodeo

stock. Their Oscar is one of the best bulls on the northern circuit,' the man was saying to Hamish as they lifted the second body from the wreck. 'Dunno who'll take over from—'

He stopped abruptly, looked around, then said, 'Cripes, where's Lily?'

'Lily?' Hamish and Kate both echoed the name.

'Little 'un,' the ambo explained, holding out his hand to measure off about three feet from the ground. 'She was at the rodeo.'

Hamish and Kate looked at each other, but Kate was the first to move, scrabbling into the blood-covered seat from which they'd taken the adults, searching desperately through the twisted metal.

Although it hadn't been immediately obvious, the truck was a dual cab, with a second row of seats behind the front ones. Hamish pulled Kate out, explaining the crane would lift the damaged front seats out of the way.

'She might be alive. She might be injured and moving the seats will harm her.' Kate knew her anxiety was unprofessional, but the thought of a child trapped in the twisted mess of metal had her heart racing erratically.

The firemen hooked a chain to the less-damaged passenger seat and gave the signal for the crane to lift.

The little girl was curled in a foetal position in the footwell behind the seat, which had been tipped backwards on top of her. Blonde hair, a pink dress and blood. Blood everywhere.

Kate broke away from Hamish's restraining hand and knelt beside the child, talking quietly while her hand slid beneath the girl's chin, feeling for a pulse—praying for a pulse.

'Damn it, be alive!' she ordered, and felt not a pulse but a movement.

'She moved,' she cried, as Hamish squatted beside her, resting one hand on her shoulder while reaching out to touch the little girl's head, then sliding his hand down to the far side of her neck, seeking a pulse where Kate had found none.

It seemed to Kate that he took for ever, then one word.

'Pulse!'

Kate closed her eyes and uttered a little prayer of thanks. She wasn't certain anyone was listening to her prayers these days, but it didn't hurt to say thank you just in case.

'Lily!' Hamish's voice was gentle. 'Sweetheart, we're here to help you. My hand is on your back. Can you take a deep breath for me?'

Katie tensed as she waited, then Hamish nodded, shifting his hand so it followed the skinny little arm as it curled inwards.

'Now I've got your hand, sweetheart. Can you squeeze my hand?'

Another pause. 'Great!'

Kate heard the genuine delight in that one word.

'I can't reach your toes to tickle them,' Hamish continued, 'but can you wiggle them?'

The blonde head moved just slightly but it was definitely a nod, not a head shake.

'OK, so now we know we can move you a little bit. Do you want to lift your head up so Kate and I can look at you?'

This time it was definite head shake.

Kate, who'd been stroking the blood-matted hair, looked across at Hamish.

'There's a scalp wound here, above her right ear, that I think explains most of the visible blood, but if she was wearing her seat belt there could be soft-tissue damage to her chest or abdomen and even organ damage.'

'I wasn't wearing my seat belt. Mummy will be cross.'

The muffled words pierced Kate's heart, and she put her arms around the little curled-up ball of misery and gave her a hug.

'Maybe this is one case where not wearing a seat belt was lucky. Instead of flying through the windscreen, she's shot off the seat into that space,' Hamish said, sliding his arms down under the child so he could lift her out.

'Lily, we need to get you out of there so we can take a proper look at you. I'm going to lift you now, OK?'

No reply, but as Hamish lifted the little girl, she raised her head and looked at Kate, then put out her arms.

Kate nodded to Hamish and took the child, who attached herself like a limpet to Kate's chest.

'Do you think she knows?' Kate mouthed the words at Hamish above the little girl's head.

'Most probably,' Hamish muttered grimly. 'She's been there and conscious all the time and we've all been talking about things she shouldn't have heard.'

Kate rocked back and forth, holding Lily tightly, hoping human contact would help ease the shock and horror the little girl had suffered.

Hamish dressed the scalp wound, then continued his examination, hampered by the fact he could only work on the bits of Lily not clamped to Kate.

'She seems OK,' he said, shaking his head in disbelief that the child should have escaped unscathed—although it was only her physical self that had been lucky. Who knew what emotional toll losing both parents would take on her?

'That's Lily! She survived!' Harry approached, a rifle in one hand. He walked around Kate so he could see Lily's face—if she'd lift it from where it was burrowed into Kate's shoulder.

'Hey, Lily! It's Harry. How are you, little darling?'

The head lifted and while Hamish watched, Lily registered first the policeman, who was obviously a friend, and then the rifle in his hand.

'What are you going to shoot, Harry?' she asked, and Kate smiled at Hamish, sure this interest in Harry's job signalled the little girl was OK.

But it was Harry's response that surprised Hamish. The policeman frowned and looked around as if seeking something to distract the child. Then the bull, which had been mercifully silent since they'd found Lily, began to bellow again and the quiescent child who'd clung to Kate became a small tornado, kicking and fighting herself free of Kate's protective arms and dashing to the trailer.

'It's Oscar. You were going to shoot Oscar.'

She flung herself down on the torn trailer, so close to the huge head of the angry bull that Hamish reached out and lifted her away. She kicked and fought and screamed to be let down, while the bull became equally agitated.

'It's OK, Lily,' Hamish said, tightening his hold on the little girl, soothing and comforting her. 'Harry isn't going to shoot your bull, darling. No way! We won't let him.'

He handed her to Kate, who kissed her on the head and murmured, 'You stay here with me and talk to Oscar while Harry and Hamish work out how to get him out.'

'You've got to be kidding!' Hamish muttered, looking from Kate to the bull then back to Kate.

'You'll think of something,' Kate told him, hugging Lily closer to her body. 'Isn't there a vet? Couldn't you get a tranquillising dart?'

'I tried to get the vet, but he's out on the Coopers' place, seeing to the cattle Charles wanted checked.' Harry sounded defensive. 'And don't think I like the idea of shooting a healthy animal, but you tell me what else we can do.'

'We have sedatives in our bags and the ambos will have more,' Kate said. 'We only have to do the sums. Hamish, how much do bulls weigh?'

'I'm Scottish,' Hamish protested. 'We have Highland cows but they're small, hairy, docile creatures and, believe me, I have no idea how much *they* weigh, let alone this guy.'

'Can't you work it out from people? I mean, a really big fat man might weigh, what? Three hundred pounds? Then you look at Oscar and work out how many big fat men it would take to make one of him—'

'You can't be serious!'

'You have any other ideas?' Kate demanded.

'Maybe it is the best way,' Harry said, cravenly giving in to Kate's persuasion.

'And we're going to give it to him how?' Hamish asked.

Harry shook his head but Kate turned her head to look at the bull, which appeared to be communing with Lily over Kate's shoulder.

'Intramuscularly, I'd say,' she told Hamish with a smile. 'I wouldn't like to mess around looking for a vein.'

Hamish shook his head again, but now a little smile was playing around his lips and Kate knew she'd won.

'I'll see what we have,' he said, then his smile grew. 'While you work out how to get it into him.'

'He seems a nice bull,' Kate said to Lily when the two men had departed.

'He's mine,' Lily told her. 'My very own. *And* we're friends.'

'I'm kind of glad about that,' Kate said, eyeing the extremely large animal, which looked as if he ate friends for breakfast. Except he did have soft brown eyes, and now she really looked, he had a friendly face.

'Does he let you pat him?'

'Of course he does,' Lily scoffed, reaching out a skinny arm towards the tear in the trailer.

'Be careful, you'll cut yourself,' Kate warned, but the little arm snaked inside and touched the bull's soft nose.

'Would he let me touch him?' Kate pursued.

Lily turned her head to look more closely at the woman to whom she still clung.

'If I told him to,' she said, without a hint of boasting or bravado in her voice.

'Well, when Dr Hamish gets the injection for him, will you tell Oscar to let me touch him? It's not going to hurt him, just put him to sleep for long enough for the men to cut him free and lift him into a truck.'

'Where will the truck take him?'

Lily's legs and arms tightened around Kate's body again and Kate knew the little girl must know, at some level where she didn't want to go, that her parents were dead.

'Wherever you say,' Kate told her, rocking her again.

'He has to come where I go,' Lily said, her voice breaking and warm tears spilling down Kate's neck. 'He has to stay with me. He's mine, he's mine.'

'He'll stay with you, darling, of course he will,' Kate promised, knowing the bond she felt with the child was more than sympathy for her loss, but an understanding of how total that loss must be. 'I promise you he'll stay.'

Hamish and Harry returned, Hamish holding a big bulb syringe Kate knew was normally used for irrigating ears.

'You have a needle on that thing?' Kate asked, and Hamish nodded proudly at her.

'Never let it be said a Scot can't improvise,' he said, showing her his invention, which had a hard plastic cannula attached to the blunt end of the syringe and a hollow hypodermic needle attached to the cannula. 'You ready?'

'Me?'

She may have talked to Lily about touching the big bull, but she hadn't for a minute imagined either Hamish or Harry would allow her to do it. Forget women's lib, this was a very large bull they were talking about.

But Hamish was offering her the syringe!

No chance. 'Lily, tell Oscar Hamish is a friend.'

The little girl, apparently unwilling to take Kate's word for it, wriggled around to look at Hamish.

'You're not going to hurt him, are you?'

Hamish smiled and touched her cheek.

'He'll hardly feel it,' he promised.

'Then I'll hold him.'

Still clinging with one arm to Kate, she stretched out the other and with an imperious 'Oscar, come!' she reached her hand into the damaged trailer.

The big bull stretched his neck, lowered his head and nuzzled her hand, allowing her to pat his nose then reach upward to grab hold of one of his horns.

'Stay!' Lily commanded, for all the world as if she were talking to a very obedient dog not an animal the size of a small elephant. Kate eyed the set-up. If the bull moved his head, he could tear off Lily's arm.

'I'll hold him, too,' she said, and shifted Lily to one hip.

'You'll stay right out of it!' Hamish ordered, placing his body between her and the bull and reaching in to grasp the thick horn above where Lily's small hand lay.

Then he took the chance, reaching in with his right hand and jabbing the needle into the bull's neck, then squeezing the bulb hard and fast to inject as much of the sedative as he could while Oscar remained still.

'It's not going to work,' Kate said ten minutes later, as all four of them watched the bull watching them through the tear in the trailer.

'He looks sleepy,' Lily told her. 'Soon he'll lie down.'

And within moments she was proved correct. The big animal started looking confused, then shook his head, before his legs gave way and he sank down onto what was now the base of the trailer.

The firemen moved in immediately, cutting through the metal shell then calling the tow truck closer and wrapping ropes around the inert body.

'Where am I taking him?' the truck driver asked, when Oscar was settled into the back of a cattle truck.

'To the hospital,' Kate answered, and all the men involved in the rescue turned to stare at her.

'He'll be OK when he comes round,' Hamish assured her,

his voice the kindly one he probably used to people who were off the planet.

'He needs to stay with Lily,' Kate explained, resting her head against the head of the now dozing child. 'Or she needs him to stay with her. And we have to take her to the hospital to check her out and contact relatives. There's that paddock at the back of the Agnes Wetherby Garden—I asked Charles about it one day and he said in the old days the hospital had its own cows. Oscar can go into the cow paddock.'

Harry shrugged and turned to the driver.

'You heard the lady,' he said, while Hamish came over and gave her and Lily a hug.

'And how long did it take you to work out all of that?' he asked, his arm around the pair of them, leading them away from the damaged trailer then stopping abruptly within sight of the ambulance.

Kate shifted Lily so the little girl's weight was on her hip and smiled at Hamish.

'You'd have worked it out just as quickly if you'd heard Lily talk about her bull,' Kate replied, then she checked to make sure the little one was still sleeping. 'She's lost so much, Hamish. How could we not keep her bull close to her?'

He hugged her again and she realised it wasn't just shoulder shrugs and kisses she'd miss. She'd miss Hamish's hugs…

But he wasn't thinking about hugs. Or, if he was, they weren't happy thoughts for he was frowning and looking around as if he'd lost something. Then he turned her and Lily round again and walked back towards the accident.

'Wait here a moment,' he said, sounding so definite Kate didn't argue, though Lily was growing ever heavier in her arms.

He returned, this time with Harry.

'I'll send you back in the second police car,' Harry said, and Kate, glancing back towards the ambulance that was to have been their transport, looked at Hamish and understood. He hadn't wanted Lily travelling with the vehicle that held her parents' bodies.

This was the Hamish that got under her defences. He might joke and make light of things most of the time, but underneath his detached exterior there was a heart that felt the pain of others and a steely determination to do whatever was possible to alleviate it.

'You'll go straight to the hospital?' Harry asked.

'Yes, we need to check her out and the staff there can start a search for relations,' Hamish told him.

'Good luck with that,' Harry said, still frowning, though Hamish felt the frown was directed at him, not at the task that lay ahead of them. 'Brad was a runaway and although a whole crowd of locals and rodeo folk turned out for Jenny's mother's funeral, I don't know that any of them were relatives.'

'We'll do our best, and in the meantime there are plenty of people at the hospital who can keep an eye on Lily.' Hamish wasn't sure why he was getting such negative vibes from Harry, who was usually an extremely positive person. Though maybe having to deal with two dead people and an untold number of dead animals might destroy anyone's positivity.

'So, tomorrow?'

It took a moment for Hamish to realise the question hadn't been directed at him. And that Kate was already answering it!

'I don't know,' she was saying hesitantly, looking down at the blonde head on her shoulder. 'I'll stay with Lily while ever she needs me. I'll let you know.'

Harry gave Hamish another disgruntled look and walked away.

'You were going out with him tomorrow?' Hamish demanded of Kate the moment the policeman was out of earshot.

'He was going to take me out on the river,' she said, 'but now…'

They were in the middle of the highway—mercifully still closed to traffic—halfway between the wrecked vehicles and the second police car, but Hamish wasn't moving another step until he'd sorted this out.

'Take you out on the river? I've asked you to dinner at Athina's, to a beach barbeque, to the movies and to the Black Cockatoo for a drink, and every single time you've given me the same excuse—you don't want to get involved. Yet you had a drink with Harry at the pub on Wednesday and now a second date?'

Somewhere deep inside him a voice Hamish didn't recognise was suggesting he was making a fool of himself—that maybe the woman just didn't like him, or liked Harry better. But he was sure the voice was wrong about her not liking him. Hadn't she kissed him—or at least returned his kisses—just that afternoon?

Could she like Harry better?

The voice was interrupting her reply so he ignored it for a moment to listen to whatever lame excuse she was about to offer.

'I know I keep having second thoughts about finding my father, but Harry's lived here all his life and must know everyone, and I thought maybe I'd find out from him if my father *does* have a family, and what they're like, and then maybe I could judge if I should make contact or not.'

'You're going out with him so you can find your father?'

The internal voice seemed to think that would be OK, except…

'Is that fair?''

'No, probably not!' Kate snapped at him, but Hamish, caught in the grip of an emotion he'd never felt before, couldn't let it go.

'So don't go out with him. Visit him at the police station. Ask him there. Make it an official visit.'

'I don't want to make it an official visit. That's the whole point. I want to find out about him first. He mightn't even be here. He might never have been here. He might have been someone passing through, someone my mother met on holiday. Anyway, this isn't the time or place to be talking about this. We've got to get Lily back to hospital. What's more, whether I go out with Harry or not is really none of your business!'

Stunned by her final statement, Hamish could only watch her back moving further and further away from him.

He'd lost her!

Not that he'd ever really had her—he'd just had hope, quite a lot of hope.

But he'd pushed too far. Now she'd go out with Harry just to spite him.

Or maybe not. He doubted there was a spiteful bone in Kate's body.

But the 'none of his business' phrase told him she was finished with whatever small flirtation she'd allowed herself to enjoy.

Pain he didn't understand bit in again. How could this possibly have happened?

To him, who didn't do love?

Kate watched him as he slipped into the police car—not into the back where she and Lily sat, but into the front beside the driver.

She read his hurt in the slump of his usually straight shoulders and the way he turned his head to look out into the darkness of the rainforest through which the road ran.

And pain of knowing she'd hurt him swamped her heart.

She stroked the hair of the little girl who was sleeping safely strapped in but with her head resting on Kate's body.

What *was* she thinking? What was the hurt of love compared with the loss this child had suffered? How had she and Hamish got into personal stuff while this little girl needed all their attention?

But, no matter how much she felt for Lily, it didn't stop the regret clutching at her gut when she glanced at the man in front of her in the car.

# CHAPTER TEN

'NORMAL SATURDAY NIGHT chaos,' Hamish remarked as they walked into the emergency department with Lily.

He sounded OK—but, then, he did the colleague thing so well it was hard to tell.

Grace was doing admissions. She looked at the little girl in Kate's arms and shook her head, news of the accident and its devastating results having reached the hospital well ahead of them.

'You'll get her processed faster if the two of you do it,' she said. 'I know you're off duty, both of you, but if you wouldn't mind?'

'I want to check her out anyway,' Hamish assured Grace. 'Have you got a spare cubicle we can use?'

Grace tapped her keyboard.

'Room Five. I'll let Charles know you're here. He's been trying to find some close relatives.'

Hamish rested his hand lightly on the small of Kate's back and steered her and her sleeping burden towards the small examination room. She liked the touch, but she'd seen him do it to strangers, men and women.

Once inside Kate slumped down into a chair, turning the little girl so she rested against her body.

'Do you have to wake her?' She looked up into Hamish's concerned blue eyes.

Concerned or hurt?

She didn't know, though probably concerned—this was work after all.

'You know I do,' he said quietly. 'Let's get her on the table and clean her up a bit and see what we can see.'

He bent to lift Lily, the movement bringing his head close to Kate's and bringing something else to her mind—a prescience—as if this was a snapshot of the future—herself, Hamish and a child…

How could that be?

Not possible!

She must have shivered because before he lifted Lily Hamish brushed his thumb against Kate's temple.

'She'll be OK,' he said softly, then, just as she was feeling thankful he hadn't read her thoughts, he added, 'Maybe we all will be.'

Maybe? There were far too many maybes in her life right now.

Lily woke as Hamish settled her on the table and looked around in panic,which subsided when Kate reached out to hold her hand and explain what was going on. The child's eyes, a clear, pale blue, searched further, then, as if remembering what she sought wouldn't be there, they closed, shutting her off from the world and the dreadful reality it held.

'How is she?'

Charles asked the question as he and Jill came into the room.

'Miraculously all right,' Hamish replied, but his voice was sombre and no one really needed the 'physically' which he added to the sentence.

He straightened from his examination.

'She should be kept overnight anyway,' he said, 'purely for observation.'

Kate wanted to protest—to say Lily could stay with her, that she could watch her during the night—but Charles was already agreeing, and Kate knew it was the right thing for the child.

'I'll stay with her,' she said instead. 'I'm off duty tomorrow. I can sleep then.'

Charles looked at her, the frown she often saw on his face only just held at bay by a slight smile.

'Were you always bringing home stray dogs as a child, or is it only stray humans you collect?'

'I lived in the inner city—no stray dogs. And Jack's no longer my stray, he's Megan's.'

Kate wasn't sure why Charles always made her feel slightly uncomfortable. Was it just the frown, or something more?

Whatever, she edged a little closer to the table where Lily lay—and where Hamish stood beside her.

'I think Kate's one of those rare people whose compassion is like an aura she carries with her,' Jill said, startling the subject of her observation. 'People bond with her without really knowing why.'

'I think it's just that I was there—for both Jack and Lily,' Kate protested, acutely embarrassed to think she might have an aura of any kind floating somewhere around her body. 'And I'm still the person with the day off tomorrow, so it won't hurt me to stay with Lily.'

She bent over the little girl, explaining that Hamish wanted to keep her in hospital.

'Is it because my head hurts?'

'You didn't tell me your head hurt,' Hamish said.

Charles wheeled out of the room, calling for an orderly to take the child through to Radiology.

'It just started now,' Lily told him, and fear for the girl welled in Kate's chest as she thought of a deadly haematoma building pressure inside the little girl's skull.

'I should have done a CT scan earlier,' Hamish said to Kate as they stood outside the doors of the radiology department and waited for a result. He looked as anguished as Kate felt.

'Why?' Kate demanded, the argument on the road forgotten as she tried to reduce the load of guilt he was now carrying. 'She was obeying commands, talking, open-eyed, top marks in all her GCS responses. As far as we know, she hadn't lost consciousness and there was no palpable depressed fracture or other sign of skull fracture.'

'She had the cut on her scalp.'

'It bled a lot, that's all. There wasn't even swelling.'

Reassuring Hamish was helping Kate's nerves, but she was just as pleased as he was when Charles emerged to tell them the CT scan was clear.

'Her head's hurting where the cut is, and where's her Kate?' he added, smiling so warmly at Kate she wondered why she'd ever worried about his liking her.

'I'll go into her,' she said, but before she did she turned to Hamish and squeezed him gently on the arm. 'See!' she added softly, but she knew he wasn't comforted. He'd continue castigating himself for some time, although he'd followed ED rules to the letter in his examination and treatment of the little girl.

Kate walked into the X-ray room but Hamish was in front of her, lifting Lily in his arms and carrying her out, following Charles through to the four-bed children's room.

Lily grew heavy in his arms, falling so deeply asleep she didn't wake up as he laid her on the bed or protest as Kate changed her into a pair of child-size hospital pyjamas.

Still anxious about the little girl, Hamish wrote an order for half-hourly obs, then did the first himself.

'We know there's no bleeding inside her skull, and no damage to her skull. It's exhaustion,' Charles told him. 'You and Kate are showing signs of it as well. Go and get some dinner. I'll sit with Lily until you get back.'

'You'll sit with her?'

The question slipped out before Hamish could prevent it, but Charles seemed more amused than annoyed.

'I *can* sit with patients!' he said with mock humility. 'I know the way to do it!'

Then he sighed.

'Actually, it's personal as well. More in the feuding Wetherby family saga,' he said regretfully. 'Her grandmother was a cousin, but my father stopped speaking to that branch of the family before I was born. I knew about Lily's grandmother, and probably should have made more of an effort to contact her after my father died, but—'

'Families!' Kate said, and Hamish wondered if Charles heard the understanding in her voice.

Or knew her link with Lily was more than empathy.

He looked down at the pale face, thinking of how much the child had lost—of how much Kate had lost.

No wonder she didn't want to trust the love that had sprung up between them lest it be stripped away from her. Easier by far to deny it existed, or to pass it off as attraction…

Easier by far to push it away by going out with Harry!

So why did this understanding not make him feel better—not reduce the primal urge he felt to throttle Harry and carry Kate off, bodily if necessary, to his lair?

Or Scotland…

'Go!' Charles said, and Hamish touched Kate on the shoulder then steered her away.

'He's lonely, isn't he?' she asked, as they walked towards the dining room. 'I hadn't thought about it before, but you could hear it in his voice when he talked of the family feud.'

Hamish nodded, understanding—and not saying that he heard it in her voice, too.

Not saying anything at all as he thought about loneliness in all its many manifestations.

His own future loneliness not least among them…

No! That was not to be. Kate felt something for him, so somehow he had to battle through her resistance—somehow.

* * *

'Doctors' house meeting?' Kate joked as they walked into the dining room to find Cal, Gina, Emily, Grace and Susie all sitting at a table.

With Harry!

'Harry's found the missing bulls,' Gina told her, when Kate had helped herself to some roast beef and vegetables and joined them.

'Missing bulls? What missing bulls?' Hamish, who was pulling a chair out for her, asked. 'Don't tell me we've got to put more bulls in the cow paddock. Charles'll have a fit!'

The others laughed but it was Cal, not Harry, who took up the explanation.

'The Alcotts definitely had four bulls at the rodeo, but when you bravely liberated Oscar, he was the only animal in the trailer. Ergo, three missing bulls.'

'So?' Kate said, looking around the table. 'You all seem particularly happy about Harry finding these three. Why?'

'Because they're at Wygera,' Gina said, as if that totally explained the group's pleasure.

'Rob Wingererra, the uncle of one of the girls who died in the car accident some weeks back, travelled the rodeo circuit for years, and later on worked with rodeo stock animals.' Once again it was Cal telling her what she needed to know to connect the dots. 'He helped the Alcotts set up their business, but returned to Wygera recently because his mother isn't well.'

'So when he was talking to them at the rodeo, about the swimming pool and the kids being bored—' Gina took up the tale, her excitement almost palpable '—the Alcotts suggested they leave some bulls with Rob so he can get the kids interested not only in bull riding but in the care of rodeo stock. Isn't it marvellous?'

A young couple dead—two young people with names—Brad and Jenny. A little girl orphaned, a truck driver injured. Kate's mind flashed back to the nightmare horror of the scene, and pushed away her meal. She wasn't at the marvellous part yet.

Then she felt Hamish's hand on her knee, squeezing gently, and she knew he hadn't reached the marvellous goal either.

But his touch brought comfort—comfort she shouldn't be accepting—but she could no more have shifted that hand than she could have swallowed food.

'It will be another interest for the kids at Wygera, and a challenging one at that. At least equal to playing chicken in their old bombs of cars,' he said gently. 'Gina and Cal have been very involved with the community because of the pool, and can see how having the bulls to care for will help even more. I know it seems a funny kind of industry but apparently there's good money to be made in breeding and training rodeo stock, and Rob can manage the business for Lily for as long as is necessary—'

'And other members of the community can get involved.' Kate could see the reason for the smiles now.

The conversation continued around her but she wasn't thinking about bulls, but about how nice it was to have Hamish's hand resting on her knee.

Stupid, really. The last thing she should be feeling pleased about was contact with Hamish. For a start, she'd just told him that what she did was none of his business. And if she set that minor hurdle aside, there was the fact that in less than a week he'd be gone, and the closer she was drawn to him, the more she'd miss him when that day arrived.

'So, are we on for tomorrow?'

Hamish's fingers tightening their hold suggested Harry's question might have been for her, but she'd drifted so far away from the conversation it took her a few seconds to make sense of it.

Hadn't she already told Harry she wouldn't be free tomorrow?

The others were now watching her with interest. Could they know about Hamish's hand on her knee?

And could she say yes to Harry when Hamish had his hand on her knee, and she could feel the tension in it, the tension in the man beside her—the man she'd already hurt with careless words this evening?

'I'm sitting with Lily tonight so I won't get much sleep,' she said, her voice genuinely regretful because Harry was her best chance of finding out more about her father, although Harry wasn't asking her out to be helpful.

'We could go in the afternoon,' Harry pursued, but even though Hamish had now removed his hand, leaving a cold patch on her skin, she shook her head.

'No, Harry,' she said, as gently as she could, embarrassed that this conversation was taking place in front of others but needing to get it said. 'I don't think it's a good idea.'

He glanced from her to Hamish, then back to her again, and she wondered why she didn't feel shivers down her spine when Harry's cool grey eyes looked at her.

It had to be more than eye colour…

'OK!' he said easily, but she sensed he was hurt, an impression confirmed when he stood up and left the table without even a casual goodbye.

'He's a good bloke,' Grace said stiffly, then she too stood up and departed.

Following Harry, or hiding hurt Kate hadn't suspected?

'How's that for breaking up a party?' Hamish asked no one in particular, while Gina stacked dirty plates at one corner of the table.

'Grace has been in love with Harry for ages,' Emily said quietly. 'Unfortunately, until Kate arrived, he's never shown any particular interest in women—or not in any woman working at the hospital.'

'Poor Grace,' Gina said. 'Love can be the pits!'

But though her voice showed sympathy, the smile she shared with Emily showed two people, at least, who'd been there in the pits but had since clambered out—both now glowing, annoyingly for Kate, with the radiance of love.

'Gina's right,' Hamish said gloomily, now only he and Kate were left at the table. 'Love can be the pits!'

'It's not love,' Kate told him firmly. 'It can't possibly be love. We've known each other exactly two weeks—people don't fall in love in two weeks.'

He said nothing for a moment, then caught her eyes and held them.

'I have,' he said, so firmly she knew it was true. 'I know you don't want to hear it, Kate. I know you have so many other issues that you don't need to hear it. But I have to say it.'

He glanced around, then tried to make a joke of something that was obviously killing him.

'We're back at wrong time and wrong place, aren't we—me declaring my love in the hospital dining room?'

And it was this feeble attempt at a joke that hurt Kate most. It pierced her heart and left it oozing pain.

She searched for words to make things better, but couldn't find any. She could only shake her head, slowly and sadly, not knowing now if the utter sadness inside her was for herself or Hamish.

Perhaps for both of them.

She sighed and went for practicality.

'I can't eat. I'm going back to sit with Lily,' she said, pushing back her chair and standing up. 'Isn't Mike organising a fire at the beach? Shouldn't you be helping or at least on your way there?'

Hamish offered a smile so pathetic she wished he'd growled or yelled at her.

'That's tomorrow night,' he said, then the slightest of gleams returned to his dark eyes. 'You're off duty and, as it happens, so am I. It won't be a date, of course, but we'll be sure to see each other there.'

Kate felt the shiver grey eyes hadn't caused. The beach, a fire, night sky, wave music lapping at the shore…

She'd run away from all that last time—but hadn't run far enough.

Hamish was persistent. She'd pushed him away but the gleam and his words suggested he hadn't quite given up.

This time would Hamish leave her at the door?

Maybe she should have gone out on the river with Harry after all.

In the end, they both missed the fire.

It had started innocently enough, with Lily asking Kate where they were keeping Oscar's food.

Hamish, Kate and Lily, still in hospital pyjamas, were sitting on the cow paddock fence watching Oscar who, to Kate's eyes, seemed perfectly content eating grass.

Hamish had arrived not long after dawn and, once assured Lily's obs were perfect and that both she and Kate had slept most of the night, had whisked Kate off to breakfast in the dining room. They'd returned to the children's room to find Lily up and about, demanding to be taken to visit her friend.

So here they were.

'Food?' Kate repeated vaguely, her mind involved with whether she felt the effects of Hamish's presence more keenly in the morning or the afternoon. 'Isn't grass food?'

'No, silly, he needs his pellets.'

Kate had heard of pellets, but she rather thought it had been in connection with guns of some kind. Air rifles? Shotguns?

'Pellets?' Hamish repeated, saving Kate the embarrassment of mentioning firearms.

'Pellet food. It's at home,' Lily continued. 'We'll have to go and get some.'

The three of them had already had a number of conversations about Lily's missing parents but Kate wondered if the little girl really understood they were dead. Was this interest in Oscar's food an excuse to go to her place? Was she thinking her parents might be there?

And if so, would going there and not finding them make it harder or easier for her to accept their loss?

She glanced at Hamish over the child's head and read the same worries in his face and in the small shrug he gave.

'We'd better talk to Charles,' Kate said, surprising herself at how easily she'd fallen into the way of all the hospital staff who saw Charles as the solver of all puzzles large and small. Although if Charles was a relative…

'OK,' Lily said happily, climbing down from the fence and heading towards the hospital.

'How do you know where his office is?' Hamish asked, as Lily led them unerringly towards it.

'I talked to Charles and Jill this morning when you two were at breakfast,' Lily told her. 'He asked about my dad's family, if I had aunts and uncles, and I told him I didn't have any, but he's a kind of cousin and he says I can stay with him until something is sorted out.'

Lily paused in her forward progress and turned to Hamish.

'Charles knows a lot about bulls,' she confided. 'As well as a lot of other stuff. And Charles says there are plenty of people around the hospital who can take care of me when he's working. Do you know Mrs Grubb?'

Hamish smiled at the little girl.

'I do know Mrs Grubb,' he assured her, while Kate guessed the woman in question had already found her way to Lily's heart through chocolate-chip cookies.

But Charles?

Kate smiled to herself.

What could be more perfect—if Charles was lonely—than to have a lively little girl like Lily come into his life?

'Happy families?' Hamish murmured, reading Kate's thoughts again as Lily hurried ahead of them. 'Would it work?'

'It might,' Kate responded cautiously, hoping it would but knowing how ephemeral happiness could be.

Reaching the office, Lily wandered in as if she already belonged in the hospital family and greeted Charles like an equal. She then explained the food problem, far more succinctly than Kate could have.

'Ah!' Charles said, nodding and smiling at his new young friend. 'Did you explain to Kate and Hamish what the pellets are?'

'I told them they were Oscar's food,' Lily replied, and it was Charles who provided more information.

'Rodeo stock need special care. The owners work out exactly what they need and write out…a recipe, I suppose you'd call it, with the balance of protein, vitamins and minerals each particular animal requires, then stock-feed companies make it up into pellets. Oscar would be fed these in the morning and some hay when he's brought into his own pen in the afternoon. It's one of the reasons rodeo stock is easier to handle, because the animals *are* fed twice daily and are used to their handlers being around.'

Kate looked at him and shook her head, while Hamish appeared equally bemused.

'If Lily had a pet shark, would you know what to feed him as well?' Kate asked, remembering Daniel talking about some trendy friend who kept a shark in his living room.

Charles smiled at her.

'Fish, I would think,' he said, then turned his attention to Hamish.

'I'd go myself but there's a Health Department bigwig flying in this morning. Would you mind driving Lily out there? You can take the station wagon and pick up a couple of bags of the pellets. Eventually we'll get it all shifted to Wygera.'

'Can Kate come?' Lily asked, grasping Kate's hand.

Charles's eyes met Kate's above the blonde head, and Kate

knew he was thinking what she'd thought earlier—that maybe Lily needed to see for herself that there was no one there.

And maybe when she saw that, she'd need someone to hold her while she cried…

'Is it far?' Kate asked, all innocence.

'Oh, no,' Charles said. 'Two hundred—not much more.'

'Miles?' Kate said weakly.

And Hamish laughed.

'City girl!' he teased. 'Up here, it's what's known as a nice Sunday drive. Isn't that right, Charles?'

It *was* a nice Sunday drive, but the togetherness of it disturbed Kate. Too many emotions mixed and intermingled—the pleasure of being in a car with Hamish, the genuine joy she felt in Lily's presence, the heart-breaking strength of Hamish as he carried a very subdued little girl through her deserted home then knelt with her, helping her choose toys and clothes for Kate to pack. Singing silly songs as they drove home, until Lily fell asleep in the back seat.

It was family yet not family.

It was something glimpsed then snatched away.

It was very, very confusing for a bruised and aching heart.

# CHAPTER ELEVEN

THREE WEEKS AGO, Hamish had been looking forward to this dinner with Charles. It was to be Charles's private farewell to him, on the Tuesday night before Hamish's departure on the Friday.

But now…

'For a man returning home to the job of his dreams, you don't seem particularly happy,' Charles remarked, and Hamish, who was sure he'd been hiding his misery, shrugged his shoulders at the man who had become a friend.

'Kate?'

This time Hamish nodded, not wanting to talk about the woman with whom he'd so foolishly fallen in love.

'Well, it can't be that she doesn't love you,' Charles said, startling Hamish into speech.

'I beg your pardon?'

Charles smiled at him.

'I said it can't be that she doesn't love you. One only has to stand near her when you're around to feel the warmth of love radiating out of her body. Does she not want to go to Scotland? Has she reasons for wanting to stay in Australia? Perhaps she's afraid of starting a new life so far away from her family.'

'She doesn't have a family!' Hamish muttered crossly. 'That's the whole bloomin' trouble. Or I think it is. I think you're right about her at least liking me enough to give it a go, but she's been through so much…'

She'd kill him if he talked about her troubles—with a scalpel, he thought, or was that fate reserved for anyone who pitied her?

'Tell me.'

Two words, quietly spoken, but enough for Hamish to stop pretending to eat the delicious stuffed vine leaves he'd ordered for dinner and forget death by scalpel. He poured out the whole story into Charles's receptive ears.

'So she came up here to find her father?'

Charles had somehow found the main issue in the muddled tale Hamish had told.

'Has she found him?'

Hamish looked at his friend, Kate and her problems for once relegated to a position of lesser importance in his mind. Charles was sounding stressed and anxious. He'd been through some tough emotional crises recently—could they have affected his health?

'Has she?'

The abrupt demand brought Hamish back to the conversation in hand, though he'd speak to Cal about Charles's health as soon as he got back to the house.

'Well, no,' Hamish admitted. 'I think the shock of finding out she was fostered and then losing her rat of a fiancé propelled her into immediate action. She tracked down her mother first, but she had died. People in the place where her mother had lived mentioned Crocodile Creek. Kate was running on emotion and it wasn't until she arrived here that she realised a twenty-seven-year-old daughter might not be quite what her father wanted in his life. All the what ifs surfaced in her head.'

'She's twenty-seven? When is her birthday?'

Hamish was sure this was the least important part of the conversation he'd had with Charles, but he was now seriously enough worried about the man to go along with it.

'August. I only know because her birthday is the same day as Lucky's.'

'Of course it would be,' Charles muttered, making so little sense Hamish wondered about a stroke, although the words were clearly enunciated. 'What's her mother's name? Has she told you?'

Hamish tried to remember, then shook his head.

'But I've seen a photo. She was going to show it to Harry because he's lived here for ever, then she got cold feet about it all, but she showed it to me.' Hamish paused, still concerned about his dinner companion, but as Charles wasn't showing any symptoms of imminent collapse, he continued. 'Mind you, she doesn't really need the photo. She's the dead ringer for her mother.'

'Two years in the country and you're talking like a native,' Charles said, pushing his half-eaten dinner away and wheeling back from the table. 'Come on, we're getting out of here.'

He waved to Sophia Poulos, who was used to hospital staff leaving halfway through their meals, apologised when she came over and asked her to put the bill on his tab, then led Hamish out of the restaurant, down the ramp and out to his specially modified vehicle.

Hamish kept his mouth shut, although the questions he wanted to ask were clamouring to escape.

'Kate at home?' was all Charles said, as they drove back across the bridge, past the hospital and up to the house.

'She's not on duty,' Hamish managed to admit, although he was becoming more and more disturbed by Charles's behaviour.

'Good! See if you can find her, would you, and ask her to see me in the downstairs lounge. You'd better come, too. Might come as a shock to her to learn I'm her father.'

'*What?* You? Oh, come on, Charles! You can't know that! You don't even know her mother's name—'

'Oh, yes, I do!' Charles snapped. 'It was Maryanne, all one word, no hyphen. And she was, as you said, a dead ringer for Kate, only you said it the other way around.'

Hamish struggled to absorb this information, and struggled even more with his reaction to it. Loving Kate as he did, surely he should be glad for her if Charles did turn out to be her father. Charles, in fact, would be the perfect choice. No wife or children to cause awkwardness, a loving man who would take Kate into his heart without reservation and give her all the love and security she so badly needed.

But to Hamish it was the death of his last hope—the one that if Kate decided not to worry about finding her father she might give in to his pleas and join him in marriage, making a family of their own.

'I'll see if I can find her,' he told Charles, 'though I hardly think that room downstairs is the right place for this conversation. There are sure to be some of the staff down there, and Kate's a very private person.'

'The garden, then,' Charles suggested, as the hoist on his car lowered his wheelchair. 'Kate's told me how much she loves the garden, so she'll feel at ease there.'

I always seem to be waking her up, Hamish thought as he stood in the doorway of Kate's bedroom and looked at her sleeping figure. It was only ten, but she'd been on duty at six, then had played with Lily when she'd finished work.

Hamish sighed, knowing he had to wake her—knowing for her this might be the most wonderful news in the world.

Knowing it was going to break his heart.

But he couldn't yell from the door—everyone in the house would wonder what was going on—so he went quietly into the bedroom, saying her name as he did so, coming to the bed and bending to touch her shoulder.

'Kate, it's Hamish.'

She woke as quickly as most medical staff did, used to

being on call. She sat straight up, the hippo stretching out across her breasts.

'Hamish?'

Her voice was muddled with sleep, but full of…well, affection at least, though to Hamish it sounded like love.

'It's OK,' he said gently, sitting down on the bed and putting his arms around her. 'I'm sorry to wake you but Charles wants to talk to you.'

'Is it Lily?'

He tightened his arms around her when he heard the panic in her voice and reminded her that Lily was sleeping over with CJ, reassuring her Lily was just fine.

'But Charles? Me? What time is it?'

A lot less love or affection now, and who could blame her, considering the broken nights' sleep she'd been having lately?

'Just gone ten. He's in the garden. It's important, love.'

'It had better be,' his love snapped, shrugging away from his embrace so she could get out of bed. 'It had bloody well better be! Jack's OK, Lily's OK, I was looking forward to the first good night's sleep I've had since I arrived in this place.'

She was pulling on her sweatpants as she grumbled, then she ran a brush through her hair, slipped her feet into sandals—this time pink ones with a rose between the toes—and left the room.

Once again, though cravenly this time, Hamish wanted nothing more than to slide between her body-warmed sheets and stay there at least until morning—possibly until he had to leave Australia.

But he followed her out of the house, catching up with her on the back steps.

'What on earth's this about?' she demanded, slightly less aggrieved now.

'It's personal,' he said, slipping an arm around her shoulders and holding her close.

Wrong move. She stopped abruptly and turned towards him, and though it was dark he could see the flare of anger in her eyes.

'Personal? How? Don't tell me you asked him to intercede on your behalf? Asked him to talk to me about going to Scotland with you? *And* woke me up!'

Then she answered her own questions with a decisive shake of her head.

'No, you wouldn't do that. I'm sorry. But personal?'

'It's about your family.' Hamish made the admission reluctantly, knowing the anger she'd just quenched could so easily flare again. 'I'm sorry, I didn't intend to tell him anything, but he wanted to know why you wouldn't consider coming back to Scotland with me and somehow the bit about looking for your father came out.'

But Kate's only response was a sigh, then she lifted her hand and touched his cheek.

'What a mess of a person you got involved with,' she said quietly.

He forgot about Charles waiting in the garden and the bizarre turn events had taken, and took her in his arms and kissed her.

Though sure she was strong enough to handle Charles's revelation on her own, Hamish went with her. This was personal—between her and Charles—but he wasn't going to let go just yet.

Charles was waiting by the garden seat and Hamish could see his tension in the way white-knuckled hands gripped the wheels of his chair.

Maybe he should stay for Charles…

'Kate!'

Charles said her name and nodded to the garden seat. Hamish guided her towards it, sitting her down but keeping his arm firmly fixed around her shoulders, though Charles reached out to take both her hands in his.

'I don't know where to start, my dear, but when Hamish told me—'

He broke off and turned to Hamish, who knew full well he shouldn't be there—yet Charles seemed to need support now as much as Kate would later.

'Charles thinks…' Hamish paused then saw Charles nod for him to continue. 'He thinks he knew your mother.'

Kate stiffened in his arms and her lips moved, but no words came out so Hamish tucked her closer and dug deeper into his heart, trying to find a way to help two people he loved over such an awesome emotional hurdle.

'He knew and loved—' he'd bloody better have loved her, a savage voice muttered in his head '—a young woman who looked so much like you, you've been like a ghost walking through his life since you arrived.'

Hamish used his free hand to tilt Kate's chin so he could look into her eyes.

'Her name was—'

'Maryanne!'

Charles choked out the word then lifted Kate's hands in his, waiting, waiting, until finally a nod—so small if might have passed unnoticed if she hadn't at the same time begun to cry.

'My dear! Kate!' Charles raised her hands to his lips and pressed kisses on them, before looking up at her, his face whitely gaunt as he added, 'Am I right?'

Kate nodded again, more firmly this time, then dropped her head to rest on their clasped hands.

Hamish waited until Charles began to stroke the soft brown curls, then he stood up and moved quietly away.

He'd not go far—Kate might need him later—but right now these two people needed just to be together.

Hamish was dozing, his head against the iron lace that decorated the balustrade on the staircase, when Charles brought her back, stopping at the bottom of the steps and holding tightly to both Kate's hands.

Later, Kate knew, they would need to talk some more, but right now, in the early hours of the morning, they were both too overwhelmed by a multitude of emotions to do anything but cling to each other.

'You need some sleep,' Charles told her gruffly, and she bent and kissed his cheek.

'So do you,' she whispered, then she nodded to her sleeping guard. 'And so does Hamish.'

Charles released her hands and backed away so he could turn to go back to his car. Light from the house glinted on the wheels of his chair, and picked up the faint sheen of moisture on his cheeks.

Kate waited until he was no longer in sight, then she touched Hamish lightly on the head.

'Hey! You should be in bed,' she said, but instead of continuing on up the steps she sat down beside him, knowing he'd put his arm around her—needing the solidity and comfort of it.

He didn't say anything immediately, which was just as well because she was having trouble sorting it all out in her head, but when he finally said 'Well?' the words came tumbling out—the story of a young woman who had been working out at Wetherby Downs and a young man home from boarding school, barely a man at seventeen but man enough to fall in love.

'He went back to school at the end of January, promising to keep in touch. They were so in love they'd already talked of marriage when he finished school and returned to the property at the end of the year. He wrote and she replied, until the week before the Easter break. When he didn't get an answer he phoned home, to be told Maryanne had left. He flew home in the mid-year break and contacted Maryanne's aunt, who'd brought her up in Crocodile Creek, but the aunt thought she was still at Wetherby Downs. He asked around, but she'd vanished as completely as if she'd never been.'

'Charles's father, from all I've heard, was a terrible man,' Hamish said quietly. 'No doubt if he thought she posed a threat to his plans for his son, she'd have had to go. By Easter, the old man would probably have known or guessed that she was pregnant.'

Kate nodded against his shoulder, too overwhelmed by emotion to say any more. Although, somewhere in her head she was wondering why she wasn't happier. Why finding her father—knowing she had family—hadn't brought the joy and ease and peace she'd thought it would?

'Walk on the headland?'

Hamish's suggestion eased a lot of her tension. Knowing she wouldn't be able to sleep, she'd been dreading going back to her lonely room. But Hamish should be sleeping—they were both on duty in the morning—there was no reason she should keep him up.

'Come on,' he said, easing away from her to stand up and pull her up after him. 'I could use the walk myself.'

But walking on the headland where she and Hamish had first kissed was not a good idea. Sure, she'd almost managed to put Charles's revelations out of her head, but now she was far too conscious of Hamish—of the feel of his bones beneath the flesh of his fingers, of the warmth of the muscles beneath the skin of his thighs. Bits of Hamish she'd never even considered seemed to be calling to her, tempting her, pulling her towards him, so when he stopped at the highest point where the sea broke against the cliff beneath them, she turned into his arms and lifted her head for his kiss.

And what happened to not kissing Hamish any more? her conscience demanded.

Tonight's different, she reminded it, although she knew that was just an excuse. No matter what had happened, she shouldn't, definitely shouldn't, be kissing Hamish!

The pressure of his lips opened hers, and she tasted his uniqueness, tart yet sweet—addictive, as addictive as the feel of his body against hers and the strength of the arms that held her close. As addictive as the softly accented words he whispered in her ear, and the way his fingers caught a curl and twirled it round and round.

She sighed and he caught the sound in his mouth and turned it back to her, then the intoxication of the kisses took over and she stopped thinking, simply responding with her lips and hands, exploring more and more of him, knowing she needed to know him with every sense so she could keep the memory for ever.

'I love this place. I could stay—*not* go back,' he said quietly, when, sated with kisses, they walked again.

And knowing just how much the position in the paediatrics team meant to him, Kate understood the magnitude of the offer he was making.

She turned and put her arms around him, resting her head on his chest.

'Oh, Hamish! That's the sweetest, kindest, most wonderful thing you could ever have said to me, but it's not a matter of geography. I know, having just found Charles, that leaving him would be very hard to do, but there are phones and emails and even planes that fly from here to there and back again. So…'

Knowing she needed words as she'd never needed them before, she searched her tired, over-excited mind.

But how to explain?

'It's love that worries me,' she said in the end. 'And all that love entails. The giving over so completely of oneself, the responsibility for someone else's happiness—it frightens me too much, Hamish. Yes, it's magic when it works—the magic that you've talked of, a precious magic. But when it doesn't?'

She moved away from him but he drew her back, holding her in his arms as if he'd never let her go.

'It's love,' she whispered again, hating the word that was paining her so much. 'Love's—love's so full of hurt!'

And she pressed her face against his shirt and wrapped her arms around him.

They stood like that for a while, until he moved so they were side by side again. Then arm in arm, with saddened, heavy hearts, they walked back towards the old house.

Kate leaned against the gate of the cow paddock, watching Lily as she sat on the lush lawn inside the fence, pulling up handfuls of grass and feeding them to Oscar, chatting all the time, telling him she was going to live with Charles and that he'd be going to Wygera with the other bulls but Charles would take her to visit him often.

The gentle giant stood in front of her, carefully lipping the offerings from her small hand, a look of bemused benevolence on his face.

Kate felt Hamish's presence a moment before he joined her, folding his arms on the top rail and resting his chin on them so he, too, could watch the pair.

He'd asked her so often to go back to Scotland with him but Kate knew that today—the day before he left—he wouldn't ask again.

It was up to her.

She slid a glance towards him—saw the strong, angular planes of his face, the almost arrogant masculinity of this gentle, caring man, and her heart all but seized up when she considered never seeing him again…

'It's all about trust, isn't it?' she said, nodding towards the pair in the paddock. 'By trusting Oscar, she's virtually handed him her life, hasn't she?'

'It is, and she has,' Hamish replied, and the depth of emotion in his voice told Kate he knew she wasn't talking about Lily and the bull. 'But she's young,' he continued. 'She's never had reason to lose trust—never had it betrayed.'

Kate turned and looked properly at him, seeing the face she loved so dearly strained and tired.

'But she lost her parents,' she said, needing to argue with him no matter how tired he looked.

'Death isn't a betrayal,' Hamish reminded her. 'And it shouldn't be seen that way.'

'It wasn't my parents' deaths but that they hadn't told me,' Kate whispered, and Hamish took her in his arms and held her close.

'Do you think I don't know that, Kateling? Do you think I can't feel your hurt or understand your unwillingness to trust again? I can and I do, but I can't make you trust me. Trust's something that has to be given freely or it's a worthless gift.'

Kate looked up into the anguished eyes above her, then she rose on tiptoe and kissed him on the chin.

'Will you take my trust?' she murmured, and watched his anguish change to puzzlement then to something that looked like a very cautious hope.

'Are you offering it?' he asked, his voice harshly raspy with emotion.

Kate tried a tentative smile, and took a deep gulp of air.

'I am,' she said, and waited.

And waited.

Then Hamish gave a whoop that startled Oscar into skittishness and had Lily scolding both of them for giving her a fright.

'You mean it? You'll marry me?'

'I do and I will,' Kate said, her voice shaking so much she just hoped the words were distinguishable.

They must have been for Hamish's grasp tightened, but belief, she realised, was still a little way off.

'And Charles? Your family here? You do realise you have

family, don't you? Beyond Charles, you and Jack are cousins. You and Lily are related.'

'Charles said he'll bring Lily to visit us. Jack and Megan and Jackson can come, too. I thought we might give Jack and Megan money for their fares as a wedding present. Then when you've finished your paediatric training…'

'We'll come back here?' The words were hushed with disbelief, as if the last thing Hamish had been expecting was a miracle.

But something must have sunk in for he released her suddenly, stepping back and peering suspiciously down into her face.

'Whoa! Back up here,' he said sternly. 'Charles said he'll come and visit? He'll bring Lily? How come Charles knows where you'll be to visit, before you got around to telling me?'

Hamish watched the colour rise in her cheeks and wondered if he'd ever tire of looking at this woman. She raised those soft brown eyes, now brimming with embarrassment, then offered an equally embarrassed smile.

'Everyone knows Charles knows everything,' she teased, and though it was a brave try, Hamish refused to let her get away with it.

He raised his eyebrows and waited.

And waited.

'Charles had a long talk to me this morning,' Kate finally explained, then she swallowed hard and for a moment Hamish regretted pushing her. In fact, he wanted to take her in his arms and keep her there for ever, no matter how this miracle had happened.

But before he could do anything, she was speaking again.

'He talked to me about my birth mother, not who she was and what had happened between them—he'd told me all of that before. But this morning he told me how much he'd loved her and how much he's always regretted not going after her—not searching for her until he found her.'

Kate blinked but not before one tear had escaped, to roll slowly down her flushed cheek.

'He said regret was a terrible companion with whom to spend your life, but even worse was the knowledge that he'd once been offered the very precious gift of love and he hadn't grasped it with both hands. That, he said, was stupidity, and he hoped like hell he hadn't passed on the stupid gene to his daughter.'

Now more tears were following the first, hurting Hamish's heart just to look at them. He pulled her close and held her tightly, using her body to anchor his to the ground as the realisation that she was his for ever filled him with a heady, dizzying delight.

'I love you,' he managed to whisper gruffly, knowing the words needed to be said.

'And I love you,' Kate responded, drawing away from his embrace so she could look into his eyes. 'With all my heart!' she added.

Then she kissed him again, while across the fence Oscar nodded benevolently.

Everyone was there—Christina and Joe, back from New Zealand with Joe's mother and sister in tow, Emily and Mike, Cal and Gina, CJ and Rudolph. Grace was there, and Susie, Georgie and young Max, and Jill, standing quietly next to Charles, who held Lily on his lap—all lining the drive between the house and the hospital—all yelling good luck and best wishes and waving streamers.

The old house that had seen so much now saw them go—a certain warmth departing with them. But it had stood too long to think love wouldn't bloom again within its walls.

# THE PLAYBOY DOCTOR'S PROPOSAL

BY
ALISON ROBERTS

**Alison Roberts** lives in Christchurch, New Zealand. She began her working career as a primary school teacher, but now juggles available working hours between writing and active duty as an ambulance officer. Throwing in a large dose of parenting, housework, gardening and pet-minding keeps life busy, and teenage daughter Becky is responsible for an increasing number of days spent on equestrian pursuits. Finding time for everything can be a challenge, but the rewards make the effort more than worthwhile.

he must have really been asleep because he didn't remember anything else until morning.

Then there were more words—'very peaceful' and 'gone away on the most wonderful journey'—but he was so good, he didn't say anything himself in case it made Mummy…better call her Alanya…in case it made her worse. A lot of boring time went by. He wasn't allowed to see her at all. He had some meals, breakfast and lunch. Were they saying it was Alanya who had gone on the wonderful journey? When was she coming back? He didn't want to ask because that would not have been hushing and staying silent.

Raina sat him down and hugged him and kissed his forehead and told him, 'Your auntie Janey is going to come and get you, sweetheart.'

He didn't know he had an auntie Janey. He wanted to ask who she was and when she was coming but he was so, so good, he stayed quiet and silent and hushed and didn't say a word.

# CHAPTER ONE

'YOU'RE *not!*'

'Yes, I am. What's the big deal? It's only a few days off work.'

'You never take days off work. In all the time I've known you, Hannah, and that's, what—three years? You've never missed a shift.'

Senior Nurse Jennifer Bradley collected the paper emerging from the twelve-lead ECG machine and Dr Hannah Jackson cast an experienced eye over the results.

'Bit of right heart failure—there's notching on the P waves but everything else looks pretty good for an eighty-six-year-old. No sign of infarct.'

The elderly patient, who had been sound asleep while the recording was being taken, suddenly opened her eyes.

'Give it back,' she said loudly. 'You're a *naughty* girl!'

The complaint was loud enough to attract the attention of several staff members near the central desk. Heads turned in astonishment and Hannah sighed inwardly. One of them would be her fellow senior registrar, Ryan Fisher, wouldn't it? And, of course, he had a grin from ear to ear on overhearing the accusation.

Jennifer was stifling a smile with difficulty. 'What's the matter, Mrs Matheson?'

'She's stolen my handbag! I've got a lot of money in my purse and she's taken it, the little blonde trollop!'

Hannah heard a snigger from the small audience by the central desk. It would have been a good idea to pull the curtain of this cubicle but in the early hours of a Monday morning, with the emergency department virtually empty, it hadn't seemed a priority.

'Your handbag's quite safe, Mrs Matheson,' she said soothingly. 'It's in the bag with your other belongings.'

'Show me!'

Hannah fished in the large, brown paper bag printed with the label PATIENT PROPERTY and withdrew a cavernous black handbag that must have been purchased at least forty years ago.

'Give it to me!'

Hands gnarled with arthritis fumbled with the clasp. The bag was tipped upside down and several items fell onto Doris Matheson's lap. The contents of the opened packet of peppermints rolled off to bounce on the floor and a number of used, screwed-up handkerchiefs were thrown after them.

'There, I told you! There was a *thousand* dollars in here and it's *gone!*' A shaky finger pointed at Hannah. '*She's* taken it! Call the police!'

Ryan wasn't content to observe now. He was standing at the end of the bed. Faded blue eyes peered suspiciously at the tall, broad masculine figure.

'Are *you* the police?'

Ryan flashed the ghost of a wink at both Jennifer and Hannah. 'I've had some experience with handcuffs, if that's any help.'

Hannah shut her eyes briefly. How did Ryan get away with this sort of behaviour? Sometimes, if he was any more laid back, he'd be asleep. What a shame Doris hadn't stayed asleep. She was sniffing imperiously now.

'Arrest that woman,' she commanded.

'Dr Jackson?' Ryan eyed Hannah with great interest. She couldn't help the way the corners of her mouth twitched. This *was* pretty funny. It was just a shame it was going to give Ryan ammunition he wouldn't hesitate to use.

'She's stolen my money.'

Ryan stepped closer. He leaned down and smiled at Doris. One of those killer smiles he usually reserved for the women he was flirting with. Which was just about every female member of staff.

Except Hannah.

His voice was a deep, sexy rumble. *'Really?'*

Doris Matheson stared back. Her mouth opened and then closed. Hannah could swear she fluttered her eyelashes and stifled another sigh at the typical feminine reaction to being the centre of this man's attention. The coy smile Ryan received was only surprising because of the age of their patient.

'What's your name, young man?'

'Ryan Fisher, ma'am.'

'And you're a policeman?'

'Not really.' Ryan's tone was that of a conspirator revealing a secret. 'I'm a doctor.'

The charm he was exuding was palpable. Totally fake but, for once, Hannah could appreciate the talent. It wasn't being directed at her, was it? She didn't need to arm herself with the memories of the misery men like Ryan could cause the women who trusted them. It was certainly defusing a potentially aggravating situation here.

'Ooh,' Doris said. 'Are you going to look after me?'

'You're about to go to X-Ray, Mrs Matheson,' Hannah said.

'What for?'

'We think you've broken your hip.'

'How did I do that?'

'You fell over.'

*'Did I?'* The question, like the others, was directed at Ryan despite it being Hannah who was supplying the answers.

'Yes.' Hannah looped her stethoscope back around her neck. 'And we can't find any medical reason why you might have fallen.' The cause had been obvious as soon as Hannah had been within sniffing distance of her patient. She hadn't needed the ambulance officer's report of an astonishing number of empty whisky bottles lined up on window-sills.

Ryan was smiling again but with mock severity this time. 'Have you had something to drink tonight, Mrs Matheson?'

She actually giggled. 'Call me Doris, dear. And, yes, I do like a wee dram. Helps me sleep, you know.'

'I'm sure it does, Doris.' Ryan's tone was understanding. He raised an eyebrow. 'But it can make it difficult to remember some things, too, can't it?'

'Ooh, yes.' Doris was looking coy again. 'Do you know, I almost forgot where the bathroom was one night?'

'Did you forget how much money you might have had in your purse, too?'

'I *never* keep money in my purse, dear! It might get stolen.'

'It might, indeed.' Hannah got a 'there you go, all sorted' kind of glance from Ryan. She tried hard to look suitably grateful.

'I keep it in the fridge,' Doris continued happily. 'In the margarine tub.'

'Good thinking.' Ryan stepped back as an orderly

entered the cubicle. 'Maybe I'll see you when you get back from X-Ray, Doris.'

'Oh, I hope so, dear.'

Hannah held up her hand as her patient's bed was pushed away. 'Don't say it,' she warned.

'Say what?' Ryan asked innocently.

'Anything about naughty girls,' Jennifer supplied helpfully. 'Or arresting them. And especially nothing about handcuffs.'

'Not even fluffy ones?'

Jennifer gave him a shove. 'Go away. Try and find something useful to do.'

They were both laughing as Ryan walked away. Relaxed. Enjoying the diversion of an amusing incident. But Jennifer could afford to enjoy Ryan's company, couldn't she? Happily married with two adorable small children at home, she was in no danger of being led astray.

Neither was Hannah, of course. She knew too much about men like Ryan Fisher. Great-looking, *fun* men like the ones who'd made her mother's life a misery after her dad died, not to mention the guy who'd broken her sister's heart not so long ago.

Hannah only ever let herself get involved with nice, trustworthy, serious men like her father had been. She'd believed herself to be totally immune to men of Ryan's ilk.

Until three months ago.

Until she'd met Ryan Fisher.

Jennifer was still smiling as she tidied the ECG leads away. 'I still can't believe you're taking time off,' she told Hannah. 'I've never even known you to be sick. You're the one who always fills in for other people like Ryan when *they* take days off work.'

Hannah glanced towards the central desk. Ryan—the

king of holidays and all other good things life had to offer—was now leaning casually on the counter, talking to a tired-looking receptionist. Probably telling her one of his inexhaustible supply of dumb blonde jokes. Sure enough, a smile was starting to edge the lines of weariness from Maureen's face.

'I'm going to check the trauma room while it's quiet,' Hannah told Jennifer.

'I'll help you.' Hannah's news of taking time off had clearly intrigued her friend, who didn't consider their conversation finished. 'And there I was thinking that, if *I* didn't drag you out occasionally, you'd spend all your time off studying or something.'

Hannah picked up the laryngoscope on top of the airway trolley and pulled the blade open to check that the battery for the light was still functional. 'Are you saying I have no life?'

'I'm saying your career takes the prize as your raison d'etre.'

'I always wanted to be a doctor.' Hannah snapped the blade back in line with its handle, switching off the light. 'Now that I *am* one, I intend to be a very good one.'

'You *are* a very good one. The best.'

'We'll see.' The glance between the two women acknowledged the growing speculation within the department over who was going to win the new consultant position. She had been the only serious contender until Ryan had thrown his hat into the ring today. Was that why she was so aware of his presence in the department tonight? Why everything about him seemed to be rubbing her up the wrong way even more than usual?

'Anyway…' The wind had been taken out of Jenny's sails, but not by much. She opened a box of syringes to restock the IV trolley. 'You don't need to prove how good you are by living and breathing emergency medicine.'

'So you're saying I'm an emergency department geek?' Hannah tilted the ceiling-mounted, operating-theatre light so it was in a neutral position. It would be fair enough if she was. Hannah loved this space. Fabulous lighting, X-ray and ultrasound facilities, every piece of equipment they could possibly need to cover the basics of resuscitation and stabilisation of a critically ill patient. Airway, breathing, circulation. To be faced with a life-threatening emergency and succeed in saving that life was all the excitement Hannah needed in her life.

Jenny caught her expression and clicked her tongue with mock exasperation. 'I'm just saying you could do with more in your life than work.'

'And that's precisely why I'm taking a few days off.'

'Touché.' Jenny grinned, magnanimous in defeat. 'OK.' She shoved the syringes into their allocated slot and then used her forefinger to stir the supply of luer plugs and IV connectors, pretending to count. 'So where the hell is Crocodile Creek, anyway?'

'Australia. Far north Queensland.'

'Oh! Has this got something to do with your sister?'

'Yes. I've been invited to a wedding.'

'Susie's getting *married?*'

'No, though I'm sure she'd be over the moon if it *was* her wedding. She's being a bridesmaid to her best friend, Emily.'

'Do you know Emily?'

'No.'

'So why have you been invited to her wedding?'

'Well…' Hannah leaned against the bed for a moment. It wasn't often they got a quiet spell, even at 2 a.m. on a Monday morning and the break hadn't gone on long enough to get boring yet. 'Susie didn't have a partner to invite and we haven't seen each other since she jumped the ditch and came to New Zealand for Christmas. I'm starting to feel guilty about how long it's been.'

'It's only March and it's a hell of a long way to go to ease a guilty conscience. Auckland to Cairns is about a six-hour flight, isn't it?'

'It sure is.' Hannah groaned. 'And then there's the little plane from Cairns to Crocodile Creek, which will take another couple of hours, I guess.'

'It must be a long way north.'

'About as far as you can get. The hospital there is the rescue base for the whole of far north Queensland. That's why I need the Friday on top of the weekend. I have to get right into the heartland of sugar and cane toads.'

'Eew!'

'Actually, it's right on the coast. It sounds gorgeous.'

'You've never been there before?'

'No, and Susie's been living there for as long as I've been working here. It's high time I checked out what my little sister is up to.'

'I thought you were twins.'

By tacit consent, the doctor and nurse were leaving the trauma room, satisfied it was ready for a new emergency. Hopefully, they'd be back in there soon with some real work to do.

'She's four minutes younger than me.'

'And she's a physiotherapist, right?'

'Yeah. She started medical school with me but she hated it. Too much pressure.'

'You must be quite different.'

'Personality-wise, definitely. To look at, no. We're identical.'

'Wow! Do you have, like, that twin thing?'

'Which "twin thing" is that?' They were near the central desk now. Ryan had disappeared, presumably into the only cubicle with a drawn curtain. The nurse on triage duty, Wayne, was sitting, drumming his fingers on the counter.

'You know, when one twin sprains her ankle, say, here in Auckland and the other twin falls over in a supermarket in central London.'

Hannah laughed, dismissing the suggestion with a shake of her sleek head. But was it so ridiculous? Was it just that she was missing a sister who had always also been her best friend or did those niggling doubts about how happy Susie was have a basis in some form of telepathic communication? Was the urge to travel thousands of miles at a very inconvenient time to attend the wedding of two people she only knew through Susie's emails just an excuse?

'Apparently this wedding is going to be great fun.' Hannah tried to find a more rational explanation for the urge she hadn't been able to resist. 'The groom, Mike, is Greek and his parents own a boutique hotel right in the cove. Susie reckons it'll be the biggest party the Creek has ever seen.'

Jennifer's peal of laughter made several heads turn.

'What's so funny?' Hannah's eye was caught by the light on the radio receiver that linked the department with the ambulance service. It was blinking.

Jennifer could hardly get the words out clearly. 'You're going to *My Big Fat Creek Wedding*!'

Grinning, Hannah still managed to beat Wayne to the microphone. 'Emergency Department.'

'Auckland four eight here. How do you receive?'

'Loud and clear,' Hannah responded, her grin fading rapidly. 'Go ahead.'

'We're coming to you from the scene of a high-speed

multiple MVA. The chopper's just landing to collect a second seriously injured patient who's currently trapped, but we're coming to you with a status-one seven-year-old boy.'

The grin had long gone. Status one was as serious as it could get. Under CPR, not breathing or uncontrollable haemorrhage were all possibilities for the priority designation. This ambulance would be coming towards the hospital under lights and sirens.

'Injuries?'

'Head and facial trauma. Partially unrestrained front-seat passenger—the safety belt wasn't latched securely.'

This wasn't the time to feel angry at someone failing to strap a child into a car seat properly. Or to wonder why they were travelling at 2 a.m. in the first place.

'Vital signs?'

'GCS of 3.'

The child was profoundly unconscious. Quite possibly due to bleeding around his brain.

'Airway?'

'Unsecured.' The paramedic raised his voice as the siren came on in the background. The vehicle must be in heavier traffic now. At night, just having the beacons flashing could be enough warning of the urgency of their mission. 'There's severe facial trauma and swelling. We've got an OP airway in but that's all.'

The boy needed intubation. Securing an airway and optimising oxygen levels were a priority in a head injury. Especially in a child because they had a greater chance of neurological recovery than an adult after a head injury and therefore warranted aggressive treatment in the early stages. If the paramedics had been unable to intubate due to the level of trauma, it could mean that this was going to be a challenging case.

Hannah could feel her adrenaline levels rising and the tension was spreading. Nearby staff were all listening avidly and the curtain on cubicle 4 flicked back to reveal that Ryan was also aware of what was happening. Hannah's heightened awareness registered the interest and at some subconscious level something like satisfaction was added to the emotional mix. She was taking this call.

This would be her case, not Ryan's. Just the kind of case she needed to showcase the skills that would be a major consideration in choosing the new consultant for the department.

'What's the oxygen saturation level?' she queried briskly.

'Ninety-four percent.'

Too low. 'Blood pressure?'

'One-thirty over sixty-five. Up from one-twenty five minutes ago.'

Too high for a seven-year-old. And rising. It could well be a sign of increasing intracranial pressure.

'Heart rate?'

'One hundred. Down from about one-thirty.'

Too slow for Hannah's peace of mind. And dropping. It could also be a worrying sign. 'What's your ETA?'

'Approximately five minutes.'

'We'll be ready for you.' Casting a glance over her shoulder, Hannah could see Ryan moving towards the resuscitation area she and Jennifer had just checked. Not that she was about to decline any assistance for dealing with the incoming case but she didn't want Ryan taking over. It wasn't as though there was only one victim arriving, was it? She pushed the button on the microphone again.

'Do you know the ETA for the chopper?'

'Negative. Fire service is on scene, though.'

It shouldn't take them long to cut the second victim clear of the wreckage, then. 'And that's also a status-one patient?'

'Affirmative. Chest trauma. It's the mother of our patient.'

Ryan would be able to lead the team on that case. In resus 2. Or they could share the main trauma room if necessary. Hannah's plan of action was forming rapidly as she replaced the microphone.

'Put out a call for an anaesthetist, please, Wayne,' she directed. 'And let's get a neurosurgical consult down here. Sounds like we might need someone from Plastics, too. Jenny, you're on the trauma team tonight, aren't you?'

'Yes.'

'And you, Wayne?'

'Yes. Resus 1?'

Hannah nodded, already moving towards the area. She pulled one of the protective plastic aprons from the large box on the wall. Ryan was already tying his behind his back.

'Could be a tricky airway management,' he said.

'Mmm. I've called for some anaesthetic back-up but I'll see how I go.' The direct look Hannah gave Ryan could leave him in no doubt that she intended to lead this resuscitation effort. The subtle twitch of an eyebrow let her know the message had been received and understood. It also hinted at amusement rather than intimidation.

'I'll stay until the mother gets here,' he said calmly. 'In case you need a hand.'

'Thanks.' The acknowledgement was perfectly sincere. There was a child's life at stake here and Hannah would never let any personal considerations affect her performance. She would stand back in a flash if she thought Ryan's skills would improve the management. Never mind that he would get the credit for managing a difficult case.

It was just annoying that people that mattered were keeping a count of those credits at present. And disappointing that a competitive edge of any kind had crept into

Hannah's working environment when one of the things she loved best about her work was the way a team of people could work together and the only kudos that really mattered was a successful outcome to that work.

The decision on the consultant's position was only a week or two away. A position that represented everything Hannah was striving towards in a career she was passionate about. Why had Ryan decided to compete at the last minute like this? It wasn't as if he really *needed* the position. He didn't have a massive student loan, the repayments of which would benefit enormously from an increase in salary. He didn't need to prove himself in a field that was still dominated by males in senior positions. He was an Australian. Auckland wasn't even his home town.

She couldn't help flicking a glance towards the tall man who had now donned protective eyewear and a pair of gloves and was lounging at the head end of the bed. Why hadn't Ryan Fisher just stayed on his side of the ditch? In that Sydney emergency department where he'd honed his not inconsiderable skills? Life would be so much easier if he had. And it wasn't just due to that professional competition.

Jenny pushed the IV trolley into an easily accessible position and then stood on tiptoe to check that the tubes attached to the overhead suction and oxygen supplies were firmly in place. It was still a stretch for her short stature and Ryan was quick to step forward.

Without a word, he saved Jenny the awkward task and then gave her one of those killer smiles in response to her thanks. The senior nurse turned back to the IV trolley but Hannah noticed the extra glance that went in Ryan's direction.

Not that he had noticed. The registrar was lounging again, his keen glance taking in the mill of the gathering trauma team and registering the growing tension.

The few minutes before the arrival of a serious case was a strange time. A calm before a storm of unknown proportions. Equipment was primed and ready. Staff were wearing protective gear and waiting. Wayne stood behind a kind of lectern that had the paperwork necessary to document every moment of the resuscitation effort and he was fiddling with a pen.

Hannah had pulled on gloves and was unrolling the airway pack on the top of a stainless-steel trolley. Others were simply standing. Waiting. There was nothing to do until their patient came rolling through those double doors. Nobody liked to speculate in too much detail on what was about to arrive because that could give them tunnel vision. A conversation that required distraction of mental focus was just as unwanted. What usually happened was a bit of gossip or a joke. Light-hearted banter that could relieve tension before it achieved destructive proportions. Something that could be abandoned as easily as begun.

And Ryan could always be counted on to provide a joke that would make everybody laugh.

Everybody except Hannah. She made a point of never laughing at Ryan's jokes because the vast majority of them were at the expense of women with blonde hair. Like hers.

Sure enough, he was telling one now.

'So this blonde—Cindy—is in desperate financial straights and she prays for help. "Please, God, let me win the lottery or I'll have to sell my car." But she doesn't win so she prays again, "Please, God, let me win the lottery. I'm going to have to sell my car *and* my house."'

Everybody was listening. Or half listening. Waiting for the distant wail of the siren that would advertise that the calm was over. Hannah kept her gaze on the trolley, checking that there was a range of paediatric-sized tubes and that the laryngoscope was still working.

She didn't have to look at Ryan to know exactly what the image would be. He would be standing completely at ease with just a hint of a smile and a twinkle in those dark eyes that advertised an upcoming punchline. It might be a terrible joke but everybody would be listening and would be prepared to laugh because Ryan commanded that sort of attention. And popularity. Without even trying.

Hannah lips pressed themselves into a thinner line as she made sure that the more serious gear that might be needed for a surgical airway was at hand. No, it wasn't just the professional competition that irked her. It was the fact that she had been as attracted to Ryan as every other woman who'd set eyes on him from the moment he'd arrived in this department three months ago.

It had been so unexpected. He was the epitome of the type of man she had always steered very well clear of. Despised, even, thanks to the collateral damage she had seen them produce in the lives of women she cared about. One of life's golden people. She had probably been the first woman ever to freeze out an advance from him. Was that why he was persevering for so long? Did she represent some kind of challenge?

'She *still* didn't win,' Ryan was continuing. 'She's down on her knees, pleading and this time God speaks to her.' His voice dropped to a deep rumble that Hannah could actually feel in her bones. 'And he says, "Work with me here, Cindy. *Buy a ticket!*"'

Sure enough, there was a wave of laughter. A wave that faded with dramatic swiftness, drowned out by the faint wail of a siren. Then the sound of the approaching siren died as it sped onto the hospital grounds with just its beacons flashing. Seconds later, the stretcher appeared. A third crew member was moving rapidly beside the stretcher, a bag-mask unit over the face of the child, trying to keep oxygen levels up on the short journey between the ambulance and the trauma bay.

The team went into action as a unit. The transfer of the small body was smooth—made easier by the fact he was strapped to a backboard with a collar to protect his neck. And although this team was well used to seeing victims of major trauma, it was a shock to get their first close-up view of this little boy.

Waiting at the head of the bed to manage the airway, Hannah sucked in a quick breath that was almost a gasp. No wonder he hadn't been intubated and it would have been far too dangerous to attempt a nasopharyngeal airway. His nose and mouth were almost lost beneath swollen and lacerated tissue. There were obvious facial fractures and the eyelids were so swollen it was impossible to open them enough to assess the pupils with a torch.

'Do we know his name?'

'Brendon,' one of the paramedics supplied. 'His mother was initially conscious enough to be calling for him.'

He was wearing pyjamas, Hannah noticed as she leaned forward. Bright red racing cars on a blue background. 'Brendon, can you hear me?' She reached over his shoulder. Why had he been in a car in pyjamas instead of safely asleep in his bed? 'Squeeze my hand if you can hear me, sweetheart.'

A response hadn't really been expected and Hannah moved swiftly to take the tip of the suction unit Jennifer was holding. The child was moving air but there was a nasty bubbling sound and the probe on his finger revealed an oxygen saturation level that was far too low to be acceptable.

'Rapid sequence intubation?'

'If it's possible.' Hannah's gaze flicked up, relieved to find one of the senior anaesthetic registrars now standing right beside her.

Ryan was on the other side of the bed and farther down, moving in to assess IV access and flow and to look for other potential injuries as the pyjamas were cut clear of the small body.

ECG electrodes were being attached. Jennifer was using a bag mask to assist the delivery of oxygen. Hannah suctioned as much blood as she could from Brendon's mouth and nose.

'I can't see anything that clearly looks like CSF,' she said. Not that that discounted the possibility of skull fractures or spinal damage.

'Saturation's down to ninety per cent. Let's go for the intubation,' the anaesthetist advised. He took the bag mask from Jennifer and began to squeeze it rapidly, increasing the amount of oxygen reserves to cover the down time for trying to get a tube into Brendon's throat. He was clearly prepared to provide back-up rather than taking over the procedure.

Hannah drew in a slow breath to dispel any nerves. She heard herself issue instructions for the drugs needed, like suxamethonium to relax muscles and atropine to prevent the heart slowing dangerously. The formula for determining the size of the endotracheal tube was there instantly—the diameter equalled the age of the child divided by four, plus four.

'I'll need a 6 millimetre, uncuffed tube,' she informed Jennifer. 'And I want you to hold his head while we ease this collar off.'

It was a challenge, easing the blade of the laryngoscope past the swollen lips, broken teeth and a badly lacerated tongue, and Hannah had to use the suction unit more than once. It was an unexpectedly easy victory to visualise the vocal cords and slip the tube into place.

'I'm in.' The tone was one of satisfaction rather than triumph, however. There was still a long way to go but at least they were on the way to stabilising a critically ill patient.

'Well done.'

With her stethoscope now on Brendon's chest to check for correct tube placement and equal air entry, the quiet words of praise were muted and, for a moment, Hannah thought they might have come from Ryan.

But he was no longer standing beside Brendon. Hannah had been concentrating so hard on her task she had managed to block the sounds of the second patient's arrival and the stretcher was now being swiftly manoeuvred to the other side of the trauma room.

'Blunt chest trauma with tachycardia and hypotension. No sign of a tension pneumothorax.' she heard Ryan stating. 'We could be dealing with an acute pericardial tamponade.'

Would Ryan attempt a procedure to drain off the fluid inhibiting the function of the young mother's heart? It would be a very impressive coup as far as patient treatment if it was successful. Hannah couldn't help casting frequent glances towards his side of the room as she worked with the anaesthetist to get Brendon's ventilator setting right, supervised the amount of IV fluid that was being administered, started an infusion of mannitol, which could help reduce intracranial pressure, and arranged transfer for an urgent CT scan of the boy's head and neck.

Sure enough, Ryan was preparing to intubate his patient, cardiac monitoring was established and kits requested for both pericardiocentesis and chest drainage. Ryan looked determined and confident but less than happy about the challenge he was about to face. And no wonder. From what Hannah could see, the woman's condition was deteriorating rapidly.

Ominous extra beats were disrupting the line of the ECG trace on the screen of the monitor.

There was time for one more, rapid secondary survey on Brendon before he was taken to the CT suite.

'Some of these bruises look old,' she commented.

'Maybe he plays rugby,' Jennifer suggested.

'You reckon his mother does as well?' Wayne had been helping Ryan's team in the initial preparation of his patient. 'She's covered in bruises as well.'

Hannah eyed the clothing remnants Wayne was putting into a patient property bag. 'Dressing-gown?' she queried.

He nodded. 'I don't think their trip was planned.'

A police officer was standing well to one side of the now crowded area. 'Have any relatives been contacted?' Hannah asked him.

'We didn't need to. The car she was driving had just been reported stolen.' The police officer's face was grim. 'By her husband.'

Hannah absorbed the information like a kind of physical blow. Was her patient an innocent young victim caught up in a situation involving domestic violence? Had his mother's desperate bid to protect him ended in a disaster he might never recover from? Would he even still have a mother?

It seemed unlikely. Ryan was sounding uncharacteristically tense as Brendon's stretcher was taken through the double doors on the way to CT.

'We've got VF. She's arrested. Charging to 200 joules. Stand clear!' He looked up as he recharged the paddles. 'Hannah, are you free?'

Hannah's hesitation was only momentary. She had been

planning to follow protocol and accompany Brendon but he already had an expert medical escort in the anaesthetic registrar. She knew what Ryan would do if the roles were reversed and *she* asked for assistance. Hannah turned back.

'I'm free,' she said quietly. 'What do you need?'

## CHAPTER TWO

'WE'VE got sinus rhythm.'

Ryan dropped the defibrillator paddles with relief. The same kind of relief he'd noted when Hannah had turned back to help before he'd delivered that last shock. Not that he'd doubted he could count on her in a professional capacity. He could see her pulling on gloves and positioning herself beside the tray containing the pericardiocentesis and chest drain kits as he reached to check his patient's pulse.

'Carotid is barely palpable,' he reported grimly.

'Systolic pressure is fifty-nine,' Wayne confirmed.

'Let's shut down the IV. Just run it enough to keep the vein open,' Ryan ordered. 'There's been no response to a fluid challenge and if we're dealing with thoracic haemorrhage it'll only be making things worse.'

'Ventricular ectopics starting again.' Hannah had an eye on the monitor screen. 'And the systolic pressure is dropping. Down to fifty-five.'

The patient was threatening to arrest again. Ryan reached for a scalpel and Hannah had the forceps ready to hand him a moment later. Then the cannula for the chest drain. In less than a minute, blood was draining freely into the bottle. Too freely. All too soon, the bottle was almost full.

'Have we got someone from Cardiothoracic on the way?'

'No.' Jennifer shook her head at Ryan's terse query. 'Sorry. They're unavailable for fifteen to twenty minutes. They're tied up in Theatre with a post-bypass complication.'

'Have we got a thoracotomy kit?' He could almost hear a collective intake of breath. 'She's exsanguinating from a chest injury and about to go into cardiac arrest again. A thoracotomy might be a long shot but it's the only hope we've got.' Ryan knew the statistics were not on his side but at least they would be doing something other than watching this woman bleed to death.

Hannah nodded once, as though she had gone through the same thought processes and was in agreement with him. 'Want me to scrub as well?'

'Yes. Thanks.'

Wayne was sent to find the rarely used sterile kit. Jennifer took over the task of manually ventilating their patient. Ryan scrubbed fast. Ideally he should have the chest opened in less than two minutes. Faster, if there was another cardiac arrest.

'Have you done this before?' Hannah squeezed soap into her hands beside him.

'Yes. You?'

'Never even seen it.'

'Know the indications?'

'Penetrating thoracic injury with traumatic arrest or unresponsive hypotension or blunt injury with unresponsive hypotension or exsanguination from the chest tube. Overall survival is between four and thirty-three per cent but higher for penetrating injury.'

'We've got VF again,' Jennifer warned. 'No…it's asystole.'

Speed was now critical. A flat-line ECG meant that the heart couldn't be shocked into producing a rhythm again. Chest compressions on someone with blunt trauma were also contraindicated because it could worsen the injury. Opening the chest was the only option with any hope at all now.

It was good that Hannah had never seen the technique. Explaining things as he started this incredibly invasive procedure somehow eased the tension of a desperate measure to save a life.

'We'll make bilateral thoracotomies in the fifth intercostal space, mid-axillary line—same as for a chest drain.' Ryan worked swiftly with a scalpel and then a heavy pair of scissors. 'I'll be ready for the Gigli saw in a sec.'

He showed her how to use the serrated wire saw, drawing a handle under the sternum with a pair of forceps and then joining the handles and using smooth, long strokes to cut through the sternum from the inside out.

Hannah was ready with the rib spreaders. For someone who hadn't done this before, her calmness and ability to follow direction was a huge bonus.

'You can see why this is called a "clam shell" thoracotomy,' he said as he spread the ribs away from the anterior incisions. 'Suction, thanks.' Ryan sucked out blood and clots from the chest cavity, hoping it would be enough for the heart to start beating again spontaneously.

It wasn't.

'Where's she bleeding from?'

'Haven't found it yet.' Ryan placed both hands around the heart. 'I'm starting internal cardiac massage. Can you find and compress the aorta against the spine, Hannah? We want to maximise coronary and cerebral perfusion. I'll clamp it in a minute.'

* * *

She was totally out of her depth here. It was a huge relief when back-up from the cardiothoracic surgeons finally arrived. They were impressed with Ryan's management of the case so far, which was hardly surprising. Hannah wouldn't have had the confidence or skill to go further than the chest drain insertion.

The thought that Ryan might deserve the consultant's position more than she did was not a pleasant one.

Edged out as people with far more experience than she had took over, Hannah could only watch. It was hard, feeling the tension and increasing frustration as they failed to get the young woman's heart started again, having controlled the haemorrhage from the damaged aorta.

Maureen's signal, with the message that Brendon was now in the paediatric ICU and an invitation to discuss the results of the CT scan with the consultant, was welcome. Hannah slipped, unnoticed, from the resuscitation area.

She couldn't afford to stand around admiring Ryan's skill and thinking how easily he might win the position she'd wanted for so long. Or to share his disappointment at the inevitable failure he was facing. Empathy would create a connection that was too personal. Even worse than laughing at one of his stupid jokes. It would only make it that much harder to maintain the necessary distance between them.

Any reduction in that distance could only make her vulnerable.

And Hannah Jackson did not do vulnerable.

She'd always been the strong one. Ever since she was ten years old and her father's sudden death had made her small family almost fall apart. Hannah had been strong for her mother. For Susie. For herself.

The lesson had been hard but valuable. Strength was

protection. The only way to get through life without being scarred too deeply.

Being too tired didn't help when it came to being strong.

When Hannah entered the staffroom nearly an hour later, she could feel Ryan's dejection all too easily. He had his back to her as he made coffee but his body language said it all. Slumped shoulders. Bent head. The way he was stirring his mug so slowly. If it had been any other colleague she wouldn't have hesitated in offering commiseration. A comforting touch or even a hug. But this was Ryan. Distance was obligatory.

'No go, huh?'

'Nah.' Ryan straightened his back. 'Didn't really expect to win that one but it was worth a try. Want coffee?'

'Sure, but I'll make it.'

Ryan was already spooning coffee into a second mug. 'You take sugar?'

'No.'

'Milk?'

'No.'

He'd been in the department for three months and didn't know how she took her coffee but she was willing to bet he'd know the preferences of all the female staff who responded to his flirting. And that was every one of them.

Except her.

'So how's your little guy, then?'

'Not flash. He's in paediatric ICU but the scan was horrible. Multi-focal bleeds. If he does survive, he'll be badly brain damaged.'

'Might be better if he doesn't, then. You saw the father?'

'Yeah.' There was no need for further comment. The glance Ryan gave Hannah as he handed her the mug of black coffee told her he shared her opinion that the man she'd had to talk to about the serious condition of his child was an uncaring brute. Responsible for the death of his wife and quite likely his son, not to mention the admittedly less serious injuries sustained by the other drivers involved, and he hadn't given the impression of being overly perturbed about any of it. 'And they can't even charge him for anything.'

'No.' Ryan went and sat down on one of the comfortable armchairs dotted around the edge of the room.

The silence was heavy. Too heavy.

Ryan cleared his throat. 'Hey, have you heard the one about the blonde who didn't like blonde jokes?'

Hannah sighed. She sat down at the central table, deliberately putting Ryan out of sight behind her right shoulder. Maybe it wasn't good to sit in a depressed silence but this was going a bit too far in the other direction, wasn't it? She sipped her coffee without saying anything but Ryan clearly ignored the signals of disinterest.

'She went to this show where a ventriloquist was using his dummy to tell blonde jokes. You know, like,how do you change a blonde's mind?' He raised his voice and sounded as though he was trying to speak without moving his lips. "Blow in her ear!" And what do you do if a blonde throws a pin at you? "Run, she's still holding the grenade."'

'Yeah, yeah.' Hannah allowed herself to sound annoyed. 'I know.'

'Well, so did this blonde in the audience. She was furious. She jumps to her feet. "I've had enough of this", she shouts. "How dare you stereotype women this way? What does the colour of someone's hair have to do with her worth as a human being? It's people like you that keep women like me from reaching my full potential. You and your kind continue to perpetrate discrimination against not only blondes but women in general and it's *not* funny!"'

'Mmm.' Despite herself, Hannah was listening to the joke. So Ryan was actually aware of why someone like herself might take offence at his humour? Interesting. Did that mean he was intentionally trying to get under her skin? That his charm with her was as fake as it had been with Doris Matheson and he actually disliked her type as much as she did his?

Ryan's tone was deadpan. 'The ventriloquist was highly embarrassed. He goes red and starts apologising profusely but the blonde yells at him again. "Stay out of this, mister. I'm talking to that little jerk on your knee!"'

Hannah snorted. Somehow she managed to disguise the reluctant laughter as a sound more like derision. She didn't want to laugh, dammit! Not at one of Ryan's jokes and not when she'd just been through a gruelling, heart-breaking and probably fruitless couple of hours' work. She knew exactly why he was trying to make her laugh. It had to be the quickest way of defusing an overly emotional reaction to a case. But if she let him make her feel better, it would be worse than empathising with *him.* She could feel the connection there, waiting to happen. It needed dealing with. She had to push Ryan as far away as possible.

'You just can't help yourself, can you?'

'I thought you might appreciate that one.'

'What makes you think I'm in the mood for jokes right now?' Hannah swivelled so that she could give Ryan a direct look. 'Doesn't anything dent your warped sense of humour? Even a battered wife who died trying to get her child to a safe place?'

'That's precisely why I thought a joke might be a good idea,' Ryan said wearily. 'Sorry, maybe I should have left you to wallow in how awful it was. Maybe question your abilities and wonder endlessly what you might have been able to do better.'

'It might be more appropriate than telling jokes.'

'Really? What if another major case comes in in the next five minutes, Hannah? You going to be in a fit state to give that person the best you can?'

'Of course I am.'

'Well, lucky you. Some of us need to distract ourselves. Lift our spirits a bit. There's always time for wallowing later.'

'I don't believe you ever wallow,' Hannah snapped. She wasn't going to admit that even that stifled snort of laughter *had* done something to ease the emotional downside of this job. She'd rather believe that it was being able to channel her frustration and anger into a confrontation that had been building for some time. 'And you distract yourself often enough to be a liability in this department. You've been here, what, three months? And how many times have you taken time off to flit back to Australia? Four, five times? I should know—it's usually me that does extra shifts to cover the gaps.'

This distraction was working wonderfully well. Hannah was really hitting her stride.

'You know your problem, Ryan? You're shallow. You're so intent on having a fun life you can't even spare the time to think about someone else.'

'Oh?' Ryan was staring at Hannah and she'd never heard him use such an icy tone. 'Shallow, am I?'

'You might find it more beneficial to your career to review cases like we've just had. You never know. Try having a professional discussion with a colleague next time instead of telling *stupid* jokes. You might learn something.'

'From you?' Ryan snorted. 'I doubt it.'

'Why?' Hannah's tone was waspish. 'Because I'm blonde?'

'No.' Ryan stood up, abandoning his cup of coffee. 'Because you're less experienced professionally and far less competent when it comes to relationships between people. You're judgmental, Dr Jackson, and you don't even bother finding out the facts before you make those judgments.'

He stalked behind Hannah and she had to swivel her head to keep glaring at him as he made his parting shot. 'And when I'm consultant, it might be nice if you made *me* coffee, babe. Not the other way round.'

'Dream on, mate!' What a pathetic rejoinder. Hannah could only hope Ryan would take it as she meant it—referring to the consultancy position and not the coffee-making.

Jennifer came in a few seconds after Ryan had left. Her eyebrows had disappeared under her fringe.

'What on earth's wrong with Ryan? I've never seen him look so grumpy!'

'He's a grumpy man.'

Jennifer laughed. 'He is not and you know it. He's a lovely man and if you weren't trying so hard not to like him you would have realised that by now.'

'I'm not trying hard,' Hannah protested. 'It's easy. Besides, it was your friend in Sydney that told you what a reputation he had for breaking hearts. The man needs an emotional health warning attached.'

Jennifer shook her head, smiling. 'Yeah...right.' She took another glance at Hannah. 'You look pretty grumpy yourself.'

'It's been a bad night. I hate cases like that—especially when they shouldn't have happened in the first place.' She sighed again. 'And I'm tired. Roll on 7 a.m.'

'Roll on Friday more like. Isn't that when you leave for a few days' R & R in the sun?'

'Sure is.' Hannah's spirits finally lifted—a lot more than Ryan's joke had achieved. 'You know, I'm finally really looking forward to this trip.'

'I could do with some time away from this place myself. Could be just what the doctor ordered. For both of us.'

'Mmm.' Hannah's agreement was wholehearted. But it wasn't the place she needed the break from. A few days away from Ryan Fisher was definitely what this doctor was ordering.

Hannah Jackson could go to hell in a hand basket.

The glimpse of a woman with sleek blonde hair disappearing into the melee of economy class was enough of a reminder to sink Ryan Fisher's spirits with a nasty jolt.

He slid his cabin baggage into the overhead locker with the same ease he slid his long body into the comfortable window seat at the rear of the business class section of the plane. Seconds later, he returned the smile of a very pretty young air hostess.

'Orange juice would be lovely,' he agreed. 'Exactly what I need.'

The frosted glass was presented while economy-class passengers were still filing past, but Ryan killed the faintly embarrassed reaction to the envious glances. Why shouldn't he travel in comfort? He had to do it often enough to make it a boring inconvenience and he'd decided he may as well make the travel as enjoyable as possible when the destination usually wasn't.

At least this time he could look forward to what lay at the other end of his journey.

'Is there anything else you need, sir?'

Ryan suppressed a wry smile along with the temptation to ask the crew member for a thousand things. How about a miraculous cure for a little girl in Brisbane that he had far more than just a bond of family with? Or perhaps freedom from the ridiculously powerful attraction he had felt for Hannah Jackson ever since he'd first laid eyes on her three months ago?

No. He was over that. As of last Monday night when she'd told him exactly what she thought of him. She hated him. He was shallow—telling jokes when he should be taking on board the misery of others. Lazy—taking time off to flit back to Australia to have fun at regular intervals. Out to win the job she felt was rightfully hers.

Ironic that he'd actually set out to catch Hannah's attention by demonstrating his clinical ability. He hadn't expected the head of department to twist his arm and put his name forward for the upcoming consultancy position but then he'd thought, Why not? The anchor of a permanent job could be just what he needed to sort out his life. And at least that way Hannah would see him as an equal.

Would really *see* him.

How idiotic would it be to waste any more time or emotional energy hankering after someone who didn't even have any respect, let alone liking, for him?

'No, thanks.' He smiled. 'I'm fine.'

Ryan sipped his chilled juice, stretching his legs into the generous space in front of him and enjoying the fact that the seat beside him was empty. So were both the seats on the opposite side of the aisle. There was, in fact, only one other occupant of business class and Ryan found himself listening to the well-dressed man with an American accent telling the air hostess that all he wanted was to go to sleep and could he have one of those eye covers? Apparently he hadn't expected a diversion to Auckland or a night in an airport hotel and he'd had more than enough of travelling for now.

'It should have been a straightforward trip to Sydney and then Cairns,' he was saying. 'Instead, I'm bunny-hopping through the south Pacific. Inefficient, that's what it is.'

'There's been a few disruptions due to some bad weather,' the hostess responded. 'Hopefully we'll be able to bypass it on this trip.'

Ryan didn't care if they hit a few bumps. Despite what Hannah thought of him, he didn't often get a smooth ride through life. OK, so maybe he didn't wear his heart on his sleeve and go around telling everyone his problems, but it was just as well, wasn't it? Imagine how low he'd be feeling right now if he'd made it obvious just how attracted he'd been to Hannah and had been squashed like the bug she clearly thought he was?

Well, she wouldn't get the opportunity now. No way. He wouldn't have her if she threw herself at him. Wrapped up in a ribbon and nothing else.

A soft sound like a strangled groan escaped. That short flight into fantasy wasn't likely to help anything. He drained his glass and handed it back as part of the preparation for take-off. Then he closed his eyes as the big jet rolled towards the end of the runway. Maybe he should follow the example of the other occupant of business class and escape into a few hours of peaceful oblivion.

The trip promised to be anything but restful. Hannah had an aisle seat, for which she was becoming increasingly grateful. It meant she could lean outwards.

She had to lean outwards because the man beside her was one of the fattest people Hannah had ever seen. He could easily have used up two seats all by himself but somehow he had squeezed in. Apart from the parts of his body that oozed through the gaps above and below the armrests and encroached considerably on Hannah's space. Any sympathy for his obvious discomfort had been replaced by a more selfish concern about her own when the personality of her travelling companion began to reveal itself.

'Name's Blair,' he boomed at her. 'How's it going?' He certainly wasn't shy. 'They make these seats a bit bloody small these days, eh? Just want to pack us in like sardines so they make a profit.'

'Mmm.' And they were allocated the same amount of baggage weight, Hannah thought crossly. What would happen if every passenger was Blair's size? Could the plane flip over because the baggage compartment was too light? Use twice as much fuel? Drop out of the sky?

Hannah wasn't a great fan of flying. She leaned further into the aisle and gripped the armrest on that side as the plane gathered speed.

'Not keen on flying, huh?' Blair was leaning, too. 'Wanna hold my hand?'

'Ah…no, thanks.' Hannah screwed her eyes shut. 'I'm just fine.'

'It's OK. ' Blair was laughing as the wheels left the tarmac. 'I'm single.'

There was no point pretending to be asleep because Blair didn't seem to notice. He obviously liked to think aloud and kept himself amused by a running commentary on the choice of movies available, the tourist attractions of Cairns showcased in the airline magazine and the length of time it was taking for the cabin crew to start serving refreshments.

The reason for any delay was revealed when the captain's voice sounded in the cabin.

'G'day, folks. Welcome aboard this Air New Zealand flight to Cairns. We're expecting a bit of turbulence due to strong westerly winds courtesy of a tropical cyclone in the Coral Sea region going by the name of Willie. I'm going to keep the crew seated until we get through this next layer of cloud.'

Blair made a grumbling sound.

'Once we're cruising at around thirty-five thousand feet, things should get a bit smoother,' the captain continued. 'You'll be free to move around the cabin at that point but I would suggest that while you're in your seats you do keep your seat belts firmly fastened.'

Sure enough, the flight became smoother and the cabin crew began to serve drinks and meals. The steward that stopped beside Hannah cast a second glance at her companion, listened to him patiently while he complained about the delay in being fed and then winked at Hannah.

'I'll be back in a tick,' he said.

When he returned, he bent down and whispered in Hannah's ear. Then he opened the overhead locker and removed the bag she specified. Hannah unclipped her seat belt and stood up with a sigh of relief.

'Hey!' Blair was watching the removal of the bag with concern. 'Where're you going, darling?'

'We've got a bit of room up front,' the steward informed him. 'I'm just juggling passengers a bit. If you lift the armrest there, Sir, I'm sure you'll find the journey a lot more comfortable.'

Much to Hannah's astonishment, 'up front' turned out to be an upgrade to business class. Her eyes widened as she realised she was going to have a window seat—no, both the seats—all to herself.

'You're an angel of mercy,' she told the steward. 'Wow! I've never flown business class before.'

'Enjoy!' The steward grinned. 'I'll make sure they bring

you something to drink while you settle in and have a look at the breakfast menu.'

Hannah sank into the soft seat, unable to contain her smile. She stretched out her legs and wiggled her toes. Not much chance of developing a DVT here. There was any amount of elbow room, as well. She tested it, sticking her arms out like wings. She even flapped them up and down a little. Just as well there was no one to see her doing a duck impression.

Or was there? Hannah hadn't yet considered the possibility of a passenger on the other side of the aisle. She turned her head swiftly, aware of a blush starting. And then she recognised the solitary figure by the window and she actually gasped aloud.

Glaring was probably the only description she could have used for the way Ryan Fisher was looking at her.

'Oh, my God!' Hannah said. 'What are *you* doing here?'

# CHAPTER THREE

'I WAS about to ask you the same thing.'

'I got upgraded.' Hannah hadn't intended to sound defensive. Why did this man always bring out the worst in her? 'Things were a bit crowded down the back.'

'Here you go, Dr Jackson.' A pretty, redheaded hostess held out a tray with a fluted glass on it. 'And here's the menu. I'll come back in a minute to see what you'd like for breakfast.'

'Thank you.' Hannah took a sip of her juice and pretended to study the menu, which gave a surprisingly wide choice for the first meal of the day. There were hours of this flight left. Was she going to have to make conversation with Ryan the whole way?

It was some sort of divine retribution. Hannah had been feeling guilty ever since Monday night when she'd let fly and been so rude to a colleague. She couldn't blame him for either the retaliation or the way he'd been avoiding her for the last few days. The personal attack had been unprofessional and probably undeserved. He couldn't know where the motivation had come from and Hannah certainly couldn't tell him but…maybe she ought to apologise?

She flicked a quick glance from the menu towards Ryan.

He was still glaring. He wasn't about to use their first meeting away from work to try building any bridges, was he?

Hannah wished she hadn't looked. Hadn't caught those dark eyes. She couldn't open her mouth to say anything because goodness only knew what might shoot out, given the peculiar situation of being in this man's company away from a professional setting. Imagine if she started and then couldn't stop?

If she told him her whole life history? About the man her mother had really fallen in love with—finally happy after years of getting over her husband's tragic death. Of the way she'd been used and then abandoned. Hannah had known not to trust the next one that had come along. Why hadn't her mother been able to see through him that easily? Perhaps the attraction to men like that was genetic and too powerful to resist. It might explain why Susie had made the same mistake. Fortunately, Hannah was stronger. She might *want* Ryan Fisher but there was no way she would allow herself to *have* him.

Oddly, the satisfying effect of pushing him firmly out of her emotional orbit the other night was wearing off. Here she was contemplating an apology. An attempt at establishing some kind of friendship even.

Ryan hadn't blinked.

Hannah realised this in the same instant she realised she could only have noticed because she hadn't looked away. The eye contact had continued for too long and…Oh, *God!* What if Ryan had seen even a fraction of what she'd been thinking?

Attack was the best form of defence, wasn't it?

'Why are you staring at me?'

'I'm still waiting for you to answer my question.'

'What question?'

'What you're doing here.'

'I told you, I got upgraded.'

'You know perfectly well that wasn't what I meant. What the hell are you doing on this flight?'

'Going to Cairns.' Hannah didn't need the change in Ryan's expression to remind her how immature it was to be so deliberately obtuse. She gave in. 'I've got a connecting flight at Cairns to go to a small town further north in Queensland. Crocodile Creek.'

Lips that were usually in some kind of motion, either talking or smiling, went curiously slack. The tone of Ryan's voice was also stunned.

'You're going to *Crocodile Creek?*'

'Yes.'

'So am I.'

'Did you decide what you'd like for breakfast, Dr Jackson?'

'What?' Hannah hadn't even noticed the approach of the redheaded stewardess. 'Oh, sorry. Um… Anything's fine. I'm starving!'

The stewardess smiled. 'I'll see what I can surprise you with.' She turned to the other side of the aisle. 'And you, Dr Fisher? Have you decided?'

'I'll have the fresh fruit salad and a mushroom omelette, thanks.'

Ryan didn't want to be surprised by his breakfast. Maybe he'd just had enough of a surprise. As had Hannah. She waited only a heartbeat after the stewardess had moved away.

'Is there a particular reason why you're going to Crocodile Creek at this particular time?"

'Sure is. I'm best man at my best mate's wedding.'

'Oh…' Hannah swallowed carefully. 'That would be…Mike?'

Ryan actually closed his eyes. 'And you know that because you're also invited to the wedding?'

'Yes.'

Ryan made a sound like a chuckle but it was so unlike the laughter Hannah would have recognised she wasn't sure it had anything to do with amusement. 'Don't tell me you're lined up to be the bridesmaid.'

'No, of course I'm not. I don't know Emily that well.'

'Thank God for that.'

'My sister's the bridesmaid.'

Ryan's eyes opened smartly. Hannah could have sworn she saw something like a flash of fear. Far more likely to be horror, she decided. He disliked her so much that the prospect of being a partner to her sister was appalling? That hurt. Hannah couldn't resist retaliating.

'My twin sister,' she said. She smiled at Ryan. 'We're identical.'

Ryan shook his head. 'I don't believe this.'

'It is a bit of a coincidence,' Hannah agreed, more cheerfully. Ryan was so disconcerted that she actually felt like she had control of this situation—an emotional upper hand—and that had to be a first for any time she had spent in Ryan's company, with the exception of Monday night. Maybe this wouldn't be so bad after all. 'So, how come you know Mike so well?'

But Ryan didn't appear to be listening. 'There are two of you,' he muttered. 'Unbelievable!'

Their conversation was interrupted by the arrival of their food. Hannah was hungry enough to get stuck into the delicious hot croissants and jam she was served. Ryan was only halfway through his fruit salad by the time she had cleaned her plate and he didn't look as though he was particularly enjoying the start of his meal.

Hannah had to feel sorry for him but she couldn't resist teasing just a little. She adopted the same, slightly aggrieved tone he had been using only a short time ago.

'You didn't answer my question.'

'What question?' Ryan wasn't being deliberately obtuse. He looked genuinely bewildered.

'How do you know Mike? The groom at this wedding we're both going to.'

'Oh… I was involved in training paramedics in the armed forces for a while, years ago. Mike was keen to add medical training to his qualifications as a helicopter pilot, having been in a few dodgy situations. We hit it off and have stayed in touch ever since.' Ryan stirred the contents of his bowl with the spoon. 'I was really looking forward to seeing him again,' he added sadly. 'The last real time we had together was a surfing holiday in Bali nearly three years ago. After he got out of the army but before he took himself off to the back of beyond.'

'Crocodile Creek does seem a bit out of the way,' Hannah had to agree. Besides, thinking about geography was a good way to distract herself from feeling offended that Ryan seemed to think all the pleasure might have been sucked from the upcoming weekend. 'It was easy enough to hop on a plane to Brisbane to spend a day or two with Susie.'

'I got the impression you never took time off.'

'I don't take rostered time off.'

'Unlike me.' Ryan said it for her. ''Cos you're not lazy.'

Hannah wasn't going to let this conversation degenerate into a personality clash. Here was the opportunity she had needed. 'I never said you were lazy, Ryan. You work as hard as I do. You're just more inclined to take time off.'

'For the purposes of having fun.'

'Well…yes…' Hannah shrugged. 'And why not?'

Would this count as an apology, perhaps? 'All work and no play, etcetera.'

'Makes Jack a dull boy,' Ryan finished. 'And Jill a very dull girl.'

Was he telling Hannah she was dull? Just a more pointed comment than Jennifer telling her she was an ED geek? If he saw her as being more *fun*—say at a wedding reception—would he find her more attractive?

Hannah stomped on the wayward thought. She didn't want Ryan to find her attractive. She didn't want to find *him* attractive, for heaven's sake! It was something that had just happened. Like a lightning bolt. A bit of freak weather—like the cyclone currently brewing in the Coral Sea, which was again causing a bit of turbulence for the jet heading for Cairns.

The two cabin-crew members pushing a meal trolley through to economy class exchanged a doubtful glance.

'Should we wait a bit before serving the back section?'

'No.' The steward who had been responsible for Hannah's upgrade shook his head. 'Let's get it done, then we can clear up. If we're going to hit any really rough stuff, it'll be when we're north of Brisbane.'

Hannah tightened her seat belt a little.

'Nervous?' Ryan must have been watching her quite closely to observe the action.

'I'm not that keen on turbulence.'

'Doesn't bother me.' Ryan smiled at Hannah. Or had that smile been intended for the approaching stewardess? 'I quite like a bumpy ride.'

Hannah and Ryan both chose coffee rather than tea. Of course the smile had been for the pretty redhead. Likewise the comment that could easily have been taken as blatant flirting.

'I don't know Emily,' Ryan said. 'Maybe you can fill me in. She's a doctor, yes?'

'Yes. She's Susie's best friend.'

'Susie?'

'My sister.'

'The clone. Right. So how long has she been in Crocodile Creek?'

'About three years. She went to Brisbane to get some post-grad training after she finished her physiotherapy degree and she liked it so much she decided to stay.'

'I thought she was a doctor.'

'No. She started medical school with me but it wasn't what she wanted.'

'How come she lives in that doctors' house that used to be the old hospital, then?'

'She doesn't.'

'That's not what Mike told me.'

'Why would Mike be telling you about my sister?'

'He wasn't. He was telling me about his fiancée. Emily.' Ryan groaned. 'We're not on the same page here, are we?'

'No.' And they never would be. 'Sorry. I don't know much about Emily either, except that she's a really nice person and totally in love with Mike and his parents are thrilled and hoping for lots of grandchildren.'

Ryan was still frowning. 'If you don't know Emily and you don't know Mike, why have you been invited to their wedding?'

'As Susie's partner, kind of. We haven't seen each other since Christmas.'

'That's not so long ago.'

Hannah shrugged. 'It seems a long time. We're close, I guess.'

'Hmm.'

Ryan's thoughts may as well have been in a bubble over his head. As best man, he would have to partner Hannah's clone. Another woman who wouldn't be on the same page. Someone else who would think he was shallow and lazy and a liability.

Hannah opened her mouth to offer some reassurance. To finally apologise for losing it on Monday night in such an unprofessional manner. To suggest that they would both be able to have a good time at the wedding despite having each other's company enforced.

She didn't get the chance.

Her mouth opened far more widely than needed for speech as the plane hit an air pocket and seemed to drop like a rock. The fall continued long enough for someone further down the plane in economy to scream, and then they got to the bottom with a crunch and all hell broke loose.

The big jet slewed sideways into severe turbulence. The pitch of its engine roar increased. The water glass and cutlery on Hannah's tray slithered sideways to clatter to the floor. The seat-belt sign on the overhead panel flashed on and off repeatedly with a loud dinging noise. Oxygen masks were deployed and swung like bizarre, short pendulums. Children were shrieking and someone was calling for help. The stewardess who had been pushing the meal trolley staggered through the curtain dividing business class from the rest of the cabin, her face covered in blood. She fell into the seat beside Hannah.

'I can't see anything!'

Hannah was still clutching her linen napkin in her hand. She pushed the tray table up and latched it, giving her space to turn to the woman beside her, who was trying to wipe the blood from her eyes.

'Hold still!' Hannah instructed. She folded the napkin

into a rough pad. If her years of training and practice in emergency departments had done nothing else, Hannah would always bless the ability to focus on an emergency without going to pieces herself. 'You've got a nasty cut on your forehead.' She pressed the pad against the wound as best she could, with the plane continuing to pitch and roll.

'I came down on the corner of the trolley.'

'What's happening?' Ryan was out of his seat, hanging onto an armrest for support.

By way of answer, calmly overriding the noise of the engines and distressed passengers, came the voice from the flight deck.

'Sorry about this, folks. Bit of unexpected rough stuff. We should be through this pretty fast. Please, return to your seats and keep your belts firmly fastened for the moment.'

Ryan ignored the direction. 'Anyone else hurt back there?'

'I don't know.' The stewardess was leaning back in the seat, her face pale beneath smeared blood. 'We were still serving breakfast. It'll be a mess. I should go and help.'

Ryan held back the curtain to look into the main body of the cabin. Clearly, he was trying to see where he might be needed most urgently. Forgetting one's own fear and helping someone who'd happened to land in the seat beside her was nothing compared to the courage it would need to take command of the kind of chaos Hannah could imagine Ryan assessing.

Mixed in with her admiration of his intention was a desire to prove she could also rise to the occasion. Ryan's courage was contagious.

'Hold this.' Hannah took the hand of the stewardess and placed it over the pad. 'Keep firm pressure on it and the bleeding will stop soon. I'll come back and check on you in a bit.' She unclipped her seat belt and stood up. The oxygen mask bumped her head but Hannah ignored it. The jolt from the air pocket must have caused their deployment because she wasn't at all short of breath so the oxygen level had to be OK. Lurching sideways to get past the knees of the stewardess, Hannah found her arm firmly gripped by Ryan.

'What *do* you think you're doing, Hannah? Sit down and belt up.'

'Help!' A male voice was yelling loudly. 'We need a doctor!'

'Stay here,' Ryan ordered crisply. 'I'll go.'

But Hannah knew that her own courage was coming from the confidence Ryan was displaying. If he left, she might be tempted to strap herself safely back into her seat and wait for the turbulence to end.

People needed help.

'No,' she said. 'I'm coming with you.'

Something unusual showed in Ryan's eyes. Did he know how terrified she was? What an effort trying to match his bravery was?

Maybe he did. The glance felt curiously like applause. He let go of her arm and took her hand instead, to lead her through the curtain. Hannah found herself gripping his fingers. He'd only done it to save her falling if there was more turbulence, but she was going to allow herself to take whatever she needed from this physical connection. What did it matter, when it felt like they might all be going to plunge to their deaths at any moment?

She followed Ryan through the curtain to become the new focus for dozens of terrified passengers as they moved down the aisle. Some were wearing their oxygen masks, others trying to get them on. She saw a young woman with her face in her hands, sobbing. A much older woman, nursing what looked like a fractured wrist. A nun, clutching her crucifix, her lips moving in silent prayer. The steward was waving at them from the rear of the aircraft.

'Here! Help!' he shouted. 'I think this man's choking.'

'It's Blair!' Hannah exclaimed.

Her former seat neighbour was standing, blocking the aisle. His hand was around his neck in the universal signal of distress from choking and his face was a dreadful, mottled purple.

Ryan was moving fast. He let go of Hannah's hand to climb over the empty seat that had initially been hers to get behind Blair.

'I've tried banging him on the back,' the steward said unhappily.

Ryan put his arms around Blair but couldn't grasp his fist with his other hand to perform an effective Heimlich manoeuvre. There was just too much of Blair to encompass and there was no time. The huge man was rapidly losing consciousness and there was no way Ryan could support his weight unaided.

Blair slumped onto his back, blocking the aisle even more effectively. There was no way for anyone to move. Ryan looked up and Hannah could see he was aware of how impossible it was going to be to try and manage this emergency. She could also see that he had no intention of admitting defeat. It was a very momentary impression, however, because the plane hit another bump and Hannah went hurtling forward to land in a most undignified fashion directly on top of Blair.

She landed hard and then used her hands on his chest to push herself upright. Blair gave a convulsive movement beneath her and Hannah slid her legs in front of her old empty seat to try and slide clear. Ryan grabbed Blair's shoulder and heaved and suddenly Blair was on his side, coughing and spluttering. Ryan thumped him hard between his shoulder blades for good measure and the crisis was over, probably as quickly as it had begun, as Blair forcibly spat out what looked like a large section of a sausage.

'Let's sit you up,' Ryan said firmly.

Blair was still gasping for air and had tears streaming down his face but somehow, with the help of the steward and another passenger, they got him back into his seat. Hannah jerked the oxygen mask down to start the flow. At least one person was going to benefit from their unnecessary deployment.

'We're through the worst of it now, folks. Should be plain sailing from now on.'

The timing of the captain's message was enough to make Hannah smile wryly. Catching Ryan's gaze, her smile widened.

'He doesn't know how right he is, does he?'

Ryan grinned right back at her, with the kind of killer smile he gave to so many women. The kind that old Doris Matheson had received the other night. But it was the first time Hannah had felt the full force of it and for just a fraction of a second it felt like they had connected.

Really connected. More than that imaginary connection Hannah had taken from the hand-holding.

And it felt astonishingly good.

Good enough to carry Hannah through the next hour of helping to treat the minor injuries sustained. Splinting the Colles' fracture on the old woman's wrist, bandaging lacerations and examining bruises.

The other occupant of business class had been woken by the turbulence and offered his services.

'I'm a neurosurgeon,' he said. 'Name's Alistair Carmichael. What can I do to help?'

'We've got a stewardess with a forehead laceration,' Hannah told him. 'You're the perfect person to check and make sure she's not showing any signs of concussion—or worse. Mostly, I think it's going to be a matter of reassuring people.'

Hannah made more than one stop to check that Blair wasn't suffering any lingering respiratory distress.

Ryan worked just as hard. The first-aid supplies on the plane were rapidly depleted but it didn't matter. The plane was making a smooth descent into Cairns and Blair, who had been the closest to a fatal injury, was beaming.

'You saved my life, darling,' he told Hannah when he was helped from the plane at Cairns by paramedics who would take him to hospital for a thorough check-up.

'Yes.' Ryan's voice seemed to be coming from somewhere very close to Hannah's ear and she gave an involuntary shiver. 'Interesting technique, that. You should write it up for a medical journal.'

Hannah turned her head. Was he making fun of her?

'The "Jackson manoeuvre",' Ryan said with a grin.

Hannah was too tired to care whether he was laughing at her. And the incident *had* had a very funny side. 'Yeah,' she said. 'Or maybe the "Blonde's Heimlich"?'

Much to Ryan's disappointment, they weren't sitting anywhere near each other on the connecting flight to Crocodile Creek, despite the much smaller size of the aircraft. It seemed to have been taken over by a large contingent of rather excited Greek people who had to be part of Mike's family. They were too busy talking and arguing with each other to take notice of strangers, and that suited Ryan just fine. He was tired and felt like he had too much to think about anyway.

Fancy Hannah being able to laugh at herself like that! Or had it been some kind of dig at him? Ryan knew perfectly well how his blonde jokes got up her nose. They had become a kind of defence mechanism so that no one would guess how disappointed he was when Hannah took no notice of him. He might get a negative reaction to the jokes but at least she knew he existed.

And what about the way she hadn't hesitated to go and help others when she had clearly been terrified herself by the turbulence. That had taken a lot of courage. She obviously didn't like flying. Ryan had seen the way she'd looked at the size of their connecting aircraft. He hoped she was as reassured as he had been by the information that the tropical storm was now moving out to sea and their next journey would be much smoother. They were even forecasting relatively fine weather for the rest of the day.

'But make the most of it,' the captain warned. 'It could turn nasty again tomorrow.'

That caused the volume of conversation around him to increase dramatically as the Greek wedding guests discussed the ramifications of bad weather. Ryan tuned out of what sounded like superstitious babble of how to overcome such a bad omen.

Hannah was sitting as far away as it was possible to be down the back of the cabin. Had she arranged that somehow? She was beside the American neurosurgeon, Alistair, who had proved himself to be a very pleasant and competent man during the aftermath of the turbulence. Distinctive looking, too, with those silver streaks in his dark hair. He had put the jacket of his pinstriped suit back on but he was asleep again.

There was an odd relief in noticing that. Surely any other man would find Hannah as attractive as he did? And he hadn't known the half of it, had he? No wonder he hadn't recognised her from behind on the larger plane. He'd only seen her with her sleek blonde hair wound up in a kind of knot thing and baggy scrubs covering her body. The tight-fitting jeans and soft white shirt she was wearing today revealed a shape as perfect as her face.

Impossible to resist the urge to crane his neck once more and check that the American was still asleep. He was. So was Hannah, which was just as well. Ryan wouldn't want her to know he'd stolen another glance. He settled back and dozed himself and it seemed no time until the wheels touched down on a much smaller runway than the last one.

He was here. At the back of beyond, in Crocodile Creek. For three whole days. With Hannah Jackson. What had happened to that fierce resolve with which he had started this journey? That Hannah could go to hell because he was no longer interested? That he was completely over that insane attraction?

It had been shaken by that turbulence, that's what. It had gone out the window when he'd taken hold of her hand and she hadn't pulled away. Had—amazingly—held his hand right back.

Ryan sighed deeply and muttered inaudibly.

'Let the fun begin.'

# CHAPTER FOUR

HEAT hit her like a blast from a furnace door swinging open.

Thanks to the early departure from Auckland and the time difference between Australia and New Zealand, it was the hottest part of the day when they arrived in Crocodile Creek.

The bad weather that had made the first leg of the journey so memorable seemed to have been left well behind. The sky was an intense, cobalt blue and there were no clouds to filter the strength of the sun beating down. It was hot.

Very hot.

Descending the steps from the back of the small plane onto the shimmering tarmac, Hannah realised what a mistake it had been to travel in jeans.

'I'm cooking!' She told Susie by way of a greeting as she entered the small terminal building. 'How hot *is* it?'

'Must be nearly forty degrees.' Susie was hugging Hannah hard. 'What on earth possessed you to wear jeans?' She was far more sensibly dressed, in shorts, a singlet top and flip-flop sandals.

'It was cold when I got up at stupid o'clock. Our flight left at 6 a.m.' Hannah pulled back from the hug. 'You've let your hair grow. It looks fabulous.'

Susie dragged her fingers through her almost shoulder-length golden curls. 'It'd be as long as yours now, if I bothered straightening it.'

'Don't!' Hannah said in mock alarm. 'If you did that, nobody would be able to tell us apart and it would be school all over again.'

'Yeah…' Susie was grinning. 'With you getting into trouble for the things I did.'

The noise in the small building increased markedly as the main group of passengers entered, to be greeted ecstatically by the people waiting to meet them. The loud voices, tears and laughter and exuberant hugging made Susie widen her eyes.

'That's *another* Poulos contingent arriving. Look at that! This wedding is a circus.'

Why did Hannah's gaze seek Ryan out in the crowd so instantly? As though the smallest excuse made it permissible? She turned back to Susie.

'What's your bridesmaid's dress like?'

'Pink.'

'Oh, my God, you're *kidding!*'

'Yeah. It's peach but it's still over the top. Sort of a semi-meringue. Kind of like you'd expect some finalist in a ballroom dancing competition to be wearing. I could keep it to get married in myself eventually—except for the lack of originality. Five other girls will have the same outfit at home.'

'*Six* bridesmaids?'

'Yes, but I'm the most important one. Poor Emily doesn't have any family and she only wanted two bridesmaids—me and Mike's sister, Maria, but there were all these cousins who would have been mortally offended if they hadn't been included and, besides, Mike's mum, Sophia, is determined to have the wedding of the century. I think she only stopped at six because it was getting hard to find the male counterparts. Funnily enough, they weren't so keen.'

'How's Emily holding up?'

'She's loving every minute of it but going absolutely mad. And she'll need a lot of make-up tomorrow to cover red cheeks from all the affectionate pinching she's getting.' Susie's head was still turning as she scanned the rest of the arrivals. 'Let's go and find your bag before we get swamped. If Sophia starts introducing me as the chief bridesmaid, I'll probably get *my* cheeks pinched as well. Oh, my God!' Susie did a double take as she lowered her voice. 'Who is *that?*'

There were two men standing a little to one side of the crowd, their attention on the signs directing them to the baggage collection area. One of them was Ryan. His head started to turn as though he sensed Hannah's gaze so she transferred it quickly to the other man. It was easy to recognise the person who had been dozing in the seat beside her on the last leg of her long journey. In that suit, he had to be even hotter than Hannah was in her jeans.

'He's an American,' she told Susie. 'A neurosurgeon. Alistair...someone. He's here for the wedding but he didn't say much about it. I got the impression he wasn't that thrilled to be coming.'

'That's Gina's cousin, then. Gorgeous, isn't he?'

'I guess.' Hannah hadn't taken much notice. Who would, when someone that looked like Ryan Fisher was nearby? 'Gina?'

'Also American. A cardiologist. She's getting married to Cal next weekend. I told you all about her at Christmas. She arrived with her little boy, who turned out to be Cal's son. Cal's one of our surgeons.'

'Right. Whew! *Two* weddings in two weeks?'

'Wedding city,' Susie agreed. She was leading the way past where the men were standing. Hannah could feel the odd prickle on the back of her neck that came when you knew someone was watching you. She didn't turn around because it was unlikely that she'd feel the stare of someone she didn't know with such spine-tingling clarity.

'Some people are going to both weddings,' Susie continued, ' and they've had to travel to get here so everybody thought they might like to just stay and have a bit of a holiday in between.'

'He won't have much of a holiday if he stays in that suit. And I thought I was overdressed!'

'Oh! The guy in the suit is the American?' Susie threw a glance over her shoulder. 'So who's the really gorgeous one who's staring at you?'

Hannah sighed. 'That'll be Ryan.'

'Ryan Fisher? The best man?'

'Yes.'

'Wow!' Susie's grin widened. 'My day's looking up! Mike told me what a fabulous guy he is but he forgot to mention he was also fabulous looking.'

'Don't get too excited,' Hannah warned.

'Why? Is he married?'

'No, but he might not be too friendly.'

Susie's eyebrows vanished under the curls on her forehead. 'Why not?'

Hannah sighed inwardly, feeling far too hot and weary to start explaining why her sister could well have to deal with unreasonable antipathy from someone because he disliked her mirror image.

'I'll fill you in later.' It was much easier to change the subject. Very easy, in fact. 'Good grief!'

'What?' Susie's head turned to follow the direction of

Hannah's astonished stare at the small, dark woman wearing black leather pants, a top that showed an amazing cleavage and…red stiletto shoes. 'That's Georgie.' She smiled. 'You'll meet her later.'

As though that explained everything! 'She must be as hot as hell in those clothes.'

'She's got super air-con for travel. She rides a Harley.'

'In *stilettos?*' Hannah's peripheral vision caught the way Ryan was also staring at the woman. There was no mistaking the appreciative grin on his face. 'Good *grief,*' she muttered again.

'I guess Georgie's here to meet Alistair. Georgie's Gina's bridesmaid and Alistair's here to give Gina away. He was supposed to arrive yesterday but his flight from the US was delayed by bad weather, and Gina and Cal are on one of the outer islands today, doing a clinic. So wow! Georgie and Alistair…' Susie shook her head. 'Leathers and pinstripes. They look a perfect couple. Not! Is that your bag?'

'Yes. Coming off first for a change.'

'Let's go, then.'

While it was a relief to escape the terminal building—and Ryan—it was a shock to step back out into the heat. And the wind. Huge fronds on the palm trees were bowing under its strength and Hannah had to catch her hair as it whipped into her face.

'Hurry up, Hannah! My car's over here and we're going to run out of time if we don't get going.'

'But the wedding's not till 4 p.m. tomorrow.' It was too hot to move any faster. 'What's the rush?' Hannah climbed reluctantly into the interior of a small hatchback car that felt more like an oven and immediately rolled down her window.

Susie started the engine and fiddled with the air-conditioning controls. 'It's all a bit frantic. I'm sorry. There's a rehearsal later this afternoon and I've got a couple more patients I just have to see before then.' She turned onto the main road and the car picked up speed rapidly. 'If you roll up your window, the air-con will work a lot better.'

Hannah complied and a welcome trickle of cool air came from the vents.

'Are you seeing your patients at your rooms?'

'No, I've finished the private stuff for today. These are hospital cases. Old Mrs Trengrove has had a hip replacement and absolutely refuses to get out of bed unless I'm there to hold her hand, and Wally's been admitted—he's one of my arthritis patients and it's his birthday today so I'll have to go and say hello.'

'Do you want to just drop me off at your place? I'm sure I could find my way to the beach and have a swim or something.'

'No, you can't swim at the beach. The water's all horrible because of the awful weather we've had in the last few days and it's stinger season. With the big waves we've been getting, the nets might not be working too well. Besides, I want to show you around the hospital. If you take your bathing suit, you could have a dip in the hospital pool.'

'Sounds good.' Hannah tried to summon enthusiasm for the busman's holiday delight of visiting the hospital.

'It's fabulous. You'd love it, Hannah. Hey…' Susie turned to look at her sister. 'They're always short of doctors. You could come and live with me for a while.'

'I couldn't stand working in heat like this.'

'It's not always like this.'

'It *is* beautiful.' Hannah was looking past sugar-cane plantations and the river towards rainforest-covered mountains in the distance.

'Wait till you see the cove. You'll fall in love with it just like I did.'

'The roads are quieter than I expected.'

'Bit quieter than usual today. I expect it's got something to do with the big fishing competition that's on.'

They crossed the river that gave Crocodile Creek township its name, drove through the main part of town and then rattled over an old wooden bridge to cross the river again. Rounding the bend on a gentle downhill slope, Hannah got the postcard view. The picture-perfect little cove with the white sandy beach and the intriguing, smudged outlines of islands further out to sea.

'The sea's the wrong colour at the moment,' Susie said apologetically. 'It's usually as blue as the sky. That's the Athina.' She pointed at the sprawling white building with Greek-style lettering on its sign that advertised its function as a boutique hotel. 'That's where the reception is being held tomorrow. And that rambling, huge house on the other side of the cove is the doctors' house.'

'Ah! The original hospital which is now the hotbed of romance.'

'Don't knock it!' Susie grinned at her sister. 'You could live there if you didn't want to squeeze into my wee cottage. Who knows? You might just find the man of your dreams in residence.'

'Doubt it.'

'Yeah.' Susie chuckled. 'The man of *your* dreams is probably buried in a laboratory somewhere. Or a library. Or an accountant's office.'

'Dad was an accountant,' Hannah reminded her. 'It didn't stop him being a lot of fun.'

'True.' Susie was silent for a moment. 'And Trevor was a brain surgeon and had to be the most boring man I'd ever met.'

'Hey, you're talking about the man I was engaged to for three years.'

'And why did you break it off?'

Hannah laughed. 'Because I was bored to tears. OK, I agree. There should be a happy medium but I haven't found it yet.'

'Me neither,' Susie said sadly. 'There always turns out to be something wrong with them. Or, worse, they find something wrong with me.' She screwed up her nose as she turned towards her sister. 'What *is* wrong with me, Hannah?'

'Absolutely nothing,' Hannah said stoutly. 'The guys are just idiots and don't deserve you. You're gorgeous.'

'That makes you gorgeous as well, you realise.'

'Of course.' Hannah grinned.

This was what she missed most about not having Susie living nearby any more. The comfort of absolute trust. Knowing you could say anything—even blow your own trumpet—without having it taken the wrong way. Not that they didn't have the occasional row but nothing could damage the underlying bond. And nothing else ever came close to the kind of strength a bond like this could impart.

'We're both gorgeous,' she said. 'Smart, too.'

'I'm not as smart as you. You're a brilliant doctor, soon-to-be emergency medicine specialist. I'm only a physiotherapist.'

'You could have easily been a doctor if you'd wanted, as you well know, Susan Jackson. You're doing what you want to do and you're doing it brilliantly. Anyway, being seen as clever isn't an advantage when it comes to men. It intimidates them.'

Although Hannah had a feeling that Ryan Fisher would be stimulated rather than intimidated by an intelligent woman if he ever bothered trying to find out.

'Look!' Susie was distracted from the conversation now. 'That's the Black Cockatoo, our local. And that's Kylie's Klipz. Kylie's amazing—looks like Dolly Parton. She's our hairdresser and she'll be doing all the hair and make-up for tomorrow. That's the Grubbs' place with that rusty old truck parked on the lawn and…here's my place.'

Susie parked outside a tiny cottage with two front windows in the shade of a veranda that was almost invisible beneath bougainvillea.

'Cute!'

'Speaking of cute.' Susie was unlocking her front door as Hannah carried her bag from the car. 'What's wrong with Ryan Fisher? Was he rude to you on the plane or something?'

'Not exactly. I just happen to know he's a player.'

'How do you know that? Do you know someone that works with him in Sydney?'

'He doesn't work in Sydney any more. He works in Auckland.'

'As in the same place you work?' Susie had opened the door but hadn't made any move to go inside.

'Exactly.'

'He's in your ED?'

'He's the guy who's after my job. I told you about him.'

Susie's jaw dropped. '*Ryan's* the holiday king? The Aussie playboy who's been driving you nuts with all those blonde jokes?'

'That's him.'

'The one who's out to date every nurse in the department in record time?'

'Yep.'

'So why have you been calling him Richard the third in your emails?'

'Because he reminds me of that bastard that Mum fell in love with when she'd finally got over Dad's death. *And* the creep who dumped you just before you went to Brisbane. He's a certain type. Skitters through life having a good time and not worrying about hurting anyone along the way. A flirt.'

'I'll bet he doesn't have any trouble getting a response.'

'He drives a flashy car. A BMW Roadster or something.'

'Nice. Soft top?'

Hannah ignored the teasing. 'He knows I can see right through the image. He hates *me,* too.'

Susie finally moved, leading the way into one of the bedrooms at the front of the cottage. 'I didn't get that impression from the way he was staring at you at the airport.'

'He was probably staring at you. At *us*. Wondering how he could be unlucky enough to be partnered with my clone.'

'That bad, huh?'

'Yep.' Hannah threw her suitcase onto the bed and snapped it open. 'No time for a shower, I don't suppose?'

'Not really. Sorry. Put your togs on under your clothes and take a towel. You can swim while I do my patient visits.' Susie made for the door. 'I'd better throw a shirt over this top so I look more respectable to go to work. It's lucky we don't stand on ceremony much around this place.'

It was blissful, pulling off the denim and leaving Hannah's legs bare beneath the pretty, ruffled skirt that she chose. The lacy camisole top was perfectly decent seeing as she was wearing her bikini top instead of a bra. Hannah emerged from the room a minute later to find Susie looking thoughtful.

'I just can't believe that the guy Emily was telling me about is the same guy you've been describing. As far as Mike's concerned, he's a hero. Practically a saint.'

Hannah dampened the image she had of Ryan when he was about to ignore the captain's direction to stay safely seated during severe turbulence to go and help where he was needed. He certainly had the courage that provided hero material. But a saint? No saint could get away with emitting that kind of sexual energy.

'Mike's not a woman,' she said firmly. 'I doubt there's a saintly bone in that body.'

'You could be right.' Susie's forget-me-not blue eyes, the exact match of Hannah's, were still dreamy. 'He's got that "bad boy" sort of edge, hasn't he?'

'I wouldn't say it like it's a compliment.'

Susie closed the front door behind them. 'Shall we walk? It's only a few minutes if you don't mind being blown about.'

'Yes, let's blow the cobwebs away. I could do with stretching my legs after all the sitting in planes.'

With a bit of luck, the wind might blow the current topic of conversation away as well.

No such luck.

'You have to admit, it's attractive.'

'What is?'

'That "bad boy" stuff. The idea that some guy could give you the best sex you've ever had in your life because he's had enough practice to be bloody good at it.'

Hannah laughed, catching her skirt as it billowed up to reveal her long legs. A car tooted appreciatively as it shot past. Thank goodness she was wearing a respectable bikini bottom instead of a lacy number or a thong and that her summer tan hadn't begun to fade yet. Despite being blonde and blue-eyed, she and Susie both tanned easily without burning.

'I don't do one-night stands or even flings,' Hannah reminded Susie. 'You know perfectly well the kind of trouble they lead to.'

'Yeah.' But Susie seemed to have finally got over her last heartbreak. 'But you always think you might just be the one who's going to make them want to change. And they're such *fun* at the time. To begin with, anyway.'

They walked in silence for a minute and Hannah looked down the grassy slope dotted with rocks and yellow flowers that led to the beach. A quite impressive surf from the murky sea was sending foamy scum to outline the distance up the beach the waves were reaching.

'You've never done it, have you?' Susie asked finally. 'Let your hair down and gone with sheer physical attraction? Slept with someone on a first date or fallen in love just because of the way some guy *looks* at you.'

'Never.' If she said it firmly enough she could convince herself as well, couldn't she? She couldn't admit, even to Susie, how often Ryan infiltrated her thoughts in the small hours of the night. It was lust she felt for the man. Nothing more.

Or should that be *less?*

'Sometimes I wish I were as strong as you,' Susie said wistfully.

'Someone had to be, in our family. The voice of reason, that's what I was. The devil's advocate.'

'You were always good at picking out what was wrong with the men Mum brought home.'

'Just a pity she never listened to me. She lost the house because she went ahead and married that slimeball, Richard the first.'

'Yeah. At least she's happy now. Or seems to be. Jim adores her.'

'And he's comfortably off and perfectly sensible. I'm sure Mum's learned to love fishing.'

'Hmm.'

Hannah couldn't blame Susie for sounding dubious. She made a mental note to ring her mother as soon as she got home.

'Come this way.' Susie pointed away from the signs directing people to the emergency and other departments of Crocodile Creek Base Hospital. 'We'll cut through the garden to the doctors' house and I can show you the pool and then shoot off and see those patients. Might be better if we leave the hospital tour until Sunday. Your flight doesn't leave till the afternoon, does it?'

'3 p.m.'

'Bags of time. I'll be able to introduce you properly to every hungover staff member we come across instead of confusing you with too many names.'

'I'll meet them at the wedding in any case.'

'You'll meet a few of them tonight. We're hoping to whisk Emily away after the rehearsal and take her out to dinner to give her a kind of hens' night. Which reminds me, I need to pop into the house and see who's going to be around. Gina might be there and Georgie should be back by now.'

'Is the dinner going to be at the Athina?'

'Heavens, no! Sophia already has the tables set up and about three thousand white bows tied to everything. She'll be making the family eat in the kitchens tonight, I expect—or they'll be roasting a lamb on a spit down on the beach. Such a shame about this weather.'

The lush tropical garden they were entering provided surprisingly good shelter from the wind thanks to the thick hibiscus hedges, and Hannah found she was too hot and sticky again. Her head was starting to throb as well, probably due to dehydration.

'Any chance of a glass of water?'

'Sure. Come up to the house with me.'

Skirting a sundial in the centre of the garden, Hannah could hear the sound of laughter and splashing water. An irresistibly cool, swimming pool sort of sound. The pool was behind a fenced area, screened by bright-flowered shrubs that smelt gorgeous, but Hannah didn't get time for a proper look because Susie was already half way up a set of steps that led to the wide veranda of a huge old two-storey building. Following her, Hannah found herself in a large kitchen and gratefully drank a large glass of water while Susie dashed off to see who was at home.

'There's nobody here,' she announced on her return. 'Come on, I'll bet they're all in the pool as it's still lunchtime.'

The air of too much to get done in the available time was contagious and Hannah hurriedly rinsed her glass and left it upside down on the bench amongst plates that held the remains of what looked like some of Mrs Grubb's legendary chicken salad sandwiches. Susie was a woman on a mission as she sped out of the house and she was only momentarily distracted by the bumbling shape of a large, strangely spotty dog that bounded up the steps to greet her.

'Rudolf!' Susie put her arm out as though she intended to pat the dog, and Hannah had no idea what happened. A split second later, Susie was tumbling down the steps with a cry that was far from the delighted recognition of the dog and then—there she was—a crumpled heap at the bottom.

'*Susie!* Oh, my God! Are you all right?'

Hannah wasn't the only one to rush to her sister's rescue. More than one dripping figure emerged through the open gate in the swimming-pool fence.

Two men were there almost instantly. And one of them was Ryan.

'What's happened?'

'She fell down the steps. There was this dog.'

'Damn, who left the gate open?' Another dark-haired man with a towel wrapped around his waist appeared behind the others. 'CJ, you were supposed to be watching Rudolf.'

'I was being a *shark!*' A small wet boy wriggled past the legs of the adults to stare, wide-eyed, at Susie. 'I had to be underwater,' he continued excitedly. 'With my fin on top—like this.' He stuck a hand behind his neck but no one was watching.

'It wasn't Rudolf's fault.' Susie was struggling into a sitting position. 'It's all right. I'm all right.'

'Are you sure?' A man with black curly hair and a gorgeous smile was squatting in front of Susie. 'You didn't hit your head, did you?'

'No. I don't know what happened, Mike. I just… Oh-h-h!'

'What's wrong?' Ryan moved closer. 'What's hurting?'

'My ankle,' Susie groaned. 'I think it's broken.'

'Just as well Luke's here, then,' Mike said, turning to another man who had approached the group. 'And they say you can't find an orthopaedic surgeon when you need one?'

'I *don't* need a surgeon,' Susie gulped. 'I hope.'

'I'll just be on standby,' Luke assured her. 'I am on babysitting duties after all.'

'*I'm* not a baby,' CJ stated. His hand crept into Luke's. 'You said I was your *buddy.*'

'You are, mate. You are…'

'Let *me* have a look.' Ryan's hands were on Susie's ankle. He eased off her sandal before palpating it carefully. 'I can't feel anything broken.'

'Ouch!'

'Sorry. Sore in there, is it? Can you wiggle your toes?'

There was a small movement. 'Ouch,' Susie said again. She looked close to tears and Hannah crouched beside her, putting an arm around her shoulders. 'I don't believe this. How could I have done something this stupid?'

'Accidents happen,' Ryan said calmly. He laid his hand on top of Susie's foot. 'Can you stop me pushing your foot down?'

'No. Oh, that *really* hurts.'

'It's starting to swell already.' Hannah peered anxiously at Susie's ankle. She might not have been very impressed if this injury was in front of her in the emergency department, but this was no professional environment and this was her sister. And Ryan looked nothing like he did in the ED. Hannah's gaze swung back to her colleague for a moment. He was practically naked, for heaven's sake. Tanned and dripping and…gorgeous. And giving Susie that killer smile.

'I think it's just a bad sprain but we'll need an X-ray to be sure. At least you chose the right place. I believe there's an X-ray department not far away.'

'It's not funny,' Susie wailed. 'I've got to wear high heels tomorrow. Little white ones with a rose on the toe. My dress is nowhere long enough to cover an ankle the size of an elephant's. I need some ice. Fast.' Susie leaned down to poke at the side of her ankle. 'What if it's broken and I need a cast? Oh, Mike, I'm so sorry! This is a *disaster!*'

'Forget it,' the curly haired man told her. 'The only thing that matters right now is making sure you're all right. Let's get you over to A and E.'

'I'll take her,' Ryan offered. 'Isn't Emily expecting you back at the Athina?'

Mike glanced at his watch and groaned. 'Ten minutes ago. And I'm supposed to have all the latest printouts from the met bureau. The women are all petrified that Willie's going to turn back and ruin the wedding.'

'As if!' Luke was grinning. 'There's no way Sophia's going to let a bit of weather undermine a Poulos wedding.'

Hannah could feel an increasing level of tension curling inside her. This was no time to be discussing the weather. Or a wedding. Susie needed attention. Her sister's face was crumpling ominously.

'*I'm* ruining the wedding,' she wailed forlornly. 'How could I have been so *stupid?*'

Hannah glared at Ryan. If he made even one crack about anything blonde, he would have to die!

Ryan's eyebrows shot up as he caught the force of the warning. Then he looked away from Hannah with a tiny, bemused shake of his head.

'Nothing else hurting?' he asked Susie. 'Like your neck?'

She shook her head.

'Right. Let's get this sorted, then.'

With an ease that took Hannah's breath away, Ryan took charge. He scooped Susie into his arms as though she weighed no more than the little boy, CJ. 'Emergency's that way, yes?'

'Yes,' Luke confirmed. 'Through the memorial garden.'

'Can I go, too?' CJ begged. ' I want to watch.'

'No,' Luke said. 'We told Mom we'd be waiting here when she got back.'

Mike was grinning broadly. 'You sure you want to go in like that, mate?'

'No time to waste.' Ryan was already moving in the direction Hannah had approached earlier. 'We need ice. And an X-ray.'

Hannah was only too pleased to trot behind Ryan. This was exactly the action that was required and there was no way she could have carried Susie herself.

'I'll bring your clothes over,' Mike called after them. 'I'll just call Emily and let her know what's happening.'

* * *

What was happening was a badly sprained ankle.

Despite ice and elevation and firm bandaging, Susie's ankle was continuing to swell impressively and was far too painful to put any weight on at all.

'Crutches.' An older and clearly senior nurse appeared in the cubicle Susie was occupying nearly an hour later. 'At least I won't need to give you a rundown on how to use them, Susie.'

'Thanks, Jill.' But Susie took one look at the sturdy, wooden, underarm crutches and then covered her face with her hands as though struggling not to burst into tears.

There was a moment's heavy silence. The cubicle was quite crowded what with Hannah standing by the head of Susie's bed, Ryan—now dressed, thankfully—and Mike leaning on the wall and Jill at the foot of the bed, holding the horrible accessories Susie was not going to be able to manage without.

Then the silence was broken.

'What are you saying?' came a loud, horrified, female voice. 'She can't *walk?* How can we have a bridesmaid who can't *walk?*'

'Oh, no!' Susie groaned. 'Sophia!'

'I was wondering how she'd take the news,' Mike said gloomily. 'Em didn't sound too thrilled either.'

A young woman with honey-blonde hair and rather serious grey-blue eyes rushed into the cubicle.

'Susie, are you all right? Is it broken?' She leaned over the bed to hug her friend. 'You poor thing!'

Hannah's eyes widened as the curtain was flicked back decisively. It wasn't just Mike's mother who had accompanied Emily. There were at least half a dozen women and they were all talking at once. Loudly. Anxiously.

'Susie! Darling!' The small, plump woman at the forefront of the small crowd sailed into the cubicle and stared at Hannah. 'What *have* you done to your hair?'

'I'm not Susie,' Hannah said weakly, as her sister emerged from Emily's hug. 'I'm her twin, Hannah.'

'Oh, my God!' The young, dark-haired woman beside Sophia was also staring. 'You *are* identical. Look at that, Ma! You wouldn't be able to tell them apart.'

An excited babble and an inward flow of women made Hannah back into the corner a little further. Alarmed, she looked for an escape route, only to catch the highly amused faces of both Mike and Ryan. There was nothing for it but to hold her breath and submit to the squash of people both wanting to pat and comfort Susie and to touch Hannah and see if she was actually real.

Jill looked as though she knew even her seniority would be no help in trying to evict this unruly mob from her emergency department and was taking the crutches out of the way for the moment, but the movement attracted Sophia's attention.

'What are those?'

'Susie's crutches.' Jill picked up speed as she backed away.

'She needs *crutches?*' Sophia crossed herself, an action that was instantly copied by all the other relatives. 'But we can't have crutches! The photographs!'

'It's all right, Ma.' The woman who had to be Mike's sister, Maria, was grinning. 'It doesn't matter if Susie can't walk.'

'It doesn't matter? Of course it matters!' Sophia's arms were waving wildly and Hannah pressed herself further into the corner. 'There are six dresses. We have to have six bridesmaids and Susie is Emily's best friend. She has to be in the photographs. In the ceremony.' A lacy handkerchief appeared from someone's hand and Sophia dabbed it to her eyes. 'But with crutches? Oh, no, no, no…' The sympathetic headshakes from all directions confirmed that this event was cataclysmic.

'Never mind Willie,' Mike murmured audibly to Ryan. 'This is going to be worse than any cyclone, believe me.'

'Ma, listen!' Sophia's shoulders were firmly grasped by Maria. 'We can use Hannah instead.'

*'What?'* The word was wrenched from Hannah and everybody was listening now. And staring. And then talking, all at once.

'No, her hair's all wrong.'

'She's the same size. She'll fit the dress.'

'Nothing that curling tongs couldn't fix.'

'No crutches!'

'Nobody will know the difference.'

'I'll know,' Emily said emphatically. 'And so will Susie.' She still had her arms protectively around her friend.

'Would it matter?' Susie spoke only to Emily. 'I'd rather it was Hannah than me in the photos, Em. I'd just spoil them.'

'No, you wouldn't.'

'Yes, I would. It would be the first thing anyone would notice when they looked at the pictures. Or when they're sitting in the church. Instead of saying, "Look at that gorgeous bride," they'd be saying, "Why is that girl on crutches? What's wrong with her?"'

The chorus of assent from the avid audience was unanimous. Emily looked appealingly at Mike but he just shrugged sympathetically and then grinned.

'Up to you, babe,' he said, 'but it does seem fortuitous that you chose a chief bridesmaid that's got a spare copy of herself available.'

Hannah looked at Ryan. If this crazy solution was going

to make everybody happy then of course she would have to go along with it. But would Ryan?

Clearly, it *was* going to make everybody happy. Especially Susie.

'I'll still be there,' she was telling Emily. 'And Hannah's like part of me anyway.'

'Hannah? Are you OK with this?'

'Sure.' Hannah smiled warmly at Emily. 'I'd be honoured.'

'Hannah! Darling!' Sophia was reaching to squeeze Hannah's cheeks between her hands. 'Thank you! Thank you!'

Nobody asked Ryan if he was OK with the plan. Hannah caught his gaze and for a moment they just stared at each other. Another moment of connection. They were the two outsiders. Caught up in a circus over which they had no hope of exerting the slightest control.

It was a bit like dealing with the turbulence on that plane trip really. Had that been only this morning? Fate seemed determined to hurl them together. As closely as possible.

Ryan's expression probably mirrored her own. There was nothing they could do about it so they may as well just go with the flow.

There was something else mixed in with the resignation. Maybe it was due to the almost joyous atmosphere in the cubicle at having solved a potentially impossible hitch to the perfect wedding. Or maybe, for Hannah, it was due to something she didn't want to analyse.

It was more than satisfaction.

Curiously, it felt more like excitement.

## CHAPTER FIVE

CLOUDS were rolling in towards the North Queensland coast by 5 p.m.

Stained-glass windows in the small, Greek Orthodox church in the main township of Crocodile Creek were rattled with increasing force by the sharp wind gusts.

'Did you hear that?' Emily tugged on Mike's arm. 'It's getting worse.'

'Last report was that Willie's heading further out to sea. Stop fretting, babe. Spit for luck instead.'

'I've given up spitting, I told you that.' The smile Emily shared with her fiancé spoke of a private joke and Hannah found herself smiling as well. Emily and Mike had the kind of bond she had only ever found with her sister. One where an unspoken language said so much and just a look or a touch could convey a lot more than words.

If she was ever going to get married herself, Hannah would want that kind of a bond with the man she was going to spend the rest of her life with. She had known it wouldn't be easy to find a man she could trust to that extent. No, that wasn't quite true. Trevor had been as reliable and trustworthy as it was possible to be—perhaps because he was so hard working and scientific and couldn't tolerate anything that required imagination or spontaneity.

The relationship had gone from one of comfort to one of predictability. And then boredom had set in. In the end, Hannah had been quietly suffocating. The opportunity that moving to Auckland to take up her first registrar position had afforded had been too good to miss. Much to poor Trevor's unhappy bewilderment, she had also moved on from their relationship.

She hadn't been in another relationship since. Hurting another nice, kind, trustworthy man was not on the agenda. Risking personal disaster by trying the kind of man who was fascinating was also a place Hannah had no intention of going. Of course Susie was right. That 'bad boy' edge was attractive. It would be all too easy to think like most women—that *they* would be the one to make the difference—but it never happened like that. Not in real life.

Emily tore her eyes away from Mike to smile apologetically at Hannah. 'I must sound like a real worry wart,' she said, 'but I've got a long veil. Can you imagine what it's going to be like in gale-force winds?'

'There are six of us.' Hannah glanced at the lively group of young women milling behind her that included Mike's sister, Maria. 'I'm sure we'll be able to keep your veil under control.'

Sophia put the finishing touches to yet another of the large, alternating peach and white bows she was tying to the ends of the pews and then clapped her hands.

'Another practice!' she ordered. 'Michael! What are you doing? Go back up to the front with the others. Ryan! You're supposed to be making my son behave.'

'That'll be the day,' Ryan muttered. 'Come on, mate. Let's get this over with and then we can hit the bright lights of Crocodile Creek for a stag party, yes?'

'That really *would* be the day,' Mike responded with a grimace. 'There's a lamb on a spit turning as we speak and every member of the family has about six jobs to do later. I think you're down for potato-peeling duties. Or possibly painting the last of the damn chicken bones.'

'Chicken bones?'

'Quickly!' Sophia's tone suggested that there would be trouble if co-operation did not take place forthwith.

The two men shared a grin and then ambled up the red carpet of the aisle, and the rear view made Hannah realise how similar they were. Both tall and dark and handsome. They were wearing shorts and T-shirts at the moment but Hannah could well imagine what they'd look like tomorrow in their dark suits, crisp white shirts and bow ties. Just…irresistible.

Emily was watching the men as well and she sighed happily. 'I can't believe this is really going to happen,' she whispered. 'It's just too good to be true.'

Her eyes were shining and Hannah could feel the glow. What would it be like, she wondered, to be *that* happy? To be so sure you'd chosen the right person and that that kind of love had a good chance of lasting for ever? Mike looked like Ryan in more than an outward physical sense. They both had that laid-back, mischievous gleam that advertised the ability to get the most enjoyment possible out of life. And that did not generally include settling down with one woman and raising a family. Had Emily been the one to change Mike? Did being Greek make the difference? Or was she heading for unimaginable heartbreak?

No. Hannah didn't believe that for a moment. She had seen the way Mike and Emily had looked at each other.

They had found the real thing, all right. Standing in this pretty church, about to rehearse the steps for a ceremony to join two lovers in matrimony, Hannah couldn't help a flash of envy. It was a bit like winning the lottery, wasn't it? Only it was a human lottery and you couldn't buy tickets. And even if you were lucky enough to find one, you might forget to read the small print and think you'd won, only to have the prize snatched away. It had happened to both her mother and to Susie, and Hannah knew why. Because 'the Richards' had had that hint of a 'bad boy' edge. They had been playboys. Fun-seekers. Like Ryan.

The pageboys and flower girls were being rounded up from their game of chase between the empty pews. They were holding plastic beach buckets as a prop to represent the baskets of petals they would hold tomorrow. Sophia herded them into place and repeated instructions they had apparently misheard on the first rehearsal.

'Gently!' she insisted. 'You are throwing rose petals, CJ, not sticks for Rudolf!'

Maria was examining her nails. 'They're full of silver paint,' she complained. 'I never want to see another chicken bone in my life.'

'What's with the chicken bones?' Hannah queried. 'I heard Mike saying something about them as well.'

'Wishbones.' Emily was moving to take her place in the foyer. 'Painted silver. Sophia's planning to attach them to the little bags of almonds the guests will be given. Not that anyone's found time to put the almonds in the bags yet, let alone attach the wishbones.'

'They're for fertility,' Maria added. 'The almonds, that is. And boy, do I wish they hadn't been scattered around at my wedding. Watch out for the ones in your bed, Em. I'd sweep them out if I were you or you might end up like me, with four little monsters under five.' She was peering anxiously past Hannah to see if her small children were doing what they were supposed to on reaching the end of the petal-throwing procession.

'Uncle Mike!' one of them shrieked. 'Did you see me pretending to throw petals?'

Mike swept the small girl into his arms and kissed her. Ryan held out his hands and got high-fives from two small boys—a gesture that was clearly well practised. Then he pulled them in, one on each side of his body, for a one-armed hug.

'Good job, guys,' Hannah heard him say.

When did Ryan get to spend enough time with young children to be that at ease with them? Did he have a big family with lots of nieces and nephews? Maybe he'd been married already and had his own children. The notion was quite feasible. It would explain his frequent trips back to Sydney. Not that it mattered to Hannah. She was just aware of how little she knew about her colleague. Aware of a curiosity she had no intention of satisfying.

'I hope the aisle's going to be wide enough.' Emily had come back to her cluster of bridesmaids. 'My dress is *huge.* A giant meringue. Do you think there'll be room for a wheelchair beside me?'

'A wheelchair?' Hannah was glad she'd paid attention to Susie's emails. 'Is Charles Wetherby giving you away?'

'Yes. He's the closest thing to a father figure I've got.'

Reading between the lines of those emails, Hannah had the impression that Charles was a father figure to more than just Emily. With an ability to know more about what was happening within the walls of the hospital he directed than his staff were always comfortable with. A man with a quiet strength and wisdom that provided the cement for a remarkable small community of professional medics. A community that her sister was very much a part of now.

'I'm sure there'll be room,' she said confidently.

'Susie!' Sophia was sounding flustered. She was waving frantically from the altar end of the aisle. 'Pay attention, darling!'

'It's Hannah, Ma, not Susie,' Maria shouted.

'I knew that. You know what I mean. Come on, girls. In your pairs.'

Hannah and Maria were first. They walked along the red carpet beneath the elaborate chandelier, the gilt frame of which had miniature copies of the paintings of various saints that decorated the walls of this church between the stained-glass windows. The tiny crystals tinkled musically overhead as another gust of wind managed to shake the solid brick building.

Maria glanced up at the chandelier and muttered something under her breath that could have been either a curse or a prayer. Maybe a bit of both, Hannah decided, as Mike's sister flashed a grin at her.

'It's going to be a wild wedding at this rate!'

Hannah nodded agreement but found herself swallowing a little nervously. Even if Willie was out to sea and moving in a safe direction, this was still as close to a tropical cyclone as she felt comfortable with.

The first rehearsal made it easy to remember what to do this time. Hannah and Maria climbed to the top of the three steps and then waited until the other pairs of bridesmaids were on the lower steps before they all turned gracefully in unison to watch the bride's entrance.

Hannah felt a complete fraud. If only Emily and Susie weren't so set on her standing in. She couldn't even follow someone else's lead. She was the chief bridesmaid. It was up to her to make sure all the others did the right thing at the right time. There was a point when she would actually be a closer part of this ceremony, too. When the bride and groom were wearing the matching orange-blossom wreaths on their heads that were joined by satin ribbons, they would take their first steps as man and wife with a tour three times around the altar. It would be Hannah's job to hold up the train of Emily's dress and keep her veil in order. As best man, Ryan would be right beside her, holding up the ribbons joining the wreaths.

He would be wearing his tuxedo and Hannah would be so dressed up and groomed she wouldn't even feel like herself. She would have to be Ryan's partner in this ceremony and probably at the reception. She might even have to dance with him, and she was going to feel so uncomfortable she would be hating every minute of it.

And you'll look miserable, a small voice at the back of her mind warned. You'll make Susie miserable and probably Emily and definitely Ryan, and they'll all wish you'd never been invited to this wedding. Hannah noticed the nudge that Mike gave his best man by bumping shoulders. There was a whispered comment and then a frankly admiring stare from both men as the girls behind Hannah proudly arranged themselves on the steps. The men grinned approvingly. The girls giggled. They were all enjoying every moment of this circus.

And why not? It was going to be a huge party. The wild weather would probably only enhance the enjoyment of those safely tucked away inside. It was play time, not work time. Why couldn't she just relax and have fun, like they were?

Everybody thought she was boring. Too focussed on her career. Too ready to troubleshoot problems before they even occurred. It should, and probably did, make her a very good doctor, but too many people had criticised that ability in the last few days. Jennifer thought she had no life of her own outside work. Ryan thought she was dull. Even her own sister had commented on her lack of spontaneity or willingness to reap the rewards of taking a personal risk.

Hannah had never allowed sheer physical attraction to be the deciding factor when it came to men. Or slept with someone on a first date. Not that she intended to jump Ryan's bones, of course. Or fall in love with him because of a look, or, in his case, more likely due to the kind of smile she'd experienced in the plane that morning. The kind her junior bridesmaids were enjoying right now.

She could, however, throw caution to the winds for once, couldn't she? Given the current weather conditions in Crocodile Creek, it would be highly likely to be blown a very long way away, but would that be so terrible?

For the next twenty-four hours or so, she was going to have to pretend to be Susie. Someone with a rather different perspective on life and taking risks. This could be the perfect opportunity to step outside her own comfort zone. To really let her guard down and simply enjoy the moment, without trying to see down the track to locate potential hazards.

What did she have to lose? On Sunday she would get on a plane again to go home. Back to being herself. Back to working hard enough to ensure the success she craved. Hopefully, back to a new position as an emergency department consultant. And how much time would she get to have fun after that? This weekend could be seen as a kind of hens' party really. A final fling before Hannah became wedded to a new and intense phase of her career.

And it wouldn't hurt to show Ryan Fisher that she *did* know how to enjoy herself. That she wasn't all work and no play and as dull as ditchwater.

*Yes!*

Hannah hunched her shoulders and then let them drop to release any unconscious tension.

And then she smiled at Ryan. Really smiled. Here we are, then, her smile said. Let's have fun!

Good grief!

What had he done to deserve a smile like that? One that actually touched Hannah's eyes instead of just being a polite curve of her lips.

Ryan had to fight the urge to glance over his shoulder to see whether the real recipient of the smile was standing nearby.

Hell, she was gorgeous. It was going to be more than rather difficult to stick to his resolution if she was going to do things like smile at him like that. Almost as bad as discovering it had been Hannah and not Susie wearing that frilly skirt. The one that the wind had whipped up to reveal a pair of extremely enticing legs as he and Mike had driven up to the hospital earlier that afternoon. He'd never be able to see her wearing scrubs trousers in the ED again without knowing what lay beneath the shapeless fabric.

Mind you, that hadn't been half as disconcerting as what had happened later. Ryan had been entertaining hopes of finding Susie's company perfectly enjoyable. Of maybe being able to learn why his attractive colleague was so uptight and had taken such an instant dislike to him.

To have Susie incapacitated and Hannah stepping in to fill the breach had been a cruel twist of fate. Not that he'd allowed his disappointment to show, of course. Not when Emily had looked so happy. When Emily looked that happy, Mike was happy. And if his best buddy was happy, Ryan certainly wasn't going to do anything to tarnish the glow.

He'd go through with this and he'd look as if he was enjoying every moment of it. It would be hard *not* to enjoy it, in fact, and if he could only make sure his resolution regarding Hannah Jackson didn't go out the window, he could be sure he wouldn't spoil that enjoyment by getting some kind of personal putdown.

But it would help—a lot—if she didn't smile at him like that. As though she had put aside her preconceived and unflattering opinions. Opened a window in that wall of indifference to him and was seeing him—*really* seeing him—for the first time.

She did look a bit taken aback when he offered to take her home after the rehearsal but she rallied.

'Sure. I guess it's on your way, seeing as you're staying in the doctors' house. I might even go as far as the hospital and check on Susie.'

'It's good that she decided she would stay in overnight and get that intensive RICE treatment. It should help a lot.'

'Mmm.' Hannah's tone suggested that nothing would help enough unless, by some miracle, Susie awoke after a night of compression bandages and ice and elevation to find her foot small enough to wear her shoe and the ability to stand and walk unaided, which was highly unlikely. 'I need to stop at her house and collect a few things she might need, if you're not in too much of a hurry.'

'Not at all.' Ryan lowered his voice. 'With a bit of luck, I'll arrive at the Athina *after* all the potatoes are peeled.'

Hannah made no response to that and Ryan kicked himself mentally. What was he trying to do here? Prove how shallow and lazy he was?

'Tell Susie I'll be up to see her later,' Emily said as they left the church. 'If she can't come to the hens' party, we'll just have to take the party to her.'

'I think Jill might have something to say about that,' Mike warned. 'She's not big on parties happening in her wards.'

'Yeah.' Emily nodded sadly. 'She'd say that I should know the R in RICE stands for rest. Tell Susie I'll come and get her later in the morning, then, so she can come and supervise. Kylie can still do her hair and make-up.'

To Ryan's disappointment, Hannah was ready for the wind when they stepped outside. She had wrapped her skirt firmly around those long brown legs and was holding it in place. On the positive side, the action affected her balance and a good gust sent her sideways a few moments later to bump into Ryan. She could have fallen right over, in fact, if he hadn't caught her arms.

Bare arms.

Soft skin.

Enough momentum in the movement for Ryan to feel the press of her breasts against his hands. It wasn't the first time he had touched her skin but the tension of that incident in the plane hadn't really afforded an opportunity to analyse the effect. It was, quite simply, electrifying. Or was that because this contact had come about so unexpectedly?

No. He'd known, all along, that there would be something very different about touching this woman.

Something very special.

He didn't want to let go. The urge to pull her even closer and kiss her senseless was as powerful as what felt like hurricane-force winds funnelling through the church car park, whipping their hair and buffeting their bodies.

Simply irresistible.

Oh...*God!*

The strength of the grip Ryan had on her arms was

sending shock waves through Hannah, not to mention the delicious tingle of what had to be that latent lust kicking in.

And he looked…as though he wanted to *kiss* her!

Even more shocking was the realisation that she *wanted* him to.

Letting her hair down and being prepared to enjoy this weekend was one thing. Making out with Ryan Fisher in a church car park was quite another. And quite unacceptable.

Hannah wrenched herself free. 'You've got Mike's car?'

'Yes. That Jeep over there.'

The vehicle was vaguely familiar. Hadn't that been the one that had hooted when her skirt had blown up around her neck on that walk around the cove? Had it been Ryan getting a close-up view of her legs?

The tingle became a shaft of something much stronger that was centred deep in Hannah's abdomen but sent spirals all the way to the tips of her fingers and toes. Battling with the door of the Jeep so it didn't catch in the wind and fly outwards was a welcome diversion. Why was she feeling like this? Had she somehow flicked a mental switch back there in the church that could lead her rather too far into temptation?

How inappropriate.

But intriguing.

Ryan wouldn't think twice about following his inclinations, would he? Sleeping with someone on a first date or having a little weekend fling? Hannah couldn't help casting a speculative glance at her companion as he started the Jeep and they moved off. His hands gripped the steering-wheel with enough strength to keep the vehicle straight despite the strong winds but they didn't look tense. Strength and a capacity to be gentle. What had Susie said about bad boys and getting the best sex you ever had?

Maybe her thoughts were too powerful. Something made Ryan turn his head. He held her gaze for only a heartbeat and then gave her one of those smiles.

Oh…help! Hannah spent the next few minutes until they were driving over that rickety bridge wondering if Ryan was discreet. Whether what happened on camp would stay on camp. Seeing as she'd never actually heard any firsthand gossip about his previous conquests, it seemed likely that the answer was yes. The added bonus of dealing with that distracting attraction as well as proving she could be fun might well mean that her working relationship with Ryan could be vastly improved. Even when she got the consultancy position and, effectively, became his boss.

It was quite difficult to rein in her thoughts and focus on her immediate intentions.

'I might change my clothes before I go and visit Susie.' Thinking out loud was partly to ensure Ryan didn't know what she'd really been thinking about. 'I've still got my bikini on under this and it's not as if I'm going to get a chance to swim.'

'That's a shame. The pool's great. Very refreshing.'

'It has been a long day, hasn't it?' Hannah agreed. 'Feels like for ever since we left Auckland.' A different time. A different place. Different rules were definitely allowable.

'You could have a swim after you've been visiting.'

'I'd still need a change of clothes and, besides, it gets dark early here, doesn't it?'

'About eight, I think. But there are lights around the pool. People often swim at night over summer from what Mike was telling me.'

'Tempting. I might just do that. This heat is really getting to me.' It wasn't the first time that day that Hannah had lifted the weight of hair off her neck to try and cool down a fraction. 'I don't think I've ever felt this hot in my life.'

'Mmm. You look pretty hot.' Ryan's grin suggested that he was commenting on her sexual appeal rather than her body temperature but, for once, Hannah wasn't put off. Was that because the flirtatious comment was acceptable under the new rules that seemed to be forming?

She laughed. 'You're hopeless, Ryan.' Then she pointed ahead. 'Stop here—that's Susie's cottage.'

Ryan followed her as far as the veranda. When Hannah emerged a few minutes later, wearing light cargo pants and a shirt over her bikini and with a towel and underwear and things for Susie in a carry bag, he was lounging against one of the posts framing the steps. Strands of bougainvillea snapped in the wind and a shower of dark red petals had left blooms caught in the dark waves of his hair.

'Why am I hopeless?'

Had he been stewing over the casual reprimand the whole time he had been waiting for her?

'Because you're an incorrigible flirt,' Hannah informed him. 'You can't talk to women without…' She had to leave the sentence unfinished. 'Without making them feel like you're attracted to them' had been the words on the tip of her tongue but what would happen if he responded by saying he *was* attracted to her? In theory, letting her hair down was great, but this was actually quite scary. What if he said she had nothing to worry about because there was no way he could be attracted to her? Hannah's mouth felt oddly dry.

'Most women appreciate a compliment,' Ryan was saying. 'I try to be nice. To establish a good rapport with the people I work with.'

'Hmm.' Hannah didn't have to try and make the sound

less than understanding. Professional rapport had boundaries that Ryan clearly took no notice of.

He hadn't moved from the support of the post. To get to the car, Hannah had to go down the steps, which meant moving closer to the stationary figure.

'I work with you, Dr Jackson.'

'You do, Dr Fisher.' Hannah gripped the handles of her carry bag more firmly and made the move to the top of the steps.

'I'd like *us* to establish a good rapport. I don't think we've really got one yet, have we?'

'No.' She was close to Ryan now. She could almost have reached out and plucked petals from his hair.

'Why is that, Hannah?'

'I…ah…' It had been a mistake to make eye contact at this proximity. Words totally failed Hannah.

'Maybe we could try again,' Ryan suggested softly. 'We're in a new place that has nothing to do with work. We could make this weekend a new start.'

'Ah…' Something had already started. Hannah watched the way Ryan's gaze slid from her eyes to her mouth. The way his head was tilting slightly. She had to close her eyes as a wave of desire threatened to make her knees wobble and send her down the steps in an undignified stagger.

Had she mirrored that tilt of his face? Leaned closer to Ryan? Or had he just closed the gap of his own accord so that he could kiss her?

Not that it mattered. The instant his lips touched hers, *nothing* else mattered.

Yes, it was the start of something new, for sure. Something Hannah had never experienced. The first brush of paint on a totally new canvas.

Soft lips. A gentle pressure. Long enough to be intensely arousing but not nearly long enough. Hannah wanted more.

A *lot* more.

She wanted to taste this man. To touch him. To have him touch her. To fill in more of that canvas because she had no idea what colours and textures it would encompass or what the finished picture might be like. What that brief kiss *had* told her, however, was that the picture would be bigger and more exciting than any she'd ever seen.

It was Ryan who bent to pick up the carry bag, which had slipped, unnoticed, from Hannah's fingers.

'This way, Dr Jackson,' he murmured. 'Your chariot awaits.'

Hannah didn't want to move. Unless it was to go back into the cottage and take Ryan with her. It was disappointing that he hadn't suggested it himself. Surely he would normally follow through on a kiss like that?

Perhaps he intended to. He smiled at Hannah.

'Maybe,' he said lazily, 'we can do something else about establishing that rapport later.'

'Rapport, huh? That's a new word for it.' Susie lay on her hospital bed with her leg elevated on pillows, bandaged and packed in ice. 'So what was it like, then?'

'The kiss?' Hannah chewed the inside of her cheek. 'Not bad, I guess.'

Susie pulled a pillow from behind her back to throw at her sister.

'OK, it was great. Best kiss I've ever had. Satisfied?'

'No. Are you?'

Hannah smiled wryly. 'No.'

'So what are you going to do about it?'

'What can I do? OK, he might have been tempted to kiss

me for some reason but I can't see it going any further. He doesn't even like me. I don't like him. I'm just…attracted to him physically.'

'Maybe he's pretending not to like you because he's really attracted to you and you haven't given him any encouragement.'

'I kissed him! What more encouragement could he need?'

'Maybe he likes to take things slowly.'

'Ha!'

'Yeah.' Susie grinned. 'He doesn't look the type to take things slowly. Never mind, you've got the whole weekend in a tropical paradise. Something's bound to happen.'

'Forty-eight hours isn't that long.'

'But weddings are very romantic. And it's not as if you won't be seeing each other after you go home.'

'We won't be "seeing" each other when we go home. This is purely physical, Susie. An opportunity to get it out of my system. I mean, what if I'm sitting in a rest home when I'm ninety-five and I regret never trying a one-night stand? Doubt that I'd have the opportunity then.'

'So Ryan's not a long-term prospect, then?'

'Are you kidding? Would you take up with Richard the second with the benefit of hindsight?'

'No… Yes… Maybe…' Susie sighed. 'But Ryan might be different. He might not take off as soon as he spots greener pastures.'

*'Ha!'* Hannah put even more feeling into the dismissive response this time.

'Will you be seeing him again tonight?'

'No. I'm going to finish watching this movie with you, go and have a quick dip in the pool and then go home to sleep. I'm stuffed.'

'Why don't you skip the movie and see if you can find

him over at the doctors' house? I've got some stuff about Emily I was going to tell him so he could put it in his best man's speech.'

Hannah groaned. 'He's probably got it written already. One long string of blonde jokes.'

'It's a good excuse to talk to him.'

'He'll be at the Athina. Peeling potatoes or something.'

'He might be back by now. He got up as early as you did so he's probably equally stuffed.'

'I could go and have a swim.'

'What's the weather like out there now?'

'Horribly windy but still hot. It's not raining.'

'The pool's nice and sheltered. You probably won't be the only one there. Lots of people like to cool off before they go to bed. You sleep a lot better that way.'

Hannah wasn't the only one in the pool.

Ryan was there.

'I've done my potato-peeling bit,' he told Hannah. He was watching her shed her outer clothing. 'I really needed to cool off.'

Hannah slid into the water with a sigh of pleasure. The pool area was sheltered but it was still windy enough to make the water slightly choppy and the wind on wet skin pulled the heat out quickly enough to raise goose-bumps when Hannah stood up at the shallower end of the pool. She ducked down and swam breaststroke into deeper water. 'This is gorgeous.'

'Isn't it?' Ryan was swimming towards her. Only his head was showing but, thanks to Susie's accident, Hannah was only too well aware of what the rest of Ryan looked like. She took a determined breath.

'Susie's been telling me things about Emily that might

be useful for your best man's speech. Or have you finished writing it?'

Ryan grinned. 'No. Haven't started. Thought I might just wing it.'

'Well, there's a funny story about her spitting on Mike's helicopter.'

'Why did she do that?'

Hannah trod water, edging further away from Ryan. 'She was terrified of flying in helicopters and there's this Greek thing of spitting for luck. Only when the Greeks do it, it's kind of a token spit.' Hannah turned and swam a few strokes before shaking wet strands of hair from her eyes and taking another breath. 'When Emily did it, Mike had to clean the helicopter and there's a long-standing joke between them now about the paintwork getting corroded.' Hannah trod water again and turned. She should be a safe distance away from Ryan now.

She wasn't. He had kept pace with her.

'Interesting,' he said. 'I did know that Em hated helicopters. The night Mike proposed to her, they'd been sent on a mission that got cancelled and he landed them on a secluded beach. She thought they were crashing so she was really angry but Mike said that emergency measures had been necessary because he really needed to talk to her.'

'It all worked out, then.'

'Mmm. They have a very good rapport.' Ryan twisted his body in the water so that he was floating on his back. 'How's our rapport coming along, Dr Jackson?'

'Pretty good, I think.' Was it a feeling of insecurity that made it a relief to find her feet could touch the bottom of the pool here?

'Could be better, though, couldn't it?' With a fishlike movement, Ryan turned again, moving sideways at the same time so that he was within touching distance of Hannah. He caught her shoulders and Hannah seemed to simply float into his arms.

Not that she tried to swim away. She could have. Her feet were secure on the tiles at the bottom of the pool as she stood up and it would have been possible to get enough momentum to escape.

But she had no intention of escaping. This was it. She just had to get over the fear of doing something so out of character. Falling into what looked like a matching desire in Ryan's dark eyes, it became possible to step over that boundary.

'Yes,' she managed to whisper.

And then he was kissing her again and it was totally different to that kiss on the veranda. This one had a licence to continue. This one rapidly deepened so that Hannah had to wind her arms around Ryan's neck to keep her head above water. She could feel his hands on her bare skin, along with ripples from the disturbed water that seemed to magnify the sensation. His fingers trailed from her neck down her back, held her waist and then stroked their way up to cup her breasts.

At the same time, his lips and tongue were doing things that were arousing Hannah more than she would have believed possible. His face and lips were cool, thanks to the relentless wind, but the inside of his mouth was far from cool. It was hot enough to fuel an already burning desire. Hannah kissed him back, sucked headlong into that desire until she totally forgot herself. When he held her closer, Hannah found herself winding her legs around Ryan so that she couldn't float away.

Ryan groaned. 'God,' he murmured, pulling her hips even closer with an urgent strength to his grip. 'I want you, Hannah. You know that, don't you?'

Hannah tried to swallow, but couldn't. 'I want you, too.'

'Not here. Somewhere dry.'

Hannah had all the incentive she needed to throw caution to the winds for at least one night of her life. She even managed to sound as though she was quite used to being carried away by physical passion.

'Your place or mine?' she asked with a smile.

'Mine's closer. Just up those steps. It's Mike's old room. You can get in through a door on the veranda so nobody will see us.' Ryan bent to kiss her again and then he took her hand in his to lead her from the pool. 'You sure about this, Hannah?'

'What's not to be sure of? As you said, it's important to establish a good rapport with the people you work with.' She tightened her fingers around his, shivering as she climbed the steps of the pool and the wind caught at more of her exposed skin. Or was it the thought of where she was going and what she knew they would do that caused that shiver? Not that she had any intention of backing out. No way.

'Lead on, Dr Fisher.'

## CHAPTER SIX

IT WAS the curious howling sound that woke Ryan.

The first fingers of light were stretching under the roof of the wide veranda to enter his room and he could just make out the smooth hump of the feminine shoulder beside him.

Without thinking, Ryan touched the skin with his lips. A butterfly kiss that was as gentle as the way he traced the delicious curve of Hannah's hip with his hand, loving that dip to her waist that was accentuated by her lying on her side.

Loving everything about this woman. This new version of Hannah Jackson.

Her intensity. Softness. Suppleness. The way she accepted everything he had to offer and had responded in kind.

Thank God he hadn't stuck to that resolution to stay well away from her.

If he had, he would have missed out discovering just how good it was possible for sex to get. His experience last night had been the best he'd ever had in his life.

And Ryan knew what had made the difference. It was knowing he'd been right the moment he'd first laid eyes on Hannah. That there was a reason why the attraction had been so powerful. It was just possible he had found what he desperately needed in his life.

More of an anchor than a permanent job represented. The haven of a relationship that could be trusted. Could grow into something strong enough to last a lifetime. Could become a whole family even.

Something *good*. Love that wasn't darkened by the grim side of life. He was so tired of being strong for the people he loved. Not that he'd ever stop, but he badly needed something that would let the sunshine back into his own soul.

Someone he could be totally honest with. Someone that he could actually allow to see that things ripped him apart sometimes. He was fed up with hiding. Being flippant because he couldn't afford to share how he really felt. Making other people laugh because he'd discovered that was the best way to escape his own fear or misery.

Not that he'd ever made Hannah really laugh and, in a way, that was scary. Could she see through him? Despise him for being less than honest with himself and others? Had she been hurt in the past by a man who hadn't been able to connect on an emotional level and was that why that prickly barrier had been between them since that first meeting? If so, he could understand. Forgive and forget any of the putdowns.

Ryan pressed another soft kiss to Hannah's shoulder. Then he lifted her hair to kiss the side of her neck. She'd dropped that barrier last night, hadn't she?

One night.

A perfect night.

Ryan let his breath out in a contented sigh. Never mind that dawn was breaking. Last night had been just the beginning. The connection had been established and it could be the foundation for something that was going to last for ever.

Right now, Ryan had no doubt that it was entirely possible he could spend the rest of his life loving Hannah—in bed and out of it.

* * *

The dream took on colours that were so beautiful they took Hannah's breath away. She could actually *feel* them and the building excitement was something she remembered from childhood, waking up to a longed-for day that was going to bring something very special.

She was flying in her dream. Soaring over some incredible tropical landscape towards the place she most wanted to be. But she wasn't going to reach her destination because the edges of reality were pushing the dream away. The sense of loss was only momentary, however, because the reality was the touch of Ryan's lips. They were on the side of her neck, delivering a kiss so gentle it made her want to cry. Instinctively, she turned towards him, seeking the comfort of being held, only to find his lips tracing a line from her neck all the way to her breast. Stopping when they reached the apex and the cool flick of his tongue on her nipple took Hannah's breath away for real.

There was still a dreamlike quality to this, though, and Hannah kept her eyes closed even as her hands moved to find and touch Ryan where she now knew he most liked to be touched. The whole night had been a dream—the stuff of erotic fantasy—so why not keep it going just a little longer?

Thank God she had given in to that urge to experience something new. To find out if Susie was right and she'd discover the best sex of her life. Even in her wildest dreams until now, she hadn't had any idea what it could be like. Hannah could understand perfectly what had drawn her mother and her sister and probably countless other women into relationships that could only end in heartbreak.

Not that she was going to allow this to go that far. This was just a perfect ending to a perfect night. A one-night stand that Hannah could treasure the memory of for the rest of her life.

With a small sound of absolute pleasure, she slid her arms completely around Ryan to draw him closer.

It was raining when they woke again. Rain driven sideways by a wind that hadn't abated at all during the night. If anything, it was worse.

'What's the time?'

Ryan reached to collect the wristwatch he'd dropped by the side of the bed. 'Nearly nine.'

'Oh, my God, I can't believe we've slept in!' Hannah slid out from the tangled sheets, covering her bare breasts with her hands while she looked for her clothes. 'I've got to get back to Susie's place and get sorted. We're supposed to be at Kylie's salon by nine-thirty. It's probably chaos out there by now.'

'It would be chaos whatever time it is.' Ryan put his arms behind his head, clearly intending to watch Hannah getting dressed. 'Don't worry about it.'

'Where's my phone?' Hannah felt more in control now that she had her underwear on. 'Susie's probably been trying to text me. I put it on silent mode at the rehearsal yesterday and I completely forgot to reset it.'

'You got distracted,' Ryan said with satisfaction. 'The wedding's not till 4 p.m. Don't stress.'

Hannah pulled on crumpled cargo pants. Impossible not to feel stressed with the sound of rapid footsteps on the wooden boards of the veranda behind the thin curtain and then the excited bark of a dog.

'I need to get out of here without anyone seeing me.'

'Why?'

'It would be embarrassing if everyone knew I'd spent the night here.'

'Why?' Ryan repeated. 'It's nothing to be ashamed of. We're both single, consenting adults, aren't we?'

'Yes…' But there was an element of shame as far as Hannah was concerned. She'd never done anything like this in her life. This kind of selfish physical indulgence might be normal for Ryan and the women he chose, but it couldn't be more out of character for her. She'd always made sure she was ready to commit to an exclusive relationship before going to bed with someone.

'And it was fun, yes?' Ryan wriggled his eyebrows suggestively. 'I certainly enjoyed it.'

'Mmm.' Hannah tore her eyes away from the sight of Ryan getting out of bed. He obviously felt no need to cover himself. This was a man who was quite comfortable in his own skin. An enviable confidence that Hannah could only aspire to. She did her best. 'Me, too,' she added with a smile.

Ryan covered the floor space between them with an easy couple of strides. He drew Hannah into his arms and kissed her. 'I *really* enjoyed it,' he murmured. 'You're amazing.'

'Mmm.' The sound was a little strangled this time. Hannah wasn't so sure about daylight kisses. Sexual fantasy needed the cover of dark. She drew away. 'Could you keep an eye out and tell me when the coast is clear on the veranda? I can go down the other end, away from the kitchen, can't I?'

'Yeah.' Ryan turned away and picked up his shorts. 'I'll come with you.'

'No need. It'll only take me a few minutes to walk and I could do with the fresh air.'

'It'll be fresh all right. Might feel quite cold after yesterday with this rain. Did you bring a jacket?'

'No.'

'Then why don't you let me drive you home? I've got to take Mike's Jeep back up to the Athina, anyway. I'd better check in and see what my best-man duties involve. I suspect I'll have to stick with Mike for the rest of the day.'

And Hannah would need to be with Emily. She probably wouldn't see Ryan again till later that afternoon. No more daylight kisses to contend with. The odd sensation in her stomach had to be relief, rather than disappointment, surely?

'A ride would be good,' she said. 'That way I can get sorted faster.'

The veranda was deserted and no one interrupted their journey through the garden to the car park. As they scrambled from the end of the veranda, Ryan took hold of Hannah's hand and it felt so natural it would have been rude to pull hers away. As they left the gardens behind them, Hannah glanced at the hospital buildings but there had been no message from Susie yet and she would be back here in no time. Would she tell her sister about last night?

Maybe not. Not yet, anyway. The experience was still too fresh. Private and…precious?

Would Ryan say anything?

Maybe not. The way his hand still held hers was comforting. As though he shared a reluctance to break the illusion of a bond they'd created last night. Hannah was even more confident he could be discreet when he dropped her hand at the sight of someone running towards them.

Wet curls of black hair were plastered around Mike's face. 'I was just coming to find you, mate. Hi, Hannah.'

'What's up?' Ryan wasn't smiling. Neither was Mike.

'There's been an accident up at Wygera. Harry called me to see if I can do a first response with the Jeep. I've got a good paramedic kit in the back.' Mike was still moving and both Ryan and Hannah followed. 'I was on the way to the house to find a doc to come with me, but you'll do just fine.'

'Do you want me to come as well?' Hannah queried.

'Please.' Mike caught the keys Ryan threw and unlocked the doors of the Jeep. 'Sounds like there are at least three casualties. All teenagers.' He opened the back of the vehicle and pulled out a light, which he stuck to his roof. A cord snaked in through his window and he plugged the end into the cigarette lighter. A bright orange light started flashing as he turned on the engine.

'Where's Wygera?' Ryan pulled his safety belt on as Hannah climbed into the backseat.

'It's an aboriginal settlement about fifty miles from here. We'd normally get the chopper out for something like this but there's no way anyone's going to be flying today.' Gears crunched and the Jeep jerked backwards as Mike turned with speed and they took off. Hannah clicked her safety belt into its catch.

'What's happened?' she queried. 'And don't you have an ambulance available?'

'They're all busy on other calls right now and it'll take time to get a vehicle on the road. There's been trouble with the bloody bulls, by the sound of it—thanks to this weather.'

They were on the main road now, and Hannah could feel how difficult it was going to be, driving fast in the kind of wind gusts they were being subjected to. The windscreen wipers were on high speed but the rain appeared to be easing a little. Hannah shivered. She was damp and still hadn't had the opportunity to get any warmer clothing. Wrapping her arms around herself for warmth, she listened as Mike continued filling them in.

'There's a guy up at Wygera by the name of Rob Wingererra. They've acquired a few rodeo bulls. Long story, but they're a project for the teenagers up there. Huge animals with wicked horns. Apparently the wind caused some damage last night and brought a fence down and damaged a shed. The kids went out to try and get the bulls rounded up and into shelter and they got out of hand. Some kid's been cut by corrugated iron, one's been gored by a bull and another sounds like he might have a crush injury of some kind after getting caught between a bull and a gate.'

'How long will it take us to get there?'

'It's an hour's drive on a good day but I'm hoping to get there sooner than that. Hang on tight back there, Hannah, but don't worry. I know this road like the back of my hand. We'll just need to watch out for slips or rubbish on the road.'

He certainly knew the road. Having gone over the bridge and through the township, Mike headed towards the foothills of the mountains that divided the coastal plain from the cattle country Hannah knew was further inland. At the speed they were going, they would arrive there as fast as any ambulance was capable of. As they rounded one corner, Ryan threw a glance over his shoulder.

'You OK, Hannah?'

The tone was caring. How long had it been since a man had been this concerned for her well-being? It was dangerous to allow it to matter.

'I'm fine,' she said hurriedly.

'No, you're not—you're freezing!' Ryan twisted his body beneath the safety belt, pulling off the lightweight jacket he was wearing. 'Here. Put this on. '

'Thanks.' Hannah slid her arms into sleeves that were still warm from Ryan's skin. 'Are you sure you don't need it?'

But Ryan wasn't listening. 'What information have you been given about these kids so far?'

'There's a health worker at the settlement, Millie, who's

very good. Rob called her after he found the kids and they've got them inside at his place. She's controlled the bleeding on the boy that got cut but it sounds like he might have lost quite a bit of blood. The one who got poked by a horn isn't feeling too good. He's been vomiting but Millie thinks that might have something to do with a heavy night on the turps. The other one has sore ribs, maybe a fracture, so he's finding it painful to breathe.'

'Sounds like a mess.'

'I'm glad I've got you two along.' Mike flashed a grin over his shoulder at Hannah. 'Not the chief bridesmaid duties you were expecting this morning, eh? Sorry about that.'

Hannah smiled back. 'Actually, this is probably more within my comfort zone.'

'We'll have back-up pretty fast. There'll be an ambulance not far behind us and they'll send another one as soon as they're clear. We just need to do the initial triage and make sure they're stable for transport. Couldn't ask for more than two ED specialists on my team.'

'Let's hope it's not as bad as it sounds,' Ryan said. 'At least the rain's slowing down.'

'I've put in a good word to try and get some sunshine for Em this afternoon.'

Ryan laughed. 'You think the big guy's going to listen to you?'

'Hey, I've collected a few brownie points in my time. At least as many as you. Or maybe not.' Mike glanced at his friend. 'How's your dad doing?'

'Not so great. It's hard on Mum.'

'She must be delighted to have you in Auckland now.'

'Yeah.'

'Few trips to Brisbane still on the agenda, though, I guess? How's Michaela?'

Ryan shrugged. 'You know how it is,' was all he said.

'Yeah, buddy.' Mike's response was almost too quiet for Hannah to catch. 'I know.'

What was wrong with Ryan's father? And who was Michaela? An ex-wife? Hannah slumped back a little in her seat. How ridiculous to feel jealous. A timely reminder that this was just one weekend of her life; she didn't need to get caught up in Ryan Fisher's personal business. That was the road to the kind of emotional disaster Hannah had carefully avoided in her life thus far.

Caught up in her own thoughts and then a text conversation with Susie, who had heard about the drama at Wygera and was happy to wait for Emily to collect her, it seemed only a short time later that a tall water tower came into view. The cluster of houses nearby had a sad, tired air to them, with the rusting car bodies on the sparse greenery of surrounding land adding to an impression of poverty.

The eucalyptus trees were huge. They had been here far longer than the housing and would no doubt outlast most of these dwellings. Right now, the majestic trees were dipping and swaying in the strong wind, participating enthusiastically in a form of elemental ballet. Small branches were breaking free, swirling through the air to join the tumble of leaves and other debris on the bare ground. A larger branch caught Ryan's attention as it landed on the steep roof of the tidiest building they'd seen so far.

'It's the local hall,' Mike told him. 'Built to withstand snow, from what I've heard.' He grinned. 'Really useful, huh? It should manage the odd branch or two, anyway. We've got a turn-off up here and then we should almost be at Rob's place.'

A young woman could be seen waving frantically as they turned onto a rough, unsealed road.

'Target sighted,' Mike said. 'One windmill!'

Hannah was amazed he could sound so relaxed. And that Ryan could share a moment of amusement. She felt completely out of her depth here. They had one paramedic kit between the three of them and three potentially seriously injured teenagers. Hannah had never worked outside a well-equipped emergency department before.

'Hell, you took a long time,' the young woman told them. 'The boys are hurt bad, you know.' She led the way into the house. 'Stupid bulls,' she added with feeling.

'They weren't being nasty,' an older woman said. 'They were scared by the wind and that flapping metal on the shed. Hi, Mike!'

'Hi, Millie.' Mike smiled at the health worker and then at a man who was holding bloodstained towels to the leg of a boy on the couch. 'G'day, Rob. How's it going?'

'I'll let you tell me,' Rob said. His weathered face was creased with anxiety. 'I think I've finally managed to stop the bleeding in Jimmy's leg now, anyway. I've been sitting on the damn thing for an hour.'

Mike had set his backpack-style kit down on the floor and was unzipping it to pull out a stethoscope. 'This is Ryan,' he said, 'and that's Hannah. They're both doctors.' He glanced at the two other boys, who were sitting on the floor, leaning against the wall. They both had a rug over their legs and they both looked miserable. One had a plastic basin beside him. He shifted his gaze to Millie questioningly.

'Hal's got the sore ribs and Shane's got the puncture wound.' She smiled at Hannah and Ryan. 'Guess you've all got one patient each. Who wants who?'

Hannah swallowed a little nervously. An abdominal goring from a long bull's horn could have resulted in nasty internal injuries that would be impossible to treat in the field. Broken ribs could result in a tension pneumothorax and there were no X-ray facilities to help with diagnosis. A cut leg seemed the safest option. Even if Jimmy had lost enough blood to be going into shock, the treatment was easy. Stop the bleeding, replace fluid and supply oxygen.

'I'll have a look at Jimmy,' she said quickly. 'Have you got a sphygmomanometer in that kit, Mike?'

'Yep.' Mike pulled it out. 'You want to check Shane, Ryan?'

'Sure.'

'Mary?' Mike spoke to the girl who'd shown them inside. 'Could you go back to the road, please? There should be an ambulance arriving before too long and it was really helpful to have you show us where to stop.'

'But I wanted to watch,' Mary protested. 'Are you going to sew Jimmy's leg up?'

'Probably not,' Hannah responded. 'Not until we get him to hospital anyway.'

'Do as you're told,' Millie added firmly.

Hannah moved towards Jimmy, who looked to be about fourteen. 'Hi.'

The youth stared back silently for just a second before averting his eyes, which gave Hannah the impression he'd taken an instant dislike to her.

'I'm going to be looking after you for a bit, Jimmy,' she said. 'Have you ever had your blood pressure taken?'

He shook his head, still avoiding eye contact.

'It doesn't hurt. I'm going to wrap this cuff around your arm. It'll get a bit tight in a minute.'

Ryan had gone to Shane who looked younger than the other two. He was holding a teatowel to his side and it, too, was blood soaked.

Hannah unwound the blood-pressure cuff from Jimmy's

arm. His baseline recording for blood pressure was within normal limits but he was young enough to be compensating well for blood loss. She would need to keep monitoring it at regular intervals.

'I'm going to put a small needle in the back of your hand,' she warned Jimmy. 'OK?'

'Why?'

'You've lost a fair bit of blood. We need to give you some fluid to get the volume back up. Blood doesn't work as well as it should if there isn't enough of it going round. Is your leg hurting?'

'Yeah, course it is. It's bloody near chopped off.'

'Can you wiggle your toes?'

'Yeah.' The tone was grudging and Jimmy still wouldn't make eye contact. Was it just her or were all strangers not welcomed by these teens?

'I don't think it's in too much danger of dropping off, Jimmy, ' she said calmly. 'I'll check it properly in a minute. When I've got this needle in your hand, I'll be able to give you something to stop it hurting so much.'

Ryan seemed to be getting a similar suspicious response for being a stranger. Shane didn't look too happy when he put his hand out to touch the teatowel.

'Mind if I have a look, buddy?'

'Are yous really a doctor?'

'Sure am. Just visiting from New Zealand.'

'He's a mate of mine,' Mike told the boys. 'He's going to be the best man at my wedding.'

'Oh, that's right!' Millie exclaimed. 'You're getting married today, Mike. Crikey, I hope you're not going to be late for your own wedding. Dr Emily would be a bit cheesed off.'

'We'll get sorted here in no time,' Mike said calmly.

'Hal, I'm just going to listen to your chest while you take a few breaths, OK?'

'But it hurts.'

'I know, mate. I want to make sure those ribs haven't done any damage to your lung, though. Try to lean forward a bit.'

Hannah had the IV line secured and a bag of fluids attached and running. She got Rob to hold the bag. Having been given the kudos of being Mike's best friend, Ryan now had a more co-operative patient.

'Does it hurt if you take a deep breath?'

'Yeah.'

'Can I have a look at it?'

'I guess.'

'Wow, that's a pretty impressive hole! These bulls must be big fellas.'

'Yeah.'

'Does it hurt if I touch here?'

'Nah. Not much.'

For the next few minutes a rather tense silence fell as they all worked on assessing and treating their patients. Hannah didn't want to disturb the makeshift dressing on Jimmy's leg in case the bleeding started again, but she made a careful examination of his lower leg and foot to check for any serious damage to blood supply and nerves.

Mike was worried about a possible pneumothorax from Hal's broken ribs and got Ryan to double-check his evaluation.

'I think you're right,' Ryan said. 'Breath sounds are definitely down on the left side but it's not showing any signs of tensioning. One of us should travel with him in the ambulance, though.'

The need for constant monitoring and the potential for serious complications from the injury went unspoken, but

Hannah could feel the level of tension in the room creep up several notches.

Ryan glanced around him. 'Anyone heard the one about the blonde and the bulls with big horns?'

Hannah almost groaned aloud. Just when she'd been impressed by the professional, *serious* manner in which Ryan was approaching a job that should have been as much out of his comfort zone as it was for her, he was about to revert to type and tell one of his stupid jokes. Make light of a serious situation.

And then she caught Ryan's gaze.

This was deliberate. He knew exactly what he was doing. This was a ploy—as much of a skill as applying pressure to stop heavy bleeding, only it was intended to work in the opposite direction. A safety valve to relieve pressure. A way of defusing an atmosphere that could be detrimental if it was allowed to continue.

What if Hal picked up on how dangerous a pneumothorax could be and got frightened? He would start to breathe faster, which would not only hurt but interfere with his oxygen uptake. Shane might start vomiting again and exacerbate an internal injury. Jimmy might get restless and open the wound on his leg, with further blood loss.

They were all listening already.

'So, she tells him exactly how many bulls there are in this huge paddock and demands that he honours his side of the bargain and gives her the cute baby one.'

If this was a practised skill, as that almost defensive glance had suggested, what did that tell her about the man Ryan *really* was? Was the fun-loving, laid-back image simply a veneer?

'And the farmer says, "If I can tell you the real colour of your hair, will you give me back my baby bull?"'

Maybe the times Hannah saw Ryan so focussed on his patients—as he had been with Brendon's mother on Monday night and with Shane only minutes ago—said more about who he really was. Or the concern she'd heard in his voice when he'd asked if she was OK on the trip up here. Or…that incredible ability to be so gentle she'd discovered in his touch last night.

No. Hannah couldn't afford to believe in the serious side Ryan was capable of presenting. That was the short cut to disaster that her mother and sister had followed so willingly. She was stronger than that. She could push it away. It was easy, really. All she had to do was remember the way he flirted. The way women flocked to queue up for a chance to go out with him.

He might have the ability to be serious but it couldn't be trusted to last. Serious stuff couldn't be allowed to continue for too long. It just had to be broken by the injection of fun.

'"Now…give me back my dog!"'

Even though she'd only been half listening, Hannah found herself smiling. Shane and Jimmy were giggling. Hal groaned because it hurt, trying to laugh, but he still managed a big grin. Rob and Millie were still laughing when two ambulance officers came through the door with Mary. Eyebrows shot up.

'We heard there was an accident here,' one of them said, 'not a party!'

How many doctors would be able to achieve that? Hannah wondered. Then her own smile broadened. How many doctors had such a supply of awful jokes that could seemingly be adapted to suit the situation? As a demonstration of how useful it could be to be so laid back, this had been an eye-opener. The tension that had filled this room when Hannah had arrived and had threatened to get worse later had gone. Much of the anxiety had left the faces of Rob and Millie and even the boys were all still grinning, even when faced with imminent transport to hospital.

It didn't take long to sort out the transport arrangements. Mike would travel in the ambulance with Hal and Jimmy. Shane demanded to travel with Ryan in the Jeep.

'You can't do that,' Millie said. 'You'd better wait for the other ambulance. You've got a hole in your guts.'

'It's pretty superficial, luckily,' Ryan told her. 'It's going to need a good clean-out and examination under local, but I don't see any harm in Shane riding in the Jeep to start with, anyway. We can meet the other ambulance on the road and transfer him then.'

'Guess that'll be quicker.' Millie waved at Mike as he climbed into the back of the ambulance. 'You'd better get back in time to get your glad rags on, eh?'

Hannah was in the backseat of the Jeep again and Ryan kept up an easy conversation with Shane, interspersed with the occasional query and frequent glance that let Hannah know how closely he was monitoring the lad's condition.

They got back to Crocodile Creek before a rendezvous with the second ambulance. Hannah gave herself a mental shake when she realised that she was disappointed. It wouldn't do to be shut in the confines of a vehicle with no company other than Ryan's, she told herself firmly. It would make it impossible not to feel the strength of the connection that daylight and even a semi-professional working environment had failed to dent.

Disturbingly, it seemed to have become stronger. Hannah stood back in the emergency department of Crocodile Creek Hospital after doing a handover for Jimmy. When Ryan finished transferring the care of Shane to the hospital staff, he turned to look for her. When he spotted her, standing near the water cooler, he smiled.

A different sort of smile. It went with a questioning expression that suggested he really cared about whether she was OK. Like his tone had been when he'd given her his jacket to keep her warm. It touched something deep inside Hannah and made it impossible not to feel happy.

Dangerous, dangerous territory.

She wasn't going to fall in love with Ryan Fisher.

Hannah simply wasn't going to allow it to happen.

## CHAPTER SEVEN

WHEN had it happened?

*How* had it happened?

It wasn't just the atmosphere. The way Mike and Emily were looking at each other as they walked around the altar, taking their first steps as man and wife. Or the chanting of the priest as he gave them his blessing. Or the collective sigh of approval coming from the packed church pews.

There was no question it *had* happened, however.

With her arms full of the white silk train of Emily's dress and the soft tulle of her veil, Hannah was walking very slowly, her arm touching Ryan's as he held the silk ribbons joining the wreaths on the heads of the bridal couple. They got a little tangled at the last corner and there was a momentary pause.

And Ryan looked at her.

There could be no mistaking that sensation of free-fall. The feeling that all the cells in her body were charged with some kind of static electricity and were desperately seeking a focus for their energy.

Or that the focus was to be found in the depths of the dark eyes that were so close to her own. This was a connection that transcended anything remotely physical. The caress of that eye contact lasted only a heartbeat but Hannah knew it would haunt her for life.

It was a moment of truth.

A truth she hadn't expected.

One she most certainly didn't want.

She was in love with Ryan Fisher. She could… incredibly…imagine that this was a ceremony to join *them* in matrimony, not Mike and Emily and the notion only increased that delicious sensation.

Fortunately, Hannah had a huge armful of fabric she could clutch. It brought back memories of the cuddly blanket Susie had dragged around with her for years as a small child, much to Hannah's disgust. The fleecy square had become smaller and smaller over the years and was finally abandoned but somehow the last piece had emerged just after their father had died and Susie had slept with it under her pillow and had genuinely seemed to derive comfort from the limp rag.

Hannah had never needed an inanimate object for comfort.

Until now.

How stupid had it been to go to bed with Ryan?

She *knew* she didn't do one-night stands. She had always believed that that kind of intimacy should be reserved for a relationship that meant something because it was too hard to separate physical and emotional involvement.

Had her subconscious tricked her into believing that, for once, she could do just that? Or had she known all along that her attraction to Ryan had only needed a push to become something far deeper and she had been drawn towards it as inevitably as her mother and sister had been drawn to involvement with the Richards? Had she despised his flirting because, deep down, she had been jealous?

Stupid, stupid, stupid!

How horrified would Ryan be if he guessed how she was feeling? Or, worse, would he take advantage of it, in the Richards style, making the most of having some female fall at his feet—just until he got bored and moved on to a more exciting playground?

Any of those wayward thoughts, generated by the chaos and excitement of the afternoon's preparation for this ceremony, of allowing her one-night stand to become a one-weekend stand had to be squashed.

This had all the makings of a painful ending already. If even a tiny bit more was added to the way Hannah was feeling, it could be just as disastrous as spending weeks or months in a relationship, only to have it end. She might have had no intention of making an emotional investment but something had been automatically deducted from her account without her realising.

Hannah liked that analogy. It wasn't possible to withdraw the sum but she could, at least, stop throwing good money after bad and pull the plug.

Firmly enough to break the chain so she could throw it away.

Facing the congregation as they made their final circuit, Hannah looked up, finally confident she had control again. There was a woman in the second row in the most extraordinary hat she had ever seen. A vast purple creation with bright pink artificial flowers, like giant gerberas, around its brim.

In front of the hat sat Mike's mother, a handkerchief pressed to her face to mop up her tears of joy. His father was using his sleeve to wipe his. Beside them sat a little row of children—the pageboys and flower girls who had done a wonderful job of petal-strewing and had had to sit quietly for the more serious part of the proceedings.

As a sensible insurance policy, Susie sat at the end of

the pew, hemming the children in, her crutches propped in front of her, and beside her, in the aisle, was Charles in his wheelchair with one of the flower girls sitting on his lap. The adults were both smiling happily but there was an almost wistful element in both their expressions.

It *had* been a gorgeous service. Sophia must be thrilled that everything had gone so perfectly despite the worry that the worsening weather that afternoon had caused.

Not that any of the bridal party had had time to fret. Kylie, the gum-chewing, self-confessed gossip queen, had worked like a Trojan to make them all as beautiful as possible. Hannah had been startled by how she looked with her soft, natural curls bouncing on her shoulders and more make-up than she would normally have worn. By the time she was encased in her peach silk, sheath dress with the big flower at the base of a plunging halter neckline that matched the explosion of froth at knee level and the sleeveless, silver bolero jacket, Hannah felt almost as gorgeous as Emily looked in her cloud of white lace and flowers.

The men had peach silk bow ties to match the bridesmaids' dresses and silver waistcoats to match their jackets. Hannah hadn't been wrong in thinking they would look irresistibly handsome in their dark suits and white dress shirts. And Ryan, of course, was the best looking of the lot, with his long, lean frame encased in tailored elegance and his dark hair groomed to keep the waves in place. Even a very recent shave hadn't been enough to remove the dark shadow, however, and Hannah couldn't help remembering the scratch of his face that morning on some very tender areas of her skin.

With some difficulty, she dragged her thoughts back to the present. Yes. It had been an over-the-top, fairy-tale wedding ceremony for two people who were obviously very deeply in love and that had the potential to make any single person like Susie or Charles Wetherby reflect on what was missing from their own lives.

It had to be contributing a lot to Hannah's own heightened emotional state. With a bit of luck, she would see things quite differently once they were away from the church.

It was nearly time for the bridal procession. Hannah could see Charles moving his wheelchair and Susie whispering to the children to give them their instructions. They would come at the end of the procession after each pair of bridesmaids and their male counterparts had moved into the aisle. Hannah's partner was, of course, Ryan. She would have to take his arm at least until they got to the foyer, where she would need both hands to help Emily with her veil.

It might take all twelve available bridesmaids' hands, judging by the howl of the wind that could now be heard over the trumpet music. The blast of air inside that came as someone opened the main door of the church was enough to catch Emily's veil and threaten to tear it from her head. The chandelier overhead rattled alarmingly and a crashing sound brought a gasp from everybody standing to watch the procession.

People were craning their necks to see what had happened but they were staring in different directions.

'It was the flowers!' someone near Hannah exclaimed. 'Look!'

Hannah looked. She could see the huge vase of exquisitely arranged peach and white blooms that had toppled from its pedestal near the altar. A large puddle was spreading out from the mound of scattered blooms amongst the shards of broken china.

'No, it came from outside,' someone else shouted. 'Everybody, sit down!'

The priest was looking as alarmed as his congregation. Hannah caught a glimpse of Sophia crossing herself as the priest hurried down the side aisle. Another loud splintering noise was heard as he reached the foyer and his robes were whipping around his legs.

'Close the door,' they heard him order. He came back to where Emily and Mike had halted a few seconds later. 'There are slates coming off the roof,' he reported. 'You can't go out that way.'

A buzz of consternation rippled through the crowded pews. What was happening? Was this a bad omen for the bridal couple? The noise level continued to increase as the priest spoke to Mike and Emily, pointing towards another door at one side of the church.

'You'll have to go out through the vestry. It's not safe this way.'

'No, no, no!' Sophia was powering down the side aisle, gesticulating wildly. Hannah saw a pretty young woman in a dark blue dress with a matching ribbon in her curly hair get up hurriedly to follow her. 'They can't go backwards,' Sophia cried. 'It's bad luck!'

A chorus of assent came from the congregation nearby. The priest was looking deeply concerned and even Mike and Emily exchanged worried glances.

'How about "take two"?' Ryan suggested calmly. 'We'll push rewind. You guys go back to the altar, have another snog and then go down the side and out the vestry door. That way, you won't be going backwards before you leave the church.'

'How about it, Ma?'

'It's a great idea,' the young woman beside Sophia said firmly. 'Isn't it, Mrs P.?'

'I don't know. I really don't know. This is bad....'

'Don't cry, Ma,' Mike ordered. 'Have you got a spare hanky there, Grace?'

The sound of more slates crashing into the courtyard decided the matter. As one body, the bridal party turned and moved swiftly back towards the altar. The sound of spitting for luck from everybody at the end of the pews was clearly audible despite continuing, excited conversation.

'Hey!' Ryan leaned towards Hannah. 'Aren't you supposed to be hanging on my arm?'

'I don't think we rehearsed this bit.' But Hannah obligingly took the arm being offered.

'I haven't had a chance to tell you but you look fabulous in pink.'

'It's peach, not pink.'

The second kiss that Mike and Emily shared in front of the altar was a little more hurried than the first. They were all aware of the priest now standing by the vestry door, virtually wringing his hands with anxiety. He wanted his church emptied, preferably without anyone being decapitated by flying slates.

Sophia looked as though she would benefit from smelling salts. Unplanned happenings were threatening to disrupt the most carefully orchestrated wedding that Crocodile Creek was likely to experience.

The loose slates weren't the only surprise. Hannah was close behind the bride and groom as the priest opened the vestry door and there, in front of them, was a couple locked in a rather passionate embrace.

It had to be that girl, Georgie, she had seen at the airport. Hannah would have recognised those red stiletto shoes anywhere.

Ryan nudged her. 'Isn't that Alistair—that American neurosurgeon?'

'Yes, I think so.'

'Seems like they've been having their own little ceremony.'

'Mmm.' What was it about this place? Something in the tropical air? Romance seemed to be around every corner.

Maybe *that* was the problem. She'd get over Ryan in a flash once she was breathing nice clean, sensible New Zealand air again. Not that there was time to think even that far into the future. Some of the male guests had braved the front entrance to make sure it was safe to leave the church from this side. Vehicles were being brought right to the door and the mammoth task of shifting the whole congregation to the Athina for the reception was under way.

Any hint of blue patches between the boiling clouds had long gone. It looked as though another heavy, squally rain shower was imminent.

'Quickly, quickly,' Sophia said to everyone passing her at the door. She had clearly abandoned her carefully thought-out transport arrangements and was planning to move everybody as fast as possible. 'We must get home!'

She made Emily, Mike, Ryan, Hannah and Susie squeeze into the first of the limousines. 'The bride mustn't get wet!' she warned. 'It's bad luck!'

Sophia spat three times as Emily and Mike climbed into the spacious rear of the car. What with the huge wedding dress and then Susie's crutches, there wasn't much room left for Ryan and Hannah. They ended up on the same side as Susie with Hannah in the middle. A crutch pressed against her thigh on one side but that discomfort paled in comparison to the disturbing effect of having such close contact with Ryan's thigh on the other side.

'Well, that was fun.' Mike had a huge grin on his face. Then he turned to Emily and his smile faded before he kissed her tenderly.

'Don't mind us,' Ryan drawled.

Mike surfaced reluctantly. 'You should try this some time, mate. It's not that bad.'

'Mmm.' Ryan's sidelong glance at Hannah involved a subtle quirk of an eyebrow. *I know,* the glance said. *I've enjoyed that particular pastime quite recently myself.*

'Hey!' Mike was grinning again. 'If you got around to it soon enough, we could give these suits another airing. I'll return the favour and be *your* best man.'

'I'll keep that in mind.'

Why did Ryan choose that moment to slide his hand under the peachy froth of Hannah's skirt to find her hand? To hold it and give a conspiratorial kind of squeeze?

Had he got some crazy notion himself during that ceremony—as she had? Was Hannah going to be tricked into believing she was a candidate for his bride?

*No!*

She pulled her hand free but the gesture lost any significance because the driver of the limousine chose precisely that moment to slam on his brakes and she, Ryan and Susie tumbled forward.

'Ouch!' Susie cried.

'Are you all right?' Ryan helped her back onto the leather seat.

Mike slid the glass partition behind his head open. 'What's going on?'

'Rubbish bag flying around in this wind,' the driver told him. 'Sorry—but it landed on the windscreen and I couldn't see a thing. You guys OK back there?'

'Fine,' they all chorused.

Including Hannah. She *was* fine now that Ryan wasn't holding her hand. Now that they'd all been shaken out of the romantic stupor emanating from the bridal couple.

'Crikey!' The car slowed again as it crossed the old wooden bridge into the cove. 'If that water comes up any more, this'll get washed out to sea.'

The creek was more like a raging torrent and the wind was whipping up small waves on its swift-moving surface. The strings of fairy-lights adorning the exterior of the Athina were seriously challenging the staples holding them in place and Mike heroically gathered Emily's dress together to scoop his bride into his arms and carry her the short distance from the car to the restaurant doors.

Huge, fat drops of rain were starting to fall but Mike moved fast enough to prevent Emily's dress getting damp.

'Thank goodness for that.' She laughed. 'Sophia will be feeling my dress the moment she walks in.'

'Let me check.' Mike ran his hands down the embroidered bodice of the dress and then yanked Emily close. Laughing again, she wrapped her arms around his neck and lifted her face for a kiss.

Ryan's voice was close to Hannah's ear. Too close.

'They have a good rapport, don't they? Just like us.'

Hannah swallowed hard. Even his voice was enough to stir desire. A sharp yearning that was painful because she couldn't allow herself to respond.

'Later,' Ryan murmured. The word was spoken too softly for anyone else to overhear.

*'No!'*

She hadn't expected her response to come out with such vehemence but the promise Ryan's word had contained was too much. *Pull the plug,* her brain was screaming. *Now!*

The momentary freezing on Ryan's part was strong enough for Hannah to sense his shock at the rebuttal but there was no time to try and soften the rejection with any kind of explanation or excuse. The second and third cars from the church had pulled up and Mike's parents spilled out, along with several more clouds of peach-tulled women and dark-suited men.

'Your dress!' Sophia wailed. 'Let me feel your dress, darling! Is it wet?'

'No, it's completely dry. See?' Emily did a twirl in front of the mass of wedding presents piled up in the restaurant entrance.

Mike's father, George Poulos, beamed happily. 'Inside. Everybody inside. Our guests are arriving. It's time to eat, drink and be merry!'

The next hour was a blur of posing for the photographer and then introductions amongst a loud, happy crowd who were determined to ignore the shocking conditions outside. The howl of the wind, the intermittent thunder of rain on the roof and the crash of huge waves on the beach below the restaurant windows were largely drowned out by the enthusiastic live band and even more enthusiastic guests.

Hannah did her best to ignore the rather dark glances that were coming her way from Ryan. It was easy to avoid him by talking to other people. Like Grace, the young nurse with the blue ribbon in her hair.

'It's been my job to try and keep Mrs P. calm,' she told Hannah. Blue eyes that matched her ribbon rolled in mock exasperation. 'As if! Don't be at all surprised if there are a few doves flying around in here later.'

'Plates!' Mike's father carried a stack past them, weaving through a circle of dancers. 'For later,' he threw over his shoulder at Hannah and Grace. 'Don't tell Sophia.'

'I'd better distract her. Excuse me.' Grace hurried away.

'*Opa!*' someone shouted.

A chorus of echoes rippled through the room and Hannah saw a lot of small glasses being raised to lips.

'Ouzo?' A waiter had a tray of the small glasses, as well as the more traditional champagne flutes.

'Maybe later.' Hannah was having trouble trying to keep her head clear enough to remember all the names and she knew she would have to keep it clear to deal with the conversation that was bound to occur with Ryan.

He was right behind the waiter. 'What did you mean, "No"? "No", what?'

'I meant "no" to later,' she said with a resigned sigh.

'But I thought…is something wrong, Hannah?'

'Not at all.' Hannah smiled—reassuringly, she hoped. She would have to work with Ryan. She didn't want to offend him. 'Last night was lovely. Great fun.'

*'Fun?'* Ryan was staring at her. He had no right to look so shocked. Surely *he* did this kind of thing all the time? A bit of fun. Move on.

'This is Harry.' Grace had returned to where Hannah was standing, staring dumbly back at Ryan. 'He's our local policeman here in the cove. Hi.' She smiled at Ryan. 'You did a good job as best man.'

'I do an even better job at dancing.' Ryan's killer smile flashed as he extended his hand. 'Come on, let me show you.'

It was a snub, Hannah realised as Ryan turned away with Grace on his arm without a backwards glance. He *was* offended for some reason.

Harry was staring after the couple as though he didn't approve any more than Hannah did, but then they managed to smile at each other. In fact, it wasn't that difficult for Hannah to smile. A glow of something like pleasure curled within her. He had liked being with her, then. It had been good enough for him to want more.

If she wasn't so weak, she would have wanted it herself. How wonderful would it be to sink into a relationship with someone like Ryan and enjoy it for what it was? An interlude. One that would set the standard for the best that sex and probably companionship could offer. But to do it without losing too much of her heart and soul?

Impossible.

He would wreck her life eventually.

She would end up like her mother, settling for something that was better than nothing. Learning to enjoy fishing.

Or alone, like Susie, unable to find anyone that excited her as much as the first man who had really stolen her heart.

Harry was telling her something. Hannah made an effort to focus on the tall, good-looking man with a flop of black hair and a worried expression.

'I'm trying to keep tabs on what's happening with Willie,' he told her. 'They're making noises about upgrading it from a category 3 to a 4.'

'Is that serious?'

Harry nodded. 'Cyclones are all dangerous. 'Specially Aussie ones—they're known for exhibiting a more erratic path than cyclones in other parts of the world. The higher the number, the more danger they represent. A category 3 is a severe tropical cyclone. You can get wind gusts up to 224 kilometres per hour and can expect roof and structural damage, and a likely power failure.'

'The slates were certainly flying off the church.'

'There's a few people with tarps on their roofs already. They'll lose them if things get any worse.'

'And they're expected to?'

'It's been upgraded to a 4. It's running parallel to the coast at the moment but if it turns west we'll be in trouble.

A 4 has winds up to 279 kilometres per hour. You'll get significant structural damage, dangerous airborne debris and widespread power failures.'

As though to underline Harry's sombre tone, the lights inside the Athina flickered, but there was still enough daylight for it not to matter and they came back on almost immediately.

'I'm with the SES—State Emergency Services,' Harry finished. 'In fact, if you'll excuse me, I should make a call and see what's happening.'

Just as Harry disappeared, Ryan emerged from an animated group of Greek women nearby.

*'Fun?'* he queried with quiet menace. 'Is that all it was for you, Hannah? *Fun?'*

This was disconcerting. She would have expected a shrugged response from Ryan by now. A 'there's plenty more fish in the sea' kind of attitude.

'It *was* fun.' She tried to smile. To break the tension. 'But we both know it could never be any more than that.'

'*Do* we?' Ryan held her gaze. Challenging her. 'Why is that?'

'Oh, come on, Ryan.' Hannah looked for an escape. Someone to talk to. A new introduction. Where was Susie when she needed her? Nothing seemed readily available. They were marooned. A little island of hostility that was keeping all the happy people away with an invisible force field. 'We're not on the same page, remember?'

'Obviously not,' Ryan snapped. 'There I was thinking that we had made a fresh start. The start of something that could actually be meaningful.'

Meaningful? Oh, help! It would be so easy to believe that. Hannah so *wanted* to believe it. To believe *she* could be the one to tame this particular 'bad boy'. To have him love her so much he would be content to settle down and never get bored.

The wheelchair arrived beside them so smoothly neither had noticed.

'I'm Charles Wetherby,' the man said unnecessarily. 'I must apologise for this awful weather Crocodile Creek is turning on for you. I hope you're still managing to enjoy yourselves.'

Hannah had the weird feeling that Charles had known exactly how much they were enjoying themselves and was there to do something to defuse the atmosphere.

Ryan controlled the flash of an ironic smile and managed to introduce both himself and Hannah to Charles without missing a beat.

And then he excused himself, as though he couldn't stand being in Hannah's company any longer.

He was hurt, she realised. She hadn't expected that at all. It was confusing. Why would he be hurt…unless he was being honest. Unless he really had thought there was something meaningful going on.

No. He might think that—for now. He might even believe it long enough for Hannah to trust it, but he was a type, wasn't he? He was, what, in his mid-thirties? At least a couple of years older than she was, given his professional experience. If he was into commitment he wouldn't still be playing the field. And what about Michaela? Was she someone who had believed in him and had now been discarded?

Hannah had to paste a smile onto her face to talk to Charles.

'You look so like Susie,' he was saying. 'It's a real treat. Must be wonderful to have a sibling that you're so close to.'

'It is.'

'Uncle Charles! Look at me! I'm dancing!'

The small blonde flower girl who had been sitting on Charles's knee during the ceremony was part of a circle of dancers, between two adults. She wasn't watching the steps any more because her head was twisted in Hannah's direction and she had a huge smile on her face.

'This way, Lily.' Mike's sister, Maria, had hold of one of Lily's hands. 'We go this way now.'

*'Opa!'* The cry to signal a new round of toasting the bridal couple rang out.

'Ouzo?'

'No, thanks.' Hannah shook her head at the attentive waiter. Lily had given her an excuse to watch the dancers and Ryan was now part of the circle. So was Mike. And then the circle disintegrated as Sophia bustled through.

'Eat! Eat! The food will be getting cold.'

Ryan and Mike took no notice. With an arm around each other's shoulders and their other arms extended, they were stepping in a dance of their own. Happy. Relaxed. The bond of a deep friendship was obvious to everyone and they all approved. They were clapping and stamping their feet in time with the music and calling encouragement.

And then George was on the dance floor, a plate in each hand.

'No!' Sophia cried.

But the sound of smashing crockery only brought a roar of approval and more people back to the dance floor.

Hannah turned away. She spotted Susie sitting with a very pregnant woman. They had plates of food from the buffet.

Not that Hannah felt hungry. Watching Mike and Ryan dance had left her with a curious sense of loss. How long had Ryan known his best friend? Ten years? More? Their bond appeared unshakable. Mike trusted him completely.

But Mike wasn't a woman. The ending of a friendship, however close, could never destroy someone as much as the ending of the most intimate relationship it was possible to have.

It was really quite straightforward so why was her heart winning the battle with her head right now?

Why did she feel this sense of loss? As though she had just made a terrible mistake?

Because it was already too late. She was in love with this man.

She was already prepared to believe in him.

And if he gave her another chance, she would take it.

Take the risk.

Do whatever it took to spend as much time as possible with him. In bed and out of it.

The rest of her life, even.

# CHAPTER EIGHT

THIS had to be the ultimate putdown.

And he had only himself to blame.

It had only been one night. Hannah Jackson was only one of hundreds of women Ryan had met since he'd grown up enough to be interested in the opposite sex. Thousands, even, and he'd dated a fair few in those early years. Slept with enough to know how rare it was to find a woman who could be both intellectually and physically stimulating.

He could have dealt with that attraction, however powerful it had been, when that was all it was. Moved on with maybe just a shrug of regret. But Hannah had taken down that barrier. Taken him by the hand and shown him a place he had never been to before. A place he didn't want to leave.

And now she was shoving him out. Had put that barrier back up and….it *hurt,* dammit! Nobody had ever treated him like this before—and she'd accused *him* of being shallow? What reason did she have? She might have been hurt in the past, he reminded himself. Some bastard might have treated her badly enough to leave scars that hadn't healed yet.

No. It didn't matter how good the reason might be. Or how fresh the scars. Why the hell would he set himself up for another kick in the guts like the one she'd just delivered? With a smile, no less. A damning with faint praise.

*Fun?* Like a night out? A party? A game of tennis?

'What's up, mate?' Mike's fingers dug into his shoulder. 'You look like you're at a funeral, not a wedding.'

'Sorry. Miles away.'

'Not in a happy place, by the look of that scowl. Forget it. Come and eat. The lamb's wonderful and Ma will be force-feeding you soon if she doesn't see you holding a plate.'

'Good idea. And I think a drink or two is overdue as well.'

'Just don't get trollied before you have to make that speech and tell everyone how wonderful I am.'

Ryan laughed. 'More like seeing how many stories of your disreputable past I can dredge up. What time am I on?'

'Just before the cake-cutting. I think Ma's got it down for about 8:30 p.m.'

'Cool. Gives me half an hour to see how much I can remember. What was the name of that girl in Bali? The one with all the tattoos?'

'Don't you dare! You might get Em worried I haven't settled down.'

'And have you?'

'No question, mate. I'll never look at another woman. I've found the one for me. Oh, great—a slow song! Catch you later. Go and eat. I'm hanging out for a waltz with my wife.'

Lucky man, Ryan thought, watching Emily's face light up as Mike reached her and the way she seemed to float dreamily in his arms as they found a space on the dance floor.

Lucky, lucky man.

The lights had flickered more than once in the last hour but this time they went out and stayed out.

Hannah, sitting with Susie, the very pregnant doctor

called Christina and her gorgeous, dark-skinned husband Joe, who had turned out to be a fellow New Zealander, had also been watching the bridal couple dance. And Harry and Grace, who were dancing towards the edge of the crowd. And the woman who hadn't taken off that extraordinary purple hat with the huge flowers.

'That's Dora for you,' Susie was saying. 'She's so proud of that hat she'll probably wear it when she's polishing floors at the hospital for the next week or—'

She stopped as the room plunged into semi-darkness. The candles on tables provided only a dim light that would take a few moments to adjust to. People were just shadowy figures. The dancing had stopped and there was an uncertain kind of milling about, both on the dance floor and around the tables. The couple who were not moving at all in the corner caught more than Hannah's attention.

'Who *is* that?' Susie whispered loudly. 'I can't see in this light.'

'Whoever they are, they seem to like each other.' Joe grinned.

Susie winked at Hannah. 'Yeah. I'd say they've got a pretty good rapport all right.'

Hannah elbowed her sister. A reminder of what had started this small life crisis she was experiencing was not welcome.

They found out who the male of the pair was almost immediately, as Charles Wetherby rolled past their table accompanied by a young police officer who was holding a candelabrum. The flames on several candles were being dragged backwards to leave little smoke trails due to the speed with which the men were moving.

'Harry Blake!' The tone was urgent enough for conversation to die amongst everyone within earshot and the reaction to it spread rapidly. A lot of people could hear what

Charles had to say as Harry seemed to attempt to shield the woman he'd been kissing so passionately by steering her further into the dark corner and then striding forward to meet the hospital's medical director.

'Bus accident up on the mountain road,' Hannah heard him say.

'I think it was *Grace* he was kissing,' Susie whispered. 'Woo-hoo!'

'Shh!' Hannah warned. 'This sounds serious.'

Joe's chair scraped as he got up and moved towards the knot of men. Christina's bottom lip was caught between her teeth and she laid a protective hand, instinctively, on her swollen belly. Tension and urgency were radiating strongly from their centre of focus.

Everybody who could hear was listening avidly. Others were trying to find out what was being said.

'What's going on?' someone called.

'Why are the police here?'

'Why haven't the lights come back on?'

'The hospital's four-wheel drive is on its way here to pick up whatever hospital staff you think you might need on site. Have you seen Grace? If we've got to set up a triage post and then get people off the side of the mountain, we'll probably need an SES crew up there, as well....'

Mike was heading towards the expanding knot of male figures. So was Ryan. Hannah got to her feet. If this was a major incident, they would need all the medical expertise available.

Charles would be magnificent in any crisis, Hannah decided. So calm. So in touch with what was happening everywhere in his domain.

'We've been on standby to activate a full code black disaster response, thanks to the cyclone watch on Willie,' he told the cluster of medics now around him. 'I'm going to go ahead and push the button. We have no idea how many casualties we might get from this bus but it looks likely we're in for trouble from Willie so it'll give us a few hours' head start. A dry run, if you like.'

'What's happening?' Sophia pushed her way towards Charles. Dora Grubb was not far behind her, the pink flowers on her hat wobbling nervously.

'There's been an accident, Sophia,' Charles said. 'A bus full of people has vanished off the road near Dan Macker's place. Big landslide, thanks to all the rain we've had this week.'

'Oh… *Oh!*' Sophia crossed herself, her face horrified. 'This is bad!'

'I'm going to have to call in all available medical staff, starting with everyone here. Including Mike and Emily. I'm sorry, Sophia.'

*'Oh!'* Sophia looked stricken now. 'But the cake! The speeches!' Then she rallied, visibly pulling herself together. She stood as tall as possible for a short, plump person. 'Of course you need my boy,' she said proudly. 'And our Emily. Who else can look after those poor people if they need an operation? Emily! Darling! Let me help you find something else to wear.'

Hannah looked down at the froth of peach tulle around her knees and on to the flimsy white shoes with the flowers on the toes.

Mike noticed the direction of her glance. 'I've got spare flight suits in our room and Em's probably got a spare set of boots. Ryan? You'd better come and grab a suit, too.'

'Thanks, mate.'

'At least you won't have to roll up the sleeves and legs. Come with me, you guys. Let's get kitted up.'

It was Susie's turn to look stricken. 'I want to help but I'm useless with these crutches!'

'Not at all,' Charles said. 'You can stay with me and Jill. There's a lot of admin we'll need to do at the hospital. Code black means we've got to empty as many beds as we can. Set up a receiving ward. Mobilise stores. Reorganise ED…'

The list was still continuing as Hannah hurried in the wake of Mike and Ryan. She could also hear Dora Grubb talking excitedly to Sophia.

'They'll need food, all these rescue people.'

'We *have* food. Too much food. All this lamb! I'll tell the chef to start making sandwiches.'

It took less than ten minutes for the four young medics to encase themselves in the helicopter service issue overalls.

Emily sighed as she took a glance over her shoulder at the mound of white lace and silk on the bed. 'It was nice while it lasted,' she said, 'being a princess.'

'You'll always be a princess, babe,' Mike assured her. 'And I reckon you know how sexy I think you look in those overalls.'

Hannah carefully avoided looking anywhere close to Ryan's direction. She could understand the look that passed between Mike and Emily because she had stolen a glance at Ryan moments before, when he'd bent to lace up the spare pair of Mike's heavy steel-capped boots, and there had been no danger of him catching her glance.

It was a completely different look to civvies. Or scrubs. Or the white coat that doctors never seemed to bother with any more. He looked taller, somehow. Braver. Ready to get out there and save lives. And there was a very determined tilt to his chin that she hadn't seen before. Tension that visibly knotted the muscles in his jaw.

Was he anticipating a tough job at the scene of the bus crash or was it controlled anger? Directed at her?

Whatever.

Sexy didn't begin to cover how he looked.

Hannah scraped back her carefully combed curls and wound an elastic band to form a ponytail. Would Ryan see *her* as looking adventurous and exciting in these overalls with the huge rolled-up cuffs on the arms and legs?

Not likely.

Especially as he appeared determined not to actually look directly at her at all.

Even in the back of an ambulance a commendably short time later, when they had collected gear and co-ordinated with other personnel at the hospital, he was avoiding anything as personal as direct eye contact.

Mike was with them. Emily had ended up staying behind at the hospital to oversee the set-up and preparation of Theatres. Because of the weather conditions, with injured people exposed to the rain and wind, she needed to organise fluid warming devices and forced-air warmers on top of making sure she was ready to administer a general anaesthetic at short notice.

A second ambulance was following with another crew and all Crocodile Creek's available fire appliances had gone on ahead. Police had been first on scene, and by the time Hannah arrived, the road was lined with vehicles—a chain of flashing lights they had glimpsed from miles away as they'd sped up the sometimes tortuous curves of the mountain road. Lights that had haloes around them right now thanks to the heavy curtain of rain.

A portable triage tent was erected on the road to one side of the massive obstacle of mud, rocks and vegetation. Guy ropes had it anchored but the inflatable structure was looking alarmingly precarious in the high wind and its sides were being sucked in and then ballooning out almost instantly with a loud snapping sound.

The generators used to fill the outlines of the tent with compressed air were still running, powering lights, including some that were being directed downhill from the point where large skid marks were visible. There was more noise from the fire engines whose crews were rolling out winch cables from the front of the heavy vehicles. Pneumatic tools like the Jaws of Life were being primed and tested. As a background they were already tuning out, the wind howled through the treetops of the dark rainforest around them.

Harry Blake, wearing a fluorescent jacket that designated him as scene commander, met the ambulance, framed by the back doors Mike pushed open and latched.

'Who's in charge?' he queried briskly.

'I'm liaising with the medical director at the ED.' Mike clipped his radio to his belt. 'What frequency are we using on site?'

'Channel 8.'

Mike nodded. 'Channel 6 is the hospital link.' He leapt out of the back of the ambulance. 'I'll go down and triage with these two doctors and then we'll deploy all the other medical crews we get. What's it looking like down there?'

'It's a bloody mess,' Harry said grimly. 'The bus must have come off the road at speed and it rolled on the way down. The windows have popped out and we've got people and belongings all over the place. Some of the seats have come adrift inside and there's people trapped, but we can't get inside until the fire boys get a line or two onto the bus.'

'It's not stable?' Mike was sliding his arms into the straps of his backpack containing medical supplies.

'Hell, no. It could slide farther, especially if it keeps raining like this.'

Hannah and Ryan were out of the ambulance now, standing beside Mike. 'Don't forget your helmets,' he reminded them. Then his attention was back on Harry. 'Any fatalities?'

'At least one.' Harry raised his voice to a shout to be heard as they started walking and got closer to the generators. 'There's a guy who's been thrown clear and then caught under the bus. He's at the front and we think he's probably the driver. We won't be able to shift him until we can jack up the front corner somehow.'

'The fire guys going to be able to use their cutting gear down there? Is it safe to have them clambering around?'

'We've got nets anchored on the slope. It's not too bad for climbing. There's an SES crew down there at the moment, trying to clear the scene of everybody who's able to move.'

'How many are we dealing with?' Ryan had jammed his hard hat on and was pulling the strap tight.

Harry shook his head. 'Haven't been able to do a head count yet. There's injured people over quite a wide area. We think there's two or three still trapped in the bus, from what we can see. One of the passengers who's not hurt thinks the bus was quite full. There's about ten people we can bring up now. Could be fifteen or twenty still down there needing attention.'

Mike and Ryan shared a glance. This was huge. It was going to stretch their resources and everybody's skills.

'Let's do it.' Ryan pulled on latex examination gloves and then heavier ones for climbing. He gave Mike a thumbs-up and Mike responded with a terse nod and another shared glance. They had faced difficult situations before. They were more than ready to tackle this one. Together.

Hannah felt oddly excluded. Even when Mike put her after Ryan and before himself to protect her as she climbed down the steep, slippery slope, she didn't really feel a part of this small team.

Ryan hated her. He didn't want her there.

Within the first few metres of their climb, however, any thoughts of personality clashes or anything else that could affect a working relationship were forgotten.

A woman lay, moaning. 'My leg,' she groaned. 'I can't get any further. Help…'

This was an initial triage. No more than thirty seconds could be allocated for any patient to check for life-threatening injuries like uncontrolled haemorrhage or a blocked airway. Mike had triage tags in his pocket. Big, brightly coloured labels with an elastic loop that would alert all other personnel to the priority the victims had for medical attention. This woman was conscious and talking. It took less than thirty seconds for Ryan to examine her.

'Fractured femur. Closed. No external bleeding. Airway's clear.'

Mike produced a yellow label. Attention needed but second priority. 'Someone will be with you as soon as possible,' he reassured the woman as they moved on. 'We've got to check everybody else first and then we'll be back.'

'But it *hurts*…Oh-h-h….'

It was hard, leaving her to keep descending the slope. A huddle of people near the base of the nets were bypassed. They were all mobile and being looked after by SES people. Grace was there, organising the clearance of the less injured from the scene. Mike gave her a handful of green triage tags that designated the lowest priority. Hannah saw a young Asian couple clinging to each other, looking terrified, and she could hear someone talking in a foreign language that sounded European. Had the bus been full of tourists? It could make their job more difficult if they couldn't communicate with their patients.

A young woman lay, unconscious, against the base of a huge eucalyptus tree.

'Hello, can you hear me?' Hannah pinched the woman's ear lobe. 'Non-responsive,' she told Mike. She laid a hand on the woman's neck and another on her belly. 'She's breathing. Good carotid pulse. Tachy.'

The elastic of a pink triage label went over her wrist. Highest priority. This case was urgent, with the potential to be saved and the likelihood of rapid deterioration if left. They moved on.

'There's one over here,' a fire officer yelled at them. 'He's making a weird noise.'

'Occluded airway.' Mike repositioned the man's head and the gurgling sound ceased. Another pink tag.

Winch hooks were being attached to the bus. There were no big lights down here and the rescue workers had to make do with the lamps on their helmets. A curious strobe effect to viewing the disaster was evident as lights intersected and inspected different areas. It made it easier to deal with, Hannah decided, because you could only see a patch at a time. A single patient, a broken window, dented metal, broken tree branches, strewn belongings and luggage.

Just the top half of the unfortunate man who had been caught beneath the front wheel of the bus. It took only a moment to confirm the extinction of life and give the man a white tag to signify a fatality so that nobody would waste time by checking him again.

'Don't go downhill from the bus.' A fire officer with a winch hook in his hand shouted the warning. 'We haven't got this thing stable yet.'

The doors of the bus were blocked because it was lying, tilted, on that side. The emergency hatch at the back was open, however, and must have been how some of the less injured had escaped the wreckage.

Mike saw Ryan assessing the access. 'Not yet, buddy,' he said firmly. 'You can just wait until it's safer.'

*Safer,* Hannah noted. Not *safe.* It could never be really safe to do something like this, could it? And yet Ryan was clearly frustrated by having to hold back.

Hannah shook her head to clear the water streaming down her face from looking up at the hatch. She was soaked now and the wind was chilling. She flexed increasingly stiff fingers and cast a glance at her colleagues.

There was certainly no doubting Ryan's commitment to his work and the people he cared for. How many ED specialists would be prepared to work in conditions like this? To risk their own lives without a moment's hesitation to try and save others?

Mike might have been off the mark in making people think Ryan was some kind of saint, but he hadn't been wrong in advertising him as a hero. They both were. The way these two men worked together suggested they had been in situations before that had not been dissimilar. There was a calm confidence about the way they worked that was contagious.

Like Ryan's courage in that plane turbulence had been.

What if she couldn't redress the antipathy Ryan now held towards her and the one who didn't win that consultancy position in ED felt obliged to go and work elsewhere? If she never had the chance to work with him again?

The sense of loss she had experienced watching him dance with Mike came back strongly enough to distract Hannah for several seconds. Was it always going to haunt her? Did she have to be ruthlessly squashed at frequent intervals in order for her to perform to her best ability? Like now?

Hannah continued the triage exercise with grim determination. They found another five people with fractures and lacerations who needed yellow tags. One more pink tag for a partially amputated arm and severe bleeding. An SES worker had been doing a great job of keeping pressure on the wound. Then they were given the all-clear to check out the bus.

'Not you, Hannah,' Mike stated. 'You can check in with the SES guys. Make sure we haven't missed anyone. Get someone to check further afield as well. We've got debris over a wide area and injured people could have moved or even fallen further down the slope.'

Hannah moved to find someone to talk to but she couldn't help stopping for a moment. Turning back to watch as the two men climbed into the bus.

Turning back again a moment later, when alarmed shouting heralded a noticeable shift in the position of the bus.

'Oh, my God…' Was the bus going to move with the extra weight? Slide and possibly roll again down the side of this mountain?

Remove any possibility of repairing the rift she'd created with Ryan?

Remove Ryan from her life with the ultimate finality of death?

*'No-o-o!'*

It was a quiet, desperate sound, snatched away and disguised by the howl of the wind. If it was a prayer, it was answered. Having taken up some slack from one of the winch cables, the movement stopped. Mike actually leaned out a broken window with his thumb and forefinger forming the 'O' of a signal that they were OK.

It was only then that Hannah realised she had been holding her breath. A couple of minutes later and Ryan and Mike emerged from the bus.

'One pink, one yellow, one white,' Mike reported. 'One's unconscious and another's trapped by a seat.' He reached for his radio. Medical crews could now be co-ordinated, specific tasks allocated, patients treated and evacuated. The most seriously injured patients would be assigned a doctor who would stabilise and then escort them to hospital.

Hannah was joined by a paramedic by the name of Mario, issued a pack of gear and assigned the case of the woman who had been pink-ticketed at the base of the eucalyptus tree. Mike and Ryan were going to work on the pink-ticket patient inside the bus. Hannah watched them climb inside again. A scoop stretcher was passed in along with the pack of resuscitation gear by firemen who then waited, knowing their muscle would be needed to assist with extrication.

Once again Hannah felt that sense of loss as Ryan vanished from view and this time she couldn't quite shake it off.

She *needed* him, dammit! This was so far out of her comfort zone, it wasn't funny. The rain might be easing but she was still soaked and cold and her fingers felt uselessly stiff and clumsy.

The effort to concentrate seemed harder than it had ever been. Hannah was trying to recall the workshop she'd attended at a conference once, on the practice of emergency medicine in a hostile environment. Control of the airway was the first priority, of course, with cervical spine control if appropriate.

It was appropriate in this case. Hannah's gloved hand came away streaked with blood after touching the back of the young woman's head. Had she been thrown clear of the bus and hit the tree she now lay beside? If the blow had been enough to cause her loss of consciousness, it had potentially caused a neck injury as well.

'I need a collar,' she told Mario. She placed her hand, side on, on the woman's shoulder, making a quick estimate of the distance to her jaw line. 'A short neck, please. And a dressing for this head wound.'

It was difficult, trying to assess how well their patient was breathing. Hard to see, given the narrow focus of the beam of light from her helmet. Hard to feel with her cold hands and impossible to hear with the shouting and noise of machinery. And over it all, the savage wind still howled. Large tree branches cracked ominously and small pieces of debris like broken branches flew through the air, occasionally striking Hannah in the back or hitting the hard helmet she wore with a bang, magnified enough to make her jump more than once.

'I don't think we can assess her for equal air entry until we get her into an ambulance, at least,' she said. 'She's certainly breathing on her own without any respiratory distress I can pick up.'

Which was a huge relief. While this woman was probably unconscious enough to be able to be intubated without a drug regime, the lecturer at that conference had discussed the difficulties of intubation in a situation like this. Often, the technique of cricothyroidotomy was more appropriate and that wasn't something Hannah wanted to attempt with limited light and frozen fingers.

IV access was more manageable. Hannah placed a large-bore cannula in the woman's forearm and started fluids. She remembered to use extra tape to secure both the cannula and the IV fluid lines. The lecturer's jocular warning was what she'd remembered most clearly about that workshop. "If it can fall out," he'd said, 'it *will* fall out.'

Mario had the expertise and strength to move the woman onto a backboard and strap her securely onto it. And then the firemen took over, inching their way up the mountainside with the help of ropes and the net.

Moving to follow them, the beam of Hannah's light caught something that made her stoop. She picked the object up. It was a shoe. A rather well-worn sneaker with a hole in the top and what looked like a picture of a bright orange fish done in felt pen or something similar. What startled her was its size. It was small.

Very small.

A child's shoe.

But they hadn't come across any children in their triage, had they? Hannah had the awful thought that it could be the fatality inside the bus. But maybe the owner of this shoe was uninjured? Not seen amongst that huddle of frightened people who had been waiting for help up the slope? Hannah certainly hoped so. And if they were, they might have one bare foot and be grateful to see that shoe. Hannah stuffed it into the large pocket on the front of her overalls.

It wouldn't have been easy for a child to climb, even with the hand- and footholds the net provided. They were wet now and very muddy. Hannah slipped, more than once, and had to save herself by grabbing the netting or a tree root or branch.

How could fifty metres seem such a long way? And how long had they been on scene? Certainly no more than an hour, but she felt as though she had just completed a full night shift in the ED and a busy one at that.

The third time she slipped, Hannah might well have fallen but she was caught by her arm in a vice-like grip.

'Are you OK?' Ryan asked.

It had to be her imagination that she could hear the

same kind of caring in the query that she had heard in the car on the way to Wygera that morning. An aeon ago. In her current state it was enough to bring the sting of tears to her eyes. She blinked them away.

'Yeah…thanks…'

'Not easy, this stuff, is it?' Ryan was climbing beside her. Just below them, the scoop stretcher containing his patient was making slow progress upwards. 'How's your woman?'

'Still unconscious but breathing. A head injury but I have no idea how bad it is yet.'

'You'll be able to do a more thorough assessment in the ambulance. We won't be far behind you if you run into trouble. Mike says they're going to stage departures so we arrive at the ED at about six-minute intervals. Just pull over and keep your lights on and we'll stop to help.'

'Thanks,' Hannah said again. Professional assistance but at least he was talking to her. She was almost at the top of the slope now. A fire officer had his hand out to help her onto the road and the noise level increased markedly. She could still hear Ryan's call, though.

'Hey, Hannah?'

'Yeah?'

'You're doing a fantastic job. Well done.'

Those tears were even closer all of a sudden. They couldn't be allowed to spill. Hannah clenched her fists as she got to her feet on the road and her hand struck her bulky pocket. She peered down at Ryan.

'Hey, did you come across any children in the bus?'

'No. Why?'

'I found a shoe. A kid's size shoe.' She pulled it from her pocket. 'See?'

'Could have come from anywhere,' Ryan said. 'Maybe there's a kid amongst the green tickets.'

'Yes, I thought of that. I'll check with Grace later.'

'It could have come from spilled luggage as well. Or even been thrown away. Looks pretty old.'

'Hannah?' Mario, the paramedic, was calling. She could see the backboard supporting her patient being lifted into the back of an ambulance. 'We're nearly ready to roll.'

'On my way.' Hannah turned to give Ryan a smile of thanks for his help but he wasn't watching. He had already turned back to his patient.

'I'll take over the ventilations there, Mike. You've done a fantastic job up the hill.'

A fantastic job. Like her. So the praise hadn't really been personal, had it? The doors of the ambulance slammed shut behind her and someone thumped on the back to give the officer driving the signal to go. Hannah took a deep breath.

'Let's get some oxygen on, Mario. A non-rebreather mask at ten litres a minute. And I want a slight head tilt on the stretcher. Can we do that with a backboard in the way?'

'Sure, we'll just use a pillow under this end.'

'Let's get some definitive baseline measurements, too. Blood pressure, heart rate and rhythm, oxygen saturation.' She pulled a stethoscope from the kit. 'I'm going to check her breathing again.'

It felt good to be on the move towards a fully equipped emergency department and hospital. Hannah would feel far more in control then. Far less likely to be thrown off balance by overly emotional reactions to someone else's words or the way they looked at her. Or *didn't* look at her.

It helped to know that Ryan would be on the road within minutes, though. Travelling in the same direction she was. Sharing the same experiences and goals that had arrived in their lives so unexpectedly. To get through this ordeal and help as many people as possible.

They were on the same page now, weren't they?

What a shame it was just too late.

## CHAPTER NINE

THE contrast couldn't have been greater.

The Poulos wedding had been a happy circus. Crocodile Creek Base Hospital was hosting a miserable one.

Injured, bewildered people filled the cubicles and sat on chairs. A moving sea of professional staff was doing everything necessary. Doctors, nurses, clerks, radiographers and orderlies were doing their jobs. And more. The fact that it was late at night and the majority of people here were not rostered on duty meant nothing. A disaster response had been activated and there was nobody associated with this medical community who wasn't prepared to do whatever they could to help.

There was a lot to be done. Hannah's case was the first serious one to arrive so she had the initial advantage of all the staff she could possibly need to assist.

Luke hadn't yet gone to the receiving ward where he would be available on the surgical team, along with Cal and Alistair. Emily was still in the department as well, because minor cases needing surgery were going to have to wait until all the majors had been dealt with. They both came to assist Hannah. Charles wasn't far behind.

'You should get changed out of those wet overalls,' he

told Hannah. 'There's plenty of people here to take over. Susie can show you where the scrubs are kept.'

'Soon,' Hannah promised. 'I just want to make sure she's stable.' Having come this far with the injured woman, Hannah was reluctant to hand over. 'If that's OK with you, Dr Wetherby?'

Ryan might be registered to work in Australia but Hannah wasn't. It was Charles who could give her permission. It was up to him whether he trusted that she was competent enough not to cause problems he would have to take ultimate responsibility for.

The look she received was assessing but Charles had obviously seen enough to make a decision.

'Go ahead,' he said.

Mario and a male nurse had moved the woman, still strapped to her backboard, onto the bed.

'Right.' Hannah nodded, tucking away the pleasure that someone like Charles Wetherby was prepared to trust her. 'This woman was apparently thrown clear of the bus and was found unconscious. There's been some response on the way in but nothing coherent. I'd put her GCS at seven. She was initially tachycardic at 120 but that's dropped in the last fifteen minutes to a rate of 90, respirations are shallow but air entry is equal and the oxygen saturation has been steady on 97 per cent on 10 litres.'

Standard monitoring equipment was being attached to the woman, like ECG leads, a blood-pressure cuff and an oxygen saturation monitor. Someone was hanging the fluids from a ceiling hook and another nurse was taking the woman's temperature.

'Thirty-five point six degrees centigrade,' she reported.

'Not hypothermic, then,' Emily commented.

'Blood pressure was initially one-twenty on eighty. Last measurement was one-thirty on seventy.'

'Widening pulse pressure,' Luke said. 'Rising intracranial pressure?'

'Quite possible. She has an abrasion and haematoma in the occipital area. No obvious skull fracture. Pupils were equal and reactive.'

'They're not now.' Emily was at the head end of the bed, shining a bright torch into the woman's eyes. 'Right pupil is two millimetres larger and sluggish.'

'Do we know her name?' Luke asked.

'No.' Hannah glanced at one of the nurses. 'Perhaps you could check her pockets? She may have some ID.'

'We need some radiography,' Luke said. 'Preferably a CT scan. And where's Alistair? If we've got a neurosurgeon available, this is where he should be.'

Charles pivoted his wheelchair. 'I'll find him.'

The movement of the woman on the bed was unexpected. Restrained, due to the straps still holding her to the backboard, but unmistakable.

'She's going to vomit,' Emily warned.

'Let's turn her side on,' Hannah ordered. 'I'll need suction.'

It was easy to turn the woman onto her side and keep her spine protected, thanks to the backboard, but it was another sign that the pressure could be building dangerously inside her head.

The nurse checking her pockets had easier access with the patient tipped to one side. 'I've found something,' she said. 'It's a passport. An Australian one.'

'Great. At least she'll understand the language. And we'll be able to use her name.' Hannah glanced up at the monitor, to see what was happening with the blood pressure. 'What is it?'

'Janey Stafford.'

*'What?'* The startled query came from Luke. 'Did you say *Janey Stafford?*'

'Do you know her?' Hannah asked. It could be helpful for an unconscious person to hear the voice of someone she knew.

'I… I'm not sure.' Luke was looking stunned. He reached over and lifted the oxygen mask the woman had on. Was he looking for a feature he might recognise? Hannah wondered. Like that small mole at the corner of her top lip?

Luke was backing away. Shaking his head.

'You don't know her, then?'

'Not really. It was her sister I knew.' The tone was dismissive. An 'I don't want to talk about this' sort of tone. 'It was a long time ago.'

Emily was staring at Luke. Then she blinked and refocussed. 'Do you want me to intubate?' she asked Hannah.

Alistair walked into the resus bay at that moment.

'I'll hand over to an expert,' Hannah said. Having given Alistair a rundown on their findings so far, she found herself stepping back. Luke did more than step back. He left the resus bay completely.

But then a new emergency was coming in. Luke hadn't pulled the curtain closed behind him and Hannah could see Ryan arriving with his multi-trauma case from the interior of the bus. They were still using a bag mask to ventilate this patient. There were two IV lines in place and Ryan looked worried.

'Bilateral fractured femurs,' Hannah heard him tell Charles. 'Rib fractures and a flail chest. GCS of nine.'

Charles directed them to resus 2 and Luke disappeared behind the curtain along with them.

The picture of Ryan's face was not so quick to disappear for Hannah. She had seen him work under duress before. Seen him tired and even not a hundred per cent well himself, but she had never seen an expression like the one he had walked in with.

So grim. Determined. So…lacking in humour.

Instinct told her that it wasn't just the grim situation that was making Ryan look like that. He was the one who always made an effort to defuse just such an atmosphere. He seemed like a different person. Gone completely was that sparkle. The laid-back, golden-boy aura that had always seemed to cling enough to be easily resurrected.

It didn't look like Ryan intended smiling for a long time to come and Hannah didn't like it. He was being professional and she knew he would have the skills to match anything he had to face, but something was wrong. Something big was missing. The real Ryan seemed shut off. Distant.

Was it sheer arrogance to wonder if his anger at her had something to do with his demeanour?

Hannah shivered and wasn't even surprised to hear Charles's voice from close by.

'Go and get out of those overalls. Get some dry scrubs on and get a hot drink. I don't want to see you back in here for at least ten minutes.'

It did feel better, being in dry clothes. And the hot chocolate and a sandwich she found in the staffroom were wonderful.

'At least you're getting a bit of the wedding breakfast.'

Hannah smiled back at the plump woman. Susie would be surprised to see that Dora had taken off her hat. 'It's delicious,' she said. 'Thank you so much.'

'You're all doing such a wonderful job. Those poor people out there. There are a lot that are badly hurt, aren't there?'

Hannah nodded, her mouth full of the first food she had eaten since a hurried lunch too many hours ago. She had taken a moment to check on Janey's progress, to find she'd gone for a CT scan and that Alistair was planning to take her to Theatre immediately afterwards, if necessary, to relieve any pressure building from a bleed inside her skull. Emily had gone to get ready to administer an anaesthetic.

Ryan was still busy stabilising his patient, ready for the surgery Luke would have to perform to deal with the major fractures sustained.

More cases were coming in, prearranged to arrive at a steady but not overwhelming rate. Susie had hopped past on her crutches, a sheaf of papers scrunched in one hand.

'I've got to locate a new supply of O-negative blood,' she told Hannah. 'And there's so many other things to do. We're still trying to discharge people to one of the rest homes and find accommodation for everyone from the bus. You OK?'

She was, surprisingly, more than OK, thanks to the food and hot drink.

In the corner of the staffroom sat two tired-looking children. Lily was still in her flower girl's dress and CJ hadn't changed out of his small suit.

'Can we go now?' CJ asked Dora.

'We're supposed to stay here,' she replied. 'You know what they said about my house. It's not fit to be in when the cyclone comes.'

'Is it definitely coming, then?' Hannah's appetite faded and she swallowed with difficulty.

'They reckon it's going to hit us by morning. Susie's arranged some beds for the children to stay in here overnight. Dr Wetherby and CJ's parents are going to be busy all night by the look of things.'

'But you said—' CJ's lip wobbled ominously '—you *said* we could go and see if the puppies have arrived before we have to go to bed.'

'My dog's due to whelp again,' Dora explained to Hannah. 'Goodness knows why Grubby keeps letting her get in pup. It's me who ends up doing all the work.'

*'Ple-ease?'* begged CJ.

Dora looked at the clock. 'I guess we've got a fair few hours before the weather gets dangerous. If we went home quick and then came back again, I guess Dr Wetherby won't notice we've gone.'

'Don't tell,' CJ ordered Hannah. 'Will you?'

'I'm sure nobody will ask me,' Hannah responded. She watched as Dora took a small hand in each of hers and led the children away. A very capable woman, Dora. Hannah was sure no harm would come to the children.

And that reminded her of the shoe.

Over the next hour, as Hannah assisted in the treatment of several people, she had two things on her mind. One of them was watching for glimpses of Ryan, to see whether he was still looking so distant and miserable.

He was. More than once he passed Hannah with barely more than a glance. Never a smile. Or a comment that might have lifted her spirits. To imagine him telling a joke seemed ridiculous. He had changed into scrubs as well so he looked like the Ryan she had always known.

She just wished she could see a flash of him behaving the way he always had.

The other thing on her mind was the shoe. At every opportunity she asked different members of the staff whether they had come across a small child amongst the patients. Someone advised her to check with one of the clerks and, sure enough, when she did, she struck gold.

'There *was* a kid. A little blonde girl,' she was told. 'Chloe, I think her name was. She had a broken arm.'

'How old was she?'

'I can't remember. Four or five.'

The right sort of age to fit a shoe the size of the one Hannah had found.

'Where would she be now?'

'I have no idea, sorry. Maybe the plaster room? It was ages ago, though. She might have been sent home.'

Except that she had no home to go to, did she?

The thoughtful frown on Hannah's face must have looked like fatigue to Charles. He rolled towards her.

'You've been on duty for more than four hours,' he said. 'It's time you took a break. At least two hours' standdown before I see you back in here, please. It's going to be a long night and it might be just the beginning of what we need you for with the way Willie's decided to behave.'

Hannah nodded. A break was exactly what she needed right now, wasn't it?

The soaked pair of overalls lay where she had left them, in the corner of the women's locker room. Nobody had had time to tidy yet. Hannah fished the shoe out of the pocket and went looking for the child she now knew existed.

Jill Shaw, the nursing director, passed her in the corridor, with her arms full of a fresh supply of IV fluids.

'Have you seen a little girl?' Hannah asked. 'About five? With blonde hair?'

'You mean Lily? I think Mrs Grubb's looking after her. She should be in the hospital somewhere.'

'No, not Lily. A child from the bus crash. I need to know if this is her shoe.' Hannah showed Jill the worn sneaker with the faded fish picture on the toe.

Jill shook her head. 'Sorry.'

Ryan emerged from the door to the toilet just behind where Jill and Hannah stood.

He still looked grim. Distant. Lines of weariness were etched deeply into his face. He looked so…serious.

*Too* serious for Ryan Fisher under any circumstances. It just didn't fit. Hannah could feel her heart squeeze into a painful ball. She wanted to touch him. To say something that could raise just a hint of smile or bring back just a touch of life into those dark eyes.

But she couldn't. Partly because Jill was there and mostly because Ryan wasn't even looking at her. He was looking at the object in her hand.

'For God's sake, Hannah. There are more important things to be worrying about right now than a bloody *shoe!*'

Jill raised an eyebrow as she watched him stride away. 'It's time he had a break, I think.' She turned back to Hannah. 'They're collecting all the unclaimed property in Reception. Why don't you leave it there?'

Reception was crowded. People with minor injuries from the bus crash that had been treated were waiting for transport to the emergency shelters. Other accidents attributable to the awful weather conditions were coming in in a steady stream. And there were still the people that would normally present to Emergency with the kind of injuries and illnesses they could have taken to their GP in working hours. Many of these people had been bumped well down any waiting list. Some were giving up and going home. Others were still waiting—bored, miserable and increasingly impatient.

'I don't give a stuff about bloody tourists off a bus,' an irate man was shouting at the receptionist. 'I pay my bloody taxes and I want to be seen by a doctor. *Now!* I've been waiting hours. Is this a *hospital* or what?'

Hannah gave the receptionist a sympathetic smile. Near her desk was a sad-looking pile of wet luggage, some back-packs and other personal items like handbags, hats and sunglasses.

The angry man stormed back to his seat. Then he jumped to his feet. 'I've had enough of this,' he shouted. 'I'm bloody going home.'

Casting a glance around the waiting room, Hannah could tell nobody was sorry to see him go. She doubted there had been much wrong with him in the first place. He should see the kind of injuries that were having to wait for attention inside the department.

Hannah didn't really need a two-hour break. Maybe she should go back and help. She could leave the shoe on the pile because it probably did belong to the little girl and she might come looking for it.

Something made her turn back before she reached the pile, however. Something niggling at the back of her mind since her gaze had skimmed the more patient people still waiting for attention.

And there she was. A drowsy little blonde-headed girl, almost hidden with her mother's arms around her. She had a pink cast on her arm.

Hannah walked over to them, absurdly hopeful.

'Is this Chloe?'

The mother nodded, a worried frown creasing her fore-head. 'Is there a problem? I thought we were all finished. We were just waiting for a ride to the shelter.'

'No problem,' Hannah assured her. 'I just wondered if this could be Chloe's shoe?' She held the small sneaker out but the hope that she might have solved this small mystery bothering her was fading rapidly.

Chloe was wearing some white Roman sandals. Two of them.

The little girl opened her eyes. 'That's not my shoe,' she said. 'It's the boy with the funny name's shoe.'

Hannah caught her breath. 'What boy?'

'The boy on the bus.'

'I didn't see a boy,' her mother said.

'That's because he was hiding in the back of the bus. With his friend.'

'A friend?' Hannah blinked. Surely the searchers couldn't have missed *two* children? And where were the parents? They would be frantic. Everybody would know by now if they had missing children.

'He had a dog called Scruffy,' Chloe added. 'They were hiding so the driver wouldn't see Scruffy.'

So the friend was a dog? There had been no reports of a dog at the accident site that Hannah was aware of and that would be something people would talk about, surely? Chloe's story was beginning to seem unlikely.

'Chloe has a very good imagination,' her mother said fondly. 'Don't you, darling?' Her smile at Hannah was apologetic. 'It was a pretty long, boring bus ride.'

'I can imagine.'

'I *did* see them,' Chloe insisted. 'I went down the back of the bus when you were asleep, Mummy. His name was F-F-*Felixx*,' she said triumphantly. 'Like the cat.'

'I don't think so, darling. I've never heard of a little boy being called Felixx.'

'But it's *true*, Mummy.' Chloe was indignant. She wriggled away from the supporting arm and twisted her head sharply up to glare at her mother.

And then the small girl's eyes widened in surprise.

A split second later she went completely limp, slumped against her mother.

For a stunned moment, Hannah couldn't move. This was unreal. Talking one moment and apparently unconscious the next? Automatically she reached out to feel for a pulse in Chloe's neck.

Chloe's mother was frozen. 'What's happening?' she whispered hoarsely.

Hannah's fingers pressed deeper on the tiny neck.

Moved and pressed again.

'I don't know,' Hannah said, 'but for some reason it seems that Chloe's heart might have stopped.'

Another split second of indecision. Start CPR here in the waiting room and yell for help or get Chloe to the kind of lifesaving equipment, like a defibrillator, that she might desperately need? There was no question of what could give a better outcome.

She scooped the child into her arms. 'Come with me,' she told Chloe's mother as she ran towards the working end of the department.

'I need help,' she called as soon as she was through the door. *'Stat!'*

Ryan looked up from where he was squatting, talking to a man in a chair who had a bloodstained bandage on his hand. He took one look at Hannah's face and with a fluid movement he rose swiftly and came towards her.

'What's happened?'

'I have no idea. She just collapsed. I can't find a pulse.'

'Resus 2 is clear at the moment.' Charles was rolling beside them. 'I'll find help.'

Hannah laid Chloe on the bed. It had been well under a minute since the child had collapsed but, horribly, her instincts were screaming that they were too late. There had been something about the feel of the child in her arms.

Something completely empty.

Her fingers trembled as they reached for the ECG electrodes and stuck them in place on a tiny, frail-looking chest.

Ryan was reassessing her for a pulse and respirations. 'Nothing,' he said tersely. He reached for a bag-mask unit. 'What the hell is going on here?'

'Could it be a drug reaction? Anaphylaxis? What analgesia has she had for her arm?'

'Do you know if there were any prior symptoms?' Ryan had the mask over Chloe's face and was delivering enough air to make the small chest rise and then fall.

The normal-looking movement of breathing gave Hannah a ray of hope. Maybe they *weren't* too late. But then she looked up at the monitor screen to see a flat ECG trace. Not even a fibrillation they could have shocked back into a normal rhythm. She moved, automatically, to start chest compressions.

'She was fine,' she told Ryan. 'A bit drowsy but fine. She was talking to me. Telling me about the shoe and a boy who was on the bus.'

Any worries about a potentially missing child were simply not part of the picture right now.

More staff were crowding into the resus area to assist. One of the doctors, Cal, was inserting an IV line. One nurse was rolling the drugs trolley closer, the airway kit open on top of the trolley.

Charles was there. A solid presence. Beside him, Chloe's mother was standing, white faced, a nurse close by to look after her.

'An undiagnosed head injury?' Charles wondered aloud.

'A lucid period before total collapse?' He shook his head. 'Couldn't have been that dramatic.'

Ryan looked over to Chloe's mother. 'Does she have any medical conditions that you know of? Heart problems?'

'No-o-o.' The word was torn from the woman in the form of a sob. The nurse put her arms around the distraught mother. As awful as this was, it was better for a parent to see that everything possible was being done, in case they had to deal with the worst possible outcome.

Hannah kept up the chest compressions. It wasn't physically hard on someone this small. One handed. Rapid. It didn't take much pressure at all.

'Stop for a second, Hannah.'

They all looked at the screen. The disruption to the trace that the movement of CPR was causing settled.

To a flat line.

'I'm going to intubate,' Ryan decided. 'Someone hold her head for me, please?'

'I'll take over compressions.' Cal stepped up to the bed and Hannah nodded. She moved to take hold of Chloe's head and keep it in the position Ryan required.

'Oh, my God,' she murmured a moment later.

'What?' Ryan snapped. His gaze caught hers as though challenging her to say something he didn't want to hear. She had never seen anyone that determined. Ever.

'It's her neck,' Hannah said quietly. 'The way it moved. It's...' She was feeling the top of Chole's spine now, her fingers pressing carefully. Moving and pressing again. 'There's something very wrong.'

It was hardly a professional evaluation but she couldn't bring herself to say what she thought.

It fitted. Chloe must have had a fracture that had been undisplaced. She might have had a sore neck but that could have been masked by the pain relief administered for her fractured arm.

A time bomb waiting to go off. That sharp, twisting movement when she'd looked up at her mother could have displaced the broken bones. Allowed a sharp edge to sever the spinal cord.

Death would have been instantaneous.

And there was absolutely nothing any of them could do about it.

In the end, she didn't have to say anything. Her face must have said it all. Cal's hand slowed and then stopped. He stepped back from the bed.

Chloe's mother let out an agonised cry and rushed from the room. The nurse followed swiftly.

Everybody else stood silent.

Shocked.

Except for Ryan. He moved to where Cal had been standing and started chest compressions again.

And Charles rolled silently to the head of the bed where he could reach out and feel Chloe's neck for himself.

'We don't *know* her neck's broken,' Ryan said between gritted teeth. 'Not without an X-ray or CT scan. We can't just give up on her. Cal, take over again. Hannah, I want an ET tube. Five millimetre. Uncuffed.'

Nobody moved. Only Ryan, his face a frozen mask, his movements quietly desperate.

Charles dropped his hand from Chloe's neck. 'Ryan?'

The word wasn't spoken loudly but it carried the weight of an authority it would be impossible to ignore. So did the next word. *'Stop!'*

For a few seconds it looked as though Ryan might ignore the command. Keep fighting to save a life when there was absolutely no chance of success. Hannah could feel his pain. She reached out to touch his shoulder.

Ryan jerked away as though he'd been burnt. Without a glance at anyone, he turned and strode away. Long, angry strides that didn't slow as he flicked the curtain aside.

'Everybody take a break,' Charles ordered. 'Jill and I will deal with what needs to be done here.'

The shock was dreadful. Hannah could understand why Ryan hadn't been prepared to give up. If there was anything that could have been done, she would have done it herself. *Anything.*

They all faced terrible things like this, working in any emergency department. That it was part of the job didn't make it easy. Somehow they had to find a way to cope or they couldn't be doing this as a career.

What was making it worse than normal for Hannah was the feeling that Ryan *couldn't* cope with this particular case. There had been something in his body language as he virtually fled from the room that spoke of real desperation. Of reaching the end of a personal, if not professional, tether.

There was no way Hannah could leave him to deal with that on his own.

She had to try and help. Or at least *be* with him. To show him that she cared. That she understood.

An ironic smile vied with the tears she was holding back.

To wallow with him, even?

# CHAPTER TEN

HE WAS disappearing through the doors to the ambulance bay.

Going outside into the storm.

As scary as that was, Hannah didn't hesitate to go after him. An ambulance was unloading another patient by the time she got there and Hannah had to wait a moment as the stretcher was wheeled through the doors. Mario had done the round trip again. He was holding a bag of IV fluid aloft with one hand, steering the stretcher with the other.

'How's it going, Hannah? OK?'

Hannah could only give him a tight smile and a brief nod, unable to think of anything but her personal and urgent mission. She skirted the end of the stretcher to dash outside before the automatic doors slid shut again.

The wind caught the baggy scrub suit she was wearing and made it billow. It teased her hair out of the band holding it back and whipped strands across her face. Her eyes stung and watered but Hannah barely registered any discomfort. It was too dark out here. The powerful hospital generators were being used for the vital power needed inside. Energy was not being wasted on outside lighting.

Where was Ryan?

Where would *she* go if she was in some kind of personal crisis and couldn't cope?

Just anywhere? Was Ryan even aware of the wild storm raging around him? Would he be thinking of his personal safety? Not likely. What if he went towards the beach? That surf had been wild and couldn't you get things like storm surges with an approaching cyclone? Like tidal waves?

If he had gone somewhere that dangerous, Hannah would still follow him. She *had* to. The bond she felt was simply too strong. If ever there was a case for following her heart, this was it.

Ryan *was* her heart.

Maybe he was heading for a safer personal space, Hannah thought as her gaze raked the swirl of leaves in the darkness and picked out the looming shapes of vehicles in the car park. He only had one space that could qualify in Crocodile Creek. His room in the doctors' house.

The room she had spent the most magical night of her life in.

Headlights from another incoming rescue vehicle sent a beam of light across the path Hannah was taking. Strong enough to show she was heading in the right direction to take her to either the beach or the house. The faded sign designating the area as the AGNES WETHERBY MEMORIAL GARDEN was tilted. Had it always been like that or was it giving up the struggle to stay upright under the duress of this storm?

Hannah wasn't about to give up.

She had to pause in the centre of the garden, just beside the sundial. She needed to catch her breath and gather her courage. The crack of a tree branch breaking free somewhere close was frightening. She would wait a few seconds in case the branch was about to fall on the path she intended to take.

It must have been instinct that alerted her to Ryan's presence in the garden. Why else would she have taken a second and much longer look at the dark shape in the corner which anyone could have taken as part of the thick hibiscus hedge behind it? Or was it because that shadow was immobile whilst the hedge was in constant motion, fuelled by relentless wind gusts?

He was sitting on a bench seat, his hands on his knees, staring blankly into the dark space in front of him.

Hannah licked lips that were dry from more than the wind. 'Ryan?'

'Go away, Hannah. Leave me alone.'

'No. I can't *do* that.' With her heart hammering, Hannah sat down beside him. Close enough to touch but she knew not to. Not yet. Ryan was too fragile. Precious. A single touch might shatter him.

So she just sat.

Very still.

They were two frozen shapes as the storm surged and howled above them.

A minute went past.

And then another.

Hannah wanted to cry. She had no idea how to help. What would Ryan do if the situation were reversed? When had she ever been this upset over a bad case at work? The closest she could think of was that little boy, Brendon, with the head injury and the dead mother and the abusive father who hadn't given a damn.

And what had Ryan done?

Told a joke. A stupid blonde joke. His way of coping or helping others to cope. Trying to make them laugh and thereby defusing an atmosphere that could be destructive.

No atmosphere could be worse than this. The pain of

loving someone and being totally unable to connect. To offer comfort.

Hannah chewed the inside of her cheek as she desperately searched her memory. Had she even *heard* a blonde joke that Ryan wouldn't already know?

Maybe.

'Hey…' Surprisingly, she didn't have to shout to be heard. The wind seemed to have dropped fractionally and the hedge was were offering a small amount of protection. 'Have…have you heard the one about the blonde who went to pick up her car from the mechanic who'd been fixing it?'

There was no response from Ryan. Not a flicker. But he'd never been put off by Hannah's deliberate indifference, had he? It took courage to continue, all the same. More courage than heading out into a potentially dangerous storm.

'She asked, "Was there much wrong with it?" and the mechanic said, "Nah, just crap in the carburettor."' Hannah had to swallow. This was so hard. How could anything be funny at a time like this? The punchline might fall like a lead balloon and she would seem shallow. Flippant. Uncaring. The things she had once accused Ryan of being. The *last* things she wanted to be seen as right now.

'And…and the blonde thought about that for a minute and then she nodded and she said, "OK…how often do I have to do that?"'

For a heartbeat, and then another, Hannah thought her fears were proving correct. The stone statue that was Ryan was still silent. Unmoving.

But then a sound escaped. A strangled kind of laughter. To Hannah's horror, however, it morphed into something else.

Ryan was *crying*.

Ghastly, racking sobs as though he had no idea *how* to cry but the sounds were being ripped from his soul.

Hannah felt tears sliding down her own face and there was no way she could prevent herself touching him now. She wrapped both her arms around him as tightly as she could, her face pressed against the back of his shoulder.

Holding him.

Trying to absorb some of the terrible grief that he seemed to be letting go.

Maybe it was Chloe's case that had caused it or maybe she'd been the straw to break the camel's back. The reason didn't matter. Ryan was hurting and if Hannah hadn't known before just how deep her love for this man went, there was no escaping that knowledge now.

She would never know how long they stayed like that. Time had no relevance. At some point, however, Ryan moved. He took Hannah's arm and pushed her away.

He couldn't bear it if Hannah felt *sorry* for him.

Adding weakness to the list of faults she already considered him to have.

He had to push her away. However comforting her touch had been, he didn't want her pity.

Searching her face in the darkness didn't reveal what he'd been afraid to find. The shine of tears on Hannah's face was unexpected.

'Why are *you* crying?'

'Because…' Hannah gulped. 'Because *you're* crying.'

Why would she do that? There was only one reason that occurred to Ryan. She cared about him. Cared enough to be moved by his grief, even if she didn't know where it was coming from.

A very new sensation was born for Ryan right then. Wonderment. He had revealed the rawest of emotions. Exposed a part of himself he'd never shared with another living soul and Hannah had not only witnessed it, she had accepted it.

Was *sharing* it even.

Oh, man! This was huge. As big as the storm currently raging over their heads.

Bigger even.

Ryan sniffed and scrubbed his nose with the palm of his hand. He made an embarrassed kind of sound.

'First time for everything, I guess.'

'You mean this is the *first* time you've ever cried?'

'Yeah.' Ryan sniffed again and almost managed a smile. The grief had drained away and left a curious sort of peace. Had the crying done that? Or Hannah's touch? A combination of both maybe. 'Well, since I was about five or six anyway.'

'Oh…' And Hannah was smiling back at him. A gentle smile that was totally without any kind of judgement. 'I'm glad I was here.'

'Yeah…' It was still difficult to swallow but the lump in his throat seemed different. A happy lump rather than an agonised one. How could that be? 'Me, too.'

They listened to the wind for a moment. Felt the fat drops of rain ping against their bare arms.

'I'm sorry, Ryan,' Hannah said.

'What for?'

'Lots of things.'

'Like what?'

'Like that we couldn't save Chloe.'

'We could have, if we'd only known.' Ryan felt the weight of sadness pulling him down again but he knew he wouldn't go as far as he had. Never again. Hannah had stopped his fall. Made something right in the world again. 'It shouldn't have happened.'

'No, of course it shouldn't, but I can see why it did. If there hadn't been so many injuries it would have been standard protocol to check her out a lot more carefully. To collar and backboard her until X-rays were done, given the mechanism of injury. But she was part of the walking wounded group. She only complained about her sore arm.'

'Tunnel vision.'

'Not entirely. With so many to care for, you don't have time to think outside the square. Tick the boxes that don't seem urgent. Anyway, it happened and it's dreadful and I know how you must feel.' A tentative smile curved Hannah's lips. 'I'm available for a spot of wallowing.'

Ryan shook his head. 'I don't do wallowing, you know that.' He snorted softly. 'Hell, if I went down that track with the kind of material I've got to keep me going, I'd end up like a character in some gloomy Russian novel. Chloe *did* get to me more than usual, though. Too close to home.'

'I don't understand.'

Of course she didn't. Why had Ryan thought that keeping his private life private would make things easier?

'I've got a niece,' he told her. 'Michaela. She's six and blonde and it could have been her in there instead of Chloe. Not that there's anything that could save Mikki so to have another little girl that didn't *have* to die and still did seemed just too unfair to be acceptable.'

'Mikki *has* to die?'

'It's inevitable. She's got neuroaxonal dystrophy. It's an autosomal recessive genetic disease and it's incredibly cruel. They seem perfectly normal at birth and even for the first year or two, and then there's a steady deterioration until they die a few years later. Mikki can't move any more.

She can't see or talk. She can still hear and she can smile. She's got the most gorgeous smile.'

When had Hannah's hand slipped into his like that? Ryan returned the squeeze.

'I love that kid,' he said quietly. 'She's got a couple of older brothers but she was special right from day one.'

'And she lives here, in Australia?'

'Brisbane. She's my older brother's child. He's taking it hard and it's putting a big strain on the marriage. He's a bit like me, I guess—not good at sharing the hard stuff in life. Easier to bottle it up and have a laugh about something meaningless.'

'Like a joke.' Hannah was nodding.

'Yeah. Shallow, isn't it?'

'You're not shallow, Ryan. You care more than anyone I've ever met. You've just been good at hiding it.' She cleared her throat. 'So Mikki's the reason you come back to Australia so often?'

'Yeah. I try to be there whenever things get really tough or when she has a hospital appointment. I can explain things again to her parents later.'

'It's a huge commitment.'

'I would have moved there to make it easier to be supportive but my parents live in Auckland. Dad had a stroke a couple of years ago. Quite a bad one and Mum's finding it harder to cope. So there I was in Sydney, commuting one way and then another. The travel time was playing havoc with my career so I had to choose one city and the job in Auckland happened to come up first. It doesn't seem to take any longer to get to Brisbane from Auckland than it did from Sydney and I'm only doing half the travelling I used to do.'

Hannah's smile was rueful. 'And I was thinking that Michaela was a girlfriend. Or an ex-wife.'

Ryan snorted. 'For one thing, any wife of mine would never become an "ex". For another, I haven't had time in my life for a relationship for years. Who would, with the kind of family commitments I've got?'

'But you go out with everyone. You never miss a party.'

'I'm in a new city. I need to find friends. Sometimes I just need to escape and do normal, social things. I still feel lonely but if you can't find some fun somewhere in life, it takes all the sense out of struggling along with the bad bits.'

'I can't believe I accused you of being shallow, Ryan. I'm really, really sorry.'

'Don't be. I can see why you did. I've never told anyone at work what goes on in my private life. I had a feeling that if I started I'd never be able to stop and it would be too hard. I'd end up a mess and people would just feel sorry for me. I've got too much pride to take that on board.'

'*I* don't feel sorry for you.'

'You don't?'

'No.'

'What *do* you feel, Han?'

'I…feel a lot.' Hannah was looking down, avoiding his gaze. 'I'm…in love with you, Ryan.'

There.

She'd said it.

Opened her heart right up.

Made herself as vulnerable as it was possible to get, but what choice had she had? There was no escaping the truth and she couldn't live a lie.

And hadn't Ryan made himself just as vulnerable? He hadn't cried in front of anyone in his adult life. He could have hidden it from her. Stormed off and shut her out before he let himself go. He'd been exercising control over his emotions for year after year. He could have done the same for a minute or two longer.

But he hadn't. At some level he had trusted her enough to show her who he really was.

An utterly amazing, caring, committed man.

How could she have been so wrong about him?

Ryan deserved nothing less than the absolute truth from her, no matter how painful the repercussions.

She was too afraid to look at him. It was too dark to be able to interpret expressions accurately enough in any case.

She didn't need to be able to see, though. She could feel the touch under her chin as Ryan tilted her face up to meet his.

Could feel the touch of his lips on her own, the rain-slicked smoothness of her skin against the grating stubble of a jaw that hadn't been near a razor since what was now yesterday.

The kiss was as gentle as it was powerful.

It told Hannah she didn't need to be afraid. Ryan understood that vulnerability and he wasn't going to break her trust if he could help it.

The first words he spoke when he drew away had to be the most important Hannah would ever hear.

She wasn't disappointed.

'I love you, too, Hannah Jackson.'

The rain was pelting down now. Ryan smoothed damp strands of hair back from Hannah's forehead.

'We need to find somewhere dry,' he said.

Hannah laughed. Incredible as it seemed, in the wake of what they had just been through and with the prospect of more gruelling hours of work ahead, there was joy to be found in life. In each other.

'Where have I heard that before?'

'We're on a break. We've got two hours to escape. To

forget about the world and be dry. And warm. And safe.' Ryan kissed her again. 'You'll always be safe with me, Hannah. I promise you that.'

She took his face between both her hands. 'And so will you be,' she vowed. 'With me.'

She let Ryan pull her to her feet and she smiled. 'I'd like to go somewhere dry with you. Very much.' Her smile broadened. 'Even though I already know how good our rapport is.'

'Yeah…' Ryan growled. 'I'm *fun.*'

'I didn't mean that, you know. It was so much more than that. I was just trying to protect myself.'

'From *me?*' Ryan sounded baffled.

'Yes. I thought it was far too dangerous to fall for someone like you.'

'Who, exactly, is someone like me?'

'Oh, you know. Someone fun. Clever. Exciting. Great looking. Too good to be true.'

'I'm someone like that?' Now he sounded very pleasantly surprised.

'Someone exactly like that. A bit too much like the man my mother fell head over heels in love with. And the one that Susie fell in love with. And they both got bored or hadn't been genuine in the first place, and it was me who had to pick up all the pieces. Do you know how many pieces you can get out of *two* broken hearts?'

'No. How many?'

'Heaps,' Hannah said firmly. 'Way *too* many.'

Ryan pulled her to a stop. Pulled her into his arms. 'Your heart's going to stay in one piece if I have anything to do with it,' he said seriously. 'I'm going to make it my mission in life.'

The promise was too big. Hannah didn't want anything

to make her cry again. She had to smile and try to lighten the emotional overload. 'Could be a full-time job.'

'I intend to make sure it is.'

'It might be a lifetime career.'

'I certainly hope so.'

'Of course, there's always the prospect of promotion.'

'Really? What kind of promotion?'

Why had she started this? Suddenly it didn't seem like a joke. 'Oh, maybe being an emergency department consultant?'

'I might not get that job. I've heard that I've got some pretty stiff competition.'

Hannah's heart was doing some curious flip-flops. 'I might not mind very much if I don't get that job.'

'Why not?'

'I might have more important things in my life than my career.'

Ryan was smiling. 'Such as?' He raised a hopeful eyebrow. 'You mean *me?*'

Hannah nodded shyly. 'Maybe even… How would you feel about a promotion to being a father?'

'Dr Jackson! Is that a proposal?'

'I don't know.' Hannah caught her bottom lip between her teeth. 'Would you like it to be?'

'No.'

Hannah's heart plummeted. But then she saw the gleam of Ryan's teeth.

'I'm old-fashioned,' he announced. 'If there's to be any proposing going on around here, *I'll* do it.'

And that's exactly what he did. In the heart of a tropical storm, in the middle of a garden, just beside a sundial, Ryan got down on one knee, holding both of Hannah's hands in his own.

'I love you.' He had to shout because the wind had risen again to snatch his words away and the rain was thundering down and the wail of a siren close by rose and fell.

'I love you, Hannah. You are the only person in existence that I can really be myself with. The only time in my life I felt no hint of being alone was when I had you in my bed. You make me whole. I don't ever want to live without having you by my side. Will you—please—marry me?'

'Oh, I think so.' Hannah sank to her knees on the wet flagstones of the path. 'I love you, too, Ryan.' It was easier to hear now that their heads were close together again. 'You are the only person in existence that I've ever…had such a good rapport with.' They were grinning at each other now, at the absurdity of choosing this particular place and time to make such declarations. Then Hannah's smile faded. It had just happened this way and because it had, it was perfect. 'Yes,' she said slowly. 'I would love to marry you.'

Ryan shook the raindrops from his hair after giving Hannah a lingering, wonderful kiss.

'Can we go somewhere dry now?'

Hannah nodded but the wail of the siren was still going and she hesitated when Ryan helped her up and then tugged on her hand.

'What's up, babe?'

'I can't stop thinking about it.'

'The bus crash? The cyclone that's on its way that we'd better find some shelter from pretty damn quick?'

'No…the shoe.'

'Did Chloe really tell you there was a boy on the bus?'

'Yes.'

'And you believe her?'

'Yes.'

'We'd better find Harry or someone, then, and let them know.'

Hannah nodded. 'I'd feel a lot better if we did. Do you mind?'

'Why should I mind?'

'It'll take a bit longer to find somewhere dry. To have that break.'

'Babe, we've got all the time in the world to work on our rapport.' Ryan had his arm around Hannah, sheltering her from some of the wind and rain. They had to bend forward to move against the force of the elements and get themselves back towards Crocodile Creek Base Hospital's emergency department.

But it felt so different than when Hannah had been going in the opposite direction on her search for Ryan. With his strength added to her own, she knew there was nothing she wouldn't be prepared to face.

Ryan paused once more as they reached the relative shelter of the ambulance bay. 'It *is* real, isn't it?'

'What, the cyclone? Sure feels like it.'

'No, I mean, how we feel about each other. The love.'

'As real as this storm,' Hannah assured him. 'And just as powerful.'

'What happens when the sun comes out?'

'We'll be in a dry place.' Hannah smiled. 'Having fun.'

Ryan looked over her shoulder through the doors into the emergency department. 'I don't think fun's on the agenda for a while yet.'

'No.' Hannah followed the direction of his gaze. Chloe was still somewhere in there. So were a lot of other people who needed attention. And when the aftermath of the bus crash had been mopped up, they could be on standby for the first casualties from a cyclone.

'It's not going to be easy.'

'No.'

'Are you up for it?'

'With you here as well? Of course I am. We can do this, Ryan. We'll be doing it together.'

'Together is good. Oh, and, Han?'

'Yes?'

'Can I have that blonde joke? The one about the carburettor? It was great.'

'You can have anything and everything I have to give,' Hannah told him. 'Always.'

Ryan took hold of her hand once more and they both turned towards the automatic doors. Ready to step back into a place that needed them both almost as much as they needed each other.

'Same,' Ryan said softly. 'For ever.'

# THE NURSE HE'S BEEN WAITING FOR

BY
MEREDITH WEBBER

**Meredith Webber** says of herself, 'Some years ago, I read an article which suggested that Mills & Boon were looking for new medical authors. I had one of those "I can do that" moments, and gave it a try. What began as a challenge has become an obsession, though I do temper the "butt on seat" career of writing with dirty but healthy outdoor pursuits, fossicking through the Australian Outback in search of gold or opals. Having had some success in all of these endeavours, I now consider I've found the perfect lifestyle.'

# PROLOGUE

AS A cyclone hovered off the coast of North Queensland, threatening destruction to any town in its path, several hundred miles away a small boy sneaked on board a bus. Terrified that his father, who was arguing with the bus driver, would discover the dog he'd threatened to drown, Max ducked between the two men and climbed the steps into the warm, fusty, dimly lit interior of the big vehicle. Mum would sort everything out when he got to Crocodile Creek—the fare, the dog, everything.

Mum would like a dog.

'Don't call her Mum—she's your flippin' sister! Or half-sister, if you really want to know.'

Echoes of his father's angry rant rang through Max's head, but Georgie hadn't ever minded him calling her Mum, and it stopped kids at school teasing him.

The kids that had mums, that was.

Mum would love Scruffy.

He shifted the backpack off his shoulder and hugged it to his chest, comforted by the squirming of the pup inside it, checking out the passengers as he made his way up the aisle. He'd been shunted back and forth across Queensland often enough to be able to pick out who was who among his fellow travellers.

The bus was nearly full and all the usual ones were there. A group of backpackers chattering away in a foreign language, a fat woman in the seat behind them—bet she'd been to visit her grandkids—bloke on the other side of the aisle—he'd be late back on the bus at all the rest stops—an old couple who looked like they'd been on the bus for all of their lives, and a tired, sad-looking woman with a little boy.

Max slipped into the seat behind them. He'd never told Mum and certainly wouldn't bother telling Dad, but scary things could happen on a bus, and he'd worked out it's always best to stick with someone with a kid, or to sit near a youngish couple, so he looked like part of a family.

Though with Scruffy to protect him…

He slid across the seat to the window, looking for his father, wondering if the argument was over—if his father had actually paid to get rid of him this time.

Wanting to wave goodbye.

The footpath was deserted, the bus driver now talking to someone in the doorway of the travel office. Twisting his head against the glass, Max could just make out a shambling figure moving through a pool of lamplight well behind the bus—walking away from it.

So much for waving goodbye.

'It doesn't matter!' Max told himself fiercely, scrunching up his eyes and blinking hard, turning his attention to the zip on his backpack before thrusting his hand inside, feeling Scruffy's rough hair, a warm tongue licking his fingers. 'It doesn't matter!'

But when you're only seven, it did matter…

# CHAPTER ONE

MIDNIGHT, and Grace O'Riordan lay on one of the examination couches in the emergency department of the Crocodile Creek Hospital and stared at an amoeba-shaped stain on the ceiling as she contemplated clothes, love and the meaning of life.

In truth, the meaning of life wasn't overtaxing her brain cells right now, and she'd assured herself, for the forty-hundredth time, that the dress she'd bought for the wedding wasn't too over the top, which left love.

Love, as in unrequited.

One-sided.

Heavens to Betsy, as if she hadn't had enough one-sided love in her life.

Perhaps loving without being loved back made her unlovable. In the same way old furniture, polished often, developed a rich deep shiny patina, so loved people shone and attracted more love.

What *was* this? Sensible, practical, Grace O'Riordan indulging in wild flights of fancy? She'd be better off napping.

Although she was on duty, the A and E dept—in fact,

the entire hospital—after a particularly hectic afternoon and early evening, was quiet. Quiet enough for her to have a sleep, which, given the frantic few days she'd just spent checking on cyclone preparations, she needed.

But she needed love, too, and was practical—there was that word again—enough to know that she had to get over her present love—the unrequited one—and start looking to the future. Start looking for someone who might love her back, someone who also wanted love and the things that went with it, like marriage and a family. Especially a family. She had been family-less for quite long enough…

This coming week would provide the perfect opportunity to begin the search, with people flying in from all over the globe for the weddings of Mike and Emily tomorrow and, a week later, Gina and Cal. Surely somewhere, among all the unattached male wedding guests, there'd be someone interested in a smallish, slightly plump, sometimes pretty, Irish-Australian nurse.

She pressed her hand against her heart, sure she could feel pain just thinking about loving someone other than Harry.

But she'd got over love before, she could do it again.

'Move on, Grace!' she told herself, in her sternest voice.

'Isn't anyone on duty in this place?' a loud voice demanded.

Harry's voice.

Grace slid off the table, pulled her uniform shirt straight, wondered, briefly, whether her short curls looked like a flattened bird's nest after lying down, and exited the room to greet the man she was trying to get over.

'If you'd come in through the emergency door, a bell would have rung and I'd have known you were here,' she greeted him, none too warmly. Then she saw the blood.

'Holy cow, Harry Blake, what have you done to yourself this time?'

She grabbed a clean towel from a pile on a trolley and hurried towards the chair where he'd collapsed, one bloody leg thrust out in front of him.

Wrapping the towel tightly around the wound to stem at least some of the bleeding, she looked up into his face. Boy, was it ever hard to get over love when her heart danced jigs every time she saw him.

Irish jigs.

She looked at his face again—as a nurse this time. It was grey with tiredness but not, as far as she could tell, pale from blood loss.

'Can you make it into an examination cubicle or will I ring for help?' she asked, knowing full well he was so stubborn he'd refuse help even if she called for it. But when he stood he wobbled slightly, so she tucked her shoulder into his armpit to take some of his weight, and with her arm around his back for added support she led him into the room.

He sat down on the couch she'd occupied only minutes earlier, then, as she pushed at his chest and lifted his legs, he lay down.

'What happened?' she asked, as she unwrapped the towel enough to know there was no arterial bleeding on his leg, then wrapped it up again so she could check his vital signs before she examined the wound.

'Carelessness,' he muttered at her. He closed his eyes, which made her wonder if his blood loss was more serious than she'd supposed. But his pulse was strong, his blood pressure excellent and his breathing steady. Just to be sure, she slid an oxygen saturation meter onto one of his fingers, and turned on the monitor.

'What kind of carelessness?' she asked as she once again unwrapped the towel and saw the torn, blood-stained trouser leg and the badly lacerated skin beneath the shredded fabric.

'Chainsaw! Does that stain on the ceiling look like a penguin to you?'

'No, it looks like an amoeba, which is to say a formless blob.' She was using scissors to cut away his trousers, so she could see the wound. Blood had run into his sock, making it hard to tell if the damage went down that far. Taking care not to brush against his wound, she took hold of his boot to ease it off.

'You can't do that,' he said, sitting up so quickly his shoulder brushed against her and his face was kissing close.

Kissing Harry? As if!

'Can't take your boot off?' she asked. 'Is there some regulation about not being a policeman if you're not wearing both boots?'

He turned towards her, a frown pleating his black eyebrows, his grey eyes perplexed. 'Of course not. You just wouldn't get it off.' He tugged and twisted at the same time and the elastic-sided boot slid off. 'I'll get the sock, too,' he added, pulling off the bloodstained wreck, but not before Grace had noticed the hole at the top of the big toe.

In a dream where Harry loved her back, she'd have mended that hole—she'd like doing things like that—the little caring things that said *I love you* without the words.

'Lie back,' she said, dream and reality coming too close for comfort with him sitting there. 'I'll flush this mess and see what's what.'

She pulled on clean gloves and set a bag of saline on a drip stand. She'd need tubing, a three-way tap, syringe and a nineteen-gauge needle to drip the liquid onto the wound while she probed for foreign particles.

Packing waterproof-backed absorbent pads beneath his leg, she started the saline dripping onto the wound, a nasty contusion running eight inches in length, starting on the tibia just below the knee and swerving off into his calf.

'The skin's so chewed up it's not viable enough to stitch,' she told him, probing a few pieces of what looked like mangled treetrunk, or possibly mangled trouser fabric, from the deepest part. Organic matter and clay were among the most likely things to cause infection in tissue injury. 'Ideally it should be left open, but I guess you're not willing to stay home and rest it for the next few days.'

'You *are* joking!' Harry said. 'I need it patched up now, and maybe in three days' time, when we know for sure Cyclone Willie has departed, I can rest it.'

'Harry, it's a mess. I'll dress it as best I can but if you don't look after it and come in to have it dressed every day, you're going to end up with ulceration and needing a skin graft on it.'

She left the saline dripping on the wound while she

found the dressings she'd need and some antibiotic cream which she would spread beneath the non-adhesive dressing once she had all visible debris removed from it.

Harry watched her work, right up until she starting snipping away torn tatters of skin, when he turned his attention back to the penguin on the ceiling.

'Would you like me to give you a local anaesthetic while I do this? It could hurt.'

'It *is* hurting,' he said, gritting his teeth as a particularly stubborn piece of skin or grit defied Grace's efforts to be gentle. 'But, no, no needles. Just talk to me. And before you do, have another look—maybe the stain looks like the little engine on a cane train.'

Grace glanced towards the ceiling but shook her head as she turned back towards him.

'Since when do a penguin and a cane train engine share similarities in looks?'

'It's a shape thing,' he said, grabbing at her hand and drawing the shape on the back of it. 'Penguin, blob, train engine, see?'

'Not even vaguely,' she told him, rescuing her hand from his grasp then changing her gloves again before she continued with her job. 'And I can see right through you, Harry Blake. You're babbling on about penguins and cane trains to keep me from going back to the question you avoided earlier.'

She stopped talking while she spread cream across his leg. He didn't feel much like talking either.

Grace sealed the wound with a broad, long dressing, and bandaged over it with crêpe bandages, then pulled a long sleeve over the lot, giving it as much security and padding as she could because she knew he'd be putting himself in situations where he could bump it.

'That should give it some protection from physical damage, although, with the cyclone coming, who knows what you'll be called on to do? Just make sure you come in to have it checked and re-dressed every day.'

'You on duty tomorrow?'

Grace smiled sadly to herself. Would that he was asking because he was interested!

'You already know the answer to that one. I finish night duty in the morning and have three days off so I can cope with the wedding and the cyclone preparations without letting any one down here at the hospital.'

Harry sat up and swung his legs over the side of the bed, ready to leave.

'Not so fast,' she warned him. 'I need to check your tetanus status and give you some antibiotics just in case there's some infection already in there.'

She paused and her wide blue eyes met his.

'*And* you're not leaving here until you tell me how you did it.'

Harry studied her as he debated whether to tell her. Tousled curls, freckled nose—Grace, everyone's friend.

His friend, too. A friendship formed when he'd been in need of a friend in the months after Nikki's death. True, he'd had friends, good friends, among the townspeople and the hospital staff, but all the locals had known Nikki since she'd been a child while the hospital staff had all drawn close to her as they'd nursed her through the last weeks of her life.

And though these friends had all stood by him and

had wanted to offer support, he'd avoided them, not wanting sympathy, needing to be left alone to sort out the morass of conflicting emotions warring within him.

Grace had arrived after Nikki's death, so there was no connection, no history, just a bright, bubbly, capable young woman who was willing to listen if he wanted to talk, to talk if he needed conversation, or just to share the silence when he didn't want to be alone.

A true friend…

'I'm waiting!'

She had her hands on her hips and a no-nonsense look on her face, but though she was trying to look serious a smile lurked in her blue eyes.

A smile nearly always lurked in Grace's eyes…

The thought startled him to the extent that confession seemed easier than considering what, if anything, noticing Grace's smiling eyes might mean.

'I hit my leg with the blade of a chainsaw.'

'And *what* were you doing, wielding a chainsaw, may I ask?'

'A tree had come down, out along the Wygera road, but part of the trunk must have been dead because the saw bounced off it when it hit it.' He waved his hand towards his now securely bandaged leg. 'One wounded leg.'

'That wasn't my question and you know it, Harry. It's one o'clock in the morning. You're a policeman, not a rescue worker. The fire service, the electricity workers and, or when requested, the SES crews clear roads. It's what they're trained to do. The SES manual has pages and pages on safe working with chainsaws.'

'I've been using chainsaws all my life,' Harry

retorted, uncomfortably aware this conversation might not be about chainsaws but uncertain what it was about.

'That's not the point,' Grace snapped. 'What if the accident had been worse? What if you'd taken your leg off? Then who's in charge here? Who's left to co-ordinate services to a town that could be struck by one of the worst cyclones in history within the next twenty-four hours?'

'Give over, Grace,' he said, standing up on his good leg and carefully putting weight on the injured one to see how bad it felt.

Very bad. Bad enough to make him feel queasy.

'No, I won't give over.' No smile in the blue eyes now. In fact, she was glaring at him. 'This is just typical of you, Harry Blake. Typical of the stupid risks you take. You mightn't care what happens to you, but you've got family and friends who do. There are people out there who'd be deeply hurt if you were killed or badly injured, but do you think about them when you pull on your superhero cape and go rushing blindly into danger? No, you don't! You don't think of anyone but yourself, and that's not noble or self-sacrificing or even brave—it's just plain selfishness, Harry.'

Harry heard her out, growing more annoyed every second. He'd had a shocking day, he was tired, his leg hurt and to accuse him of selfishness, well, that was just the last straw.

'And just what makes you think you have the right to sit in judgement on me?' he demanded, taking a careful stride towards the cubicle curtain so he could escape any further conversation. 'What makes you think you know me well enough to call me selfish, or to question my motives in helping people? You're not my mother or my wife, Grace, so butt out!'

He heard her gasp as he headed out of the cubicle, across the deserted A and E waiting room and out of the hospital, limping not entirely because of his leg but because he was only wearing one boot. The other he'd stupidly left behind, and that made him even angrier than Grace's accusation. He looked up at the cloud-massed sky and wanted to yell his frustration to the wind.

Perhaps it was just as well there was no one around, although if he'd happened on someone he knew he could have asked that person to go back in and retrieve the boot for him. The hospital was quieter than he'd ever seen it, with no one coming or going from the car park.

He was contemplating radioing the constable on duty to come over and collect it for him when he heard the footsteps behind him.

Grace!

Coming to apologise?

'Here's your boot, and some antibiotics, directions on when to take them on the packet. And in answer to your question about rights, I thought, for some obviously foolish reason, I had the right of a friend.'

And with that she spun on her heel and walked briskly back into the hospital.

Wonderful! Now Grace had joined the throng of people he'd somehow managed to upset, simply because they refused to let him get on with his life his way.

Alone! With no emotional involvement with anyone or anything.

Except Sport, the three-legged blue heeler cattle dog he'd rescued from the dump one day.

And his parents—he liked his parents. And they'd known him well enough to back off when Nikki had died…

He climbed into his vehicle and slumped back against the seat. Was the day over? Please, God, it might be. On top of all the damage and power disruptions caused by the gale-force winds stirred up by Cyclone Willie, he'd had to handle traffic chaos at the fishing competition, an assault on Georgie Turner, the local obstetrician, Sophia Poulos, mother of the groom at the next day's wedding, phoning every fifteen minutes to ask about the cyclone as if he was personally responsible for its course, and to top it all off, he'd had to visit Georgie again.

She was still shaken from the assault by a patient's relative earlier that day, and nursing a hairline fracture to her cheekbone. Now Harry had to tell her there was a summons out for her stepfather's arrest—her stepfather who currently had custody of her little brother Max.

Did Georgie know where he was?

She hadn't known where the pair were, and he'd hated himself for asking because now she'd be even more worried about Max, whom she'd loved and cared for since he'd been a baby, bringing him up herself—except for the times when the worthless scoundrel who'd fathered him swooped in and took him away, no doubt to provide a prop in some nefarious purpose.

Max was such a great kid, growing up around the hospital, loved and watched out for by everyone in the close-knit community.

So Harry had been driving away from the doctors' house, seething with frustration that he couldn't offer anything to help the white-faced, injured woman, when the call had come in about the tree coming down to block the Wygera road. His chainsaw had already been in the vehicle so he'd decided to take out some of his anger and frustration on a tree.

None of which was any excuse for being rude to Grace…

Not wanting to think about Harry or the crushing words he'd used, Grace retreated to cubicle one once again and climbed back onto the examination couch. She stared at the stain on the ceiling, trying to see a penguin or a cane train engine but seeing only an amoeba.

Was it because she lacked imagination?

Not that she couldn't see the penguin but that she couldn't let Harry alone to get on with his life his own way.

Did her lack of imagination mean she couldn't understand his grieving process?

Hurt enveloped her—that Harry could say what he had. And while she knew she should have welcomed his angry comment because now she knew for sure she had to move on, such rational reasoning didn't make the pain any less.

She studied the stain.

'Is this place totally deserted?'

Another male voice, this one deep and slightly husky. Grace sprang off the couch and was about to emerge from the treatment cubicle when the curtain opened.

Luke Bresciano, hunky, dark amber-eyed, black-haired, Italian-Australian orthopod, stood there, smiling at her.

'I always napped on examination couches when I was on duty in the ER, and for some reason it's always treatment room one,' he teased.

He had a lovely smile but it didn't reach his eyes—a tortured soul, Dr B. And although, this being Crocodile Creek, stories about his past abounded—a woman who'd left him, a child—no one really knew any more about him than they had the day he'd arrived. Age, marital status and qualifications.

'You're here late. Do you have a patient coming in?' Grace asked, being practical and professional while wondering if she remembered how to flirt and if there was any point in trying a little flirtation on Luke. Although was there any point in swapping one tortured soul for another?

'I find sleep comes when it wants to and it wasn't coming so I drove up to see a patient I'd admitted earlier. I looked in on Susie while I was here—'

'Susie? Our physio Susie? In hospital? But she can't be.' Grace was stumbling over her disbelief. 'She's Emily's bridesmaid tomorrow. Mrs Poulos will have a cow!'

Luke offered a kindly smile—much like the one Grace usually offered drunks or people coming out of anaesthetic who were totally confused.

'You obviously haven't heard the latest. Susie had a fall and sprained her ankle earlier today—or is it yesterday now? But the bridesmaid thing's been sorted out. Her twin sister Hannah is here—they're identical twins—and she's going to do bridesmaid duties so the photos won't—'

'Be totally spoilt by Susie's crutches,' Grace finished for him, shaking her head in bemusement that such a wonderful solution—from Mrs P.'s point of view—had been found. Grace was quite sure Emily wouldn't have minded in the least.

Nodding agreement to her ending of the story, Luke finished, 'Exactly! So after visiting Susie, who was sound asleep anyway, I was taking a short cut out through here when I realised how empty it seemed.'

He smiled at Grace but although it was a very charming smile, it did nothing to her heart. She'd really have to work on it if she wanted to move on from Harry. 'I thought I'd better check we did have someone on duty.'

'Yes, that's me. I can't believe how quiet it is. All I heard from the day staff was how busy they'd been and I was busy earlier but now…'

She waved her arms around to indicate the emptiness.

'Then I'll let you get back to sleep,' Luke said.

He turned to depart and she remembered the stain.

'Before you go, would you mind having a look at this stain?'

The words were out before she realised just how truly weird her request was, but Luke was looking enquiringly at her, so she pointed at the stain on the ceiling.

'Roof leaking? I'm not surprised given the rain we've been having, but Maintenance probably knows more about leaking roofs than I do. In fact, they'd have to.' Another charming smile. 'I know zilch.'

'It's not a leak. It's an old stain but I'd really like to know what you think about the shape. You have to lie down on the couch to see it properly. Would you mind checking it out and telling me what it looks like to you?'

'Ink-blot test, Grace?' Luke teased, but he lay obediently on the couch and turned his attention to the stain.

'It looks a bit like a penguin to me,' Luke said, and Grace was sorry she'd asked.

She walked out to the door with Luke, said goodbye, then returned to the cubicle.

It *must* be lack of imagination that she couldn't see it. She focussed on the stain, desperate to see the penguin and prove her imaginative abilities.

Hadn't she just imagined herself darning Harry's socks?

The stain remained a stain—amoeba-like in its lack of form. She clambered off the couch, chastising herself for behaving so pathetically.

For heaven's sake, Grace, get over it!

Get over Harry and get on with your life.

She stood and stared at the stain, trying for a cane train engine this time…

Trying not to think about Harry…

Failing…

It had come as a tumultuous shock to Grace, the realisation that she was love with Harry. She, who'd vowed never to risk one-sided love again, had fallen into the trap once more. She'd fallen in love with a man who'd been there and done that as far as love and marriage were concerned.

A man who had no intention of changing his single status.

They'd been at a State Emergency Service meeting, and had stayed behind, as they nearly always did, to chat. Grace was team leader of the Crocodile Creek SES and Harry, as the head of the local police force, was the co-ordinator for all rescue and emergency services in the area.

Harry had suggested coffee, as he nearly always did after their fortnightly meetings. Nothing noteworthy there—coffee was coffee and all Grace's defences had been securely in place. They'd locked the SES building and walked the short distance down the road to the Black Cockatoo, which, although a pub, also served the best coffee in the small community of Crocodile Creek.

The bar had been crowded, a group of young people celebrating someone's birthday, making a lot of noise and probably drinking a little too much, but Harry Blake, while he'd keep an eye on them, wasn't the kind of policeman who'd spoil anyone's innocent fun.

So he'd steered Grace around the corner where the bar angled, leaving a small, dimly lit area free from noise or intrusion.

The corner of the bar had been dark, but not too dark for her to see Harry's grey eyes glinting with a reflection of the smile on his mobile lips and Harry's black hair flopping forward on his forehead, so endearingly her fingers had ached to push it back.

'Quieter here,' he said, pulling out a barstool and taking Grace's elbow as she clambered onto it. Then he smiled—nothing more. Just a normal, Harry Blake kind of smile, the kind he offered to men, women, kids and dogs a million times a day. But the feeble defences Grace O'Riordan had built around her heart collapsed in the warmth of that smile, and while palpitations rattled her chest, and her brain tut-tutted helplessly, Grace realised she'd gone and done it again.

Fallen in love.

With Harry, of all people…

Harry, who was her friend…

## CHAPTER TWO

GRACE fidgeted with the ribbon in her hair. It was too much—she knew it was too much. Yet the woman in the mirror looked really pretty, the ribbon somehow enhancing her looks.

She took a deep breath, knowing it wasn't the ribbon worrying her but Harry, who was about to pick them all up to drive them to the wedding.

The hurtful words he'd uttered very early that morning—*you're not my mother or my wife*—still echoed in her head, made worse by the knowledge that what he'd said was true. She *didn't* have the right to be telling Harry what to do!

It was a good thing it had happened, she reminded herself. She had to get past this love she felt for him. She'd had enough one-sided love in her life, starting in her childhood—loving a father who'd barely known she'd existed, loving stepbrothers who'd laughed at her accent and resented her intrusion into their lives.

Then, of course, her relationship with James had confirmed it. One-sided love was not enough. Love had to flow both ways for it to work—or it did as far as she was concerned.

So here she was, like Cinderella heading for the ball, on the lookout for a prince.

Harry's a prince, her heart whispered, but she wasn't having any of that. Harry was gone, done and dusted, out of her life, and whatever other clichés might fit this new determination.

And if her chest hurt, well, that was to be expected. Limbs hurt after parts of them were amputated and getting Harry out of her heart was the same thing—an amputation.

But having confirmed this decision, shouldn't she take her own car to the wedding? She could use the excuse that she needed to be with Mrs P. Keeping Mrs P. calm and rational—or as calm and rational as an over-excitable Greek woman could manage on the day her only son was married—was Grace's job for the day.

A shiver of uncertainty worse, right now, than her worry over Harry feathered down Grace's spine. Mike's mother had planned this wedding with the precision of a military exercise—or perhaps a better comparison would be a full-scale, no-holds-barred, Technicolor, wide-screen movie production.

Thinking now of Mrs Poulos, Grace glanced towards the window. Was the wind getting up again? It sounded wild out there, although at the moment it wasn't raining. When the previous day had dawned bright and sunny, the hospital staff had let out their collective breaths. At least, it had seemed, Mrs P. would get her way with the weather.

But now?

The cyclone that had teased the citizens of North Queensland for days, travelling first towards the coast then veering away from it, had turned out to sea a few days earlier, there, everyone hoped, to spend its fury without any further damage. Here in Crocodile Creek, the river was rising, the bridge barely visible above the water, while the strong winds and rain earlier in the week had brought tree branches crashing down on houses, and Grace's SES workers had been kept busy, spreading tarpaulins over the damage.

Not that tarps would keep out the rain if the cyclone turned back their way—they'd be ripped off by the wind within minutes, along with the torn roofing they were trying to protect—

'Aren't you ready yet?'

Christina was calling from the living room, although Grace had given her and Joe the main bedroom—the bedroom they'd shared for a long time before moving to New Zealand to be closer to Joe's family. Now Grace rented the little cottage from Christina, and was hoping to discuss buying it while the couple was here for the birth of their first child as well as the hospital weddings.

'Just about,' she answered, taking a last look at herself and wondering again if she'd gone overboard with the new dress and the matching ribbon threaded through her short fair curls.

Wondering again about driving herself but thinking perhaps she'd left that decision too late. Harry would be here any minute. Besides, her friends might think she was snubbing them.

She'd just have to pretend—she was good at that—

only today, instead of pretending Harry was just a friend, she'd have to pretend that all was well between them. In a distant kind of way.

She certainly wasn't going to spoil Mike and Em's wedding by sulking over Harry all through it.

'Wow!'

Joe's slow smile told her he meant the word of praise, and Grace's doubts disappeared.

'Wow yourself,' she said, smiling at him. 'Christina's pregnant and you're the one that's glowing. You both look fantastic.'

She caught the private, joyous smile they shared and felt it pierce her heart like a shard of glass, but held her own smile firmly in place. She might know she'd lost her bounce—lost a little of her delight in life and all the wonders it had to offer—but she'd managed to keep it from being obvious to her friends. Still smiling, still laughing, still joking with her colleagues, hiding the pain of her pointless, unrequited love beneath her bubbly exterior.

Pretence!

'And you've lost weight,' Christina said, eyeing Grace more carefully now. 'Not that it doesn't suit you, you look beautiful, but don't go losing any more.'

'Beautiful? Grace O'Riordan beautiful? Pregnancy affecting your vision?' Grace said, laughing at her friends—mocking the warmth of pleasure she was feeling deep inside.

Harry heard the laugh as he took the two steps up to the cottage veranda in one stride. No one laughed like Grace, not as often or as—was 'musically' the right word? Grace's laugh sounded like the notes of a beautiful bird, cascading through the air, bringing pleasure to all who heard it.

Beautiful bird? Was all this wedding business turning him fanciful?

Surely not!

While as for Grace…

He caught the groan that threatened to escape his lips. He was in the right—he had no doubt about that. What he did and didn't do wasn't Grace's business. Yet he was uneasily aware that he'd upset her and wasn't quite sure how to fix things between them.

Wasn't, for reasons he couldn't fathom, entirely sure he wanted to…

At least it sounded as if they were ready. He'd offered to drive the three of them, thinking his big four-by-four would be more comfortable for the very pregnant Christina than Grace's little VW, but now he was regretting the impulse. With the possibility that the cyclone would turn back towards the coast, he had an excuse to avoid the wedding altogether, which would also mean not having to face Grace.

Although Mike had been a friend for a long time…

A sudden gust of wind brought down a frond from a palm tree and, super-sensitive right now to any change in the atmospheric conditions, Harry stopped, turned and looked around at the trees and shrubs in the cottage's garden. The wind had definitely picked up again, stripping leaves off the frangipani and bruising the delicate flowers. He shook his head, certain now the cyclone must have swung back towards them again, yet knowing there was nothing he, or anyone else, could do to stop it if it continued towards the coast this time.

They would just have to check all their preparations then wait and see. Preparations were easy—it was the waiting that was hard.

'You look as if you're off to a funeral, not a wedding,' Christina teased as she came out the door, and though he found a smile for her, it must have been too late, for she reached out and touched his arm, adding quietly, 'Weddings must be hard for you.'

He shook his head, rejecting her empathy—not deserving it, although she wasn't to know that. Then he looked beyond her and had to look again.

Was that really Grace?

And if it was, why was his body stirring?

Grace it was, smiling at him, a strained smile certainly, but recognisable as a smile, and saying something. Unfortunately, with his blood thundering in his ears, he couldn't hear the words, neither could he lip-read because his eyes kept shifting from her hair—a ribbon twined through golden curls—to her face—was it the colour of the dress that made her eyes seem bluer?—to her cleavage—more stirring—to a slim leg that was showing through a slit in the dark blue piece of fabric she seemed to have draped rather insecurely around her body.

His first instinct was to take off his jacket and cover her with it, his second was to hit Joe, who was hovering proprietorially behind her, probably looking down that cleavage.

He did neither, simply nodding to the pair before turning and leading the way out to the car, trying hard not to limp—he hated sympathy—opening the front door for Christina, explaining she'd be more comfortable there, letting Joe open the rear door for Grace, then regretting a move that put the pair of them together in the back seat.

Mental head slap! What was *wrong* with him? These three were his friends—good friends—Grace especially, even though, right now, he wasn't sure where he stood with Grace.

Very carefully, he tucked Christina's voluminous dress in around her, extended the seat belt so it would fit around her swollen belly, then shut the door, though not without a glance towards the back seat—towards Grace.

She was peering out the window, squinting upwards.

Avoiding looking at him?

He couldn't blame her.

But when she spoke he realised just how wrong he was. He was the last thing on Grace's mind.

'Look, there's a patch of blue sky. The sun *is* going to shine for Mike and Emily.'

Harry shook his head. That was a Grace he recognised, always thinking of others, willing the weather to be fine so her friends could be blessed with sunshine at their wedding.

Although that Grace usually wore big T-shirts and long shorts—that Grace, as far as he'd been aware, didn't have a cleavage…

Christina and Joe had both joined Grace in her study of the growing patch of blue sky, Christina sure having sunshine was a good omen for a happy marriage.

'Sunshine's good for the bride because her dress won't get all wet and her hair won't go floppy,' Joe declared, with all the authority of a man five months into marriage who now understood about women's hair and rain. 'But forget about omens—there's only one thing that will guarantee a happy marriage, and that's a willingness for both partners to work at it.'

He slid a hand onto Christina's shoulder then added, 'Harry here knows that.'

Grace saw the movement of Harry's shoulders as he winced, and another shard of glass pierced her vulnerable heart. She hadn't been working at the hospital when Harry's wife, Nikki, had died, but she'd heard enough to know of his devotion to her—of the endless hours he'd spent by her side—and of his heartbreak at her death.

*You're not my wife!*

The words intruded on her sympathy but she ignored them, determined to pretend that all was well between them—at least in front of other people.

'What's the latest from the weather bureau, Harry?' she asked, hoping to divert his mind from memories she was sure would be bad enough on someone else's wedding day. 'Does this wind mean Willie's turned again and is heading back our way, or is it the early warning of another storm?'

He glanced towards her in the rear-view vision mirror and nodded as if to say, I know what you're doing. But his spoken reply was crisply matter-of-fact. 'Willie's turned—he's running parallel to the coast again but at this stage the bureau has no indication of whether he'll turn west towards us or continue south. The winds are stronger because he's picked up strength—upgraded from a category three to a category four in the last hour.'

'I wouldn't like to think he'll swing around to the west,' Joe said anxiously, obviously worried about being caught in a cyclone with a very pregnant wife.

'He's been so unpredictable he could do anything,' Harry told him. 'And even if he doesn't head our way, we're in for floods as the run-off further upstream comes down the creek.'

'Well, at least we're in the right place—at a hospital,' Christina said. 'And look, isn't that sunshine peeking through the clouds?'

Harry had pulled up in the parking lot of the church, set in a curve of the bay in the main part of town. Christina was right. One ray of sunshine had found its way through a weakness in the massed, roiling clouds, reflecting its golden light off the angry grey-brown ocean that heaved and roared and crashed into the cove beneath the headland where Mike's parents' restaurant, the Athina, stood.

He watched the ray of light play on the thunderous waves and knew Joe was right—omens like that meant nothing as far as happiness was concerned. The sun had shone on his and Nikki's wedding day—for all the good it had done.

Grace felt her spirits lift with that single ray of light. Her friends were getting married, she was looking good, and so what if Harry Blake didn't want her worrying about him? This was her chance to look at other men and maybe find one who might, eventually, share her dreams of a family.

Unfortunately, just as she was reminding herself of her intention to look around at the single wedding guests, Harry opened the car door for her, and as she slid out a sudden wind gust ripped the door from his hands and only his good reflexes in grabbing her out of the way saved her from being hit by it.

It was hard to think about other men with Harry's strong arm wrapped around her, holding her close to his chest. Hard to think about anything when she was dealing with her own private storm—the emotional one—raging within *her* chest.

*You're not my wife.*

He's done and dusted.

She pulled away, annoyed with herself for reacting as she had, but determined to hide how she felt. He'd taken her elbow to guide her across the windswept parking lot outside the church and was acting as if nothing untoward had occurred between them. He was even pretending not to limp, which was just as well because she had no intention of asking him how his leg was. Because, Mr Policeman, two could play the pretend game.

She smiled up at him.

'Isn't this fun?'

Harry stared at her in disbelief.

Fun?

For a start, he was riven with guilt over his behaviour the previous night, and on top of that, the person he considered—or had considered up until last night—his best friend had turned into a sexpot.

That was fun?

Sexpot? Where on earth had he got that word?

He cast another glance towards his companion—golden hair gleaming in the sunlight, the freckles on her nose sparkling like gold dust, cleavage…

Yep. Sexpot.

'You OK?'

Even anxious, she looked good enough to eat.

Slowly…

Mouthful by sexy mouthful…

'Fine,' he managed to croak, denying the way his body was behaving, wondering if rain had the same effect cold showers were purported to have.

Although the rain appeared to have gone…

Bloody cyclones—never around when you needed them.

'Oh, dear, there's Mrs P. and she looks distraught.'

Grace's voice broke into this peculiar reverie.

'Did you expect her to be anything but?' he asked, as Grace left his side and hurried towards the woman who was wringing her hands and staring up towards the sky.

'I'm on mother-in-law watch,' Grace explained, smiling back over her shoulder at him. Maybe they *were* still friends. 'I promised Em I'd try to keep Mrs P. calm.'

Harry returned her smile just in case the damage done was not irreparable.

'About as easy as telling the cyclone not to change course,' he said, before hurrying after Christina and Joe.

Grace carried his smile with her as she walked towards Mrs Poulos, although she knew Harry's smiles, like the polite way Harry would take someone's elbow to cross a road, were part of the armour behind which he hid all his emotions.

And she was through with loving Harry anyway.

Mrs P. was standing beside the restaurant's big catering van, though what it was doing there when the reception was at the restaurant, Grace couldn't fathom.

'What's the problem, Mrs P.?' Grace asked as she approached, her sympathy for the woman whose plans had been thrown into chaos by the weather clear in her voice.

'Oh, Grace, it's the doves. I don't know what to do about the doves.'

'Doves?' Grace repeated helplessly, clasping the hyperventilating woman around the shoulders and patting her arm, telling her to breathe deeply.

'The doves—how can I let them fly?' Mrs P. wailed, lifting her arms to the heavens, as if doves might suddenly descend.

Grace looked around, seeking someone who might explain this apparent disaster. But although a figure in white was hunched behind the wheel of the delivery van, whoever it was had no intention of helping.

'The dove man phoned,' Mrs P. continued. 'He says they will blow away in all this wind. They will never get home. They will die.'

'Never get home' provided a slight clue. Grace had heard of homing pigeons—weren't doves just small pigeons?

Did they home?

'Just calm down and we'll think about it,' she told Mrs P. 'Breathe deeply, then tell me about the doves.'

But the mention of the birds sent Mrs Poulos back into paroxysms of despair, which stopped only when Grace reminded her they had a bare ten minutes until the ceremony began—ten minutes before she had to be ready in her special place as mother of the groom.

'But the doves?'

Mrs P. pushed past Grace, and opened the rear doors of the van. And there, in a large crate with a wire netting front, were, indeed, doves.

Snowy white, they strutted around behind the wire, heads tipping to one side as their bright, inquisitive eyes peered out at the daylight.

'They were to be my special surprise,' Mrs P. explained, poking a finger through the wire to stroke the feathers of the closest bird. 'I had it all arranged. Albert, who is our new trainee chef, he was going to release them just as Mike and Emily came out of the church. They are trained, you know, the doves. They know to circle the happy couple three times before they take off.'

And heaven only knows what they'll do as they circle three times, Grace thought, imagining the worst. But saving Em from bird droppings wasn't her job—keeping Mrs Poulos on an even keel was.

'It was a wonderful idea,' Grace told the older woman. 'And it would have looked magical, but you're right about the poor things not being able to fly home in this wind. We'll just have to tell Mike and Emily about it later.'

'But their happiness,' Mrs P. protested. 'We need to do the doves to bring them happiness.'

She was calmer now but so determined Grace understood why Emily had agreed to the plethora of attendants Mrs P. had arranged, and the fluffy tulle creations all the female members of the wedding party had been pressed into wearing. Mrs P. had simply worn Em down—ignoring any suggestions and refusing to countenance any ideas not her own.

'We could do it later,' Mrs P. suggested. 'Maybe when Mike and Emily cut the cake and kiss. Do you think we can catch the doves afterwards if we let them out inside the restaurant? All the doors and windows are shut because of the wind so they wouldn't get out. Then we could put them back in their box and everything will be all right.'

Grace flicked her attention back to the cage, and counted.

Ten!

Ten birds flying around inside a restaurant packed with more than one hundred guests? A dozen dinner-jacketed waiters chasing fluttering doves?

And Em was worried the sea of tulle might make a farce of things!

'No!' Grace said firmly. 'We can't have doves flying around inside the restaurant.'

She scrambled around in her head for a reason, knowing she'd need something forceful.

More than forceful…

'CJ, Cal and Gina's little boy—he's one of the pages, isn't he?' She crossed her fingers behind her back before she told her lie. 'Well, he's very allergic to bird feathers. Think how terrible it would be if we had to clear a table and use a steak knife to do an emergency tracheotomy on him—you know, one of those operations where you have to cut a hole in the throat so the person can breathe. Think how terrible that would be in the middle of the reception.'

Mrs Poulos paled, and though she opened her mouth to argue, she closed it again, finally nodding agreement.

'And we'd get feathers on the cake,' she added, and

Grace smiled. Now it was Mrs P.'s idea not to have the doves cavorting inside the restaurant, one disaster had been averted.

Gently but firmly Grace guided her charge towards the church, finally settling her beside her husband in the front pew.

'Doves?' Mr Poulos whispered to Grace above his wife's head, and Grace nodded.

'No doves,' she whispered back, winning a warm smile of appreciation.

She backed out of the pew, her job done for now, and was making her way towards the back of the church, where she could see friends sitting, when Joe caught her arm.

'We've kept a seat for you,' he said, ushering her in front of him towards a spare place between Christina and Harry.

Sitting through a wedding ceremony beside Harry was hardly conducive to amputating him out of her heart.

Although the way things were between them, he might shift to another pew. Or, manlike, had he moved on from the little scene last night—the entire episode forgotten?

Grace slid into the seat, apprehension tightening ever sinew in her body, so when Harry shifted and his sleeve brushed her arm, she jerked away.

'Problems?' Harry whispered, misreading her reaction.

'All sorted,' she whispered back, but a flock of doves circling around inside the restaurant paled into insignificance beside the turmoil within her body.

Remembering her own advice to Mrs P., Grace closed her eyes and breathed deeply.

Harry watched her breasts rise and fall, and wondered just how badly he'd hurt her with his angry words. Or was something else going on that he didn't know about? He glanced around, but apart from flowers and bows and a lot of pink and white frothy drapery everything appeared normal. Mike was ready by the altar, and a change in the background music suggested Emily was about to make an appearance.

So why was Grace as tense as fencing wire?

She'd seemed OK earlier, as if determined to pretend everything was all right between them—at least for the duration of the wedding.

So it had to be something else.

Did she not like weddings?

Had something terrible happened in her past, something connected with a wedding?

The thought of something terrible happening in Grace's past made him reach out and take her hand, thinking, at the same time, how little he knew of her.

Her fingers were cold and they trembled slightly, making him want to hug her reassuringly, but things were starting, people standing up, kids in shiny dresses and suits were scattering rose petals, and a confusion of young women in the same pink frothy stuff that adorned the church were parading down the aisle. Emily, he assumed, was somewhere behind them, because Mike's face had lit up with a smile so soppy Harry felt a momentary pang of compassion for him.

Poor guy had it bad!

Beside him Grace sighed—or maybe sniffed—and

he turned away from the wedding party, sorting itself with some difficulty into the confined space in front of the altar, and looked at the woman by his side.

'Are you crying?' he demanded, his voice harsher than he'd intended because anxiety had joined the stirring thing that was happening again in his body.

Grace smiled up at him, easing the anxiety but exacerbating the stirring.

'No way,' she said. 'I was thinking of the last wedding I was at.'

'Bad?'

She glanced his way and gave a nod.

'My father's fourth. He introduced me to the latest Mrs O'Riordan as Maree's daughter. My mother's name was Kirstie.'

No wonder Grace looked grim.

And how it must have hurt.

But her father's fourth marriage?

Did that explain why Grace had never married?

'His fourth? Has his example put you off marriage for life?'

No smile, but she did turn towards him, studying him for a moment before replying, this time with a very definite shake of her head.

'No way, but I do feel a trifle cynical about the celebratory part. If ever I get married, I'll elope.'

'No pink and white frothy dresses?' he teased, hoping, in spite of the stirring, she'd smile again.

Hoping smiles might signal all was well between them once again.

'Not a froth in sight! And I think it's peach, not pink,' she said, and did smile.

But the smile was sad somehow, and a little part of him wondered just how badly having a marriage-addicted father might have hurt her.

He didn't like the idea of Grace hurting…

Handling this well, Grace congratulated herself. Strangely enough, the impersonal way Harry had taken her hand had helped her settle down. But just in case this settling effect turned to something else, she gently detached her hand from his as they stood up. And although he'd put his arm around her shoulders and given her a hug, it was definitely a friend kind of a hug and had reminded her that's what she was to him.

Now all she had to do was close her mind to the words being spoken at the front, pretend that Harry was nothing more to her than the friend she was to him, and keep an eye on Mrs P. in case she thought of some new reason for panic.

Fun!

It *was* fun, Grace decided, some hours later.

True, Harry had excused himself and left the church not long after the ceremony began, but whether because he couldn't bear to sit through it or to check on the latest weather report and weather-related incidents, she didn't know. Something had certainly happened—tiles or something coming off the roof—because there'd been loud crashing noises then the minister had insisted everyone leave through the vestry, disrupting the wedding party to the extent Grace had to calm Mrs P. down once again, persuading her the wedding was still legal even if the happy couple hadn't left as man and wife through the front door of the church.

Grace had driven to the restaurant with Mr and Mrs Poulos so hadn't caught up with Christina and Joe until the reception.

People milled around, sipping champagne, talking and even dancing. Luke Bresciano came up to her, took the champagne glass out of her hand, set it down on a handy table, and swept her onto the dance floor.

'I was looking for you,' he said, guiding her carefully around the floor. 'Have you heard the ink-blot joke? I remembered it after we looked at the stain last night.'

Grace shook her head, and Luke launched into the story of the psychologist showing ink-blot pictures to a patient.

'So the fellow looks at the first one, and says that's two rabbits having sex. The psychologist turns the page and the fellow says, that's an elephant and a rhino having sex. The psychologist is a bit shocked but he offers a third. That's three people and a dog having sex. Floored by this reaction, the psychologist loses his cool. "You've got a dirty mind," he tells his patient. "Me?" the patient says. "You're the one showing filthy pictures."'

Grace laughed, looking more closely at this man she barely knew. The lines around his eyes suggested he was older than she knew he was. Signs of the unhappiness she'd heard was in his background?

She asked about his early life but somehow the questions ended up coming from him, so by the end of the dance she knew no more than she had at the beginning.

Except that he had a sense of humour, which was a big point in his favour.

But when she glimpsed Harry across the room,

bending down to speak to Charles, the excited beating of her heart told her she had a long way to go in the getting over him stakes. Fortunately the best man—some friend of Mike's who'd come across from New Zealand—appeared and asked her to dance, so Harry was not forgotten but tucked away behind her determination to move on.

The dance ended, and she noticed Harry heading in her direction. Dancing with Harry was *not* part of the plan, so she picked up her glass of now flat champagne and pressed into an alcove of pot plants, hoping to hide in this corner of the greenery festooning the restaurant.

Could one hide from a policeman?

'You know I can't dance with my leg!'

It wasn't exactly the greeting she'd expected. In fact, the slightly petulant statement made no sense whatsoever.

'What are you talking about? What do you mean?' she demanded, looking up into Harry's face, which seemed to be flushed with the same anger she'd heard in his voice.

'That I can't dance with you,' he said, his words as cross as his first statement had been.

'Then it's just as well I'm not your mother or your wife,' Grace retorted, unable to keep up the 'friends' pretence another second. 'Because if I was, you'd be expected to dance with me.'

She tried to turn away but the greenery defeated her—the greenery and Harry's hand on her shoulder.

'I shouldn't have said that to you,' he said, tightening his grip when she tried to shrug it off. 'I'm sorry.'

Grace looked at him for a long moment. The flush

had faded, leaving his face pale and so tired-looking she had to sternly stem the flash of sympathy she felt towards him.

'No,' she told him, knowing this was the perfect time to begin to distance herself from Harry. 'I think it needed to be said. You were right, it's not my place to tell you what to do or what not to do. I overstepped the boundaries of friendship but it won't happen again, I promise you.'

Harry stared at her, totally befuddled by what had just occurred. Hadn't he apologised? Said what had to be said to make things right again between himself and Grace? So why was she rejecting his apology? Or, if not rejecting it, turning things so it had been her fault, not his?

He opened him mouth but what could he say? *Please, keep telling me stuff like that? Please, stay concerned for me?*

Ridiculous!

He should let it go—walk away—and hope everything would come right between them in time.

Hope they could go back to being friends.

But if he walked away she'd dance with someone else, and seeing Grace in that Italian doctor's arms, laughing up at some funny thing he'd said, had made Harry's gut churn.

'I can shuffle if you don't mind a shuffling kind of dance,' he heard himself say, and saw astonishment similar to what he was feeling reflected on Grace's face.

Her 'OK' wasn't overwhelmingly enthusiastic, but he was happy to settle for even grudging acceptance.

He put his arms around her, tucked her body close to his, and felt her curls tickle the skin beneath his chin.

Grace knew this wouldn't do much for her distancing-Harry plans, but surely a woman was allowed a little bit of bliss. She slid into his arms and put her arms around his back—allowable, she was sure, because it was going to be a shuffling kind of dance.

You are stupid, the sensible voice in her head muttered at her.

It's just pretence, she told her head. Everything else seemed to be about pretence these days so why not pretend, just for a short while, that they were a couple? After all, she could go back to distancing tomorrow.

It was heaven.

The band was playing a slow waltz, or maybe a slow two-step. Dancing was something she did naturally but had little knowledge about, and she and Harry were at the edge of the dance floor, barely moving to the music, content, as far as Grace was concerned, just to be in each other's arms.

What Harry was thinking was a mystery but, then, Harry in a social setting—apart from coffee at the pub—was something of a mystery as well.

No matter—he had his arms around her and that was enough.

Well, nearly enough. Outside the wind had gathered strength again and rain lashed the garden beyond the restaurant and flung itself against the windows. It was definitely 'snuggling closer' weather. If she moved just slightly she could rest her head against his chest, and for a little while she could dream.

Later, she couldn't remember whether she'd actually

made this daring move or not, but what she did remember was that the lights went out, then Harry spun her around, into even denser blackness in a corner of the restaurant.

And bent his head.

And kissed her.

Harry kissed her…

Folded in his arms, her curls tickling at his chin, Harry had ignored the cleavage as much as possible as he'd shuffled back and forth with this different Grace on the corner of the dance floor. But when the lights went out, he lost the slim reins of control he'd been clinging to and whisked her into the shadows of one of the palms that dotted the restaurant.

He bent his head, and kissed her, curls first, then her forehead, finding the salt of perspiration on her skin and a sweetness he knew by instinct was pure Grace.

His lips moved to her temples, felt the throb of a vein, then claimed her mouth, more sweetness, but this time mingled with heat as Grace responded with a fire that lit his own smouldering desire, so need and hunger fought common sense and a determination to not get involved.

A losing battle—as useless as trying to stop the wind that now raged again outside—as useless as trying to stop a cyclone…

He clamped Grace's curvy body hard against his leanness, and drank in the taste of her as his mouth explored and challenged hers. She met his challenge and responded with her own, so he was lost in the wonder and sweetness and fire that was this new Grace.

Gripped in the toils of physical attraction, a voice whispered in his head, but he ignored it and kept kissing the woman in his arms.

Lamplight. Flickering candles. Maybe the voice wasn't in his head. Someone was calling his name.

Urgently.

'Harry Blake.'

## CHAPTER THREE

CHARLES WETHERBY, the wheelchair-bound head of the hospital, was illuminated by candelabrum, held aloft by a young policeman, Troy Newton, the newest member of Harry's staff.

'Charles?'

Harry eased Grace gently away, tucking her, he hoped, into deeper shadows, and took the two long strides needed to bring him close to Charles.

'Bus accident up on the mountain road—road's subsided and the bus has slid down the mountain. Dan Macker called it in.'

'Do we know exactly where, and who's on the way?' Harry asked, looking towards the windows and knowing there was no way the rescue helicopter, based at the hospital, could fly in this wind.

'Where? This side of Dan's place. He saw the bus go past, then later heard a noise, and when he investigated he saw the landslide. Who's on the way? The fire truck, two ambulances each with two crew and the hospital's four-wheel-drive is on its way here to pick up whatever hospital staff you think you might need on site. Have you seen Grace? If we've got to set up a triage post and then get people off the side of the mountain, we'll probably need an SES crew up there as well—she can organise that.'

'I'll tell her,' Harry said, 'and head out there myself.'

Charles made an announcement aimed mainly at the hospital staff, telling them the hospital would go to the code black disaster plan, then Harry spoke, reminding people who would be taking part in the rescue on the mountain that there were open diggings and mine shafts on the slopes, legacy of the gold rush that had led to the birth of the township that had become Crocodile Creek.

He looked around the room, wondering who he'd take, picking out hospital staff he knew were fit and active, telling them to take the hospital vehicle while he'd check on his other staff and be right behind them.

He turned back towards the shadows but Grace had gone, no doubt because she'd heard the news. More candles had been lit, but it was impossible to pick her out in the milling crowd. Joe touched his arm.

'You go, I'll organise a lift back to the cottage for Grace and Christina then go up to the hospital to see if I can help.'

Harry nodded to Joe but his eyes still searched for Grace, although common sense told him she'd be in a corner somewhere, on her mobile, starting a phone relay to gather a crew at SES headquarters in the shortest possible time. Then she'd head to the headquarters herself to organise the equipment they'd need.

As he left the restaurant, striding towards his vehicle, that thought brought with it a sense of relief he didn't quite understand. Was it tied up with the fact that Grace was safer at headquarters, organising things, than on the side of a slippery mountain riddled with old mineshafts, fighting cyclonic winds in pitch darkness?

Surely not!

Although, as a friend, he was entitled to feel some concern for her safety, so it had nothing to do with the aberration in his feelings towards her—which was purely physical.

The wind was now so strong he had to struggle to open the car door—memories of a soft body held against his chest…

Get your mind focussed on the job!

He started the car and turned out of the car park, concentrating on driving through the lashing wind and rain.

*Ignoring the physical aberration?* That was the voice in his head again.

Of course he was ignoring it. What else could he do? Physical attraction had led him into a terrible mistake once before and had caused pain and unhappiness, not only to himself but to Nikki as well. It had flung him into an emotional swamp so deep and damaging he'd blocked emotion out of his life ever since.

So there was no way he could allow whatever physical attraction he might be feeling towards her to touch his friendship with Grace.

If he still had a friendship with Grace. Her words before the dance had indicated she was backing away from whatever it was they'd had.

Yet she'd kissed him back—he was sure of that.

He'd have to put it aside—forget about the kiss and definitely forget about the lust he'd felt towards his friend.

Determinedly setting these thoughts aside, Harry

drove cautiously down towards the town, automatically noting the level of the water beneath the bridge, forcing himself to think rescue not Grace.

He had to go, of course he did, Grace told herself as she watched Harry leave. She was on the phone to Paul Gibson, still the nominal head of the local SES, although since he'd been undergoing treatment for prostate cancer, Grace, as senior team leader, had taken over a lot of his responsibilities. But Paul's knowledge and experience were still invaluable, so Grace forgot about Harry and listened, mentally repeating all Paul had said so she'd remember.

Rolls of netting—she'd seen them in the big shed and often wondered about them—were useful in landslides. You could anchor them on the level ground and unroll them down the slope to make it easier for rescuers to clamber up and down.

'Belongings,' Paul continued. 'Gather up what you can of people's belongings. They're going to be disoriented enough, ending up in a strange hospital—if we can return things to them, it helps. And remember to search for a hundred yards all around the bus—people can wander off. As soon as my wife gets back from checking on the family, I'll get her to drive me up to Headquarters. I mightn't be much use out in the field, but I'll handle the radio calls and relays up there, which will leave you free to be out in the field.'

Through the window Grace saw Harry's big vehicle leave the car park.

'Thanks, Paul,' she said, staring out the window at the vehicle, hope sneaking in where wonder and amazement had been.

Harry had kissed her.

Surely he wouldn't have done that if he wasn't interested in her?

The sneaky scrap of hope swelled like a balloon to fill her chest.

Maybe, just maybe, she wouldn't have to get over Harry after all.

Or was she being stupid? The way she'd been with James? Thinking flowers and dinners out and a physical relationship meant love?

Not that she'd had any of that with Harry. Only one interrupted kiss.

The balloon deflated as fast as it had filled, leaving her feeling empty and flat.

One thing she knew for sure—she'd been stupid for kissing him back, for letting her lips tell him things her head knew she couldn't tell him.

She tucked her phone back into her beaded handbag and looked around the room, checking who was leaving, who might give her a lift home so she could change before going to Headquarters. Charles was leading the way out the door, Jill Shaw, director of nursing, moving more slowly to guide Susie, who was swinging along on crutches, thanks to her accident the previous day.

'Would you lot drop me home?' Grace asked, coming up to them. 'I can hardly organise my crew dressed like this.'

'No problem,' Charles told her, while Jill, who must have been running through the nursing roster in her head, added, 'You're off duty until Tuesday, aren't you, Grace?'

Grace nodded. Her month on night duty had finished at seven that morning and the change in shift meant she had three days off.

'But I grabbed a few hours' sleep this morning so I'm happy to be called in. If Willie's really heading back towards us, we'll need all available staff standing by.'

'We might need all staff back on duty, not standing by, if the bus that's come off the mountain had a full load of passengers,' Charles said, as the women ducked behind his wheelchair to escape some of the wind that was ripping across the car park, grabbing at Charles's words and flinging them into the air. 'With this weather, we can't fly people out, and at last report the coast road was flooding. We could have a very full hospital.'

Jill confirmed this with a quiet 'I'll be in touch' as she dropped Grace at the cottage, but nursing was forgotten as Grace stripped off her dress and clambered into her bright orange SES overalls, fitted on the belt that held her torch, pocket knife and radio then grabbed her keys and headed for Headquarters. The crews would be gathering. She'd send one support vehicle straight up the mountain, and hold the second one back until she heard from Harry in case some special equipment not on the main rescue vehicle was needed.

Or…

She went herself, with the first crew, partly because Paul had arrived to handle the office but also because she knew an extra person with nursing skills would be useful in the rescue mission. This truck held the inflatable tent they'd use for triage and the generator that kept it inflated. They'd have to make sure the tent was anchored securely in this wind.

The men and women chatted casually, but Grace, huddled in a corner, mentally rehearsed the jobs that lay ahead as she watched the wind slice rain across the windscreen and cause the vehicle to sway from side to side. Willie had turned and was heading their way—the cyclone warnings on the radio had confirmed what increased velocity in the wind had already told most locals.

How much time did they have to get ready?

Who would need to be moved from their homes? An evacuation list would have been drawn up but before she, or anyone else, could start moving people to safety, they had to get the accident victims off the mountain…

'Your crews finished?'

Grace was kneeling by a young woman, the last person to be pulled from the bus after the jaws of life had been used to free her. Unconscious and with probable head injuries, she lay on an undamaged part of the road, her neck in a collar, her body strapped to the cradle stretcher on which she'd been pulled up the muddy slope. Now, as the wind howled around them, they awaited the return of one of the ambulances that had been shuttling back and forth to the hospital for hours.

About half an hour earlier, once most of the accident victims had been moved out of it and ferried down the mountain, Harry had deemed the inflatable tent too dangerous. So Grace's crew had packed it and the generator back into the SES truck prior to departure.

A makeshift shelter remained to protect this final patient, but the wind was getting stronger every minute and now blew rain and forest debris beneath the sodden tarpaulin. Grace had angled her body so it shielded the young woman's face. She smoothed the woman's hair and removed leaves that blew onto her skin, but there was little else she could do for her—just watch and wait, holding her hand and talking quietly to her, because Grace was certain even unconscious people had some awareness.

'Are your crews finished?'

As Harry repeated his question, Grace turned to look at him. She'd heard him the first time but her mind had been too busy adjusting to his abrupt tone—and trying to work out what it meant—for her to answer.

'Just about,' she said, searching his face, lit by the last emergency light, for some hint of his mood. Disappointment because they'd failed to save the bus driver? No, deep down Harry might be gutted, but he would set it aside until the job was done.

Was his leg hurting?

It had to be, though if she offered sympathy it was sure to be rejected.

She stopped guessing about his mood, and explained, 'One of the team is already on its way back to base and the other is packing up the gear and should be leaving shortly. Why?'

'Because I want everyone off the mountain, that's why,' Harry said, his voice straining against the wind, but Grace's attention was back on her patient.

'She's stopped breathing.'

Grace leant forward over the young woman, tilted her head backwards then lifted her chin upward with one hand to make sure her airway was clear, and felt for a pulse with the other. Her fingers pushed beneath the woman's chin, and found a flutter of movement in the carotid artery.

She stripped off the oxygen mask and gave the woman two breaths, then checked the pulse again. Looked at Harry, who was now squatting by her side.

'You monitor her pulse—I'll breathe.'

They'd practised so often as a team, it seemed effortless now, Grace breathing, Harry monitoring the young woman's vital signs. Yet it was taking too long—were their efforts in vain?

'We'll get her,' Harry said, and the conviction in his voice comforted Grace, although she knew he couldn't be as certain as he sounded.

Or could he?

Grace stopped, and held her breath. The rise and fall of the young woman's chest told them she'd resumed breathing on her own.

'Yes!' Grace said, lifting her hand for a high-five of triumph, but Harry's hands were by his side, and the bleak unhappiness on his face was far from triumph.

Whatever pretence at friendship they'd managed during the wedding was gone.

Burnt away by the heat of that kiss?

Though why would *he* be upset over the kiss? Because it had broken some rule he'd set himself when his wife died?

Thou shalt kiss no other after her?

That was weird because Harry wasn't stupid and he must know that eventually nature would reassert itself and he'd want a sexual relationship with some woman—sometime.

Although as far as she knew, monks didn't…

'I want you off the mountain,' he said.

'I want us all off the mountain,' Grace retorted, battling to understand his mood. OK, he was worried about the cyclone, but they all were, and it certainly hadn't made the other rescuers go all brisk and formal. In fact, the others had made an effort to smile even as they'd struggled up the steepest parts of the slope—everyone encouraging each other.

All but Harry, who'd frowned at Grace whenever they'd passed, as if he couldn't understand who she was or perhaps what she was doing there.

'But that's hardly possible,' she continued crisply, 'without magic carpets to whisk us all away. The second SES crew will be leaving soon. The rest of the hospital personnel have gone back to deal with the patients as they arrive. I'm staying with this patient and I'll go back in the ambulance when it gets here.'

'This place is dangerous. The wind's increasing all the time. More of the road could slip, trees could come down.'

He was worrying about her safety. That was the only explanation for Harry's strange behaviour. The thought brought such warmth to Grace's body she forgot about distancing herself. She forgot about the cruel words he'd flung at her, and reached out to touch his arm.

'This is my job,' she said softly. 'We've had the risk-taking conversation, Harry, and while you mightn't like me talking about it you have to admit, as part of your job, you do it all the time. So you should understand I can't just get in the truck and go back to town, leaving this young woman with no one.'

'*I'm* here!' Harry said, moving his arm so her hand slid off—squelching the warmth.

It had been such a stupid thing to say Grace didn't bother with a reply. She checked the oxygen flowing into the mask that was once again covering the young woman's mouth and nose, and kept a hand on the pulse at her wrist.

Harry stood up and walked away, no doubt to grump at someone else. But who else was still here? Grace had no idea, having seen the last of the SES crew heading down the road towards their truck. The first truck had taken a lot of the less badly injured passengers back to the hospital to be checked under more ideal conditions than an inflatable tent and arclamps in lashing wind and rain. The team leader of that truck would then assist in finding accommodation for those not admitted to hospital, while the other members would begin preparations for the arrival of Willie, now on course to cross the coast at Crocodile Creek.

'That you, Grace?'

She turned at the shout and saw two overalled figures jogging towards her.

'Mike! Not on your honeymoon, then?'

Mike Poulos, newly married helicopter pilot and paramedic, reached her first and knelt beside her patient.

'Could hardly leave without Em, who's in Theatre as we speak, so I decided I might as well make myself useful. I can't fly in this weather but I still remember how to drive an ambulance. Who's this?'

'We don't know,' Grace told him, watching the gentle

way he touched the young woman's cheek. 'Maybe a young backpacker—there were quite a few young people among the passengers. No one seems to know for certain who was on the bus.'

'Mainly because the driver was killed and we can't find a manifest in the wreckage.' Harry was back, nodding to the two paramedics as he explained. 'This patient's the last, but we need to take the driver's body back to the hospital.'

'She's unconscious?' Mike asked Grace, who nodded.

'And though there are no obvious injuries, she's very unstable. She stopped breathing after she was brought up from the bus,' Grace told him.

'I hate transporting a dead person with a live one, but the bus driver deserves the dignity of an ambulance,' Mike said. He looked towards Harry.

'If we take the bus driver, can you take Grace?'

Harry looked doubtful.

'As against leaving me up here all night? Taking two patients means I won't fit in the ambulance,' Grace snapped at him, aggravated beyond reason by this stranger in Harry's body.

'I'll take Grace,' he conceded, then he led the two men away to collect the driver's body, before returning for Grace's patient.

Grace walked beside the young woman as the men carried her to the ambulance, then watched as she was loaded, the doors shut, and the big four-by-four vehicle took off down the road.

'My car's this way,' Harry said, and strode off into the darkness. He was carrying the last of the lights and the tarpaulin they'd used as a shelter, and though he looked overladen he'd shaken his head when had Grace asked if she could carry something.

Still puzzling over his strange behaviour, she followed him down the road to where it widened enough for a helicopter to land—*when* weather permitted. His was the only vehicle still there.

She waited while he stacked the gear he'd carried into the back, then she made her way to the passenger side, opened the door—no chivalry now—and climbed in.

'What is with you?' she demanded, as soon as he was settled into the driver's seat. 'Is your leg hurting? Should I have a look at it?'

He glanced towards her, his face carefully blank, then looked away to turn the key in the ignition, release the brake and start driving cautiously down the wind- and rain-lashed road.

'My leg's fine.'

Grace knew that was a lie—it couldn't possibly be fine—but she wasn't his mother or his wife so she kept her mouth shut.

Between them the radio chattered—the ambulance giving the hospital an ETA, a squad car reporting on more power lines down. Yet the noise barely intruded into the taut, chilly atmosphere that lay between the two of them as they crawled at a snail's pace down the mountain road.

'Is it the bus driver? I know there's nothing worse than losing a life at an accident, but he'd have been dead the moment the bus rolled on him, poor guy. There was nothing anyone could have done, and from what the rescuers were saying, he did all he could to save the bus from being more badly damaged—all he could to save more lives.'

'So he dies a hero. Do you think that makes it better for his kids? His name was Peter. He had two kids. Photo in his wallet.'

Making him a person in Harry's eyes. No wonder he was upset.

'Someone's father,' Grace whispered, feeling the rush of pity such information always brought, but at the same time she wondered about Harry's reaction. She'd seen him bring in dead kids from car accidents without this much emotional involvement. 'No, I'm sure, at the beginning at least, the hero stuff won't make a scrap of difference to two kids growing up without a father. But all we can do is help the living, Harry. We can't change what's past.'

Harry sighed.

'You're right, and if I think rationally about it, the simple fact of having a father is no guarantee of happiness,' he said glumly. 'Georgie's Max—his father's just a nasty waste of space—and yours doesn't sound as if he brought you much joy.'

'It might not have been all his fault. I kind of got dumped on him,' Grace told him, defending blood ties automatically. 'I didn't ever know him as a small child, then, when I was seven, my mother died and my aunt got in touch with my father, who'd emigrated from Ireland to Australia, and I was sent out here.'

She paused, remembering the small sad child who'd set off on that long journey, scared but somehow, beyond the fear, full of hope. She'd lost her mother, but ahead had lain a father and a new family, a father who'd surely love her or why else had he sent the money for her ticket?

'What number wife was he on at that stage?' Harry asked, and Grace smiled.

'Only number two, but, looking back, I think the marriage was probably teetering at the time and my stepmother had only agreed to take me because she thought it might keep my father with her. Poor woman, she was kind, but she was stuck with me when he took off again, so to her I always represented a terrible time of her life. And the little boys, my stepbrothers, well, I can't blame them for hating me—I arrive and their father leaves. In their young minds there had to be a connection.'

'No one could have hated you, Grace,' Harry said, but although the words were kind his harsh voice suggested that there was more than the dead bus driver bothering him.

She listened to the radio calls, not knowing what to guess at next, but certain she needed things sorted out between them because the success of both the preparations for, and the work after, Willie's arrival depended on them working harmoniously together.

With a sigh nearly as strong as one of the wind gusts outside, she tried again.

'Is that all that's bothering you? The bus driver? His kids?'

He turned to look at her and even in the dimly lit cabin she could read incredulity.

'We're in a serious situation here,' Harry said, spacing the words as if he'd had to test each one in his head before letting it out.

'We've been in serious situations before, Harry,' Grace reminded him, ducking instinctively as a tree-fern frond careened towards her side of the car. 'Remember the time we went out to the reef in a thunderstorm to rescue the diver with the bends? That wasn't serious?'

No comment.

Grace sighed again.

Was she becoming a sigher?

Surely not. And if she considered it, being at odds with Harry could only help her getting-over-him decision. A sensible woman would welcome this new attitude of his and get on with her life. But this was, as Harry had just pointed out, a serious situation and Grace knew she wouldn't give of her best if there was added tension between the two of them.

She knew too that they'd be in some dangerous situations in the future, and if they didn't have one hundred per cent attention on the job, a dangerous situation could become a disaster.

She had to sort it out.

But how?

Bluntly!

There was only one other thing that had happened this evening that could explain his attitude.

Or maybe two things.

'Are you still annoyed about me nagging you to be careful?' she asked, thinking it was easier to bring this up than to mention the kiss.

'I apologised for that.'

More silence.

That left the kiss.

Grace's last remnant of hope that the kiss might have meant something to Harry died.

For sure, he'd started it, but the worst of it was, she'd kissed him back.

She knew it had been a mistake from her side of things, but had it also worried Harry? Had she revealed too much of how she felt?

Was that what was bothering him?

If so, she had to get around it somehow. Act as if it had meant nothing to her—pretend it had been nothing more than a casual smooch in the darkness.

More pretence!

She took a deep breath, and launched into the delicate conversation.

'Is this because we kissed? Has one kiss turned you into some kind of cold robot? If so, that's ridiculous. It was a mistake so let's get past it. We've been friends for more than two years, Harry, and friends talk to one another. We can talk about this. Isn't that easier than carrying on as if we've broken some immutable law of nature? I mean, it was a nice kiss as kisses go, but it's not likely that we'll ever do it again.'

As the flippant words spun around the cabin of the vehicle, mingling with the radio's chatter and the wind that whirled outside, Grace felt her heart break.

But this was how it had to be. She didn't want Harry thinking the kiss meant any more to her than it had to him.

He glanced her way, his face still betraying nothing.

'*Do* we talk to one another?' he asked, delving so far back into Grace's conversation it took her a moment to remember she'd made the comment.

'Yes,' she said, although doubts were now popping up in her head.

They did talk, but about their work, their friends, the hospital, the town, the price of sugar cane—Harry's father being the owner of the local mill—the weather, and just about everything under the sun.

'Not about ourselves,' Harry said, still staring resolutely through the windscreen, although, given the debris flying through the air, that was a very good idea. 'Today's the first time I've heard you mention a father.'

'Everyone has one,' Grace said glibly, but the look Harry gave her told her flippancy wasn't going to work.

'OK, you're right. We don't talk much about ourselves,' Grace admitted, though she wasn't sure what this had to do with the kiss, or with Harry's mood. 'But talking's a two-way street, Harry. Talking—really talking—means sharing small parts of yourself with another person, and it's hard to do that if the other person isn't willing to share as well. Sharing that kind of talk leads to intimacy in a friendship and intimacy leaves people vulnerable. You treat everyone the same way probably because you don't want that intimacy—don't want anyone coming that close to you. The last thing in the world you'd want to seem is vulnerable.'

Harry glanced her way, frowned, then turned his attention back to the road, slowing down as the branch of a blue fig tree crashed onto the road right in front of them. He manoeuvred the car carefully around it.

'So you start the talking,' he finally said, totally ignoring her comments about his behaviour. 'Is it just because of your father you don't like weddings?'

It was the very last conversational gambit Grace had expected.

'Who said I don't like weddings?'

'You were so tense you could have snapped in half in there this afternoon.'

Because it *was* a wedding and I was sitting next to you, and it was hard not to indulge, for just a wee while, in a pointless daydream.

Grace was tempted to say it—to tell him of her feelings. The way the wind was blowing, literally, and sending tree limbs onto the road, they could both be killed any minute.

Would it be better or worse if Harry died knowing she loved him?

The thought of Harry dying made her heart squeeze into a tight little ball, while memories of the one time she *had* told a man she loved him made her cringe back into the seat.

She could still hear James's voice—his snide 'Love, Gracie? How quaint! What a sweet thing you are! Next you'll be telling me you're thinking of babies.'

Which she had been.

No wonder she could still feel the hurt…

'Well?' Harry persisted, and Grace had to think back to his question.

'It wasn't the wedding,' she managed to say, as Harry slammed on the brakes and his left arm shot out to stop her forward momentum.

'Thank heaven for traction control,' he muttered as the car skidded sideways towards the edge of the road then stopped before plunging off the side of the mountain. 'What was it, then?'

Grace shook her head.

'I can't believe we're having this conversation,' she said. 'Any minute now a tree's going to land across us and you're worried about why I was tense at the wedding.'

She paused, then added crossly, 'Anyway, this conversation isn't about me—it's about you. I didn't change from a friend to a frozen robot in the time it took to drive from town up the mountain.' She peered out through the windscreen. 'Why have we stopped?'

'I don't like the look of that tree.'

Harry pointed ahead and, as Grace followed the line of his finger, the huge forest red gum that had been leaning at a crazy angle across the road slid slowly downwards, the soaked soil on the mountainside releasing its tangle of roots so carefully it was only in the last few feet the massive trunk actually crashed to the ground.

'Oh!'

The nearest branches of the tree were right in front of the bonnet of Harry's vehicle, so close some of their smaller limbs were resting on it.

'We'll never clear it by hand. I'll radio for a car to come and get us on the other side, but we'll have to climb around the tree. For the moment, we'll just sit here until we're sure it's settled.'

Even as he said the words Harry regretted them. Of course they were safer in the vehicle than out there in the maelstrom of wind, rain and flying debris, but out there, talk would be impossible. In the car—in the dry warm cocoon it provided—even with the radio going, there was a false sense of—what?

He shuddered—Grace's word 'intimacy' seemed to fit.

What's more, there was no excuse to not talk...

He finished his call, telling base not to send someone to clear the tree as the conditions were too dangerous and the exercise pointless because the road was cut further up at the landslide. He glanced at Grace, who was still staring at the tree that hadn't collapsed on top of them, and he felt the stirring her blue dress had triggered earlier. She'd changed into her bulky but protective SES overalls, but hadn't removed the ribbon from her hair, so it now snaked through her wet curls, slightly askew so a bit of it crossed the top of her delicate pink ear.

He'd never looked at Grace's ears before, he realised as he reached over and used his forefinger to lift the ribbon from the ear then tease it gently out of her sodden hair. He had, of course, intended giving it back to her, but when she eyed the tatty wet object and muttered, 'What a fun way to end a wedding,' he decided she didn't want it, so he dropped it into his shirt pocket, did up the button and patted it into place.

He wasn't going to accept Grace's 'frozen robot' description, but he couldn't deny anger had been churning around inside him for the last few hours. Why *was* he so cranky?

Because he was worried, sure, but if he was honest with himself it was more than that. He could only suppose it was because Grace had added to his worries. From the moment she'd appeared at the accident site, he'd felt a new anxiety gnawing at his gut, and every time he saw her, each time wetter and paler than the time before, anxiety had taken another vicious bite.

That it was related to the kiss and the new attraction he felt towards her he had no doubt, but on a treacherous mountain road as a cyclone roared towards them and trees came crashing down, this was neither the time nor the place for introspection.

Or distraction.

Although maybe if he kissed her again, it would sort itself out. He could spend the waiting time kissing her, which would also make talking impossible. His body liked the idea, but his head knew that was the worst possible way to pass the time.

However appealing it might seem.

'You didn't answer about the kiss.'

Her statement startled him. There she was, still staring at the tree, yet picking up on some vibe he didn't know he was giving out.

But this was Grace—she deserved an honest answer.

'It was physical attraction, Grace,' he began, and waited to see if she'd turn towards him. Perhaps speak and save him the necessity of saying more.

She didn't, although she did glance his way momentarily.

'Strong physical attraction—we both felt it—but physical, that's all.'

Another glance, then all he got was her profile, although he fancied now she might be frowning, so he waited some more.

'And that's bad?' she finally queried.

'I believe it is. Well, not necessarily bad in a right and wrong sense, but dangerous, Grace. Misleading. Troublesome.' There, it had been said. Now they could get back to being friends.

Or as close to friends as they'd be able to get after his comments earlier.

## CHAPTER FOUR

GRACE stared out through the windscreen at the fallen tree as she ran the explanation through her head, suspecting it might be Harry's way of saying that physical attraction was all he could feel for a woman these days. Putting it like that was less blunt that telling her he was still in love with his dead wife and always would be.

And although she'd always kind of suspected this, the confirmation of the idea caused Grace pain—physical pain, like a cramp around her heart.

The hateful, hurtful words, *you're not my wife*, took on a whole new meaning.

Perhaps she was wrong, and he wasn't saying that at all. One last gulp of hope remained in the balloon. Forgetting she was supposed to be distancing herself, she turned back towards him, determined to sort this out once and for all.

'Why is it dangerous? Misleading?'

Harry was staring at her, frowning slightly as if he wasn't certain who she was, and showed no sign of understanding her questions, let alone answering them.

'You must have a reason for believing it's bad,' she persisted.

Harry, who'd been thinking how pretty her eyes were and wondering why he'd never considered Grace's eyes before any more than he'd considered her ears, shrugged off the remark, although he suspected she wasn't going to let this go. But how could he explain the still bruised part of his heart that was Nikki? Explain the magnitude of their mistake?

'We should start walking.'

'No way!' She nodded towards the radio which had just advised them the car was forty-five minutes away. 'Even if it takes us half an hour to get over or around the tree, we'd still be waiting in the rain for fifteen minutes, and that's if the road's not blocked further down.'

He nodded, conceding her point, but said nothing, pretending fascination with the babble on the radio—trying to forget where physical attraction had led once before *and* trying to block out the insidious desire creeping through his body every time he looked at Grace.

He patted his pocket.

One more kiss won't hurt, his physical self tempted, but a glance at Grace, wet curls plastered to a face that was pinched with tiredness, told him that it would hurt.

If not him, then definitely her.

And he hated the idea of hurting Grace any more than he had already.

Hated it!

Another glance her way told him she was still waiting for an answer.

Would wait all night…

'It confuses things,' he said. 'I mean, look at us, good friends, and suddenly we're all hung up over a kiss.'

'We weren't exactly good friends when it happened,' she reminded him. 'And *I'm* not hung up over it.'

'Maybe not, but you're only pushing this kiss business because you don't want to talk about why you were so uptight at the wedding.' Good thinking, Harry, turn defence into attack. 'That, if you remember, Grace, was where this conversation started. With the fact that we don't really talk to each other. And now I know about your father, I would think you'd be as wary of physical attraction as I am. Or did he fall madly and totally in love with all four of his wives?'

It was a low blow, and he sensed she'd cringed a little from it, making him feel a bastard for hurting her. But it would be better this way—with the kiss passed off as the aberration he was sure it was and the two of them getting on with the friendship they'd always shared.

Not totally convinced by this seemingly sensible plan, he checked the weather, acknowledged an ETA call from the car coming to collect them, waited until the wail of the three hourly cyclone warning coming from the radio stopped, then pushed his companion a little further.

'Do you know what I know about you, Grace? Really know about you?' He didn't wait for her to answer, but held up two fingers. 'Two personal things—that's all. You hate being called Gracie, and you think you're too short.'

'I think I'm too short?' Grace repeated, confused by

that accusation and disturbed by the 'Gracie' echo of her own thoughts earlier. 'What makes you think I think I'm too short?'

He had the hide to smile at her! Smug smile of a man who thought he'd scored a point.

'Because of the way you throw yourself into things—especially the SES. You told me you joined the equivalent operation down there in Victoria the moment you were old enough—why? I bet it was because people had always seen you as small and cuddly and cute but in need of protection, and you had to prove to them and to yourself that you could hold your own both with bigger, taller women and with men. I see it every time we're on calls together and even when we're doing exercises—you have to go first and go highest, or deepest, or whatever. You're proving you're not only equal to other team members but better than most of them.'

'And you think that's because I'm short?' Grace demanded, hoping she sounded incredulous, not upset because he'd read her so well—although she'd got past proving her stuff a long time ago.

'I know it was, but now it's probably because you are the best—or one of the best—that you do the things you do.'

Conceding her point was definitely a low blow but, unable to refute this statement, she went back to the original bit of the 'short' conversation.

'You can add a third thing to what you know of me—I hate being thought cute!'

Harry smiled again, causing chaos in Grace's body—palpitations, tingling nerves, butterflies swarming in her stomach. Not good things to feel towards a man who'd more or less admitted he'd never love again. Not good things to feel when she was in her getting-over-him phase.

'You're especially cute when you're angry,' he teased, sounding like her friend Harry once again, although the palpitations persisted, accompanied by a twinge of sadness for what couldn't be.

Attack—that would be a good distraction for both her heart and her head.

'Well, I don't know how you can talk about always going highest or deepest—at least I don't take risks,' she told him. 'You're the one who plunges into situations the rest of us feel are too dangerous.'

'I'm not a volunteer like you guys. It's my job.'

No smile, and he'd turned away so all she could see was his profile. Hard to read, Harry's profile, although it was very nice to look at. Very well defined with its straight nose and black brow shadowing a deep-set eye. High cheekbones with shadows underneath, and lips—

She had to stop this! She had to push her feelings for Harry back where they belonged—deeply hidden in her heart.

For the moment.

Just till she got rid of them altogether.

Returning to the attack might help…

'Oh, yes? Like every policeman in Australia would have gone down in those shark-infested waters, with a storm raging, to rescue that diver?'

'Every policeman who can swim,' he said, smiling to lessen the lie in the ridiculous statement.

'Rubbish!' Grace dismissed both smile and lie with

a wave of her hand. 'If your guess—and I'm not admitting it's right, Harry—is that I went into the SES because I was short, then my guess is you do all this dangerous stuff because you don't give a damn about what happens to you. That's understandable to a certain extent, given the loss of your wife. Taking risks might have helped dull the pain at first but now it's become a habit.'

Sheesh! Was she really doing this? Talking to Harry about his wife, and his attraction to danger? The very subject he'd warned her off last night?

And how was he reacting now?

He'd turned away, the profile gone, and all she had was a good view of slightly over-long hair.

Silky hair—she'd felt it when her fingers had somehow made their way to the back of his head as they'd kissed.

Her fingers were remembering the slide of his hair against her skin when he turned back to face her.

Half smiling…

'I asked for that,' he said quietly, reaching out and touching her face, perhaps pushing a wet curl off her forehead. 'Saying that we never talked.'

Then he leaned towards her and very gently pressed a kiss against her lips.

'Time to move, my tall, brave SES friend. Where's your hard hat?'

The tender kiss and Harry's softly teasing voice caught at Grace's heart and made her vision blur for an instant. But Harry was right—they had to move, and she had to get her mind off kisses and tenderness and concentrate on getting around the tree.

She felt around her feet for the hard hat then remembered she'd given it to the volunteer who'd climbed into the bus to tend that final passenger while others had cut her free. The helmet had a lamp on it that meant he'd been able to see what he'd been doing.

She explained this to Harry who made a huffing noise as if such an action had been stupid.

'Not that it matters now,' she told him. 'They never do much to keep off the rain.'

But Harry had other ideas, reaching behind him for the wide-brimmed felt hat issued to all police officers up here in the tropics and plonking it down on her head.

'There, it suits you,' he said, and she had to smile.

'Because it's so big it covers all my face?'

The hat had dropped to eyebrow level, but she could still see Harry's face, and caught the frown that replaced the smile he'd offered with the hat.

'That's another thing I know about you,' he said crossly. 'You're always putting yourself down. Not like some women do when they're looking for compliments, but it's as if you genuinely believe you're not smart, and pretty, and…'

Grace had her hand on the catch of the door, ready to open it and brave the wild weather outside, but Harry's pronouncement stopped her.

'And?' she asked, half wanting to know, half uncertain.

'And tonight in that blue thing you looked beautiful,' he said. 'Bloody beautiful!'

He was out the door before Grace could react. Actually, if he hadn't opened her door for her he could have been halfway to Crocodile Creek before she reacted, so lost was she in a warm little cloud of happiness.

Harry thought she'd looked beautiful…

Bloody beautiful…

Harry shut the car door, took Grace's hand and drew her close to his body. Since Grace had forced him to think about it, he'd realised his problem was physical attraction mixed with angry concern. The combination was so unsettling it was muddling both his mind and his body at a time when his brain needed to be crystal clear and all his senses needed to be on full alert.

On top of that, his inability to do anything about their current precarious situation—to protect Grace from this fury Nature was flinging at them—had his jaw clenched and his muscles knotted in frustration.

And his leg hurt…

He tried to tuck Grace closer as they followed the beam of light from his torch, clambering over the lesser boughs and branches, heads bent against the wind and rain. She was so slight—had she lost weight lately and he hadn't noticed?—she could blow away.

He gripped her more tightly.

'Harry!'

Had she said his name earlier that this time she pressed her lips against his ear and yelled it?

'What?'

'I think that way's clearer,' she yelled, pointing towards the base of the tree. 'There's a branch there we can use to climb onto the trunk, and even if we have to jump off the other side, it might be better than scrambling through the tangle of branches up this way.'

She was right and he should have worked it out himself, but the mess on the road was nothing to the mess in his head. He had to get past it—to rid his mind of all extraneous thoughts. Tonight, more than ever before, he'd need to be clear-headed in order to protect the people of his town.

She'd moved away though still held his hand, leading him in the direction she'd indicated, picking her way over the fallen branches. A sudden whistling noise made him look up and he dived forward, seizing Grace in a flying tackle, landing with her against the protective bulk of the huge treetrunk.

The branch that had whistled its warning crashed to the ground in front of them.

'This is ridiculous. I want you to go back and wait in the car,' he said, holding her—too tightly—in his arms, desperate to keep her safe.

'Are you going back to sit in the car?' she asked, snuggling up against his chest, which didn't help the mess in his head.

'Of course not. There's a cyclone coming. I have to get back to town.'

She reached up and patted his cheek.

'So do I,' she said softly. 'So maybe we'd better get moving again.'

'No thank-you kiss for saving your life?'

Oh, no! Had he really said that? What was wrong with him? The very last thing he needed to be doing was kissing Grace.

'I think kissing has caused enough problems tonight, don't you?' she replied, but the hand that was resting on his cheek moved and one fingertip traced the outline of his lips, reminding him of the heat the kiss had generated earlier—stirring the glowing coals of it back to life.

He stood up, still holding her, controlling breathing that was suddenly erratic, while looking around for any new source of danger. But though the wind still blew, it seemed relatively safe.

'I'm going to boost you up onto the trunk. Get over the top and into the shelter of it on the other side as quickly as you can.'

He lifted her—so light—and set her on the trunk, then heaved himself up, his leg objecting yet again to the rough treatment it was getting. Then he followed her as she dropped swiftly down to road level again. There were fewer branches to trip or slow them down on this side, so he took her hand again and hurried her along the road, sure the car would meet them before long, although driving through the storm had its own problems.

'Lights!'

Grace pointed as she yelled the word at Harry. Even if he didn't hear her, he'd surely see the lights. She couldn't wait to get to the car, not because the wind and rain and flying leaves and branches bothered her unduly but to get away from Harry—out of touching distance, where it was impossible to make sense of all that had happened during the course of this weird evening.

The thought that Harry might be physically attracted to her had filled her with joy, but his evident distrust of such attraction could only mean he still had feelings for his wife. In his mind, physical attraction to another woman must seem like betrayal—a form of infidelity—although Nikki had been dead for nearly three years.

Then there was the question of whether they were still friends.

*And* her determination to move on from Harry—now made harder than ever because of the kiss.

Grace sighed. If she wanted a husband and family, she *had* to move on. She may have looked beautiful in her blue dress earlier today, but what chance did she have against the memory of a woman who'd not only been tall and slim and elegant, but a former local beauty queen—the Millennium Miss Caneland—and a popular television personality?

Even when she was dying, Nikki Blake had been beautiful. Grace had seen enough photos of her to know that much.

And nice with it, according to the staff who'd nursed her.

Grace sighed again.

'Not right. The lights aren't getting closer.'

She caught the end of Harry's sentence and peered ahead through the worsening deluge. Not only weren't the lights moving, but they appeared to be pointing upwards.

'He's slid off the road.'

Harry's words confirmed her thoughts and she broke into a jog, running behind him as he dropped her hand and raced towards the lights.

Hairpin bends around the mountain—they rounded one, then two, and were on the outward curve of a third when they saw the vehicle, which had come to rest against a pillar-shaped rock, its headlights pointing uselessly into the blackness of the forest.

'Stay here,' Harry ordered, but Grace was already picking her way carefully down the slope, testing each foothold before shifting her weight.

The torch beam cut through the useless illumination provided by the vehicle's headlights, but revealed nothing more than a cloud of white behind the windscreen. The air bags had obviously worked.

Then, as the torch beam played across the vehicle, Grace saw a movement, a hand, pushing at the cloud of white, fighting against it.

'It's Troy!'

Harry's voice held all the anxiety and pain she knew he'd feel about this, the youngest of the men on his staff.

'Sit still,' he yelled, scrambling faster down the slope, cursing his bad leg, and unheeding of the danger to himself as he plummeted towards the young policeman. 'The less you move, the less risk there is of the vehicle moving.'

Grace followed more cautiously, aware, as Harry was, that Troy wouldn't hear the warnings over the wind and through windows wound up tightly against the weather.

Harry reached the car, more careful now, not touching it—not touching anything—but circling, motioning with both hands for Troy, whose face was now visible, to be still. Grace stopped a little further up the hill, then turned to look back the way they'd come.

'Would you trust that red gum to hold the car if we wind the winch cable around it?'

She pointed towards a tree not unlike the one that

had fallen close to them earlier, but this one was on the far side of the road.

'We'll have to,' Harry said. 'For a start, we'll just use it to anchor the vehicle while we get Troy out. I won't risk using the winch with him in the cabin. You stay clear of everything while I take the cable up to the tree.'

He made his way to the front of the vehicle where the winch was sited and bent to release the cable.

Grace watched the careful way he touched the winch and understood his caution. The vehicle might seem secure enough, resting as it was against a massive rock, but with all the rain they'd had, the rock could have been undermined and any change in the dynamics of the vehicle could send it and Troy plummeting into the gully.

'Damn! I can't get in the back to get a bag,' Harry muttered, looking helplessly around then focussing on Grace. 'I don't suppose you're wearing something—no, of course you're not. It'll have to be my jacket.'

He handed the hook of the winch cable to Grace to hold and for the first time she realised he was still in his dinner suit. The bow-tie was gone but, yes, that was definitely a filthy, sodden dinner jacket he was removing.

'What do you need it for?' Grace asked as he took the cable hook from her and turned towards the road.

He looked back at her and smiled.

'To wrap around the tree. We all keep bags in the back of our vehicles to use as tree protection but as I can't get at a bag, the jacket will have to do. If there's no protection the steel cable can ringbark the tree and possibly kill it.'

Grace shook her head. Here they were in the rainforest, with gale-force winds and torrential rain whipping the vegetation to ribbons, and Harry was protecting a gum tree?

She watched him clamber and limp his way back up to the road, seeing the way his wet shirt clung to his skin, defining the muscles and bones as well as if he'd been naked.

She shut her eyes, trying to blot images of a naked Harry from her mind, then turned back to Troy, using her hands as Harry had, to motion him to stillness, smiling encouragement. And something worked because although all his instincts must be screaming at him to escape the confines of the vehicle, he stayed where he was—statue still.

'I'll just hook this up—doubling the cable back to the vehicle halves the weight on the winch, although the vehicle's only a couple of tons and the winch's weight capacity is five tons.' Harry explained, returning with the hook end of the cable, which he attached to a towing point at the front of the vehicle. 'Now, I'll take up any slack in the cable then get in the cab to check the lad.'

'*I'll* get in the cab to check him,' Grace said. 'And don't bother arguing because you know it makes sense. I weigh half as much as you do so, like with the cable, we're halving the risk of the vehicle moving.'

Even in the torchlight she saw Harry's lips tighten, going white with the pressure of not arguing, but in the end he gave a nod.

This wasn't anything to do with the new physical attraction, Harry assured himself as he very carefully opened the passenger door of the cambered vehicle—

the door not jammed against the rock. His anxiety was for Grace, his friend.

'You OK?' he asked, peering through the maze of white towards the young constable.

'I think I've hurt my leg.'

Troy's voice wavered slightly and Harry understood. Barely more than a kid, he'd had to drive out through the wind and rain and flying missiles, then the car had skidded and he'd thought he'd had it.

'Grace will check you out,' Harry told him, turning towards Grace so he could help her into the cabin.

Beneath his wide-brimmed hat, her face was pale and streaked with dirt, and the embattled smile she gave him tweaked at something in his heart.

Concern, that's what it was. The same concern that was making his stomach knot as she slid across the seat, cutting at the air bags with the penknife off her belt, talking all the time to Troy about where he hurt and how he felt.

'There'll be a torch snapped in grips underneath the dash,' he told Grace when she'd collapsed the air bags and pulled them out of the way.

'Thanks!'

She found the torch and turned it on, setting it down so its light shone on her patient. Then, as her small but capable hands slid across Troy's head, feeling for any evident damage, Harry remembered this was only the beginning of the salvage operation. Unless they wanted to walk the forty-odd kilometres back to Crocodile Creek, he had to get this vehicle back up onto the road.

He prowled around it, checking the tyres—all intact—and damage to the body that might inhibit movement of the wheels. The mudguard, which had taken the brunt of the collision with the rock, was pushed in, but he found a strong branch and levered it off the rubber of the tyre. Everything else looked OK, which wasn't surprising as his reading of the accident had the vehicle going into a slow slide, first across the road, then down the slope to where it had come to rest against the rock.

'Where do you keep the first-aid kit in these new vehicles?' Grace called to him, and he turned to see she'd clambered over the back of the front seat and was now searching around behind the back seats.

'It should be strapped against the back of that seat you're on,' he told her, managing to answer although his lungs didn't want to breathe while she was moving in the cabin.

'Got it. I think Troy's right leg might be broken. I'll give him a painkiller before I try to move him, then splint it as best I can.'

She turned back to her patient, the small medical kit already open on her lap.

'Actually, Troy, it might be best if you fainted when we move you. That way you mightn't feel the pain so much.'

The lad grinned at Grace and Harry shook his head. They were like two kids playing doctors, seemingly unaware that a twisted metal cable was all that held them from the very real possibility of death.

'Do we really need to get him out?'

Grace had skidded across the seat to speak quietly to Harry, while Troy's eyelids were closing, no doubt in response to the drug she'd given him.

'I don't want to try winching it with anyone inside,' Harry told her once again. 'In ordinary circumstances it's better for have someone steering, but not in this situation where we don't know if the anchoring tree will hold the weight. The winch will pull the front around this way, then drag the vehicle up the slope.'

'We hope,' Grace said, and for the first time since their adventure together had begun she sounded tired.

'The cable's holding—let me in there!' Harry said, his stomach knotting with more anxiety.

'No, I'll manage and I need you there to help Troy out and lift him down to the ground. Would there be something in the back we can wrap him in? He's already shocky from the accident and his leg. I don't want that getting worse.'

Harry pictured the gear they all carried in the back of the big police vehicles.

'There'll be a small waterproof tarp folded in the pocket behind the driver's seat and a space blanket in a pouch beside it. Get them both out and we'll wrap him in the space blanket then the tarp. It will make moving him easier as well.'

Grace found them both and wriggled across the seat to drop them out the door to Harry, then, satisfied the painkiller had had time to work, she turned her attention back to her patient.

Her first examination of him had told her he was holding up well. His pulse and breathing were steady, his pupils responding evenly to light, and he was able to move all his limbs so the front and side air bags seemed to have done their jobs, protecting his head and holding his body firmly in the seat belt so his spine wasn't compromised.

But even with a painkiller circulating in his blood and blocking messages to and from his brain, he was going to be in agony when he moved his leg.

'Troy, I need to get you over onto this passenger seat before we can get you out. The best way I can see to do it would be for you to lie sideways across the centre console so your head and shoulders are on the passenger seat behind me, then if you can bring your good leg up onto your seat and use it to help you inch your way towards the door until your butt's on this side. Can you do that?'

Troy looked at her, his eyes glazed by the medication, but he nodded and turned so he could wiggle across the seat. His groan as he moved confirmed her thoughts, but she had to get him out of the vehicle before she could splint his leg and stabilise him properly.

She was squatting in the footwell on the passenger side, her body canted across the gear lever as she reached out to take a firm grip on his injured leg. She had to get it up onto the seat of the car before she could examine the damage and was concentrating on doing this is carefully as possible, trying not to hurt him, when the vehicle moved.

Troy let out a yelp, and Harry roared, 'Keep still!'

'As if I needed to be told that!' Grace muttered to herself, frozen in place with Troy's calf held gingerly in her hands.

'It's my weight coming onto this side,' Troy said.

But it was Harry's 'I need to get you both out now!' that caught Grace's attention.

She couldn't see anything from where she was so she continued with her job, lifting Troy's injured leg up onto the seat.

He gave a whistling sigh then slumped against the seat, the pain making him pass out.

Swelling around his ankle suggested the problem was there, or at the base of his tib and fib, but there was no time to do anything but get him out, preferably while he was still unconscious.

'How are we going to do this?' she called to Harry, who now had the door propped or tied open in some way.

'You push his shoulders down towards me, and I'll ease him out. Do what you can to protect his leg as we move him.'

Back in the footwell on the passenger side, she eased Troy's body around so his shoulders slid out the door. Harry's hands caught him, then lifted him as Grace grasped the injured limb to lift it over the centre console and gently out the door.

Harry cradled the young man in his arms, holding him as easily as she'd have held a baby, then he knelt and rested his burden on the spread-out covers on the ground, so carefully Grace shook her head in wonder at his gentle strength.

'The space blanket's a bit wet but it will still keep his body warmth in,' he said, wrapping first it and then the tarp around Troy's upper body, leaving his legs unwrapped so Grace could see to his injury.

Again using her knife, she cut through the leather of

his boot, wanting to ease the constriction on his blood vessels that the swelling would be causing.

'Does he need this to order a new pair?' she asked Harry, tossing the wrecked boot to one side, cutting off Troy's sock now so she could put a half-splint around his foot to hold it steady while allowing for more swelling.

The police car's first-aid kit didn't run to splints, but there were plenty of sticks which she could pad with torn strips of sock before binding them into place around his foot and ankle.

Harry watched her work—small, capable hands moving so steadily she might have been in A and E, not on a dangerous, slippery slope with wind and rain raging about her.

She was good!

'OK?'

Had she said something that he'd missed while thinking about her, that now she was standing beside him, waiting for a response?

'He's done?'

Harry looked down at the young policeman who was now fully wrapped in the space blanket and tarp.

'We just need to get him up the hill,' Grace said, nodding up the slope. 'I'll take his legs.'

For a moment Harry considered arguing but although he'd been able to lift Troy free, he knew he couldn't carry him all the way up the slippery hill when he was healthy, let alone with a bung leg. Between them they lifted the injured man and carried him up the slope, slipping and sliding, Troy groaning from time to time, but eventually they had him safely on the road.

Grace took off Harry's hat and placed it, carefully tilted, on Troy's head to keep the worst of the rain from his face, then she watched as Harry made his way back down the slope and, using a hand-held remote control, started the winch.

She heard the winch motor whirr and held her breath then, oh, so slowly, the front of the big police vehicle swung around and, with wheels churning the surface of the slope to mud, it began to move, inch by inch, towards the tree that held its weight.

Harry had placed Troy well away from where the car would reach the road, and out of danger should the tree fall, but still Grace felt her nerves tighten, fear for all of them should the tree come down, or the vehicle not make the road, clutching at her stomach.

It was nearly up, front wheels on the verge, the winch whining complaints all the way, when the back wheels skidded, sending a final flurry of slush into the air before ploughing forward onto the bitumen.

'You did it!' Grace yelled, abandoning her patient to jump up in the air in excitement. She'd have hugged Harry if their earlier conversation hadn't suggested even friendly hugs should be avoided. 'You got it up!'

'But will it go?'

Harry's question tempered her delight, but she sensed satisfaction in his voice and knew he was fairly confident the vehicle would be drivable. He was unhooking the towing cable, then using the winch to wind it up, while Grace walked over to the tree to retrieve his dinner jacket.

'Beyond repair?' Harry asked, seeing the muddy, crumpled garment in her hands.

'We'll see,' she said, clutching the jacket to her chest, holding onto something that was Harry's, barely restraining an urge to sniff at it in the hope of picking up something of his scent.

'You're so tired you've gone loopy!' she muttered to herself, returning to her patient, who was peering out from underneath the hat, no doubt wondering if there was any chance he could be moved out of the rain.

Harry started the car then drove slowly towards them, checking the vehicle was safe to drive. He stopped beside Troy and Grace, leaping out to open the back door and lift Troy inside.

'See if you can strap him in there so he's comfortable,' he said to Grace, who scrambled in beside her patient. 'Then you hop in the front and put on your seat belt. We don't want any more patients delivered to the hospital today.'

Grace obeyed, making Troy as comfortable as she could, checking his pulse again before abandoning him to climb over into the front seat and strap on her seat belt.

'OK?' Harry turned towards her as he asked, and the smile he offered was so kind Grace felt tears prickle behind her eyelids. She knew it was relief that they were all safe, and tiredness as it had been a very long day, but try as she may she couldn't answer him, making do with a very watery smile instead.

She was exhausted, Harry realised, remembering something she'd said that morning when they'd been called out to an accident at Wygera—something about just coming off night duty.

'When did you last sleep?' he demanded, anxiety making his voice more abrupt than he'd intended.

But Grace didn't answer. She was already asleep.

At least he'd got everyone off the mountain…

'Scruffy!'

Max slid and scrambled down the hill, stumbling over rocks, ducking around the ferns, yelling until he thought his chest would burst.

The bus had been on its side, that's all he remembered. The bus being on its side and no windows where the windows should have been.

No Scruffy either.

His dog was gone.

'Scruffy! Come on, boy. Scruffy!'

He listened for the yelp that Scruffy always gave in answer to his name, but how to hear a small dog's yelp when the wind was howling and stuff was crashing in the bush all around him?

'Scruffy!'

## CHAPTER FIVE

HARRY drove carefully down the road, one hand fiddling with the radio, which seemed to be the only thing not working in the vehicle. Had a wire come loose? He twirled knobs and banged his hand against it, but couldn't pick up even a burst of static.

No distraction there…

He checked the rear-view mirror. Troy appeared to be asleep as well. So he looked back at Grace, at her pale face and almost translucent eyelids, at the shadows under her eyes and the spread of freckles now dark against her skin.

Grace!

He shook his head, unable to deny the attraction that still stirred within his body.

What was happening to him? Why had his body chosen this of all times to remind him of his physical needs?

And chosen Grace of all women?

He guessed a psychologist would tell him it was because the grieving process was finally over, but he knew what had kept him celibate since Nikki's death had been as much guilt as grief. Guilt for the pain he'd caused her. Yes, there'd been grief as well, grief that someone as young and lovely as Nikki should have to die. Grief for the child he'd lost. And grief for the friendship he'd damaged somewhere along the way in his relationship with Nikki.

He looked at Grace, knowing a similar close friendship was at risk here.

Grace! Every now and then, in the past, he'd caught a fleeting glimpse of another Grace behind the laughing, bubbly exterior most people saw—a glimpse of a Grace that disturbed him in some way.

Tonight, learning about her father—thinking about a small child flying all the way from Ireland to Australia in search of the love she hadn't found—he'd found a clue to the hidden Grace and understood a little of the pain and tears behind the laughter.

So now, more than ever, he didn't want to hurt her…

'Did I sleep?'

Grace peered blearily around her. They were in the emergency entrance at the hospital and, outside the car, Harry was holding the rear door while a couple of orderlies lifted Troy onto a stretcher.

'Like a log,' Harry told her, his smile lifting the lines tiredness had drawn on his face.

'No, stay right where you are,' he added, as she began to unbuckle her seat belt. 'I'm taking you home. Quite apart from the fact you're exhausted, you're so filthy you're the last thing anyone would want in a hospital.'

'You're not so sprucy clean yourself,' Grace retorted,

taking in the mud streaks on the wet shirt that clung to Harry's chest.

Then, remembering, she clutched his dinner jacket more tightly.

Pathetic, that's what she was, but the filthy, ragged garment in her hands had become some kind of talisman.

Though it would hardly have the power to ward off a cyclone.

'Willie?' she asked, looking beyond the well-lit area to where the wind still lashed the trees and threw rain horizontally against the building.

'Definitely heading our way.' Harry watched the orderlies wheel Troy towards the hospital, obviously torn between wanting to follow and getting Grace home. 'We're down to hourly warnings.'

'Then I've got work to do,' Grace said, unbuckling her seat belt once again. 'You go with Troy, I'll grab a hospital car, go home and change, then see what's happening on the evacuation front. I assume the SES crews started with the nursing home down by the river, so most of those people should be in the civic centre hall by now. I'll get the list and organise for all the others to be collected or chivvied into shifting under their own steam.'

She'd opened the car door while she'd proposed this eminently sensible plan, but Harry took the door from her grasp, used one firm hand to push her back into the seat and shut the door again.

'I'll take you home,' he repeated. 'Two minutes to see someone's attending to Troy and I'll be right back. We need to do the individual evacuations on our list together. We discussed this in the contingency meetings. You'll need police presence to get some of those stubborn elderly die-hards in the most flimsy of old houses to move.'

Grace acknowledged his point with a pathetically weak smile. Battling wind and rain and an approaching cyclone was bad enough, but battling all the conflicting emotions the evening had stirred up at the same time was making the job doubly—no, a hundred times—more difficult.

Harry followed Troy's stretcher into A and E, where the scene resembled something from the film set of a disaster movie.

Only this wasn't a movie, it was real.

'How's it going?' he asked Charles, who had rolled towards him as Troy was taken into a treatment cubicle.

'It looks worse than it is. I think we've got things under control, although we've some badly injured people here in the hospital. There's one young woman with head injuries. Thank heavens Alistair—you know Alistair? Gina's cousin?—was here. He's a neurosurgeon with skills far beyond anyone we have on staff. He's put her into an induced coma for the moment—who knows how she'll wake up? We lost one young girl, and that last patient…' Charles paused and shook his head. 'She died before she got here.'

He seemed to have aged, but Harry understood that—he felt about a hundred years old himself.

'How's everything out there? Did you get everyone off the mountain?'

Harry nodded then looked around again, looking ahead, not thinking back. He'd done enough of that lately.

'You've obviously cleared the walking wounded. Where are they?'

'If they weren't locals with homes to go to, they were sent to the civic centre hall. Volunteers there are providing food and hot drinks.'

Charles paused then added, 'Actually, if you're going that way and I'm sure you will be some time, you might take the belongings we haven't matched to patients with you and see if you can find owners for them at the hall. The gear's in Reception.'

Someone called to Charles, who wheeled away, while Harry strode through to Reception, aware he'd been longer than the two minutes he'd promised Grace. Perhaps she'd fallen asleep again.

Wet, squashed, some muddy, the belongings rescued from the bus formed a sorry-looking heap on the floor in one corner of the usually immaculate reception area. How was he going to ferry this lot out to the car? He'd walked through from the corridor, thinking about the belongings, and now saw the two people who stood beside it.

Georgie Turner and Alistair—the doctor Charles had mentioned. They would have been working flat out since the casualties had begun coming in, but they weren't thinking medicine now. Georgie was staring down at the small, muddy backpack in her hands. She'd emptied it—a pathetic bundle of child's clothing and a ragged teddy bear had tumbled out and were lying at her feet.

While he watched, she knelt and lifted the teddy bear. The face she raised to him was terror-stricken.

'Max was on that bus,' she whispered.

'Your Max?'

Harry found himself staring helplessly at her. Georgie's beloved Max—hell's teeth, they all loved Max.

'Harry, have you found any kids?' Georgie demanded. And then the remaining colour drained out of her face. 'He's not…he's not one of the bodies, is he? Oh, God, please…'

'He's not,' Harry said, crossing swiftly to her, kneeling and gripping her hands. 'Georgie, I've been up there. We searched the surrounding area. We found no kids.'

'His dad… Ron's on the run. They might both…'

'I know Ron, Georgie. He wasn't on the bus.'

'But he might be hiding. He might—'

'Georgie, any person in that bus would be far too battered to be thinking about hiding. And the wind's unbelievable. Ron might be afraid of jail but there are worse things than jail, and staying out in the rainforest tonight would be one of them.'

'But Max is definitely there,' Georgie faltered. She looked up at Harry. 'He is,' she said dully, hugging the bear tighter. 'This is Spike. Max has just stopped carrying Spike round but Spike's never far from him.'

Behind them the phone rang, but the pile of child-size clothes on the floor reminded Harry of something.

'There's a shoe,' he told her, looking through the mass of wet belongings and not finding it. 'I'll just ask someone.'

He left the reception area, remembering the bridesmaid, Hannah, had found the shoe. Where was it now? He tracked it down at the desk of the children's ward.

The shoe was small and very muddy, with an orange

fish painted on it, the eye of the fish camouflaging a small hole.

Harry held it in his hand and hurried back to Georgie, showing her the shoe then seeing a quick shake of her head.

'That's not Max's.'

Her dismissal of it was so definite, Harry shoved the shoe into his pocket to think about later.

'We've got to go back out there,' Georgie added.

Images of young Max, a kid who'd had enough problems in his life thanks to his wastrel, drug-running father, alone in the bush, maybe injured, definitely wet, and probably terrified, flashed through Harry's mind. His gut knotted as he realised the impossibility of doing what she'd suggested.

'There's a tree across the road—we can't get through. I'd go myself and walk in, Georgie, but I can't leave town right now.'

He could feel her anguish—felt his own tearing him apart—but his duty had to be to the town, not to one small boy lost in the bush while a cyclone ripped the forest to shreds above his head.

'Of course you can't, go but I can. I'm going out there now.'

He saw the determination in her eyes, but could he stop her?

He had to try…

'Georgie, there's a cyclone hitting within hours. There's no way I can let you go, even if you could get through, which you can't. The tree's crashed down across the road not far from the landslide. We were lucky to get the last of the injured out.'

'I'll take my dirt bike,' she snapped. She tried to shove Harry aside but he wouldn't move.

Harry ignored the fists beating at his chest, trying desperately to think through this dilemma. Georgie could throw her bikes around as competently as she wore the four-inch heels she fancied as her footwear. She'd be wearing a helmet—

As if that would help!

'Georgie, he might not even be out there. You said yourself it's not his shoe.'

'Then there are two kids. Let me past.'

Georgie shoved at him but Harry held her, and made one last attempt to persuade her not to go.

'We've got no proof he's there. It's suicide.'

'We do have proof,' Alistair said from behind them. 'We've had confirmation Max was on the bus. Suicide or not, there's a child's life at stake. I'll go with her.'

Harry's mind processed what he knew of Alistair. Gina's cousin—Harry had met him at a fire party on the beach some months ago when the American had come to visit Gina—or more to check out Gina's fiancé Cal, the locals had thought.

Stuffed shirt had been Harry's immediate reaction.

Stuffed shirt who could ride a bike?

The pushing stopped. Georgie whirled to face Alistair, her face a mixture of anguish and fear. 'You can't.'

'Don't you start saying can't,' Alistair said. 'Harry, the tree's blocking the road, right? Who else in town has a dirt bike?'

'I've got one,' Harry told him, thinking it through. If Max *was* out there…

Maybe he had no choice but to let them go. 'It's in the shed, Georgie, fuelled up, key above the door. And be careful, keep in mind at all times that there are open mineshafts on that mountain.'

But Georgie wasn't listening. She was staring at Alistair.

'You really can ride?'

'I can ride.'

'You'd better not hold me back,' she snapped.

'Stop arguing and get going—you don't have long,' Harry told them. 'You've got a radio, Georg? Of course not. Here, take mine and I'll pick up a spare at the station. Your cellphone might or might not work. And take a torch, it's black as pitch out there. Rev your bikes, he might hear the noise.'

Harry watched them go then pulled the shoe out of his pocket, grasping it in his hand, feeling how small and insubstantial it was.

Were there two children lost in the bush?

Surely not.

But his heart clenched with worry, while his hands fondled the little painted shoe. Georgie had said it was too small for Max. Max was seven, so the shoe would fit…

A two-and-a-half-year-old?

Harry shook his head. Why did thoughts like that creep up on him at the most inopportune times?

And wasn't he over thinking back?

He tucked the shoe back into his pocket, gathered up a bundle of backpacks and suitcases and headed out to his vehicle, thanking someone who'd come out from behind the reception desk and offered to help carry things.

It wasn't until he'd packed them into the back of the big vehicle that he realised he'd lost his passenger.

'If you're looking for Grace, she went into A and E,' a nurse standing outside in the wind and rain, trying hard to smoke a cigarette, told him.

Harry was about to walk back inside when Grace emerged from the side door, head bowed and shoulders bent, looking so tired and defeated Harry hurried towards her, anxiety again gnawing at his intestines.

He reached her side and put his arms around her, pulling her into an embrace, holding her tightly as the wind and rain swirled around them.

'What's happened?' he asked as she burrowed her head into his chest as if trying to escape herself.

'She died.' The whispered words failed to register for a moment, then Grace lifted her head and looked up into his face. 'Our woman, Harry. The last one out of the bus. I've just seen Mike. She died before they reached the hospital. Massive brain injuries, nothing anyone could do.'

'Oh, Grace!' he said, and rocked her in his arms, knowing exhaustion was adding to the regret and hurt of the woman's death. He'd felt the same extreme reaction when Charles had given him that news.

'She had a boyfriend on the bus,' Grace continued. 'He was seated with her and got out uninjured, but she had to use the bathroom and was in there when it happened. They're from Germany and now he has to phone her parents.'

'I'll do that, it's my job,' Harry said, but Grace shook her head.

'Charles is phoning now—he speaks German so

he'll support the boy. But fancy someone phoning, Harry, to say your daughter's dead.'

She began to shiver and Harry led her to the car, helping her in, wanting to get her home and dry—and safe.

Safe? Where was safe tonight? Nowhere in Crocodile Creek, that was for sure.

Grace fell asleep again on the short drive to her cottage and this time, when he stopped the car, Harry sat and looked at her for a minute. He had the list and could do the evacuations himself, although that would be pretty stupid as he was likely to be needed other places or would be taking calls that would distract him.

And on top of that, she'd be furious.

He sighed, reached out to push a wet curl off her temple, then got out of the car, walked, with difficulty as the wind was far stronger here on the coast, around the bonnet, then carefully opened the passenger door, slipping his hand inside to hold Grace's weight so she didn't slide out.

Her lips opened in a small mew of protest at this disruption, but she didn't push him away so he reached across her and undid the catch on her seat belt, conscious all the time of the softness of her body and the steady rise and fall of her breasts.

She stirred again as he lifted her out, then she rested her head against his shoulder and drifted back to sleep.

But once inside he had to wake her—had to get her out of her sodden garments for a start.

'Grace!'

He said her name so softly he was surprised when she opened her eyes immediately. Was it her nursing training kicking in that she could come so instantly awake?

And frowning.

'Harry? Oh, damn, I fell asleep again. You should have woken me. You've carried more than your share of people tonight, and your leg must be killing you.'

'You don't weigh much. I'll set you down and as you still have power, I'll put the kettle on. I want you to get dry, have a hot drink then gather some things together for yourself. I'll drop you at the civic centre and you can sleep for a couple of hours.'

He eased her onto her feet just inside the door of her cottage.

'Sleep?' She looked so astounded he had to smile.

'What you've been doing in the car. Remember sleep?'

The feeble joke fell flat.

'I can't sleep now!' she muttered at him, then added a glare for good measure. 'Unless you're going to sleep as well,' she dared him. 'Then I might consider it.'

'You know I can't—not right now—but I'll be only too happy to grab a nap whenever I can. You should be, too, and now's as good a time as any.'

'So you can run around on your own, doing all the evacuations I'm supposed to be doing, fielding phone calls and giving orders and generally doing your super-hero thing. Well, not on my watch,' she finished, her usually soft pink lips set in a mutinous line.

He was about to deny the superhero accusation when he realised that was exactly what she wanted. She was turning the argument back on him.

'Well, fine,' he grumbled. 'But you're not going anywhere until you've had a hot drink.'

He stalked towards her kitchen.

Joe had obviously remembered the cyclone preparations from his time working in the town because the windows were all taped with broad adhesive tape, and a note on the kitchen table told them he'd taken Christina to the hospital because he was working there and hadn't wanted to leave her at the cottage on her own.

'Also large as she is,' he'd added, 'she swears she can still be useful.'

Harry filled the kettle, banging it against the tap because his frustration with Grace's behaviour still simmered.

'Stubborn woman!' he muttered to himself, finding the instant coffee and spooning a generous amount into two cups, adding an equal amount of sugar. It wasn't sleep but maybe a caffeine and sugar boost would help them tackle what still lay ahead of them this night.

Still grumpy, though not certain if it was because of Grace's refusal to obey his orders or her repetition of the superhero crack, he was carrying the filled cups and some biscuits he'd found in the pantry through to the living room when a small mumble of frustration made him turn. Grace was slumped on the sofa. She had managed to remove her boots but was now fumbling with the press studs that held her overalls together down the front.

Grumpiness was swallowed by concern so strong he felt shaken by the power of it.

'Here, let me,' Harry said, setting down the coffee and stepping towards her, telling her at the same time about the note and the preparations Joe had made, hoping the conversation might mask the trembling of his fingers.

He undid the studs then the Velcro strips and eased the heavy, wet fabric off Grace's shoulders. His voice—in the midst of explaining that Joe had left the water bottles, bedding, radio and batteries in the bathroom—faltered and his fingers shook a little more as he saw the swell of Grace's breasts, clad only in some scraps of dark blue lace—the colour making her ivory skin seem even paler.

Reminding himself that this was Grace, his friend, he helped her stand so he could drag the clammy, all-concealing garment off her body, trying desperately to ignore his body's reaction to the matching scrap of blue lace lower down, and the surprisingly shapely legs the stripping off of the garment revealed.

'You'll have to do the rest yourself,' he told her, his voice coming out as a throaty kind of growl.

'I had better,' she said, a teasing smile illuminating her tired face. 'Although,' she added wistfully, 'I'm not so certain physical attraction is all bad.'

'Right now any distraction at all is bad, Grace, and you know it. Now, scat, and take your coffee with you. Get into the shower and into some dry clothes—I'll slip home and change, check that everything's organised at the station and come back for you in ten or fifteen minutes.'

Getting away from her—doing things that needed doing—would surely distract him from...

From what?

He couldn't find an answer, and she didn't scat. She just stood there for a few seconds with her blue lace and white skin and exhausted face, seemingly about to say something, then she shook her head and turned away, revealing the fact that the blue lace was a thong so the pert roundness of her butt had him almost agreeing that physical attraction couldn't be all bad.

Except that he knew it was…

Grace stepped over the pile of emergency supplies Joe had deposited in her bathroom, and reached in to turn the shower on. She stripped off the sexy underwear she'd bought to go with the dress, sighing as she did so. She may as well have been wearing a nursing bra and bloomers for all the effect it had had on Harry. Although if she'd been too tired to argue as he'd stripped off her gear, he'd probably been too tired to think about attraction.

She showered, cringing as noises from above suggested half the forest was landing on the roof. Joe had been right to put the emergency gear in here—bathrooms were usually the safest room in the house, but if the roof blew off, or if a large branch caused damage, anyone sheltering in the bathroom would still get very wet.

'Better wet than dead,' she reminded herself, and a wave of sadness for a woman she didn't know engulfed her so suddenly she had to rest her head against the wall of the shower for a few minutes, hoping the hot water would sluice away the pain for those they hadn't saved.

Another crashing noise outside reminded her she had work to do, so she turned off the shower, dried herself and dressed hurriedly, pulling on a light pair of cargo pants with a multitude of pockets, and a T-shirt. Both would eventually be soaked even underneath a heavy raincoat but at least they'd dry faster when she was indoors. Boots next—only an idiot would be outside on a night like this without solid boots.

They were wet and didn't want to go on, and within minutes her dry socks had absorbed water from them. She shrugged off the discomfort, knowing it would soon be forgotten once she was involved in her work.

She unhooked her two-way radio and pocket knife from her belt and tucked them into the big pockets on her trousers, then added some spare batteries for the radio to another pocket. In the kitchen she found a packet of health bars and put four and a small bottle of water into the pockets down near her knees. Finally the list, carefully sealed inside a waterproof plastic bag, completed her preparations. She had another hard hat from her days in Victoria, and with that on her head and her bright yellow rain jacket around her shoulders, she headed out to the veranda to wait for Harry.

She'd taken down the hanging baskets from their hooks beneath the veranda roof before she'd dressed for the wedding, but although she'd packed them under other plants in the garden, one look at the already stripped stems told her how damaged they were going to get.

'Plants are replaceable,' she reminded herself, leaning against the wall as all the veranda chairs were stacked inside, but now, as she waited, her mind turned to Harry. Had it been the sense of imminent danger that had prompted them to speak of things that had always been unsaid between them?

She had no doubt that her friendship with Harry had developed, in part, because she *hadn't* been on the staff at the hospital when Nikki had died. Harry was the kind of man who would have shunned the sympathy on offer from all those who knew him—the kind of man who'd have pulled away from friends to work his grief out on his own.

But everyone needed someone and Grace had filled the void, providing a friendship not linked to either of their pasts and not going beyond the bounds of good but casual acquaintances.

If anything, since her discovery that she loved Harry, she'd pulled further back from anything approaching intimacy, so they'd laughed and joked and shared coffee and discussed ideas connected with the bits of their lives that touched—work and the SES.

She was still mulling over the shift in their relationship—if one kiss and some personal conversation could be called a shift—when Harry pulled into the drive. Pleased to be diverted from thoughts that were going nowhere—she was putting Harry out of her life, remember—she dashed towards the car, ducking as a plastic chair went flying by.

'Some stupid person hasn't tied down his outside furniture,' Harry muttered as she did up her seat belt.

'It looked like one of the chairs from beside the pool at the doctors' house,' Grace said. 'I guess with the wedding and then the emergencies coming in from the bus accident, no one's had time to secure that furniture.'

Harry was already turning the car that way.

'We'll do it before we start on our evacuations,' he said. 'Imagine some poor person seeking help at the hospital and being knocked out by flying furniture before he even gets there.'

He drove up the circular drive in front of the old

house that had originally been built as the Crocodile Creek hospital, and which now housed an assortment of hospital staff, parked at the bottom of the front steps and told Grace to stay where she was.

She took as much notice of this order as she had of his earlier orders to do this or that, and followed him through the downstairs area of the big building and out to where the garden furniture was indeed still around the pool.

'Just throw it in the pool,' Harry told her. 'It's safest in there and it'll get a good clean at the same time.'

He picked up a plastic table as he spoke and heaved it into the pool, following it with a sun lounge, while Grace took the smaller chairs and tossed them in.

'This is fun!' she said, grabbing the last chair and tossing it high so it made a satisfying splash.

'You find the weirdest things fun!' Harry grumbled at her, then he took her hand. 'Come on, let's have more fun—getting Mr and Mrs Aldrich to move out of their house.'

OK, so it was a protective gesture and meant nothing, especially in the context of getting over Harry, but holding hands with Harry felt so good Grace couldn't help but smile.

They ran back through the big recreation room under the doctors' house, out to the car. In the cove below the headland, the sea roared and tumbled, sending spray higher than the cliffs.

Willie was flexing his muscles.

## CHAPTER SIX

'WHAT time's high tide?' Grace asked as they strapped themselves back into the vehicle.

'It was midnight, so it's going out now,' Harry said. 'I suppose we can be thankful for small mercies. The storm surge from the cyclone will be bad enough at low tide, but if it had coincided with a high tide, who knows how many places might have been washed away?'

They were driving past the pub as Harry spoke and Grace shivered, imagining a wave of water sweeping over the row of businesses beside it. The police station was directly behind the shops, although on a slight rise.

'Are you free to be doing evacuations?' Grace asked, thinking of the enormous task of co-ordination that must be going on, with the station at its hub.

'There's no room for me over there,' Harry replied, nodding towards the station. 'One of the benefits of getting a new building last year is that it's built to the stringent category five building regulations so all the staff who live in less well-constructed flats or houses have shifted their families in. It was part of our contingency plans and it works because it means I now have five trained staff there ready for emergencies and on standby for clean-up later, and also have enough people to cut down shifts on the radio to two-hourly.'

'Two-hourly shifts? Is that all they can take? Is it so tense?' Grace asked, wondering why she'd never thought about this aspect of an emergency. With the SES, all the members on duty had radios tuned to the police emergency frequency and although she and other team leaders radioed their members, they relied mainly on the police radio operator to co-ordinate their efforts.

'It's the radio operator who's under the most stress at the moment,' Harry explained. 'Taking emergency calls and relaying them to wherever they need to go, so being able to run two-hour shifts cuts down on tension and the possibility of mistakes. But having staff in the station also means I've got someone there whose sole task is to plot the cyclone's course, taking all the direction, speed and intensity readings from the Met and marking them on the map. He'll give me a call when Willie's an hour from crossing the coast and also get the radio operator to order any emergency crews off the streets. Once Willie's that close, anyone outside is in danger.'

Grace nodded her understanding. All her people had orders to return to their homes as soon as they'd evacuated the people on their lists. In times like this their families had to be their prime concern.

They were driving past the Grubbs' house and Grace nodded towards it.

'Good thing the hospital preparations included orders for all staff in older housing to take shelter there. The Grubbs' house always looks as if it will blow down in a strong wind or slide the rest of the way down the slope into the creek. Heaven knows what Willie will do to it.'

Harry looked towards the house where the hospital yardman lived with his wife, who was in charge of the housekeeping side of the hospital. The old place had been added onto so often it was starting to resemble a shed on an intensive chicken farm. The oldest part, nearest the creek, stood on timber stumps so old they'd shrunk so the veranda on that side and the small room they'd enclosed on it were cantilevered out from the rest of the house—the stumps taking none of the weight.

'Charles has been trying to talk them into letting him build them a new house for years, but the Grubbs refuse, saying the place suits them as it is.'

'Or until it blows down,' Grace commented, then, as Harry slowed down at an even older house further along the street, she wondered how it would feel to be so attached to a dwelling you wouldn't want to change it—or leave it in a cyclone.

Was that what 'home' was all about?

Although her stepmother had always been kind, the concept of home had eluded Grace. Sometimes in her dreams she saw it as a whitewashed cottage set amid green fields, but that was wrong. She knew she'd lived in Belfast and had seen enough pictures of the city to know there was nary a field nor a cottage in sight.

'You're too tired to be doing this!'

Harry's cross exclamation brought her back to the present. He was frowning anxiously at her, and his hand was warming the skin on her forearm.

'Not tired, just thinking,' she told him, pressing her hand over his. 'Thinking about homes.'

Harry shook his head and got out of the car. Why would such a simple remark—thinking about homes—get under his skin?

Because he now knew Grace had never really had a home?

But should that make him want to wrap his arms around her and hold her tight against his body?

He couldn't blame physical attraction for this urge, because it wasn't part of the equation. Not this time...

He'd parked so the passenger door was away from the wind, making it easier for Grace to get out, although walking to the front door of the old weatherboard house was a struggle, so he kept an arm protectively around her shoulders.

Mrs Aldrich greeted them with a battery-powered lantern held at shoulder height, the light good enough to show a tear-stained face *and* the attitude of belligerence written across it.

'I've got this lantern and torches and water and biscuits in the bathroom and Karen from next door has taped my windows and I'm not going,' she said, and Harry heard Grace sigh as if she understood the older woman's feelings and didn't want to argue.

'You have to, Mrs Aldrich.' Harry used his firm policeman voice. 'Your house just isn't safe. We need to move you and Bill down to the civic centre.'

'Bill's dead.'

Harry's stomach clenched. Another look at Mrs Aldrich's face told him this was true.

Floored by this unexpected development, Harry

could only stare at her. Fortunately Grace had more presence of mind.

'What happened?' she asked gently, stepping past Harry and putting her arm around the elderly woman, carefully guiding her further into the house.

'He just died,' Mrs Aldrich replied, her resolute voice abandoning her so the words quavered out. 'We knew it was close. I was sitting by him and he touched my hand like he was saying goodbye then that rattly breathing he'd had earlier just stopped.'

'Oh, Mrs Aldrich, I'm so sorry,' Grace said, completely ignoring the little hurry-up motions Harry was making with his hands. 'Have you had a cup of tea? Can I get you something? I should have a look at Bill, just to be sure. Do you mind?'

She hesitated, perhaps aware she was asking too many questions, then, as Harry wondered just how she'd handle this, she added another one.

'What if Harry makes you a cup of tea while you show me where Bill is?'

Harry wondered if she'd gone mad. OK, so Mrs Aldrich was in her nineties and she and Bill had been married for more than seventy years. Was Grace thinking they had to do this carefully if they didn't want another death on her hands?

'Strong, sweet tea,' she said to Harry, as she guided the older woman towards the rear of the house where the bedrooms were.

'Cyclone warnings are now hourly, Willie's due to hit us in two to three hours and instead of evacuating people I'm making tea,' Harry muttered to himself, but he'd known Bill and Daisy Aldrich all his life and his heart ached for Daisy and the sadness she must be feeling right now.

He made the tea, still muttering to himself, knowing in his gut that this wasn't the end of the Aldrich saga for the night.

'We've got to get her to the civic centre,' he whispered to Grace, who was sitting next to Daisy, beside the bed where Bill indeed lay dead.

'I heard that, Harry Blake,' Daisy countered. 'Seventy years Bill and I have shared this house, our kids were born here, the roof's blown off in other cyclones, but it's survived. So if you think I'm leaving Bill alone here tonight then you're very much mistaken.'

For one wild moment Harry considered the possibility of taking a dead body to the safe haven of the civic centre, then he saw Grace shake her head and wondered if she'd read his thoughts.

Of course they couldn't. All their attention had to be on the living, but he knew he'd have a battle on his hands moving Daisy.

Grace was holding the cup to Daisy's lips, encouraging her to drink, while Harry stood helplessly beside her, anxious to keep moving, knowing there was so much still to do.

'Harry, would you get a thick bedcover from one of the other beds? I'll wrap it around Mrs Aldrich's shoulders so she's got some protection should a window go. And one for Bill as well.'

Glad to have something to do, Harry went through to another bedroom where both the single beds had thick coverlets.

He brought them back and watched as Grace placed one carefully over Bill, folding down the top of it so they could still see his face.

'If the window breaks or the roof goes, you can pull it up,' she said to Daisy, now wrapping the second bedcover around the frail old woman. 'Harry and I will try to get back—or one of us will—to sit with you. But if we don't, use the cover to protect yourself, and if things get really wild, get under the bed.'

Daisy smiled through the tears that seeped down her face.

'Bill always said he'd protect me, no matter what,' she said, then she touched Grace's cheek. 'You're a good girl. If that Harry had a scrap of sense he'd have snapped you up a long time ago.'

Grace bent and touched her lips to the lined cheek.

'You take care,' she said, then she led a bemused Harry out of the room.

'You're going to leave her there? Not even argue about it? We can't just give in like that?'

'Can't we?' Grace said softly. 'Think about it, Harry. How important is her life to her right now? I know in a month or so, when the worst pain of her grief has passed, she'll find things she wants to live for, but at the moment she has no fear of death—in fact, she'd probably welcome it. And look at it from her point of view—Bill's been her whole life, how could she possibly go off and leave him now?'

Harry began to reply but Grace had turned back towards the bedroom, fishing her mobile phone out of her pocket as she went.

'Here,' she said, offering it to Mrs Aldrich. 'The

phone lines are all down but the cellphones will still work. This one is programmed to reach Harry's cellphone, the one he's carrying today. Just press the number 8 and it will ring through to Harry.'

'Won't you need the phone?' Harry demanded, although what he wanted to know was who had the number one to seven positions on Grace's cellphone.

He knew she didn't have a mother...

'I've got my radio,' she reminded him, 'and just about everyone at the civic centre will be clutching their mobiles so they can report on conditions to their relatives in far-flung places or sell their phone pictures to television stations. I think I'll manage without one.'

'Because you've no relatives in far-flung places?' Harry asked, disturbed that the question of family and Grace had never occurred to him before tonight's revelations.

'Because I'll be far too busy to be phoning anyone,' Grace replied. 'Come on, we've people to evacuate.'

They ran from the house to the car, and he struggled to open the door and let her in, but even if conversation had been possible he wouldn't have known what to say. In some vague way he sensed that Grace was right about leaving Daisy where she was, but for so long his practical self had ruled his emotional self that it took a little bit of adjusting to accept emotion might have a place even in emergency situations.

Fortunately the next four couples were more easily moved, and by the time they had the last of them settled in the civic centre, everyone had been checked off the evacuation list.

Harry looked around the crowded area. Babies cried,

and small children, excited by the different location and the thrill of being awake in the early hours of the morning, ran around excitedly. Somewhere a dog barked, and a cockatoo let out a loud squawk of complaint, but most of the refugee pets were as well behaved as their human owners.

'At least the majority took note of what we said, about making sure they had animal carriers for their pets as part of their cyclone preparations.'

Grace was by his side and he nodded, acknowledging it had been a good idea. The circular dropped in the letterbox of every dwelling in town had not only been an initiative of the SES, but had been delivered by the volunteers.

'Where's Sport?' she asked, looking at a small kelpie cross who was protesting loudly about his accommodation.

'He's at my parents' place. I couldn't risk leaving him in the house when I knew I wouldn't be there.'

'Bet he's furious he's missing all the fuss,' Grace said, and Harry smiled. He'd rescued the small kelpie pup from the local rubbish dump after a wild thunderstorm. Whether he'd been abandoned because of an injury to one leg, or the injury had happened during the storm, Harry didn't know. He'd paid to have the leg treated, and when that hadn't worked, the leg had been amputated. He'd intended giving the dog away, but the fiercely loyal animal had had other ideas, finding his way back to Harry's no matter where he'd been taken.

In the end, his sheer determination had persuaded Harry to keep him.

'I need to check on a few people,' Grace said, and

moved into the small corridor between sleeping bags, mattresses and assorted padding brought along by the evacuees.

He watched her bend to speak to a heavily pregnant woman who should probably have been at the hospital rather than here, then, mindful that watching Grace was not his job right now, he walked through to the kitchen area where volunteers were making sandwiches and handing out tea or coffee to anyone who wanted it. He grabbed a cup of coffee and a sandwich, thinking Grace was probably in need of sustenance as well.

She was at the far end of the hall, talking to one of her SES crew, her arms waving in the air as she explained some detail. And although she was wearing plain cargo trousers and a T-shirt, all Harry could see was a curvy figure in two scraps of blue lace.

Muttering to himself once again, he took his coffee into one of the meeting rooms so he could concentrate on the messages coming through on his radio. Reports told him where power lines were down and where the emergency crews on duty were handling problems. The hour when the radio operator would order everyone into safe shelters, whether at their homes, at the police station or here at the civic centre, was fast approaching. Another report told him the hospital had been switched over to generator power, and even as that message came through the lights went out in the civic centre.

There was a momentary darkness, which caused the kids to scream with pretend fear, then the generators kicked in and the lights flickered back to life, but that instant of darkness had reminded Harry of the blackout earlier.

Had reminded him of kissing Grace…

'Boy, this food is good! It's the roast lamb from the wedding. Apparently, after we left, Mrs P. set the remaining guests to making sandwiches with the leftover food. Some was delivered to the hospital and the rest here.'

Grace was munching on a sandwich as she came up behind Harry. Everything had been OK between them—maybe a trifle strained but still OK—while they'd been caught up in rescuing Troy and getting off the mountain. Then, apart from a slight altercation over sleep, while they'd organised the evacuations. But now, in this lull before the storm—literally—she wasn't sure just where she stood with Harry.

Knew where she should stand—far, far away.

'We've got about ten of the less injured people from the bus here,' she said, taking another bite of sandwich and chewing it before getting back to the conversation. 'Apparently all the belongings we gathered up at the accident site were taken to Reception at the hospital. By now most of the stuff belonging to the hospitalised people will have been matched up to them, so I wondered if we could go over and collect the rest—it must belong to those who are here and I'm sure they'll all feel better if they have their own belongings with them.'

Harry shook his head, unable to believe he'd forgotten about the stuff he'd packed into the back of his vehicle.

'It's not at the hospital, it's here. I'll grab an able-bodied male and go get it from the car.'

'Get two able-bodied men and let them do it. Take a break,' Grace suggested, but Harry wasn't listening, already talking to one of the locals who then followed him out of the hall.

Grace followed him to the door, waiting until the two men brought in the luggage and handbags, then she spread it out so people could identify their belongings. The bus passengers, recognising what was going on, moved through the crowded room, then one by one they swooped on personal possessions, every one of them clutching the piece of luggage to their chests, as if they'd found lost treasure.

'It's a security thing,' Grace murmured, thinking how she'd clutched Harry's dinner jacket—remembering she'd left it in a sodden heap on her living-room floor.

Slowly the pile diminished until all that remained was a new-looking backpack.

'I wonder if the shoe belongs to that one,' Harry said, and knelt beside it, opening the fastening at the top and spilling out the contents.

'Damn it to hell!' Grace heard him whisper, as he pushed small shorts and T-shirts into one pile and some women's clothing into another. 'There *is* another child!'

'That's my dog!'

Max knew he should be pleased he'd finally found Scruffy, but the kid from the bus was clutching the dog against his chest and looked as if he'd never let him go.

All eyes, the kid. Huge eyes Max could see even though it was as dark as dark could be.

The kid was crouched under a tree fern—stupid place to shelter 'cos the water came straight through the leaves of tree ferns.

'Come on,' he told the kid. 'We've got to find the road. Or get back to the bus so we can get out of the rain.'

The kid shook his head and must have squeezed Scruffy tighter because Scruffy gave a yelp.

'You can hold the dog,' Max offered, and watched while the kid considered this. Then he stood up and Max saw his feet. One foot—bare—the other in a sneaker, the bare one cut and scratched and probably bleeding, although it was too dark to see the red of blood.

Everything was black.

'Hang on,' he told the kid and he sat down and took off his sneakers, then his socks, then he pulled his sneakers back on over his bare feet. Hard 'cos they were wet.

'You have the socks,' he told the kid. 'Put both on your foot that's lost its shoe. I'd give you my shoe but it'd be too big. Go on, sit down and do it. I'll hold the dog.'

The kid sat and reluctantly gave up his hold on Scruffy, though when Max hugged his pup against his chest Scruffy gave a different yelp.

'He's hurt,' Max whispered, holding the dog more carefully now.

The kid nodded, but he was doing as he was told, pulling on one sock then the other over it.

The dog was shivering so Max tucked him inside his T-shirt, then he reached out and took the kid's hand.

He'd walked downhill from the bus, so it and the road must be uphill.

'Let's go, kid,' he said, hoping he sounded brave and sensible. Sensible was good, he knew, because Mum always kissed him when she said he'd been sensible.

And brave was good. All the knights he read about were brave.

He didn't feel brave. What he felt was wet and cold and scared…

# CHAPTER SEVEN

GRACE watched as Harry reached for his cellphone and dialled a number, then shook his head in disgust and slammed the offending machine back into his pocket.

Whoever he was phoning must be out of range.

Now he pulled his radio out and began speaking into it, calling to someone, waiting for a reply, calling someone to come in.

Urgently!

Harry put the radio away and began repacking the clothing into the backpack, folding small T-shirts with extraordinary care. Grace watched him work, but as he pulled the cord tight and did up the catch on the top, she could no longer ignore the anguish on his face.

She knelt beside him and took the capable hands, which had trembled as he'd folded clothes, into hers.

'Are there kids out there? Do you know that for sure?'

He nodded.

'Georgie's Max we know for sure, and now this.'

He pulled the little sneaker from his pocket, poking the tip of his finger in and out of the hole that made up the eye of the fish painted on it.

'Two kids.'

Despair broke both the words.

'We can go back,' Grace suggested, urgency heating her voice. 'Go and look for them.'

'I *can't* go, and logically nor can you. You're a team captain—this cyclone will pass and we'll both be flat out sorting the damage and running rescue missions.'

He took a deep breath, then eased his captured hand away from hers.

'Georgie's gone to look—she and Alistair. We'll just have to hope they're in time.'

In time—what a dreadful phrase.

But the second child?

'If there's a second child unaccounted for, why has no one mentioned it? Why has no one said my child's missing?'

One possible answer struck her with the force of a blow.

'The woman who died? Oh, Harry, what if it's her child?'

'That's what I've been thinking,' Harry said bleakly, 'although there's a woman at the hospital who's in an induced coma at the moment, so maybe the child belongs to her. And the woman who died had a boyfriend—surely he'd have mentioned a child.'

Grace tried to replay the rescue scene in her mind—a badly injured woman *had* been rescued early in the proceedings. Susie's sister, who'd acted as a bridesmaid at the wedding, had been looking after her.

'Let's hope it's her and that she lives and that Georgie finds both kids,' Grace said, although this seemed to be asking an awful lot.

Worry niggled at her mind—two children lost in the bush in a cyclone?

Worry was pointless, especially now with Willie so close. There were things she had to do. She looked around at the people settling down to sleep, at the two paramedics and four SES volunteers, not sleeping, watchful.

'Everything's under control here. If you wouldn't mind giving me a lift, I'll go back to Mrs Aldrich's place and sit out the blow with her.'

'Sit out the blow?' Harry echoed. 'It's obvious you've never been in a cyclone. The whole house could go, Grace.'

'So I can give her a hand to get under the bed. I had a look at that bed. It's an old-fashioned one, with solid timber posts on the corners and solid beams joining them. Safe as houses—safer, in fact, than some of the houses in this town.'

'And you talk about me taking risks?' Harry muttered, but as he, too, had been worried about Daisy Aldrich—in between worrying about two children—maybe it wasn't such a bad idea. Only…

'You stay here, I'll go and sit with her,' he said and knew it was a mistake the moment the words were out of his mouth.

'We've already been through the hero thing a couple of times tonight! But not this time, Harry. Mrs Aldrich is my responsibility—'

The ringing was barely audible in the general hubbub of the room. Harry pulled his cellphone out of his pocket and checked the screen.

'Your number,' he said to Grace as he lifted the little phone to his ear and said a tentative hello.

'Harry, Daisy Aldrich. Karen from next door is here and she's having her baby and it's early and she can't get hold of Georgie who's not at the hospital or at home so can Grace come?'

'We'll be right there,' Harry promised, closing his phone and motioning to Grace.

'You win,' he said. 'We need a nurse. Daisy's next-door neighbour is having a baby.'

'Karen? I saw her last week when she came for a check-up. She's not due for three or four weeks.'

'Tell the baby that,' Harry said, leading the way out of the hall.

Daisy was in her kitchen, boiling water on a small gas burner when Grace and Harry arrived.

'I don't know why people boil water,' she said, waving her hand towards the simmering liquid. 'No one ever did anything with boiling water when I was having my babies.'

A cry from the back of the house reminded them of why they were there.

'We dragged a mattress into the bathroom and she's lying on that. She'd never have got under the bed, the size she is.'

Grace was already hurrying in the direction of the cry. Another battery lantern was barely bright enough to light the room, but Grace could see the shadowy shape that was Karen, hunched up on the mattress which had been placed between the wall and an old-fashioned, claw-footed bath.

Fluid made dark smears across the mattress, but before Grace could check if it was water from the birth sac or blood, Karen cried out again, helplessly clutching the edge of the bath, her body contorting with pain.

'It hurts too much,' she said. 'Make it stop. Please, make it stop.'

Grace knelt beside her, sliding her hand around to rest on Karen's stomach, feeling the rigidity there.

'How long have you been having contractions?' she asked Karen as the stomach muscles relaxed.

'This morning,' the girl sobbed, 'but I thought they were those pretend ones with the silly name. The baby's not due for three weeks. And everyone was telling me first babies are always late so they had to be the pretend contractions.'

'Have you timed them at all?' Grace asked, trying to unlock Karen's death grip on the bath so she could lay the young woman down to examine her.

'No!' Karen roared, crunching over in pain again. 'You time them!'

She puffed and panted, occasionally throwing out combinations of swear words Grace had never heard before.

Grace pulled a towel off the towel rail, then looked around to see Harry and Mrs Aldrich peering in through the door.

'Could you find something soft to wrap the baby in? And some spare towels would be good. And scissors, if you have them,' she said, then looked at Harry.

'How long do we have before Willie arrives?'

'Three quarters of an hour, according to the latest alert. He's also been upgraded—definitely a category five now.'

He looked around at the walls and ceiling of the bathroom.

'This room's too big for safety—the load-bearing walls are too far apart—although the bath looks solid enough.'

But Grace's attention was back on Karen, who with a final shriek of pain had delivered a tiny baby boy.

He was blue, but as Grace cleared mucous from his mouth and nose, he gave a cry and soon the bluish skin turned a beautiful rosy pink.

'You little beauty,' Grace whispered to him, holding him gently in the towel.

Mrs Aldrich returned with the scissors, more towels and a soft, well-worn but spotlessly clean teatowel.

'That's the softest I've got,' she said, peering into the room then giving a cry of surprise when she saw the baby. 'It's the way of the world—one dies and another takes his place,' she said quietly, then she padded away, no doubt to sit beside her Bill.

'I'll call him William Harry,' Karen said, as Grace wrapped the baby in the teatowel and handed him to Karen, suggesting she hold him to her breast. But Karen didn't hear, her eyes feasting on the little mortal in her arms, her attention so focussed on his tiny form Grace had to blink away a tear. 'William after Bill, who was always kind to me, and Harry after Harry because he was here.'

Grace looked up at Harry who was pale and tense, shaking his head as if he didn't want a baby named after him. But even as Grace wondered about this reaction she became aware of the roaring noise outside the house and understood his lack of emotion. Another William—Willie—was nearly on them.

She turned her attention back to Karen, massaging

her stomach to help her through the final stage of labour, then cutting and knotting the cord and cleaning both mother and child.

Harry returned as she tucked a towel around the pair of them. He was carrying one of the bedcovers he'd found earlier, a pillow and a couple of blankets.

'I'm going to put these in the bath, Karen, then I want you and the baby to get in there. We'll put the mattress over the top to keep you both safe from falling debris. You'll still be able to breathe and it's not heavy, so if you feel claustrophobic you can lift it up a bit.'

Karen and Grace both stared at him, Karen finding her voice first.

'In the bath?'

Harry, who was making a nest of the blankets and bedcover, nodded.

'It's an old cast-iron bath—far too heavy to move even in a cyclone. Its high sides will protect you both and support the mattress. I wouldn't do it but the house has already lost a bit of roof and the walls are moving.'

Karen stopped arguing, handing the baby to Harry to hold while she stood up and clambered into the bath. Grace helped her, leaning over to make sure she was comfortable. She turned to Harry to take the baby and the look of pain and despair on his face made her breath catch in her lungs.

'I'll give him to Karen,' Grace said gently, moving closer so she could take the little bundle. Harry's eyes lifted from the baby to settle on Grace's face, but she knew he wasn't seeing her—wasn't seeing anything in the present.

Had there been a baby? she wondered as he stepped

forward and leant over, very gently settling the baby in his mother's arms.

Then he straightened up and strode out of the room, returning seconds later with a light blanket, which he tucked around the pair of them.

Karen smiled at him then tucked the baby against her breast, murmuring reassuringly to the little boy, although Grace knew the young woman must be terrified herself.

'Here,' Grace said, fishing in her pocket for the bottle of water and a couple of health bars. 'Something to eat and drink while Willie blows over.'

Karen smiled and took the offerings, setting them down on her stomach, but her attention was all on the baby at her breast.

With Grace's help Harry lifted the mattress onto the top of the bath, leaving a little space where Karen's head was so she could see out.

'Put your hand up and move the mattress so I know you can,' he said, and Karen moved the mattress first further back then up again so only the tiny space was visible.

'You OK?' Grace asked, sliding her fingers into the space and touching Karen's fingers.

'I think so,' the young woman whispered, her voice choked with fear.

'We'll just be next door, under Daisy's bed,' Harry told her, then he put his arm around Grace's shoulders and drew her out of the room.

'I hate leaving her like that. Surely we should all be together,' Grace said, looking back over her shoulder at the mattress-covered bath.

'Better not to be,' Harry said, and Grace shivered as she worked out the implications of that statement.

Daisy met them as they entered her bedroom, and handed Grace the cellphone.

'Give it to Karen. And this torch. Tell her about pressing 8 to talk to Harry. It might make her feel less lonely.'

Grace turned, but Harry stopped her, taking both the cellphone and the torch.

'You help Daisy down onto the floor. If she lies on the mat I can pull her under the bed if we need the extra protection. And turn off your radio. I'm turning mine off as well. There's nothing anyone can do out there, so we might as well save batteries.'

He walked away, leaving Grace to put a pillow on the mat, then help the frail old woman down onto the floor.

'Cover Bill so things don't fall on him,' she whispered to Grace, and Grace did as she asked, drawing the bedcover over the peaceful face of the man on the bed. Then she sat on the floor and held Mrs Aldrich's hand while outside the house the world went mad.

'We're going under the bed,' Harry announced, returning with the second mattress from the spare bedroom. 'I'm putting this on top as extra padding.'

He arranged the mattress so it rested from the bed to the floor, making a makeshift tent, then pulled the mat to slide Mrs Aldrich under the big bed.

'Your turn,' he said to Grace, who slid beneath the bed, leaving room for Harry between herself and the older woman.

Harry eased himself into the small space, wondering what on earth he was doing there when he could be in a nice safe police station or civic centre hall.

That it had to do with Grace he had no doubt, but he couldn't think about it right now. Right now he had to get these women—and the baby—through the cyclone.

He put his arm protectively around Daisy, but she shrugged him off.

'For shame, Harry Blake, and with Bill in the room. If you want to cuddle someone, cuddle Grace. She looks as if she could do with an arm around her, and you certainly need a bit of loving.'

Mrs Aldrich's voice was loud enough for Harry to hear above the roar of the approaching force, but would Grace have heard?

And if she had and he didn't put his arm around her, would she think—?

He had no idea what she'd think. Somehow this wild, erratic force of nature had blown the two of them into totally new territory.

Territory where he *did* need a bit of loving?

Surely not.

But just in case Grace had heard—or maybe just in case he did need loving—he turned so he could put his arm around Grace, and when she didn't object he drew her closer, tucking her body against his and once again feeling her curls feathering the skin beneath his chin.

'Cuddling me, Harry?' she said, her light, teasing voice defeating the noise outside because her lips were so close to his ear. 'Aren't you afraid? I mean, if a shuffling dance provoked the deadly physical attraction, what might a cyclone cuddle do?'

She was making fun of him, but still it hurt, and

somehow, because this was Grace and maybe because Bill and Daisy had loved one another for seventy years or maybe even because within minutes they could all be dead, he started telling her.

'We'd known each other for ever, Nikki and I, our parents friends enough for me to call hers Aunt and Uncle. She left town to go to university in Townsville while I went to Brisbane for my training. Then, about three and a half years ago, her parents were killed in a car accident. She came home to see to everything, I helped her—well, my parents arranged everything for her, but I was there for comfort.'

Grace felt his arms tighten around her, and kept as still as she could. She wasn't sure if she really wanted to hear about him loving Nikki, but listening to Harry was definitely better than listening to the raging fury of the cyclone and wondering if any of them would survive.

And maybe he needed the catharsis…

'Comfort is physical, as you know, and suddenly we both felt the attraction that being close had stirred. Wild attraction, heightened most probably on Nikki's side by grief.'

He paused then added in an undertone, 'I didn't have that excuse.

'We thought it love, Grace, and married, caught in a whirl of physical delight that left no room for plans or practicality, then, as suddenly as it had come, it seemed to leave. Not the physical attraction—that was always there—but when we weren't in bed there was—I can only describe it as an emptiness. Nikki was still grieving for her parents and she also missed her job, while I spent more time than was necessary at mine.'

Grace turned in his arms so she could hold him. She told herself it was because the noise of the cyclone was as loud as an express train roaring through a tunnel, but really it was so she could rub her hands across his back, offering silent sympathy he might or might not want.

Her heart ached for him—for the pain she heard in his voice and in the silence that now lay between them. But she couldn't prompt him, knowing he had to get through this story his own way.

'We didn't talk about it—in fact, I didn't know if Nikki felt it—but I was gutted, Grace, to think I'd mucked up so badly. Then I thought about it—really thought about it—and decided it would all be OK—that we could work it out. We'd always loved each other as friends, so surely that would remain as a solid foundation, and we had compatibility, so that had to count in building a future…'

He paused again and she felt his chest fill with air then empty on a sigh. She tightened her arms around him, offering the only comfort available.

'Eventually she told me she'd been offered a new television job in Brisbane. She'd been with the same station in Townsville but this was a promotion. Would I transfer to the city to be with her?'

Somewhere outside a tortured screeching noise suggested a roof was being torn apart. Mrs Aldrich's roof?

Grace snuggled closer, fear moving her this time.

'Go on,' she prompted, knowing Harry's story was probably the only thing holding at bay the terror that was coiled within her.

'I said I would, wanting so much to make it work, although all my life all I'd ever wanted was to be a policeman here where I belonged. We made arrangements, looked at housing on the internet, then she went to Townsville to see her old boss.'

The story stopped, and with it the noise.

'It's over?' Grace whispered, then heard how loud her voice sounded in the silence and realised she hadn't whispered at all.

'It's the eye passing over,' Harry told her as he slid out from under the bed and cautiously lifted the mattress aside. 'You two stay right where you are. I'll check on Karen and the baby and be straight back.'

Grace reached out to stop him, but it was too late, so she had to wait, fearful for his safety, having heard enough of cyclones to know that the eye was only the calm before the storm returned, only this time the wind would blow the other way.

'Both sound asleep, would you believe,' Harry reported as the howling, roaring noise drew close again. 'I guess having a baby and being born are both tiring experiences.'

He slid beneath the bed, lying between the two women, reporting to Mrs Aldrich that her kitchen roof had gone and a part of the bathroom wall had been damaged, but generally things looked OK. Radio calls to the station had assured him everything was OK there and at the civic centre.

'It's the second blow, once everything is loosened, that knocks houses about,' Mrs Aldrich told him, as they all squiggled around to relieve cramped muscles and tired bones. 'Will you go on talking, Harry?' she added. 'I can't hear the words but I like to hear your voice—it's very soothing and it makes the cyclone noise easier to bear.'

Horrified that Daisy had even heard his voice, Harry hesitated, but the cyclone was roaring again, and Grace had snuggled close, so it was easy to finish the tale he'd carried inside him for so long, locked away but probably festering because it hadn't ever been told.

He tucked Grace closer, held her tightly, and blurted out the words.

'She went to Townsville to have an abortion.'

There, it was said.

For the first time he'd actually told someone about the almost routine operation that had led to the discovery of Nikki's inoperable cancer.

He felt Grace stiffen, then her hand crept up to touch his face, cupping his cheek in her palm.

'No wonder seeing that new baby hurt you,' she whispered, her voice choked with tears.

He shook his head although he knew neither woman would see the gesture, frustrated at this situation. What was he thinking, lying under a bed—a bed with a dead body in it—in a category five cyclone, playing out his past like a series of episodes in a soap opera?

Fortunately—for his sanity—at that moment the roar grew louder and above the wild fury of the wind they heard the scream of metal sheets being torn from their anchors, nails screeching in protest as the rest of Daisy's roof peeled away.

'The weight of rain could bring the ceiling down so we stay here until we know the wind has eased,' Harry warned the two women, reaching out and drawing both of them closer, knowing they all needed human contact at the moment. 'Now Willie's crossed the coast, he'll lose his power.'

But what had that power done as it passed over the town? What havoc had it caused?

Anxiety tightened all the sinews in his body—anxiety for all the townsfolk but most of all for two small children out there on the mountain.

Had Georgie and Alistair reached them in time?

Were all four safe?

Max watched the light creep into the blackness of the hole in which they huddled, turning the dark shadows that had frightened him in the night into harmless posts and odds and ends of timber.

The kid was sleeping, curled up in a puddle of muddy-looking water, Scruffy in his arms. The kid had needed Scruffy, not because he'd said anything but because the way his face had looked when Max had heard Georgie calling to them and he'd answered her.

Instead of being happy they'd been found, the kid had started crying. Not bawling loudly, like CJ sometimes did when he was hurt, but silent crying, the light from the torch Mum was shining on them picking out the tears running down his face.

Max had thought at first he was crying because Mum had said she couldn't get them out straight away because it was too dangerous and that they'd have to wait until the cyclone stopped blowing trees over. But the kid had kept crying even after Mum had thrown down her leather jacket and some chocolate bars, and

Max had figured out he was crying because his Mum wasn't there.

So Max gave him Scruffy to hold because earlier, when Max had had a little cry because Mum wasn't there, holding Scruffy had made him feel really, really brave.

Max pushed the leather jacket over the sleeping kid and waited for more light to come.

## CHAPTER EIGHT

IT WAS another hour before the noise abated sufficiently for Harry to slide out from under the bed. The roof had indeed gone and the ceiling had collapsed in the far corner of the room, pouring water onto the floor, but thankfully the rest of the room was, for the moment, dry.

Grace joined him, staring about her at the devastation, then heading for the door.

'Don't go,' he said, catching her hand. 'You stay here with Daisy while I check out what's solid and what isn't.'

She turned, anxious eyes scanning his face in the murky dawn light.

'Be careful,' she said, touching her hand to his cheek, so many things unspoken in the gesture that Harry felt a hitch in his breathing.

The house was a mess. One of the bathroom walls had collapsed across the bath, so Harry had to toss boards and beams aside to get to the mattress-covered bath. Fortunately the ceiling had held so the room was relatively dry. He could hear Karen and the baby both crying, Karen hysterical when he lifted the mattress.

'Come on, I'll help you out. You can shelter in the bedroom with Daisy until it's safe enough to drive you to the hospital.'

'With Daisy and dead Bill? I can't do that. I can't take my baby into the room with a dead person.'

Harry sighed but he kind of understood. There'd been ghosts beneath that bed with him.

'All right, but I'll have to put the mattress back on top of you.'

'That's OK,' Karen said, stifling her sobs and settling back down in her nest of blankets. 'Now it's getting lighter and I know you're not all dead and that noise has stopped, it's not nearly as scary.'

He replaced the mattress—if the ceiling did come down he didn't want wet plasterboard smothering the pair of them—then did a recce through the rest of the house. To his surprise, the dining room, a square room to one side of the kitchen, was apparently unscathed, and from the kitchen he could see that the roof in that area remained intact.

Once they had tarpaulins over the rest of it, Daisy might be able to move back into her home as soon as services like electricity, sewerage and water were restored, although that could be weeks away.

Sure his charges were safe, he ducked into the dining room, sat down on a chair and pulled out his cellphone. Time to check on the damage in the rest of the town.

Unbelievable damage from all accounts, the policeman on duty at the station told him, but no reports of casualties. Harry breathed a sigh of relief.

'Just let me sort out a few problems here,' he said, 'and then I'll do a run through town to see what's what.

Expect me back at base in about an hour. In the meantime I'll be on air on the radio or you can get me on the cellphone.'

He rang the hospital. No word from Georgie but they'd despatch an ambulance to pick up Karen, the baby and Daisy Aldrich. They'd also contact the funeral home to send a car for Bill.

Grace was standing in the doorway as he ended the call.

'*Did* she have the abortion because of her career?' she asked, and the question was so unexpected he answered without thinking.

Answered honestly.

'No,' he said bleakly, remembering the terrible day he'd stared in disbelief at Nikki while she'd told him this—and then, disbelief turning to denial, added that she was dying of cancer. 'At least, she said not, but it might have had something to do with it. She said she had it because we didn't love each other. She said she knew that almost as soon as we were married—knew it was just lust between us, lust and her grief, and that I was there. She said she didn't want to bring a baby into that situation because without love we'd probably split up.'

Grace came closer and put her arms around him, holding him tightly.

'Then she told me about the cancer—that when she had the operation they found inoperable cancer.'

'She was dying of cancer?'

Harry nodded.

'Which made my anger at her—my fury that she'd gone ahead and aborted my child without discussing it with me—totally absurd. The baby wouldn't have lived anyway, but that fact couldn't penetrate the anger. I said things then that should never have been said—hard, hot, angry things, and through all that followed—her time at home and then in hospital—that was the guilt I had to carry. To have reacted with anger towards Nikki who'd been my friend for ever, to have hurt her at any time, let alone when she was dying…'

His shoulders hunched and he bent his head as if the weight of the emotional baggage he'd carried since that time still burdened his body.

'Physical attraction, Grace, do you wonder I'm suspicious of it?'

'But anger is a natural reaction to bad news,' Grace whispered to him. 'Your anger might have found an outlet in yelling about the abortion but it would have been far deeper than that—it would have been about the death sentence Nikki, your friend and lover, had just received.' She held him more tightly. 'It was natural, not cruel or unfair, Harry, and I'm sure Nikki would have understood that.'

'Would she?' he whispered hoarsely, the headshake accompanying the words telling Grace he didn't believe her.

The wailing cry of a siren told them the ambulance was close by. Grace let him go and headed for the door, wanting to help Karen and the baby out of the bath.

She heard the vehicle pull up, the sound of doors opening, the wheels on a stretcher dropping down.

'So now you know why he feels the way he does,' she muttered helplessly to herself, 'but what if it isn't just physical attraction?'

She understood so much more now—understood it was guilt and anger at himself that prompted not only Harry's risk-taking but also the emotional armour he'd drawn around himself.

Grace mulled it over as she led the paramedics first into the bathroom to collect Karen and baby William, then, once they were safely loaded, she walked with Daisy to the ambulance.

'Yes, I'll stay with Bill until the people from the funeral home arrive,' she promised Daisy, and was surprised at Daisy's protest.

'You'll do no such thing—you stay with Harry. Cyclone Willie shook a lot of things loose in that boy's heart. He's hurting and he needs someone with him.'

'As if Harry would ever admit to needing someone,' Grace said, but fortunately the funeral car arrived at that moment so she didn't have to make a choice.

Harry had returned to the dry refuge of the dining room while she'd been seeing the two vehicles depart. He looked grey with fatigue—or was it more than that? He looked…

Despairing?

'Georgie? You've heard from Georgie?'

He shook his head, then muttered, 'I'm thinking no news is good news out there. I told Alistair we'd left the vehicle beyond the fallen tree—they could have sheltered in that.'

But this not good but not precisely bad news did nothing to ease the knots of worry in his features.

'What's wrong?' Grace asked, walking towards him and reaching out to take his hands. Watching his face carefully, ready to read a too-easy lie.

But he didn't lie, saying only, 'It's Sport,' in a tone of such flat despair Grace thought her heart would break.

'Dead?' she whispered, then remembered where the dog had been. 'Your parents? They're OK?'

'Sport's not dead but gone. My parents are fine. Very little damage to the house, although the sheds have been destroyed and the sugar crop's flattened. But Sport's disappeared. Mum said he grew more and more agitated as Willie passed over, then, when Dad opened the door to look at the damage during the calm of the eye, Sport took off, last seen heading back towards the town.'

Grace pictured Harry's parents' place, not far from the sugar mill on the outskirts of town.

She could imagine the dog, hip-hopping his way through the fury of the cyclone.

Sport, a ragged, crippled mutt that had somehow wormed his way through the emotional barriers Harry had built around himself.

Wormed his way into Harry's heart.

She wrapped her arms around him and held him tightly.

'I love you, Harry,' she said, although it was the last thing she'd meant to say.

Bloody dog!

She was resting her head against Harry's chest so couldn't see his reaction, although she felt his chest move with a sharp intake of air.

'I know you don't want to hear that,' she added, anxious to get it all smoothed over and things back to normal between them again. 'But we've been through so much—touched by death then welcoming new life, our physical world destroyed around us—I had to say it, and it's OK because I don't expect you to love me back. I've got over love before and I'll get over this, but it needed to be said.'

One of his arms tightened around her and he used his free hand to tilt her chin, so in the rain-dimmed morning light she saw his face.

Saw compassion, which she hated, but something else.

Surprise?

Natural enough, but was it surprise?

Before she could make another guess, Harry bent his head and kissed her, his lips crushing hers with hot, hard insistence. She melted into the embrace and returned the kiss, letting her lips tell him, over and over again, just how she felt.

One corner of her mind was aware of the futility of it all, but this was Harry and right now he needed whatever physical comfort she could give him.

And *she* needed something that at least felt like love…

Perhaps a minute passed, perhaps an hour, although, looking at her watch as she pushed out of Harry's arms, Grace knew it hadn't been an hour.

Two, three minutes maybe—a short time out from all the chaos that lay both behind and ahead of them.

And if her heart cringed with shame that she'd told Harry how she felt—a confession prompted by pity that he'd lost his dog, for heaven's sake—then she was good enough at pretence by now to carry on as if the words had not been spoken.

Which, she knew, was what Harry would do…

'We've got to go. Sport will be looking for you,' she said, and Harry nodded.

'Damn stupid dog!'

'We'll look at your place first,' Grace said.

Harry turned towards her, frowning now.

*Grace loved him?*

'We can't go out looking for a dog,' he growled. 'I need to see the damage, talk to people, get arrangements going.'

*Talk about coming out of left field! Grace, his friend, suddenly declaring love for him?*

'You need to drive through town to see the damage,' this friend he suddenly didn't know reminded him, then she repeated what she'd said earlier. 'We'll go past your place first.'

*And now carrying on as if she hadn't just dropped a bombshell on him.*

*As if love had never been mentioned.*

He had to put it right out of his mind. The town and its people needed him—and needed him to have a fully functioning brain, not some twitchy mess of grey matter puzzling over love and Grace.

*Grace first—he'd deal with Grace the friend and that way might not keep thinking about the Grace he'd kissed. Twice...*

'What's this *we?* I'll drop you home, that's if your cottage is still standing. Or at the hospital. You need to sleep.'

'No, Harry, we'll do a drive around town then you can drop me at SES Headquarters so I can start sorting out what's needed and who we've got to help.'

Unable to think of a single argument against this—well, not one that she would listen to—he led the way out to where he'd left the police vehicle, tucked in under the Aldrichs' high-set house. It seemed to have survived the onslaught with only minor damage.

Sadness filled her heart as Grace snapped her seat belt into place. She sent a sidelong glance at the object of her thoughts, who was talking seriously to someone on his cellphone. Now those fatal words had been said, they could never be unsaid, so things could never really be the same between them again.

That was probably just as well, because although she'd spoken lightly about getting over love, she knew this was going to take a huge effort, and not seeing much of Harry would certainly help.

Although, comparing what she'd felt for James with what she felt for Harry, maybe he was right about physical attraction giving an illusion of love.

Certainly the love she'd felt for James had never hurt like this…

It was at this stage of her cogitations that she became aware of the world around her—or what was left of it.

'I don't believe it,' she whispered, trying desperately to make some sense of the devastation that lay around them. Harry was driving very slowly and carefully, picking a path along a road strewn with corrugated iron, fibro sheeting, furniture and bedding, not to mention trees, branches and telegraph poles, the latter flung about as if they'd weighed no more than matches.

The rain poured down with unrelenting insistence, as if Nature hadn't yet done enough to bring the town of Crocodile Creek and its inhabitants to their knees.

'We'll need the army. The mayor phoned earlier. He's already asked the premier for help,' Harry said as he pulled into his driveway.

'But today?' Grace asked, staring helplessly around. 'What can we do today? Where do we start? How can we help people?'

'Food and water. I'll check Sport's not here, then drive around town. We'll stop at the civic centre first, although I've had a report that everyone's OK there. We're broadcasting messages asking anyone who needs help to get out of their house to phone the dedicated line at the police station—the number we gave out at the end of all the cyclone warnings.'

'Four, zero, six, six, eight, eight, nine, nine,' Grace repeated, remembering the trouble Harry had had getting a number so easy to remember.

The radio was chattering at them. All downed power poles and torn lines would have to be removed before the authorities would consider turning power back on. No reports of casualties so far, apart from those lost in the bus crash. Banana plantations and cane fields had been flattened. The farmers were in for a grim year, but Willie, his violence spent, had continued moving westward and was now dumping much-needed rain on the cattle country beyond the mountains.

'So Willie moves on,' Grace whispered as she heard this report. 'But how do people here move on? How can anyone move on from something like this?'

Harry glanced towards her, and she knew he was thinking of her stupid declaration.

Well, so what if he was? Like Willie, she was moving on.

Moving on…

# CHAPTER NINE

THEY stopped at the house just long enough for Harry to satisfy himself Sport wasn't there. Neither was his dirt bike, which meant Georgie and Alistair were still out in the bush.

They were both sensible people, they had his vehicle out there to shelter in—or the bus—they'd be OK.

But had they found the kids?

Worry knotted inside him and he sent a silent prayer heavenward, a plea that they and the two children were all right. Then he looked around at the havoc and wondered if heaven had given up answering prayers, because plenty of people had prayed the town would be spared a cyclone.

'Do you think the old bridge will hold?' Grace asked as they approached the bridge across the creek that separated the hospital part of the town from the main commercial and residential areas.

'The council engineers looked at it when it was forecast Willie might head this way and declared it would probably outlast the new bridge across the river, but the problem is, because it's low and water is already lapping at the underside, all the debris coming down the creek will dam up behind it, causing pressure that could eventually push it off its pylons.'

'Debris piling up is also causing flooding,' Grace said, pointing to where the creek had already broken its banks and was swirling beneath and around houses on the hospital side.

'Which will get worse,' Harry agreed, concern and gloom darkening his voice.

They were driving towards the civic centre now, Grace looking out for Sport, although the streets were still largely deserted.

Except for teenagers, paddling through floodwater on their surf-skis here and there, revelling in the aftermath of the disaster.

'I'll be in meetings for the rest of the morning,' Harry said, turning towards Grace and reaching out to run a finger down her cheek. 'You do what you have to do then get someone to run you home, OK? You need to sleep.'

'And you don't, Harry?' she teased, discomfited by the tenderness of his touch—by his concern.

'I can't just yet,' he reminded her, then he leant across the centre console and kissed her on the lips, murmuring, 'I'm sorry, Grace,' and breaking her heart one last time because the apology had nothing to do with not sleeping.

One of her fellow SES volunteers drove her home to check the cottage was all right. She'd lost a window and the living room was awash with water, her garden was wrecked, but apart from that she'd got off lightly. They drove on to SES Headquarters, passing people wandering through the wreckage of countless homes, oblivious of the rain still pelting down, looking dazed as they picked an object from the rubble, gazed at it for a moment then dropped it back.

Some were already stacking rubbish in a pile, hurling boards that had once made up the walls of their houses into a heap on the footpath. It would take forever to clear some of the lots, but these people were at least doing something. They were looking to bring some order back into their lives.

Once at Headquarters, she set up a first-aid station. Volunteers would be injured in the clean-up and would also know to bring anyone with minor injuries to the building.

What she hadn't expected was a snakebite.

'Bloody snake decided it wanted to share our bathroom with us. I had the kids in there,' the ashen-faced man told her. 'I picked it up to throw it out, and the damn thing bit me on the arm.'

He showed the wound, which Grace bandaged with pressure bandages, down towards the man's fingers then back up to his armpit.

But it was really too late for bandages. The wound had been oozing blood, and snake venom stopped blood clotting properly.

'Did you drive here?' she asked, and the man nodded, his breathing thickening as they stood there.

'Good. We'll take your car.'

She called two of the volunteers who'd come in looking for orders to carry the man out to the car.

'The less effort you make, the less chance of poison spreading.'

'It didn't look like a brown or taipan,' the man said, but Grace had already taken the car keys from his hand and was hurrying towards the door. Even so-called experts couldn't always identify snakes by their looks.

The volunteers settled her patient into the car, and she took off, making her way as fast as she could through the hazardous streets. At the hospital she drove straight into the emergency entrance, leaping out of the car and calling for a stretcher.

'Bringing your own patients, Grace?' someone called to her as she walked beside the stretcher.

'Snakebite,' she snapped, pushing the stretcher in the direction of a trauma room. 'We need a VDK.'

Inside the trauma room she started with the basics, knowing a doctor would get there when he or she could. She slipped an oxygen mask over her patient's head, opened his shirt and set the pads for electrocardiogram monitoring, and fitted an oxygen saturation monitor to one finger.

IV access next—they'd need blood for a full blood count and for a coag profile, urea, creatinine and electrolytes, creatine kinase and blood grouping and cross-matching. Urine, too—the venom detection kit worked on urine.

She talked to the man, Peter Wellings, as she worked, hoping a doctor would arrive before she got to the catheterisation stage.

A doctor did arrive, Cal Jamieson, looking as grey and tired as Grace was feeling.

She explained the situation as briefly as she could, then was surprised when Cal picked up a scalpel and turned to her.

'Where exactly was the bite?'

Grace pointed to the spot on the bandaged arm.

'And it was definitely bleeding freely?'

She nodded.

'OK, we can take a swab from there for venom detection, rather than wait for a urine sample. I'll cut a small window in the bandages, and in the meantime let's get some adrenaline for him in case there's a reaction to the antivenin—0.25 milligrams please, Grace. And get some antivenins ready—the polyvalent in case we can't identify the snake, and some brown, tiger and taipan, which are the most likely up here.'

Cal was working swiftly, cutting through the bandages, swabbing, talking to Peter as well as telling Grace what he required next. He took the swab and left the room, returning minutes later to go through the antivenins Grace had set out on a trolley.

'Tiger,' he said briefly, more to Grace than to Peter, who looked as if he no longer cared what kind of snake had bitten him. 'I'm going in strong because of the delay. The Commonwealth Serum Laboratories recommend one ampoule but we're going two. I've actually given three to someone who had multiple wounds. But he'll need careful monitoring—straight to the ICU once I've got the antivenin going in his drip.'

He glanced towards Grace as he worked.

'You've obviously been outside. How bad is it?'

Grace thought of the devastation she'd seen and shook her head.

'I can't describe it,' she said. 'I can't even take in what I've seen. All the photos of floods and hurricanes and even bomb-sites you've ever seen mixed into one. I don't know how people will begin to recover. And the rain hasn't let up one bit. That's making things worse.'

Cal nodded.

'We'll see plenty of post-traumatic stress,' he said. 'Hopefully we'll be able to get the staff we need to handle it—it's such a specialist area.'

He was adjusting the flow of the saline and antivenin mix, ten times the amount of saline to antivenin, and calibrating the flow so Peter would receive the mixture over thirty minutes.

Grace wrote up the notes, and the latest observations, wanting everything to be in order as Peter was transferred.

'He'll need to be on prednisolone for five days after it to prevent serum sickness,' Cal said, adding his notes. 'And watched for paralysis, which with tigers starts with muscles and tendons in the head.'

He was silent for a minute then added, 'And renal failure.'

Grace knew he was talking to himself, adding reminders as he would be the person caring for Peter in the ICU. Mistakes happened and were more likely when people were exhausted by extra shifts, and only by constant checking and rechecking would they be avoided.

'You staying?' he asked Grace.

'Am I needed?'

He shook his head.

'I think we've got things pretty well under control. The worst of the accident victims, a young woman called Janey, is coming out of her induced coma, and everyone else is stable so, no, if you're not on duty, buzz off home. You look as if you could do with about three days' sleep.'

'Couldn't we all?' Grace said, but she was grateful for Cal's dismissal. She could walk home and look for Sport on the way. Later she'd return to SES Headquarters for another shift, but she'd be a far more effective participant in the clean-up operation if she slept first.

She tapped on Jill's office door before she left, wanting to be one hundred per cent sure she wasn't needed.

'Go home and sleep,' Jill ordered in answer to Grace's query. 'You look as if you need about a week to catch up. Go!'

She waved her hands in a shooing motion.

'We've all been able to grab a few hours—mainly thanks to all the extra staff available because of the weddings. Joe's been marvellous, and even Christina has put in a couple of shifts on the monitors in ICU. They're both safe and sleeping at my place at the moment, in case you were worrying about them.'

Grace shook her head in amazement that she hadn't given her friends a thought for the last few hours, although she *had* known they were at the hospital and so had assumed they'd be safe.

'Some friend I am,' she muttered to herself as she left Jill's office, then her weary brain remembered Georgie and the children. She poked her head back around the door.

'Georgie?'

Jill frowned in reply.

'We think she's OK. A truckie out west picked up a message that would have been sent about the time the eye was passing over. Something about finding two children, but the signal kept breaking up so he didn't catch it all.'

Jill looked worried but Grace realised there was little they could do until they heard more.

The wind had eased off, but not the rain, so she took an umbrella from one of the stands at the entrance to Reception. She'd return it when she came back on duty, although so many umbrellas were left at the hospital no one would ever notice one was missing.

The scene outside hadn't improved. The Agnes Wetherby Memorial Garden between the hospital and the doctors' house had been flattened, but the old house stood, apparently having come through the violent cyclone unscathed. Grace didn't pause to check it thoroughly—her own home was calling to her.

But as she passed the big house on the headland, she looked down into the cove, staring stupidly at the waves crashing on the shore. It was low tide, there should be beach, but, no, the storm surge had pushed the water right up to the park that ran along the foreshore so the beautifully ugly breadfruit trees and the delicate casuarinas that grew there now stood in water.

Every shop in the small shopping mall had lost its roof, while the Black Cockatoo looked as if it had lost most of its upper storey, although, from the sounds of revelry within, it was still open for business.

Grace turned down a side street, wanting to walk closer to the police station and Harry's house, hoping she'd see Sport.

Had the dog sensed Harry was in danger that it had taken off?

It seemed possible—

The scream was so loud and so fear-filled all thoughts of Harry and his dog fled. Grace turned in the direction it had come from and began to run, though to where she had no idea, until she turned a corner and saw the floodwaters. Filthy brown water swirling angrily along the street, washing under high-set homes and straight through those set lower.

Treetrunks, furniture, books and toys all rode the water, and further out something that looked like a garden shed sailed on the waters.

Another scream and this time Grace could pinpoint it. The Grubbs' house, Dora standing on her front veranda, water all around her, lapping at her feet, but seemingly safe, although she screamed and pointed and screamed again.

Grace pushed her way through shallow water towards the house, feeling how stupid it was to be carrying an umbrella with floodwaters up to her waist.

'No, no!' Dora cried, waving her arms when she saw Grace approaching. 'It's not me, it's the kids,' she yelled, pointing out into the maelstrom, towards the garden shed. 'The pantry broke off the house. I had the kids in there because it was safe and, look.'

'What kids?' Grace yelled, wondering if the cyclone had affected Dora's rationality. From what Grace had learned, Dora's 'kids' were in their thirties and living far from Crocodile Creek.

'CJ and Lily. I was minding them then Molly had the pups and the kids wanted to be there, and they're all in that room.'

Peering through the falling rain, Grace could almost imagine white, scared faces in the doorway of what she'd taken to be a shed.

'It will stop at the bridge,' she said to Dora. 'Have you got a cellphone?'

Dora shook her head.

'No matter, I've got a radio. Hopefully it's waterproof. I'll swim out to the kids and radio from there, but in the meantime, if anyone comes by, tell them to get onto the police and let them know to meet us at the bridge.'

Meet us at the bridge? she thought as she waded deeper and deeper into the murky water. As if they were going for a pleasure jaunt on the river.

Tourists went out on the river, but that was to look for and photograph crocodiles.

This was the creek, not the river, she reminded herself, but she still felt fear shiver up her spine.

'No,' she said firmly. 'Crocodiles have enough sense to stay out of flooded rivers *and* creeks.'

She bent into the filthy water to pull off her boots, then began to swim, setting her eyes on the floating bit of house, praying it would stay afloat at least until she got there.

The water fought her, pushing her one way and then another, making her task seem almost impossible. But then she looked up and saw the children. Cal's son, CJ, and Lily, Charles's ward, clinging to each other in the doorway of the floating room. Then CJ left the safety of the room, venturing out onto what must have been a bit more veranda, bending over as if to reach into the water.

'Stay back,' she yelled at him. 'Get back inside.'

He looked up as if surprised to see her, then pointed down to the water beside him.

'It's Sport!' he called, and Grace sighed as she splashed towards them. Now she had a dog to rescue as well.

'I'll get him,' she called to CJ, then she put her head down and ploughed through the last twenty metres separating her from the children.

Sport was struggling to get his one front foot onto the decking, and Grace grabbed him and boosted him up, then, fearful that her weight might unbalance the makeshift boat and bring them all into the water, she called to the kids to stay back as far as they could and eased her body up until she could sit on the wooden boards. Then, with caution, she got on to her hands and knees so she could crawl towards them.

She looked around, realising the pantry must once have been part of the veranda because a bit of veranda was still attached, working like an outrigger to keep the structure afloat.

For how long?

With legs and arms trembling either from the swim or fear, she hesitated, breathing deeply, trying to work out what might lie ahead.

She guessed they were maybe three hundred yards from the bridge, and she was reasonably sure the bridge would stop them, but whether it would also sink them was the question.

Kids first.

She crawled forward, wondering where Sport had gone, then entered the small room, where preserves and cereal and sauce bottles were jumbled in with two small children, two dogs, and too many newborn puppies for Grace to count.

'It's like being on a boat, isn't it, Grace?' CJ said as Grace knelt and wrapped her arms around the children.

'It is indeed,' she said, realising he'd been boosting Lily's confidence with talk of boats and adventure. CJ had never lacked imagination. 'And soon it's going to dock down at the bridge and we can all get off. I'm going to radio for someone to meet us there, OK?'

She detached the children, patted the wet Sport and the only slightly drier Molly—was Sport the father of this brood that he'd come through a cyclone to be with their mother? Did dog love work that way? Like human love?—and walked outside to radio SES Headquarters and explain the situation.

'Dora Grubb's been in touch,' Paul told her, 'and we've notified the police to be ready at the bridge. Have you any idea how you're going to get them off?'

'If all goes well and we don't sink, I'll pass the two kids over to rescuers then the pups and then the dogs.'

'Dogs?' Paul echoed weakly. 'Dora mentioned her dog Molly and some pups, but dogs?'

'Harry's Sport has joined the party,' Grace told him. 'Though what a policeman is doing with an un-neutered dog I'd like to know.'

'I guess Harry thought Sport had already lost a leg so didn't deserve to lose anything else,' Paul suggested.

Grace huffed, 'Men,' and stopped transmission.

Time to see to the kids and try to work out how to keep them all alive if their fragile craft sank.

Harry was in a meeting with local councillors, electricity officials and city engineers when he heard something different over the radio he had chattering quietly on the table beside him.

He'd been paying little attention to it, but had known he had to keep it on, half listening for any situation where he might be needed. Half listening for a report that Georgie and Alistair had returned with two kids.

But nothing so far.

Flood reports had begun to come in, but nothing serious as yet, until he heard a combination of words—flood, house, bridge, kids, and nurse from the hospital with them.

Instinct told him it was Grace and he turned the volume up a little, then, when he realised the transmission had finished, he excused himself to walk to a corner of the room and use his phone to call the station.

'No worries, Harry,' the constable who answered said. 'We've got it all under control. A bit of the Grubbs' house came adrift with a couple of kids inside, but Grace swam out to the kids and she's radioed in and reckons the room will stop when it hits the bridge. We'll have people there—'

'I'm on my way,' Harry said, anger and concern churning inside him. Grace accused him of taking risks and here she was, swimming through floodwaters filled with debris, snakes and crocodiles.

Stupid, stupid, stupid woman!

'Small crisis,' he said to the people gathered in the room as he strode out the door. Contingency plans could wait, or could be sorted without him—he needed to be on that bridge.

Which, please God, would hold.

How detailed had the engineer's inspection been? How minutely had he checked the structure?

He drove towards the bridge, passing more and more people on the rain-drenched streets, all with the bewildered expressions of disaster survivors. Rebuilding houses was one thing—could you rebuild people?

Maybe…

Maybe the anger he felt towards Grace was something to do with his own rebuilding process…

He swore at himself for such inane philosophising when his thoughts should be centred on rescue.

Swore at the Grubbs for their ridiculous habit of adding bits and pieces to their house—bits and pieces that could break off and be swept away by floodwaters. Damn it all, he'd seen that bit of the house—it had been ready to slide into the creek without the flood.

Then he was at the bridge and one look at the people gathered there made him shake his head. It was like a party—the fishing competition all over again. How word had got around he had no idea, but there must be fifteen people on the bridge with more arriving on foot and on surf-skis. And, far off, he could hear an outboard engine.

A boat! He should have thought of that first, but then he shook his head. With the debris in the water, whoever was running their outboard was also running the risk of hitting a submerged log and being tipped into the water.

Someone else to rescue.

He stopped the car and climbed out, looking upstream. One of his men came to stand beside him, explaining they'd stopped all traffic on the bridge and were getting the volunteers to spread out across it. Beyond his car an ambulance pulled up, then the hospital four-wheel-drive, a woman tumbling out.

The constable was saying something about ropes being in place and more equipment coming, but Harry barely heard, his eyes on the bobbing, slewing apparition riding the water towards them.

The craft looked for all the world like a Chinese junk floating on some exotic harbour, but then an eddy caught it and twirled it round and round, and above the raging noise of the water Harry heard a child's shrill scream.

His stomach was clenched so tightly it was like a boulder in his abdomen, and he wanted to plunge into the waters and swim towards the now teetering room.

'It's going to hit hard—let's get some tyres ready to give it some protection.'

Harry turned towards the man who'd spoken, recognising a member of Grace's SES team, then he saw Paul Gibson, looking grey and ill but there because a member of his service was in danger.

'There are tyres and rubber mooring buffers on the way,' Paul said, then pointed to an SES truck pulling up on the road at the end of the bridge. 'Or just arriving.'

More volunteers poured out of the truck, opening hatches to collect their booty. Soon they were walking across the bridge, mooring tyres and buffers in their arms.

'We'll wait until she gets closer,' Paul said, 'then work out where it's going to hit and use the protection there.'

Harry was glad to let him take charge. He was far too emotionally involved to be making cool decisions, and rescuing Grace and the children would need the coolest of heads.

*Why* he was so emotionally involved he'd think about later.

The wobbly room came closer, moving faster as the main current of the creek caught it and swirled it onward towards the bridge. He could see Grace now. She appeared to have wedged herself in the doorway of the room, and she had the two children clasped in her arms.

It made sense. All around town there were doorways still standing, the frames holding firm while the walls around them were blown to smithereens.

It looked like she was wearing a bikini, which, to Harry's dazed and frantic mind, seemed strange but still acceptable. Once he'd accepted a room floating on the creek, he could accept just about anything.

He moved across the bridge, trying to guess where they'd hit, needing to be right there to help her off.

And to rescue the children, of course.

A dog was barking.

Sport?

Harry peered towards the voyagers.

Grace couldn't have been stupid enough to swim out there for Sport?

Love me, love my dog?

His mind was going. It was the waiting. The room was barely moving now, pulled out of the main channel into an eddy. If he got a boat, they could row out to it.

The thought was turning practical when a child screamed again and the structure tipped, taking in water as it met the current once again, and this time hurtling towards the bridge.

Harry was there when it hit with such a sick crunching noise he couldn't believe it had stayed afloat. Now anger mixed with relief and his mind was rehearsing the lecture he was going to give Grace about taking risks.

He took a child, Lily, and passed her on to someone, took the other child, CJ, chattering away about his adventure but far paler than he should have been.

'I've got him,' someone said, and CJ was reefed out of his arms. He turned to see Gina, CJ's mother, clasping her son to her body, tears streaming down her face.

CJ kept talking but it was background noise. Harry's attention was on the rapidly sinking room.

'Here,' Grace said, coming out of the small room and passing a squirming sack to one of the SES men.

Not a bikini at all. It was a bra, but white, not blue.

Harry reached out to grab her but she disappeared inside again, returning with Sport, who saw Harry and leapt onto his chest. He fell beneath the weight of the dog's sudden assault, and was sitting on the bridge, comforting Sport, when Grace passed the Grubbs' dog Molly, a strange Dalmatian cross and no lightweight, across to rescuers.

Harry pushed Sport off him, and stepped around the crowd who'd emptied the sack—Grace's T-shirt—of puppies onto the bridge and were now oohing and aahing over them.

He was at the railing, reaching out for her, when the timbers groaned and shrieked, then something gave way and the little room was sucked beneath the water and the bridge.

'Grace!'

He saw her body flying through the air, registered a rope, and stood up on the railing, ready to dive in.

Paul stopped him.

'We slipped the loop of a lasso over her before she started passing the kids and dogs. She jumped clear as the timber gave way, so we'll just wait until she surfaces then haul her in.'

Haul her in?

As if she were a bag of sugar-cane mulch?

More anger, this time joining with the crippling concern he was feeling as he and all the watchers on the bridge searched the waters for a sight of her.

He grabbed the rope from the volunteer who was holding it and began to pull, feeling the dragging weight on the end of it, wondering if he was drowning Grace by pulling on it but needing to get her out of the water.

Others joined him, then her body, limply unconscious, surfaced by the bridge. Eager hands reached out to grab her, but as she was lifted from the water, Harry grasped her in his arms, vaguely hearing one of the paramedics giving orders, telling him to put her down, turn her on her side, check her pulse, her breathing.

But this was Grace and he hugged her to him,

although he knew he had to do as the man had said—had to put her down to save her life.

He dropped to his knees and gently laid her on the tarred surface of the road, seeing sharp gravel from the recent resurfacing—little stones that would dig into her skin.

That's when he knew, with gut-wrenching certainty, that it wasn't physical attraction—right then when he was thinking about sharp gravel pressing into Grace's skin…

# CHAPTER TEN

THE two paramedics took over, moving him aside with kind firm hands, clearing her airway, forcing air into her lungs, breathing for her, then waiting, then breathing again.

No chest compressions, which meant her heart was beating, but somehow registering this information failed to make Harry feel any better.

He loved her?

The concept was so mind-blowing he had to keep repeating it to himself in the hope the three words would eventually become a statement, not an incredulous question.

Was it too late?

He watched the two men work, saw oxygen delivered through bag pressure and a needle being inserted into the back of her hand. But mostly he just watched her face, the skin so pale it took on a bluish hue, her freckles dark against it.

One day he'd kiss each freckle, and with each kiss repeat, 'I love you.' He'd make up for all the time they'd lost, he'd—

Sport abandoned his paramour and puppies and came to press against him. Harry dug his fingers into the dog's rough coat, despair crowding his senses as he looked into the animal's liquid brown eyes and made silent promises he hoped he'd have the opportunity to keep.

'We're moving her now,' one of the paramedics said, and together they lifted Grace onto a stretcher, raised it to wheeling height, then ran with it towards their ambulance.

Running? Did running mean the situation was even more disastrous than he imagined?

Harry followed at a jog, cursing himself now that he'd sat communing with his dog, now loping unsteadily beside him, when he should have been asking questions about Grace's condition.

'What do you think?' he demanded, arriving at the ambulance as the driver was shutting the back door.

'She's breathing on her own—although we're still assisting her—and her heart rate's OK, but she's unconscious so obviously she hit her head somewhere underwater. There'll be water in her lungs, and she'll have swallowed it as well, so all we can do is get her into hospital and pump antibiotics into her and hope the concussion resolves itself.'

Totally unsatisfactory, especially that last bit, Harry thought as he drove to the hospital behind the ambulance. His radio was chattering non-stop and he really should return to the meeting, but he had to see Grace first—wanted her conscious—wanted to tell her…

But seeing Grace was one thing—speaking to her impossible.

'You're needed other places, Harry. I'll contact you if there's any change at all.'

Harry wanted to shrug off the hand Charles was resting on his arm and tell the man to go to hell, but he knew Charles was right. There was nothing he could do here, except glare at the nursing staff and grunt when the doctors told him all they could do was wait and see.

Wait and see what, for heaven's sake?

Frustration grumbled within him, and tiredness, so heavy he could barely keep upright, blurred his senses. He left the hospital, pausing in the car park to call the station and tell them he was going home to sleep for an hour then back to the civic centre to hear the latest in the evacuation and services restoration plans.

Power had to come first—without it water and sewerage systems failed to work. It would be reconnected first in the area this side of the creek, the original settlement, where the hospital and police station were. But with the flooding…

On top of that, there was still no word from Georgie—not since the one radio transmission that might or might not have come from her. She had his radio—why *hadn't* she called in?

It was the inactivity on that front that ate at him. Until the road was cleared they couldn't get vehicles in, while the heavy rain made an air search impossible. It was still too wet and windy for one of the light helicopters to fly searchers in—if they had searchers available.

Which they didn't! Sending sleep-depleted volunteers into the mountains was asking for trouble.

So all he could do was wait. Wait for the army, with its fresh and experienced manpower, and heavy-duty helicopters that could cope with wind and rain.

Or wait to hear.

And keep believing that she and Alistair were sensible people and would stay safe…

At midnight, when exhausted city officials and the first wave of army brass had headed for whatever beds they could find, Harry returned to the hospital. Grace, he was told, was in the ICU.

'Intensive Care? What's she doing in there?' he demanded, and a bemused nurse who'd probably only ever seen nice-guy Harry, looked startled.

'She's unconscious and running a low-grade fever and has fluid in her lungs so it's likely she's hatching pneumonia, in which case the fever could get worse. And on top of that there's the chance it's something nastier than pneumonia. Who knows what germs were lurking in that water?'

And having set him back on his heels, almost literally, with this information, the nurse gave a concerned smile.

'We're *all* very worried about her, Harry,' she added, just in case he thought he was the only one concerned.

Harry nodded, and even tried to smile, but that was too damn difficult when Grace was lying in Intensive Care, incubating who knew what disease.

He strode towards the isolated unit, determined to see her, but no one blocked his path or muttered about family only.

She was lying in the bed, beneath a sheet, wires and tubes snaking from her body.

So small and fragile-looking—still as death.

Gina sat beside her, holding her hand and talking to her. She looked up at Harry and, although wobbly, at least *her* smile was working.

'She always talks to coma patients when she's nursing them,' Gina said, her eyes bright with unshed tears. 'I thought it was the least I could do.'

Then the tears spilled over and slipped down her cheeks.

'She saved my son. She plunged into that filthy, stinking water and swam out to save him. She can't die, Harry, she just can't.'

'She won't,' Harry promised, although he knew it was a promise he couldn't make come true. Gina stood up and he slipped into the chair and took the warm, pale hand she passed to him.

Grace's hand, so small and slight, Grace's fingers, nails neatly trimmed.

'Does she know?' Gina asked, and Harry, puzzled by the question, turned towards her. 'That you love her?' Gina expanded, with a much better smile this time.

'No,' he said, the word cutting deep inside his chest as he thought of Grace dying without knowing. Then he, too, smiled. 'But I'm here to tell her and I'll keep on telling her. You're right, she does believe unconscious patients hear things, so surely she'll be listening.'

He paused, then said awkwardly to Gina, 'She loves me, you know. She told me earlier today.'

It must have been the wonder in his voice that made Gina chuckle. She leant forward and hugged him.

'That's not exactly news, you know, Harry. The entire hospital's known how Grace felt for the past six months.'

'She told you?' Harry muttered. 'Told everyone but me?'

Gina smiled again, a kindly smile.

'Would you have listened?' she said softly, then she gave him another hug. 'And she didn't tell us all in words, you know. We just saw it in the way she lit up whenever you were around and the way she said your name and the way she glowed on meeting nights. There are a thousand ways to say "I love you", Harry, and I think your Grace knows most of them.'

'*My* Grace,' Harry muttered, unable to believe he hadn't seen what everyone else had. Hadn't seen the thousand ways Grace had said 'I love you'. But Gina was already gone, pausing in the doorway to tell him Cal would be by later and to promise that Grace would have someone sitting with her all the time, talking to her and holding her hand so she could find her way back from wherever she was right now.

Again it was Charles who told Harry to leave.

'I don't ever sleep late—growing up on a cattle property in the tropics, where the best work was done before the heat of midday, instils the habit of early waking.'

He'd wheeled into the room while Harry had been dozing in the chair, his body bent forward so his head rested on Grace's bed, her hand still clasped in his.

'So I'm doing the early shift with Grace,' Charles continued, manoeuvring his chair into position. 'If you want some technicalities, her breathing and pulse rate suggest she's regaining consciousness but the infection's taking hold and her temperature is fluctuating rather alarmingly.'

Harry knew he had to go. He had to get some sleep then return to the planning room. Evacuation of people who had family or friends to go to close by had begun yesterday and today they were hoping to begin mass evacuation of up to a thousand women and children. Defence force transport planes would bring in water, tents, food and building supplies and fly people out to Townsville or Cairns. Power would come on in stages, and it could be months before all services were fully operational. Getting people out of the crippled town would ease the pressure on the limited services.

He left the hospital reluctantly, and was in a meeting when Cal phoned to say Grace had regained consciousness but was feverish and disoriented, mostly sleeping, which was good.

Harry raged against the constraints that held him in the meeting, knowing he couldn't go rushing to Grace's side when he was needed right where he was. But later…

Later she was sleeping, so he slipped into the chair vacated this time for him by her friend Marcia, and took her hand, talking quietly to her, telling her he was there.

Grace turned her head and opened her eyes, gazing at him with a puzzled frown. Then the frown cleared, as if she'd worked out who he was, and she said, 'Go away Harry,' as clear as day.

Nothing else, just, 'Go away Harry.' Then she shut her eyes again as if not seeing him would make him vanish.

She was feverish, he told himself, and didn't know what she was saying, but when she woke an hour later and saw him there, her eyes filled with tears and this time the knife she used to stab right into his heart was phrased differently.

'I don't want you here, Harry,' she said, her voice piteously weak, the single tear sliding down her cheek doing further damage to his already lacerated heart.

Cal was there, and his quiet 'I don't want her getting upset' got Harry to his feet.

But go?

How could he walk away and leave her lying there, so still and pale beneath the sheet?

'There's work for you to do elsewhere,' Cal reminded him, following him out of the ICU and stopping beside the wide window where Cal had propped himself. 'I'll keep you posted about her condition.'

So Harry worked and listened to Cal telling him Grace was as well as could be expected, not exactly improving but the new antibiotics they were trying seemed to be keeping the infection stable.

It was in her lungs and now he had to worry if pulling her through the water had made things worse, but there were no answers to that kind of question so he worked some more, and went home to sleep from time to time, to feed Sport and talk to him of love.

On the third day after Willie had blown the town apart, Grace was moved out of the ICU and two days later released from hospital, but only as far as the doctors' house, where resident medical staff could fuss over her and keep an eye on her continuing improvement at the same time.

So it was there that Harry went, late one afternoon, when the urgency had left the restoration programme and he could take time off without feeling guilty.

She was on the veranda, Gina told him. On the old couch. As he walked through the house he sensed Gina tactfully making sure all the other residents had vamoosed.

He came out onto the veranda and there was Grace, pale but pretty, her golden curls shining in the sun that had finally blessed them with its presence and what looked like a dirty black rag draped across her knees.

'Grace?' he said, hating the fact he sounded so tentative, yet fearful she'd once again send him away.

'Harry?'

The word echoed with surprise, as if he was the last person she expected to be calling on her.

A thought that added to his tension!

'Come and sit down. I'm not supposed to move about much. One lung collapsed during all the fuss and it's not quite better yet, so I'm stuck in bed or on the couch, but at least from here I can see the sea. It's quietened down a lot, hasn't it?'

Harry stared at her. This was the Grace he used to know. Actually, it was a much frailer and quieter and less bubbly version of her, but still that Grace, the one who was his friend. Chatting to him, easing over difficult moments—showing love?

He had no idea—totally confused by what he'd come

to realise after that terrible moment when Grace had disappeared beneath the murky floodwaters and then by the 'go away' order she'd issued from the hospital bed.

Stepping tentatively, although the old house had withstood Willie's fury better than most of the houses in town, he moved towards the couch, then sat where Grace was patting the space beside her on the couch.

'I thought I'd lost you,' he began, then wondered if she was well enough for him to be dumping his emotions on her. 'You disappeared beneath the waters and I realised what a fool I'd been, Grace. Stupid, stupid fool, hiding away from any emotion all this time, letting the mess I'd made of my marriage to Nikki overshadow my life, then, worst of all, blaming physical attraction for the kiss. I know it's too late to be telling you all this—that somehow with the bump on your head you got some common sense and decided you could do far better than me—but, like you had to say it when I thought I'd lost Sport, so I have to say it now. I love you, Grace.'

Having bumbled his way this far through the conversation, Harry paused and looked at the recipient of all this information. She was staring at him as if he'd spoken in tongues, so he tried again.

'I love you, Grace,' he said, and wondered if he should perhaps propose right now and make a total fool of himself all at once, or leave the foolish proposal part for some other time.

'You love me?' she finally whispered, and he waited for the punch-line, the 'Oh, Harry, it's too late' or however she might word it.

But nothing followed so he took her hands in his and nodded, then as tension gripped so hard it hurt, he rushed into speech again.

'I know you don't feel the same way but you did love me once, so maybe that love is only hidden, not completely gone.'

'Loved you once?' she said, and this time the repetition was stronger, and now her blue eyes were fixed on his. 'What makes you think I'd ever stop loving you, Harry?'

He stared at her, trying to work out what this question meant—trying to equate it with the 'go away, Harry' scenarios.

Couldn't do it, so he had to ask.

'You sent me away,' he reminded her. 'At the hospital, you said to go away and that you didn't want me there.'

'Oh, Harry,' she whispered, and rested her head against his chest. 'You silly man, thinking I'd stopped loving you. As soon stop the sun from rising as me stop loving you.'

This definitely made him happy, happy enough to press a kiss to her soft curls, but he was still confused. Maybe more confused than ever.

'But you sent me away when all I wanted was to be with you.'

She turned towards him and lifted one hand to rest it on his cheek.

'I didn't want you sitting by my bedside—not at that hospital—not again. I didn't want you remembering all that pain and anguish, and suffering for things that happened in the past through no real fault of yours.'

She pressed her lips to his, a present of a kiss.

'The fact that you talked about Nikki and your marriage suggested you were ready to move on, so I didn't want you being pulled back into the past because of me.'

'You'd have liked me there?' Harry asked, unable to believe that, sick as she had been, she'd still found this one way of the thousand to say 'I love you'.

'Of course,' she whispered, nestling her head on his chest. 'Loving you the way I do, I always want you near.'

She smiled up at him, then added, 'Look how pathetic I am—look at this.'

She lifted the black rag from her knee and it took a moment for him to recognise it as his dinner jacket.

'I brushed off most of the mud and when Gina said I had to keep something over my knees when I sit out in the breeze, it seemed the best knee cover any woman could have. Gina wanted to have it dry-cleaned but it would have come back smelling of dry-cleaning fluid, not Harry, so there you are.'

Her smile mocked her sentimentality but it went straight to Harry's heart, because it wobbled a bit as if she felt she'd made a fool of herself.

'Snap!' he said softly, and reached into his shirt pocket, pulling out a very tattered blue ribbon he'd kept with him since that fateful night.

Then he closed his arms around her and pulled her close, pressing kisses on her head and telling her things he hadn't realised he knew, about how much he loved her, but more, that he admired her and thought her wonderful, and how soon would she be his wife?

They'd reached the kissing stage when a voice interrupted them, a voice filled with the disgust that only a five-year-old could muster when faced with demonstrations of love.

'You're kissing, Grace,' CJ said, coming close enough for them to see he held a squirming puppy in his hands. 'I didn't think policemen did that kind of thing.'

'Well, now you know they do,' Harry said, tucking Grace tightly against his body, never wanting to let her go.

CJ sighed.

'Then I guess I'll have to be a fireman instead,' he said, passing the puppy to Harry. 'Mum said you were here, and this is the one Lily and I decided should be yours because it looks more like Sport than all the others, although it's got four legs.'

Harry took the squirming bundle of fur and peered into its face. He failed to see any resemblance at all to Sport, but knew once CJ and Lily had decided something, it was futile to argue.

'Do you mind if we have two dogs?' he asked Grace, who smiled at him so lovingly he had to kiss her again, further disgusting CJ, who rescued the pup and departed, making fire-siren noises as he raced away.

'Two dogs and lots of kids,' Grace said, returning his kisses with enthusiasm. 'Is that OK with you?'

Harry thought of all he now knew about Grace's

background. Loving without being loved must have been so hard for someone with her warm and caring nature.

'Of course we'll have lots of kids,' he promised, and was about to suggest they start on the project right now when he remembered she was just out of hospital and very frail.

But not too frail to kiss him as she whispered, 'Thank you.' Then added, 'I love you, Harry Blake,' and made his day complete.